"Dick Selvig is perceptive, original, innovative, and thorough. He is very deep in the understanding of the mechanisms and behavior of alcoholism. He is totally honest in his approach and counsel to those in need of his help."

> —Dr. Ignacio Fortuny
> Medical Oncologist
> St. Louis Park Medical Clinic
> Minnesota

"An inspiring work . . . this book encourages recovering alcoholics and explains what wonderful help is available to those who still need it. Most of all, it proves that none of us can conquer this disease without help."

> —Edward (Moose) Kraus
> Athletic Director
> University of Notre Dame
> South Bend Indiana

"I have known Dick Selvig for more than 20 years and he is one of the pioneers of our society in alcoholism rehabilitation. His philosophy of treatment has been respected and copied by treatment facilities all over the country. Dick Selvig was one of the early believers in family therapy as part of treatment of alcoholism.

> —Reverand Phil Hansen
> Director of Alcoholism Rehabilitation
> Abbott-Northwestern Hospital, Minneapolis

"It's high time for such a book as High & Dry. It deals with the average person's everyday concerns about the problems of alcohol and other drug abuse. Readable, straightforward, and very human in its approach, this book is especially recommended to persons involved with adolescents and young adults.

—Dagney Christiansen
Executive Director
Granville House Inc.
St. Paul

"Dick Selvic is the most authentic man I have ever met. His contribution to the field of addiction treatment is legendary. If I had only one source to learn from, I would choose Dick Selvig."

—Thomas R. Hedin
Director, Division of Alcoholism
and Drug Abuse
Bismark, North Dakota

Dick Selvig

ALCOHOLISM CERTIFICATIONS:

Certified Counselor on Alcoholism, State of Minnesota, Department of Public Welfare, 1241964.

Master Addiction Counselor, State of North Dakota, Department of Health, 3/21/1974.

ALCOHOLISM SCHOOLING:

Yale University Summer School of Alcohol Studies, 1959.

Summer School of Alcohol Studies, University of North Dakota, 1961.

Counselor Training Program, Willmar State Hospital, Minnesota, 1962-63.

Summer School of Alcohol Studies, Mankato State College, Minnesota, 1965.

Transactional Analysis Workshop, Bismarck, North Dakota, 1972.

ALCOHOLISM INSTRUCTOR:

Faculty member, Counselor Training Program, Willmar State Hospital, Willmar, Minnesota, 1963-1964.

Faculty member, International Summer School of Alcohol Studies, Grand Forks, North Dakota, 1966, 1970, 1973, 1978, 1979.

Faculty member, Counselor Training Program, Heartview Training Center, Mandan, North Dakota, 1974-1978.

MEMBER OF ALCOHOLISM BOARDS:

Medical, Counseling and Professional Committee of Bismarck, North Dakota, Drug Abuse Foundation, 1970-1974.

Committee on Professional Standards and Certification of Addiction Counselors, North Dakota Department of Health, 1973-1978.

State of Minnesota Credentialing Board, 1979.

MISCELLANEOUS:

Author of publications: *Alcoholism is a Family Affair and How About Your Drinking?*

Recipient of Heartview Foundation Founder's Club Award, 1969.

Dedication

We hope this book encourages the recovering alcoholic to be proud of sobriety . . . . and drinking alcoholics to look closely at their situation. Alcoholics must vow to fight this disease with zeal and determination—and learn again to love themselves, their family, their friends, their fellow beings, and their God.

CONTENTS

PART I
ALCOHOLISM—THE DISEASE

Part II
CHARACTERISTICS OF THE ALCOHOLIC

Part III
FAMILY AND FRIENDS OF THE ALCOHOLIC

Part IV
THE RECOVERING ALCOHOLIC

Part V
SYNOPSIS

"If this book helps even one alcoholic straighten out his life and eases the pain he has caused his friends and relatives, I consider it a success . . . ."

Dick Selvig

NOTE:

When I am writing about an individual alcoholic, I have decided to use the personal pronouns—he and his—rather than the clumsier he/she, his/her. I am painfully aware, however, of how many alcoholics are women. Thus, any reference to gender is to include masculine and feminine.

INTRODUCTION

"Oh, how my very soul cries out for
that one sweet drink of wonder and
mysticism. . . . nay nay, even
though I know a sorceress carries the
goblet—and the devil dwells within
the glistening drops. . . ."
The Court Jester

The purpose of this book is to enlighten and inform the millions of alcohol drinkers and their families and friends on the vagaries and mysteries of alcoholism.

No one is better qualified for this undertaking than Dick Selvig, who has devoted 23 years of his life to the professional study and treatment of the terminal illness known as alcoholism.

Selvig has been involved in the treatment of over 20,000 alcoholics, of whom a large share are recovering. No other individual has such a record of longevity and service and is still working in the in-patient field.

Selvig, himself a recovering alcoholic, is now on the staff of the Fountain Lake Treatment Center in Albert Lea, Minnesota, from where his messages of love and understanding and tolerance of alcoholics go out all over the world. He has treated patients from London, Paris, Vancouver, Los Angeles, New York, Mexico City, Panama, and Miami; from all stations of life—from the gutter bum, to the sports hero, to the teenager, to the mother, to the chairman of the board. He travels over 50,000 miles a year speaking and holding seminars on this topic.

In his first book on the subject, Selvig tears away the dark curtain which has surrounded alcoholism for centuries. As he points out, "Even great civilizations have ostracized the alcoholic more than the leper. In some societies the alcoholic has been put to death. It is time to face up to the disease and treat it for what it is—a horrible waste of man, a killing sickness which can be controlled and fought successfully."

This book, then, is not only for the alcoholic but for his family, his loved ones, his friends, employers, teachers, bosses, subordinates, and society in general. It is intended to pinpoint the disease and its ramifications in a layman's terms. It gives hope to those who are fighting it and those whose lives are affected by the alcoholic's behavior.

PART I

ALCOHOLISM —THE DISEASE

QUESTION:
WHAT IS AN ALCOHOLIC?

SELVIG:

Simple. He is a person who has lost the freedom to function in one or all of three areas—job time, leisure time, and sleep time. On the job he is not fulfilling responsibilities. On leisure or family time, he may be unpredictable and undependable. Sleeping, his pattern will be fragmented; little real worth will be derived. Few non-alcoholics with the sleep pattern of an alcoholic could function normally and remain unhospitalized.

Ironically, the observer may see that the alcoholic has lost control in only one area. It could be in work where he is late and is not functioning to satisfaction. Or it may be noticeable just in the family element where his antagonisms and remorse and fantasies find a buffer state where he can rage and rant and create scenes. Or to the alcoholic, it may be observed only in sleep where he tosses and turns, sometimes hallucinates and wakes up wrung out and hung over. But the key point is the fact that all these disturbing areas influence the others. No area—work, sleep or family—is insulated from the others.

When the alcoholic says, "I may drink too much but I never miss a day's work," it could be true. But he is not working at his maximum potential. He is just getting by.

Or the alcoholic, who says, "I never have an argument at home—not one in 20 years," may be telling the truth. But the fact probably is he has long ago lost all rapport with his family. They would prefer to ignore him rather than generate animosities. But be sure—the hate and resentment are growing.

In summation, the alcoholic is the person who has lost

his ability to make judgements and has lost his willpower to refuse an alcoholic beverage. He simply is a person who has placed the importance of alcoholic consumption over that of his family, friends, associates, and employer.

Alcohol has become his love affair. Yet one must realize that alcoholism is an internal disorder in origin:

An Alcoholic Is A Person Who Drinks Differently Than He Would Like To. Even With This Self-Knowledge The Alcoholic Is Unable To Quit Drinking Successfully By Himself For Any Length Of Time.

He is unable to taper off. He tapers on. As a result, the alcoholic finds he cannot drink and he cannot stay away from it. Now comes the alcoholic's famed alibi system, which he triggers almost automatically. The alcoholic begins making excuses, the kind that usually begin with one word—"Well."

As the problem becomes more serious and the alcoholic comes to grips with his antagonizers, the projection period, or the blaming of others, begins. Then comes real hopelessness and tormenting despair. Sudden, spontaneous denial shoots out from the alcoholic's mouth.

In other words, when all else fails, the logical thing to the alcoholic is to deny the problem. Until the alibi system is wiped out, there is no immediate chance for recovery.

Again, the irony: a terminal illness which is denied by the afflicted.

His effort to drink the way he would like to is impossible to fulfill. That's why he is an alcoholic.

Examples:

The handsome hotel manager makes the statement that, "I drink a lot but I'm no alcoholic. I use it as a relaxer. And I never have any auto accidents because I stay right in the hotel."

He doesn't tell you that twice last week he missed morning breakfast appointments with club leaders to schedule dinner parties. He doesn't seem to notice that he was curt with a group leader over assignment of rooms at 11 a.m. after drinking until 3 a.m. earlier that morning. He mentions nothing about booking in 40 visitors, forgetting to mark down the reservations, and having room for only 30 when they arrive.

True, he doesn't drive when drinking—but he forgets he slipped on the back stairs last winter and missed two weeks with a bad back. He conveniently forgets that his wife went home to her family for six weeks because she no longer could tolerate his harangue.

He never tells you that one of the children threw a $300 vase at him when he stumbled, cursing, into his apartment at 2 a.m. He is highly paid. He dresses well. He has hung onto his job and family for some 10 years. But Charles is in serious shape—an acute alcoholic.

* * *

Gregarious John is an insurance executive who finds his lunch hours running into long afternoon talk sessions. He finds himself postponing or canceling out appointments to spend more time with his drinking companions. His earning power deteriorates and, as a repercussion, arguments over his working value extend to the home where his wife and two children are affected.

The arguments create a void in family relationships and John begins to spend more time away from home, fearing the verbal exchanges and accusations. His relationship with his children becomes anxious, agitated. John loses faith in himself, his work and his ability to be a family leader. He begins to drink more alcohol, even realizing the problems it is causing. John is an alcoholic. He has a terminal disease.

* * *

Pretty Marie is a 24-year-old waitress. She parties long and heavily at night and finds herself irritable to her breakfast customers. Her tips fall off. She has two minor auto accidents through misjudgement. She loses her driver's license and job the same day. Her roommate moves out the next day. She sleeps fitfully and contemplates suicide by an overdose of sleeping pills. She continues to drink, hoping to soothe her nerves. Marie is an alcoholic. She is in dire need of help.

* * *

Take the case of a high school principal. Fastidious Edna is divorced, ambitious, bright. She is a private alcohol drinker, sipping brandy in her fashionable apartment. She drifts away from friends and work associates, preferring solitude, reading, and drinking.

Edna finds herself making rash decisions in her school work and becoming agitated with teachers and other working acquaintances. Her rapport with her students is diminishing. She is always on time, but the work seems burdensome and uneventful. She continues to drink late at night—and by herself.

Her sleep becomes erratic. She becomes tired at school more easily and slips away for a couple of alcoholic "morale lifters" at noon. Edna has injured no one. But Edna is an alcoholic and will soon endanger her health. She is intelligent but completely oblivious to her danger.

* * *

Tom is an 18-year-old freshman in college. He is ambitious but undecided about his major. His parents repeatedly ask him to make a decision about his future. He finds himself spending three or four evenings a week with his dorm roommates, bowling, attending sports events—and drinking beers after the activities.

When the others head for bed, Tom lingers, having two or three more beers. On weekends, he prefers to stay in school rather than visit his parents. He again consumes six to eight beers in the afternoon or evening. His work is slipping. He is agitated and nervous when he is at home. He refuses to discuss his future and converses openly with friends only after four or five beers. He never consumes highballs or cocktails, only beers. Tom is a young alcoholic.

* * *

Happy-go-lucky Robert is a 38-year-old executive for a large brewery. In his capacity, he promotes the sale of his beverage by calling on bars and restaurants. He has convinced himself that to be a good public relations representative he must indulge in a few drinks of his product with customers and owners.

To this end, he consumes three or four beers at lunch and another three or four in afternoon stops. He arrives home at 6 p.m., always on time, but carrying the familiar "glow." He is overly glib, quick to joke. By 8 p.m. the glow has worn off and Bob becomes either sullen or uncommunicative.

His four children are bewildered by his extreme emotional roller coaster. Bob gradually goes from beers to quick hard-liquor "eye-openers" at 9 a.m. on his way to the office. His drinking bouts with customers are lasting longer and are less productive. Many times he forgets to take orders. The seriousness of his call is replaced by jocular exchanges. Bob still has his health and job—but time could be running out. He is an alcoholic, victim of the occupational disease.

* * *

Wally, an ardent hunter, who always looked forward to heading up North with the boys and hunting Canadian Honkers, loaded his car with plenty of liquor and steaks but forgot to take his gun and shells along with him. Needless to say, Wally is an alcoholic. The bottle became more important than the sport. The trip was a mere excuse to indulge. He is a planner—one of the most pragmatic alcoholics.

* * *

Ben, a top-notch bowler, used to bowl at the local lanes but all of a sudden said, "I don't like the way the owners take care of the lanes. They are too slippery." He left because they would no longer allow him to spike his drinks. When drinking becomes the most important thing in one's life, alcoholism is present. The man who bowls to drink or hunts to drink is deeply afflicted.

QUESTION:
ARE THERE VARIOUS STAGES OF ALCOHOLISM?

SELVIG: Yes, there are three definite stages.

1-FULFILL

In the first stage, fulfillment, the drinker has a tendency to say to himself, "Hey, wow, I feel so good" or "I love everyone—even you." The drinker in the first stage may feel as light as a feather—and ready to fly. He thinks he has a freedom to function better than at any time in his life. He feels so talented he must share those talents with the less fortunate. Nobody bothers to control him now. The first stage is feeling elation. Unfortunately, the fulfillment or "wow" stage doesn't last very long.

2-FORGET

The second stage is the forgetful stage. The drinker is using more alcohol and enjoying it less. He no longer is experiencing fulfillment. In his vain search for that lost "wow" feeling he drinks more often and faster. He is shaken by the realization that the grand feeling of fulfillment is a feeling of the past. Problems begin to emerge with the drinking. Frightened, he drinks more. The bottle is now in complete control of the drinker. Strong physical symptoms come to the front—like a tightness in the head and a gnawing at the stomach. Oblivion is his goal.

3-FATAL

The third and final stage is next. The alcoholic begins to feel, "What the hell is the use?" Now drinking takes on a terrifying aspect: The drinker pours down liquor in the face of impending disaster or impending success. He begins suffering the shattering feelings of loneliness and despair. Now it is suicidal drinking as remorse, guilt, shame, and self-doubt build up inside. He feels terribly alone and forgotten. No one "understands" him. He wants to shut out the world—hoping the drinks that once brought him a world of fun and fantasy now will only bring him darkness and relief from the excruciating pressure of shame. He has corrupted himself with a voluntary madness. The realization that he has voluntarily abused his senses gnaws at his conscience and makes him very sad. No one is more alone or consumed in loss of self-worth than the drinker in this last stage. The successful one who drinks and succumbs doesn't feel he has a right to be successful.

Examples:

The young nurse named Gloria was telling about her first drinking bout. "I couldn't believe anybody could feel so good. I wanted to kiss everyone at the party."

Her friend Julia said, "Alcohol did things for me nothing else could. If I was down it pepped me up. If I was tired, it gave me energy. If I was lonesome it really acted so great on me, I could sit and daydream my fantasies. I didn't need people."

Both young ladies said that their earliest contacts with alcohol were so positive and they felt so good about themselves that they wondered why everybody didn't drink all the time!

Within a year, Gloria didn't care about anything but drinking. She lost her clerk's job in the hospital. She returned to live with her aging mother. In this period of time, she fought with her mother continually and actually stole from her purse to buy liquor. Finally, she was picked up off the streets and put in a treatment center.

After release, she fought the torments of the damned. Within two years of her first bouts with alcoholism, when she had the superlative feeling, she was now very close to killing herself. She tried an overdose of drugs but was saved in the hospital. Finally, she received treatment and today is on the road to recovery.

Listen to her words: "I don't know just where the fine

9

line between 'great' and that terrible sinking feeling came. All I know is that one day the drinks weren't doing that much for me. They stopped giving me a lift. From that point it was all downhill. I knew I was in trouble when I drank nearly a quart of gin one day and only felt sick."

Meanwhile, Julia didn't reach the third stage for nearly five years. It was a more insidious affair.

"I partied real well for about three years. I looked forward to my five or six drinks every night. I was a different person. It was really great. I wondered why everybody didn't booze it up a little.

"But then the depressions started to come. My best friends began dropping away. And then the boy I liked gave up on me. Still I wouldn't quit. I wanted to feel again that perfect feeling. I was never the same after the first three years or so. After that I had to really bomb myself to think I felt good. I really didn't feel good. Only on the way to a bad bag.

"At the end, the more I drank, the worse I felt. When I started drinking as soon as I got out of bed, desperately searching for that 'high,' I knew I'd had it." Julia today is recovering.

* * *

A former fighter who battled liquor for years told me this story about the frightening stages:

"I don't know when I hit the second stage but it came on me out of the blue. God, one night I was feeling great and then right in the middle of this big, wonderful high with all the party people around, something snapped. My temper exploded and I nearly killed a guy with my fists. It got me in deep trouble, being an ex-fighter with my hands considered lethal weapons. Anyway, the quick change in the second stage—from fun to damnation— was awful. First time in my life I became really frightened."

* * *

And in the third stage a retired rancher tells it all:
"You see your life slipping away. You can't control it.

10

For years I drank and I couldn't get off the bottle, but by the time I was 65 I'd lost my friends. My wife was dead. I was sick with loneliness, my kids hated me. I thought the drinks would help. They didn't.

"I felt so low I could crawl under a rug. Then I'd drink some more. The damn disease is tantalizing. It gets you and you think you can quit. When you hit that last stage where things are all downhill and you keep hoping the next drink will turn it all around, it's plain hell. It's hell on earth."

Like the rancher says, the worst part about the disease is that the victim actually thinks he can control the bottle. In reality, he is the slave. He can't quit. The bottle is the master. The next drink will always make things better. And then one day he can't move, he is desperately alone and his health is gone. The bottle sits there smiling. It's the smile of victory—and death.

* * *

The insidiousness of the change in stages is terrifying. I remember being at a lovely party. The host was an airlines captain. After dinner he regaled us with stories of his war escapades.

Then suddenly, when the party was almost at the breaking point, the suave pilot became a Mr. Hyde. He lashed out suddenly in a torrent of abuse on his lady friend. A bystander tried to interject and was hit in the face. The man went berserk. His lady friend was at a loss to explain his behavior. He called all his guests the next day to apologize.

I had heard he was a consistent drinker. I suspected the problem. Two years later I was not surprised to hear he had lost his proud position.

* * *

Let's look closely at the time when the drinks are "turning on" the alcoholic to the point when the fun can turn into nightmares. The 25-year-old business man was having a ball two or three nights a week after work, enjoying the conviviality of his young working friends. But

Lance, after six months of this pattern, would forget where he parked his car. It happened half a dozen times but no one took it seriously. He was suffering minor blackouts of memory. Finally, the seriousness of the situation struck his friends in almost tragic tones.

Lance was found nearly frozen in an alley one morning. He could not find his car and collapsed unconscious on the cement. Fortunately, the close call pinpointed his drinking problem.

"The maxim, 'in vino veritas—that a man who is well warmed with wine will speak the truth,' may be an argument for drinking, if you suppose men in general to be liars; but, sir, I would not keep company with a fellow, who lies as he is sober, and whom you must make drunk before you can get a word of truth out of him."
Samuel Johnson

VIEWPOINT

When the throes of the third-step disintegration take over, the alcoholic has such a dislike for himself that he would never seek help. His feeling about himself runs along these lines: "Who would want to help me? I'm not worth helping." Self-deprecation: a demoralizing attitude.

It is at this stage, when some alcoholics even seek death, that it is imperative he gets help. His first motivation for getting well comes from those who love him enough to make an effort against his will to help him.

Later, as the currents of hostility calm down, the alcoholic begins to feel better about himself. Then, in gratitude, he is able to say to the intruder who has breached his wall of desolation, "If it hadn't been for your help, I might be dead. Thanks for caring about me."

As in the three stages of alcoholism, there also are three steps to regaining health for the alcoholic: (1) I have to; (2) I should; (3) I want to. The external inspiration provided by our loved one's interjection provides the external sources for our rehabilitation. Then must come motivation from within the alcoholic himself.

His final step toward waging war on his disease is based on his internal attitude. Never should those aiding the alcoholic force the diseased to internal motivation so that he says, "I want help—help for myself only." He must see that he needs help with the suggestion by others. Forcing internal decisions on alcoholics prematurely can be disastrous. There are those who with good intentions want to make the alcoholic's crusade their crusade. Their motivation is completely wrong. They want to save a life to enhance their own self-appreciation.

Clearly and simply, most alcoholics are ready for help in the third and last stage of their drinking—and rarely before. To some this stage is reached in a few years—others in decades. And when the assistance comes, when the loved ones make their move, they must do so with exquisite care and thoughtful study. Shoving, jostling, screaming will never transform an alcoholic. He must be given a decision in such a way that he is driven from within to rebuild his life. He must be permitted the dignity of feeling he has a choice—even if his choice dictates that he is committed. In summary, "Will you go voluntarily or should I make an effort to commit you?"

Ironically, I have known alcoholics in the dying stages fight savagely for their own choice—right or wrong. Out of pride. Sheer pride. It is the pride which makes it so difficult for a man to say, "I am a sick alcoholic. I need your help."

But desperation does not belie dignity. Drunks are capable of enormous, omnipotent dignity—even lying in a gutter, covered by vomit and dirt. We must not remove a particle of that human dignity or there will be nothing upon which to build a happy sobriety. In the final analysis, "One has a right to not seek or accept help." Tragic but true.

13

QUESTION:
WHAT ARE THE SYMPTOMS OF ALCOHOLISM?

SELVIG:

When the person finds fulfillment in the bottle. When the bottle is used to feel superior to others. That may mean to each individual "feeling" more confident; "feeling" more linguistic; "feeling" strong; "feeling" happier; "feeling" more romantic; "feeling" more debonnaire.

When a person sets out to attain a certain feeling which is not natural to his personality, he's on his way to alcoholism.

When a person drinks to feel euphoria, he is in trouble; the disease has struck. The drinker becomes addicted to the unnatural high—with a crushing blow due when the low sets in. The more the drinker seeks the high or good feeling, the more the lows. The more highs and lows, the more frightening the roller-coaster. Alcoholism is an actual roller-coaster of emotions and feelings.

Examples:

Suzy is overweight. She is not comfortable in her clothes. She knows, however, that with three drinks she has a good feeling and her appearance does not bother her. She doesn't care what people think. She doesn't

14

care that she is battling a thyroid condition nobody understands. The good feeling wipes out the self-consciousness about her weight.

* * *

Jane has a hearing problem. Because she is young she refuses to wear a hearing aid. After three or four drinks, she is not disturbed about what people say about her missing the conversation. She then dominates the conversation and "feels" good about the situation. She is no longer apologetic about not hearing what others say. She feels so good inside that she can blot out the problems created by her hearing deficiency.

* * *

The rugged footballer has butter-finger hands. He is prone to fumble on the field. His ego cannot stand any of the jokes teammates or fans aim at him, no matter how harmless.

His mother used to explain that when she had a drink and took her "trouble pill" it eased the tensions. Footballer Dan does the same thing. He's now mixing valium with beer. Only instead of using it just in an atmosphere where he might hear derogatory remarks, he uses it in all difficult situations. It makes him "feel" better. It has made him an acute alcoholic at the age of 20.

* * *

Victor can't stand his boss or the pressures of his job. But at lunch, two martinis get him thinking completely differently. "Boss isn't so bad—he's got a tough job. . . . The job's pretty good at that—fair pay, good vacation . . . I guess I should be satisfied with the job. It's better than most of my neighbors. . . ."

The martinis turn him from a grumbler into a pacifist. They make him feel good inside; good all over. Victor comes to believe that martinis must be the answer since the therapy seems to do so much for his nerves. Every morning, however, he has grim doubts about his profession—only to come back from lunch bolstered, relaxed, enjoying life.

The difficulty is that the problem of his work will always be there. He should be studying his position and how to better it rather than kidding himself for a half a day that he has found a panacea for his ills. If martinis do that for his job, they'll certainly do the same thing for his relations at home with wife, children, neighbors, etc. The search for the different "feeling" has given alcoholism another victim.

"Other vices but impair the soul—but drunkenness demolishes her two chief faculties: the understanding and the will."
Francis Quarles

QUESTION:
WHAT MAKES ALCOHOLISM SUCH A DIFFERENT DISEASE?

SELVIG:

It is the only terminal disease in which the patient generally fights a known recovery. Not only does the patient fight the recovery, but he tries to hide the disease.

If a man suffers from cancer, he usually rushes to a specialist and hopes he can do all in his and the doctor's power to save his life. Alcoholism is just as fatal and terrifying as cancer or leprosy or a heart ailment. Yet the patient so often will prevent specialists from helping him. It is estimated that one out of seven alcoholics, who are aware of their disease, will die without having even tried to help themselves! Amazing but true.

That's what makes it such a mysterious disease. Even

the arresting treatment can stigmatize people in certain areas where the disease is not accepted as an illness of "socially proper" strains.

It is also the only illness on God's earth where mothers and sweethearts will kill the victim by seeking to "protect" him from scorn and themselves from embarrassment. More than a venereal disease, alcoholism today is still a hush-hush subject in millions of households and families.

Spouses can be the worst offenders—thinking they are helping alcoholic wives and husbands by not exposing them. Instead, they become willing helpmates, ushering their loved one to early disability and almost certain tragic death. They are accomplices and as guilty of killing their loved ones as if they laced their alcohol with arsenic.

I have never heard a heart attack victim or cancer casualty ever raise the havoc with others while in the throes of his illness as the alcoholic does. Alcoholism is a behavioral disease; so much guilt, remorse, and self-hate comes to the fore as a result of the inner turmoil.

Examples:

Mild-mannered Don is the father of seven children in an active Polish family. He has been an alcoholic for better than 16 years. The family accepts his stupors. They accept him falling asleep in Mass on Christmas Eve. They accept his missing work with "the shakes" a dozen times a year.

Oh, the children occasionally ridicule his weakness. But his wife staunchly defends him as a "good, loyal, religious, hard-working father who should not have to take insults."

One child and a brother of his have asked his wife to get him to a treatment center. Her answer, "Over my dead body." At the age of 63, Don has perhaps another five years of fairly healthy living ahead of him, but his memory is already failing.

Don's work production is down. He has no chance for

advancement. He is little more than another piece of furniture around the house. His wife says, "He doesn't beat the children and he minds his own business." She is as much a part of his depressing existence as the bottle itself. He will eventually lose his health and probably die of alcoholism, so typical of many addicts whose families cover up for them.

* * *

It has been pointed out to Julia that she is an alcoholic by her closest friends and priest and marriage counselor and psychologist. She is like millions "going to fight my problems in my own way." The sad commentary is that nobody fights the disease of alcoholism by themselves.

I have never seen anyone walk alone into a rehabilitation center of their own volition and free will! Julia claims she will eventually "give it up." That is impossible as long as she tries to go alone.

Imagine, if Julia were told by specialists that she had cancer and only 10 years to live unless she had an operation or treatment. I have no doubt but that she would rush to the hospital and place herself in the care of medics within minutes. Still, millions refuse to believe alcoholism is a disease and that they cannot fight it alone.

Julia believes she is whipping it when she gives up drinking during Lent or for a period of two or three weeks while dieting. Her mind, however, is incessantly on liquor and she usually comes back off the "wagon" with a vengeance, binging for three or four days.

I've told her firmly that she is letting down the loved ones around her. She replies, "It's my struggle. I'll whip it myself. Nobody need worry." The shame is that five or six close friends and relatives will worry, and unless the disease is arrested within three or four years, she will suffer irreparable physical damage.

* * *

The violence and savagery which can erupt among those who claim they can battle alone—or those who just don't give a damn—is appalling.

Let me cite the man whose periodic sprees usually end with his beating his wife. His closest friend was a county sheriff, raised with him from the time they were boys.

Three times this sheriff had brought his friend to the hospital to dry out. Finally, the sheriff convinced the wife of the alcoholic that she must commit him to a treatment center.

On a bright Sunday morning, the sheriff drove to the farmer friend's house preparing to take him to the center. He was greeted by a shotgun blast from the farmer which nearly decapitated him. The sheriff was the father of four children. He was trying to act as a friend.

But alcoholics not only preserve the sanctuary of their bottle—some will kill to protect their right to drink. Imagine the victim of any other fatal disease killing to permit himself to die of a lingering, torturing illness!

* * *

The deadly cover-up also is illustrated perfectly by the story of Edward, a college professor in the East. He has been plagued by the disease for better than a decade. In this time he has fallen down his stairs at home and crushed six vertebrae.

He has also smashed his car into a telephone pole. He has driven off the road. He has set fire to his reading chair. He has locked himself out of the house a dozen times and lost his car on three occasions. He's lost his billfold twice and been mugged once outside a bar in New York.

He has started three books—and finished no more than three chapters in each. He managed to get to school every morning and blunder through early classes until gaining his equilibrium.

His wife would like to take him to a treatment center but his mother, who lives with the family, says: "If you do, he'll be out of his profession. You'll kill him as if you used a gun." The wife can't stand the hassle with the mother-in-law. She permits her husband his almost continual drinking orgy.

Already he is showing symptoms of physical ailments

and mental distress. He is forgetting appointments. His liver is acting up. His blood pressure is high. The mother-in-law bitterly assails anyone who finds fault with her only son. "He's a good son, a hard worker and he deserves a little relaxation," his mother defends. She tells his wife that no college would hire a drunk if his drinking became public knowledge.

What she doesn't know is that eight other professors on the staff have undergone treatment, are recovering beautifully and that the college deans encourage such voluntary help. Edward is a brilliant man who is cutting short his career and his life because the women around him are afraid to seek help for the deadly illness. Stranger than fiction? Yet a common situation.

VIEWPOINT

Alcoholism, the most complex of illnesses, finds three things occurring in the verbal vocabulary of the alcoholic:

(1) Early in his drinking career, the alcoholic actually brags about how much he can drink and "can drink others under the table."

(2) When trouble arises, his only quote is, "I don't drink too much. In fact, look at how much some of the other guys are hitting it."

(3) When he is on the program of recovery and he talks, he talks about how much he used to drink. Invariably the amount he professes to have poured down is less than he says. Due to blackouts, he is not sure of how much he drank, how much he spilled or how much he gave away.

Is there any question why alcoholism is called such a complicated disorder? It literally changes the nature of the beast.

Alcoholism is the only hospitalized illness that finds visitors wondering what to say to the patient. You never have that much of a concern when you visit a friend with a broken leg, do you?

People even ask when should I go over and see him and will he want to see me. The only answer I give, "Drop in and see the loneliest guy in the world who feels so ashamed of himself. In a few minutes the embarrassment will disappear. He'll love that you show an interest."

Nobody rebounds like an alcoholic on the mend. I knew one who was so mortified by his illness he became a patient in a rehab center 2,800 miles from his home. But six weeks later, the arrested alcoholic was back in his swank neighborhood, giving lectures on the evil of drink!

Something else which is so mystifying. . . . most alcoholics will gladly recount their drinking escapades when they try to charm the opposite sex. But they steadfastly refuse to talk about the problems which forced them into treatment. Rarely will you hear an alcoholic say, "Hey, I think I set a record for blackouts in a month!" Or confess, "I got so drunk so much I hawked my wife's jewelry to pay the bar." They only seem to remember the "good times." Rarely do they talk about the pain and anguish.

I don't know of any product that is so completely poisonous to so many people and is called by them "the finest tranquilizer known to mankind" as alcohol. How it can relax one person in such a peaceful and serene way and drive another wild and violent is a dizzying paradox.

Other drugs may be counter indicated, but with alcohol the resulting behavior is sometimes completely unbelievable. One person finds alcohol sending him gracefully into the arms of the opposite sex and another fills him with the killer instinct of the Boston Strangler.

Early in the drinking of the alcoholic he gets a definite spiritual experience from liquor and a short while later, all hell breaks loose and there is no question but the devil is in charge of the soul.

The people who become accomplices to such behavior and who help expose the alcoholic to such cyclonic mood changes are usually sweet, warm, loving people. Again, the frightening aspects of this mystifying disease.

Can you imagine a mother presenting a known arsonist with a blowtorch at Christmas? Yet, the mothers and wives and husbands of alcoholics who try to explain the drunk's paranoic behavior by saying, "It's his friends" or "He's under a strain at work," are doing almost a criminal injustice to one they love.

There is nothing more difficult on this earth than for a loving wife to tell her spouse, "Darling, it's over. I can't help you any more. You are sick. But I will stay with you and love you and we'll both see this through." That's true devotion? The blind leading the blind and no vision appears.

Remember that for every alcoholic (and the numbers are vast) there are twice as many people providing him with the chemical which is killing him. Objectively, you could call them a "mass of murderers." They have no idea, but by their very loyalty and love, so many are killing the objects of their devotion. What other disease is claiming hundreds daily because their "loved" ones are destroying them as if they were actually suffocating or strangling the victims?

What other disease is claiming hundreds daily because their "loved" ones are destroying them as if they were actually suffocating or strangling the victims?

QUESTION:
HOW CAN ALCOHOLIC SIGNS BE
DETERMINED IN TEENAGERS?

SELVIG:

Euphoria. The false "good" feeling. The "I don't care" feeling. I've helped 13-year-olds in this state and it is amazing that after a drink or two they just don't care. They don't care if they attend school or do their chores. They don't care how they dress or what they say. The personality changes. Quiet youngsters many times become glib.

It is a completely foreign feeling. It is difficult for teenagers many times to separate that high feeling of elation from typical boyhood enthusiasm. But a close student of alcoholism can discover the symptoms—too much elation, too much of the smile, too much of the silly talk, too much enthusiasm.

It is the same with adults who feel just too good. But, generally, the adults will talk far more than ordinarily and become experts on any given subject. The adult will be almost overly friendly.

It gets back to our basic tenet: the alcoholic drinks for the feel of more knowledge, more enthusiasm, more wit, more talent than others. The social drinker is drinking only to feel as good as the next person. A typical tell-tale sign of alcoholism is the person who, ordinarily quiet, becomes loud; the person who ordinarily is reticent who becomes aggressive, the person who ordinarily is neat becomes untidy. Early alcoholics should look for the change, sometimes imperceptible—sometimes shocking. The person who changes after his alcohol drinking is probably an alcoholic or on his way to becoming diseased.

Examples:

Little Tommy was only fourteen but ordinarily disliked school. His parents were elated but shocked when Tommy suddenly found a great liking to school and could hardly wait to attend classes. What had happened was that one of Tommy's playmates had found a bottle of his parents' liquor in the garage and enjoyed the feeling after experimenting with a drink.

Tommy waited for the bus at his pal's house. Together, they would imbibe early in the morning and take on a glow after a drink or two, which would carry them through a good share of the day. Tommy became aggressive in classes. That might have been good, except that as the alcohol wore off his old feeling of anti-school took over his character and personality. Then he would be truculent and short-tempered, often getting in fights between classes or when school let out.

The personality transformation wasn't evaluated for three months. Fortunately, the parents and teacher managed to ascertain the problem and with the help of the parents of Tommy's friend, effected quick treatment. But the young man at fourteen was on his way to becoming a victim of the feared disease.

* * *

The twin brother was the quietest man on the main street of his small Montana town. For 16 years he was known as the "quiet one." His twin was known as "the guy who makes up for the 'quiet one.'" He would cover all subjects in a ton of wordage while his brother sat back with a half smile in the small variety store they ran as a family project. But the quiet one, at the age of 18, began to interject his opinions one day to the dismay of his twin who yelled loudly, "Either you're crazy or drunk!"

It was a cruel charge but an accurate one. The quiet twin had taken to drinking wine in his room. For perhaps six months he had been a silent drinker and then his personality changed.

The liquor overcame the shyness and he gradually

moved into the conversation. The twin could not stand sharing the stage. He presumed his brother must be doing something to give him false courage. Discovering his habit, he sought help. The drinking twin underwent treatment but during the course of rehabilitation counselors found that he needed to get away from the dominant twin. He changed schools and became a happy, caring person. True, he had been stifled. But he should have had the force of character to determine his own problem without seeking the synthetic solution. Young people who search for substances such as liquor or other drugs to change their outlook on life are heading in a dangerous direction.

* * *

It is sometimes easy to spot an alcoholic's humor. Or, rather, change of humor. Henrietta was a docile, quiet girl who never appeared to have a sense of humor. Friends would say, "Such a cute girl—but doesn't she ever smile?"

The world looked as sour to her as a rotten lemon. Gradually, however, she became a tease, a practical joker—in school, with her family and friends.

"What a delightful change," they all said. Nobody was suspicious. Somebody should have been. True, Henrietta was changing, but the new mood was synthetically produced—by the bottle. After four drinks she became a shade frivolous. After six drinks, she told me, she was absolutely giddy. After seven or eight, she became the life of the party.

The character change was fun to watch. Hitherto, she had been a drudge, a true bore. But the quickness of the new disguise was not healthy. In one of her giddy moods, she tried to balance herself on a condominium balcony on a dare she made up herself. She fell 20 feet to the pavement below. It was only then that horrified friends decided this was not a natural transformation; that Henrietta simply drank herself into a humorous, lively character. She was just 19 years old and, ironically, because of the accident, eventually became a sound, recovering alcoholic. Thankfully, she also developed an attractive personality by learning to share her feelings with other recovering alcoholics.

* * *

All too often the change in personality is often so welcomed by friends and family that no one even wants to believe it is caused by alcohol. I had a mother say, upon learning of her daughter's disease, "But Sally was so much more fun with a drink or two."

I heard another mother admit frankly, "I couldn't stand my son Jim until he had a few drinks to loosen up."

Telltale signs which, ironically, friends and relatives do not want to heed because the dullard has suddenly become a bright, enthusiastic, humorous person. It is a shame that so many tortured young lives have to endure years of pain and heartbreak because society hasn't discovered healthful, natural means to improve personalities. Because the alcoholic's way with society sometimes is jovial and warm, even though superficial, he often is encouraged to drink by his family and friends. These people find it difficult to admit the alcoholic has a problem. They remember only that he is "more fun than he used to be."

Another ironic fact about the disease: people who should recognize it don't and often don't want to. They are more comfortable with the alcoholic than with the real person. That will change, of course, when they understand a recovering alcoholic's gutsy fight for recovery.

There is another serious problem in the area of trying to discover a young alcoholic. Too often a group of companions will urge on the heaviest drinkers because they become entertainers for the crowd. The alcoholic's peers are not content just to have a gregarious companion; they want someone who makes a scene so that their own behavior looks more normal by comparison.

"Get a little tight, Dick, so you can sing those crazy songs," my companions urged me when I was 18 years old. I thought that to be accepted I had to be a clown, to be the life of the party. I wasn't intelligent enough or observing enough to realize I was making a fool of myself for their laughter. The sad part was, they weren't laughing with me. They were laughing at me.

I remember one 14-year-old who became his class clown. His story was sad. "I never had many friends. Then I'd see my folks drink and the people at parties in our house, and everybody would be laughing. I figured that bottle had magic." Tommy began using liquor out of his father's cabinet, eventually smuggling a bottle into his school locker. "I felt better than any kid when I was drinking. My folks didn't know because by the time I got home I was pretty much normal. But at school I could lead people when I had a drink or two. They'd do what I wanted them to."

Eventually, Tommy quit eating and his stomach turned on him. After several violent seizures during school lunch hours, authorities finally determined he was drinking. His folks were stunned. They didn't see him in this high condition. His friends just thought he had gained confidence as he got older.

Too often young people see the liquor and pills of their parents providing what they think is a panacea for all bad times. Young people emulate adults and too often adults don't look at their offspring closely enough to discern problems.

A close student of alcoholism can discover the symptoms— too much elation, too much of the smile, too much of the silly talk, too much enthusiasm.

QUESTION:
HOW DANGEROUS ACTUALLY IS ALCOHOLISM TO HEALTH?

SELVIG:

Alcoholism can be deadly dangerous. It is a terminal illness. Medical people find acute liver ailments are a direct result of drinking. Heart attacks can be brought on by excessive drinking. The deterioration of the skills—mental and physical—can be horrible. Lack of coordination, shakes, tidal tremors, loss of memory are painful.

The brain damage resulting from alcoholism can be even more horrifying than the physical dissipation. Blackouts, in which the alcoholic absolutely does not remember where he has been or what he has done, are terrifying. Hallucinations, in which patients have seen giant spiders and have felt the room filling with water, can virtually destroy a sick body.

Even more deadly than the ills brought on by excessive alcohol are the complications which arise from other ailments because of alcoholic consumption. I have had friends die from stomach ills, blood diseases and pancreatic ailments and all because they could not refrain from alcohol, which complicated their other physical problems.

The alcoholic becomes a sad case. I have seen strong men dissipate themselves into a state near death in a matter of two or three years. Some of the latest clinical theories are based on a belief that even a small amount of alcohol is bad for the system, shattering an old wives' tale.

The alcoholic, because of his severe drinking habits, often quits eating. There are occasional "freaks," as I call them, who can consume excessive amounts of alcohol for years and their systems built up a tolerance which is quite unbelievable. I have in mind a friend whose liver is as clean as a baby's although alcohol has irritated his ulcers to a point where he's lost most of his stomach.

In the end, the alcoholic generally dies from complications arising from excessive liquor consumption. Or, as I point out, the alcohol impedes or ruins restoration of other ailing organs. It is a mean street. Over 90 percent of the alcoholics over 50 years of age that I observed and who failed in treatment, died of the disease within a 10-year period. And for the last four or five years of their lives many were immobilized "vegetables," in disgrace from friends, relatives and the community.

Examples:

I welcomed a sturdy, tall, fifty-ish Montana rancher to the rehab center where I was working at 7 p.m. on a Tuesday evening. He shook hands, trembling fearfully. He asked me how the airport was in the adjacent city. I said, "Fine, why do you ask?" He answered, "Well I flew my own plane in, I think, and I can't remember landing."

That night he suffered hallucinations and screamed most of the sleeping hours. He died of a heart attack at 5 a.m.

* * *

The man was a successful auto agency owner named Fred. He was a complete success—on the surface. However, alcoholism had him in its steel grip. He would call me from strange bars in which either he could not navigate or was too sick to try. He had suffered two serious pancreas attacks and was warned by doctors that if he did not quit drinking they could not be responsible for his health. He collapsed on a pavement one afternoon at 3 o'clock and died two hours later. He virtually committed suicide.

* * *

The slow, agonizing liver death of a close friend stays

in my memory. At the age of 40 he was told he could live if he refrained from drinking. Doctors thought his liver would recover, being a resilient organ, at least enough to permit him a bearable existence. Nils would lay off the alcohol for two or three months, but gradually the hold of the disease began to strangle his controls.

At the age of 43 his complexion was yellowish and he was spending more time in bed than out. The next year he was in almost continual pain and died—shorn of friends and family. Had it not been for the children, his wife would not have attended the funeral, she told me.

* * *

A talented singer, very popular in the Midwest, could not live with even territorial fame. She began drinking in the afternoons and continued through her performances and into the early hours of the morning. She always blamed a "bad man." She gained weight rapidly. She began taking diet pills and then mixing pills and liquor. She added uppers and downers to her deadly arsenal and died at 39, a complete physical wreck who had begun heavy drinking only six years before.

An autopsy showed that Mae had virtually torn herself apart internally and from excruciating high blood pressure. In the end, her nerves were shot; her head a throbbing mass; her face ugly and distorted. Alcohol had ruined her in the prime of life.

* * *

The many forms of deadliness this killer takes is startling. A veteran hockey player refused to believe he was over the hill. His drinking bouts infused him with the belief he was still a terror on ice. One night he called a friend and talked about his future for two hours. He said he knew he'd quit drinking when he got a call he expected from a major league club giving him a tryout. A friend tried to explain to him tactfully, "Don't rely on the call." I heard that later that evening he drank for three hours. The call apparently never came. He asphyxiated himself at 1 a.m., alone and bewildered and certainly horribly hurt. The alcohol killed him as if he had drowned in a vat of it.

The worst part of the alcohol killer is the nefarious slowness with which it can take a life. It can cripple and deteriorate for years. Or it can strike quickly by causing hemorrhages or heart attacks with lightning devastation.

Over a million people in the country will die this year because of direct or indirect vulnerability to alcohol. That does not count the estimated 400,000 who will die on highways while intoxicated or at the hands of people who are intoxicated.

"First, man takes a drink. Then the drink takes a drink. Then the drink takes the man."
Japanese proverb

QUESTION:
IS ALCOHOL AS DANGEROUS AS OTHER DRUGS?

SELVIG:

Alcohol is a drug. A young man at a treatment center was fighting alcoholism. He was rooming with a cocaine addict. When the alcoholic found this out, he was horrified. He was insulted. He lashed out at me. "Dick, how could you put me with a dope head—a cocaine addict? My God, they're the lowest people in the world!"

He was so upset he was shaking. I quieted him down and said, "Thornton, you drink to change your feelings. The dope addict does it for the same reason. Maybe your roomie can't tolerate drunks or the smell of alcohol. He probably thinks of you as some bum under the elevated train. It doesn't matter what the substance is; you are both 'drug' addicts.

"You are both searching for the highs. He gets there one way—you use the bottle. The only difference is, he pays a helluva lot bigger chunk of cash for the privilege of getting sick."

The alcoholic had never thought of it that way. I then pointed out that his roomie had a college degree from a fine Eastern school and came from a family noted for leadership in many fields; also that the young man was as serious as Thornton was about coping and fighting off his disease.

Far too many alcoholics think of "dopies" as the worst breed of addicts. They forget that many pill, powder or hypo users come from the intelligentia—many of fine families; and that many had to have top-flight professional jobs to pay for their habit. Thornton's cocaine-addict roomie spent $100 a day on his habit.

When Thornton had time to appraise the situation, he admitted there wasn't a damn bit of difference between the alcoholic and the dope addict. In fact, many patients I treat are both.

It is amazing, too, the number of alcoholics who will stifle their disease and turn to valium as a relaxer and wind up hooked on it, abusing it in their search for a "good feeling."

In one counseling class I had of 50 patients, 14 were addicted to valium, all on the same search for that perfect feeling. Of course, alcohol is as dangerous as other drugs. In fact, there are those who suffer from "alcoholic toxicity" when using liquor as the example we gave previously. They can go completely berserk and display violent behavior as the result of taking alcohol, which many times is extremely foreign to their personalities. They cannot safety take alcohol in any measure for it is so alien to their systems. Even a small quantity can manifest wildly unpredictable behavior.

As for recovery, generally speaking, I feel the alcoholic

can begin his way back to normal behavior patterns quicker and more easily than any other drug addict. I generally recommend longer treatment in a rehabilitation center for a cocaine addict than an alcoholic but each case is individual. Ordinarily the other drug addict's system requires more time to return to stability, emotionally and physically.

After treatment it may take any other drug addict sometimes twice as long to be completely comfortable again than it does an alcoholic. But, like the alcoholic, the drug addict must build his recovery program around his own discipline, calling on a Greater Power for help and sharing his feelings with others. Both the alcoholic and drug addict are two runaway vehicles cascading down the mountain road without brakes. They both must stop before they can repair the mechanical and emotional damage. And they both must want to stop eventually—not for others but for themselves.

Of the two, the drug addict eventually can be much more costly to society. His habit costs so much more to sustain. That's why so often the drug addict turns to crime to secure big money quickly. The alcoholic can maintain his habit with a cheap $1.89 bottle of wine. This has powerful disadvantages, too, as so many more of the populace can afford the cheap alcohol.

An alcoholic should never turn away from any other drug addict. They are of the same family, the same "breed." They have both sought the elation of the high and are paying the price of the glows. Morals, status, society roles—nothing plays a part in either more than in the other. All addicts are sick. All are diseased. All of them may be fighting for their lives. However, many times one sees alcoholics and other drug users very uncomfortable with each other.

Examples:

I asked Charles, an opium smoker, why he didn't take up alcohol. After all, it is cheaper. He said honestly, "I

33

can get there quicker on the Big O. It's concealed easier in school. And it hits me faster. I also don't have the after-effects."

* * *

Terrance put it this way: "I got into cocaine because my father told me I wasn't a damn bit of good at anything. So I studied dope, and became as expert in its history, how to attain it, how to handle it, and what it does for you. I don't think there's an alcoholic in society that knows as much about his subject as I do."

It was nonsense for Terrance to blame his father for his interest in dope—and later he admitted that he needed no excuse—although he could have been looking for attention. But the truth is many druggers study their sickness and know far more about its ramifications than the alcoholics.

* * *

Handsome Jamie was 29 years old and his young body was ridden by addiction excesses when we got him off the streets of New York. I knew that the drug phase of his problem would take longer to handle than the alcoholism. His mind was keen in about three weeks. And in six weeks he was making headway with his mental outlook. But the tired body wouldn't respond and the demand for drugs gave way so grudgingly that I had him transferred to a drug ward in a major hospital.

After a seven-week stay in that environment he followed up his physical rehabilitation by again returning to alcoholic treatment. The whole process took nearly four months. Happily Jamie made it and today is a successful electrical engineer in Philadelphia and attends, I'm proud to say, three AA meetings a week.

He says, "The alcoholism bit was not nearly as tough as giving up the pills. My body could stand shutting off liquor—but not the other drugs. There were times when I didn't think I'd make it—because of my drug addiction." I've heard that from many patients.

* * *

Another point to bring out here is that there are some Alcoholics Anonymous groups which have not taken kindly to other drug addicts. There is misunderstanding and resentment. I can understand that. But I can't condone us not helping them. Some AA groups welcome other drug addicts and some don't. Such is life.

An old alcoholic told me, "I was raised with an Irish family that drank for generations. Maybe we all were alcoholics, I don't know. I do know that none of us would stand still for a drugger. My God, we'd tear him from limb to limb. Lowest scum on the earth." There was no way that old Tim was going to sit next to a drugger at an AA meeting. I know that. And I wouldn't want to be the man who was going to force a drug addict on an AA group that doesn't want one. The group sets their own guidelines. Some alcoholics help other drug users form their own group and not call it AA. Narcotics Anonymous is such an example of this.

But contrast that to a young, vibrant group of AA people in St. Paul, Minnesota, who are just about evenly split between alcoholics and other drug addicts. "There's great harmony here," one member tells me. "There is absolutely no difference between the drugger and the alcoholic. It's all drugs. It's all feeling. To win, we all have to share. I've never heard any part of a story to convince me that druggers are any more freaks than alcoholics. We are all diseased persons looking for a recovery." Beautiful.

* * *

The 30-year-old advertising executive named Louise puts it this way: "I'm, or was, a drug addict—all kinds of pills from the very brightest upper to the real 'coolers.' It would have been whiskey, except my stomach couldn't stand the liquor and my head couldn't take the hangovers."

* * *

And Ray, who's been a switch-hitter for 22 years, says: "I did crazier things drinking than when I was on drugs. I think the alcoholic is more insane than the drugger." That's a moot question. All heavy users are diseased. All are looking for the false fulfillment. None have their freedom to function. There is absolutely no difference in morale or physical values between the alcoholic and the drug addict per se but naturally there may be, as it might be with any individuals.

* * *

Youth seems much more ready to accept addicts of all kinds. I was never more impressed than while attending a halfway house rally in a Wisconsin city. The love involved was so real it could almost be cut with a knife and packaged for society. I saw a 15-year-old drug addict out of a juvenile home embrace a 30-year-old society woman, an alcoholic. I saw a rundown Navy veteran, still shaking through his recovery from cocaine, hold a 14-year-old girl alcoholic in his arms and say, "This is beautiful. We all love. We are all going to beat this thing together."

When I was leaving I asked a young black how he felt about mixing druggers and alkies. "No difference, man. We both been after our kicks. Now we see the light."

You could write a book and not put it more clearly than that.

QUESTION:
HOW IMPORTANT IS THE MEDICAL
PROFESSION IN AIDING ALCOHOLICS?

SELVIG:

First and foremost, most of us alcoholics would be dead without the help of the medical profession.

The greatest breakthrough in the history of enlightenment and treatment of the alcoholic was made when the American Medical Association defined alcoholism as an illness. Skeptics thought this might become a shield with heavy drinkers using this as an excuse to consume alcohol. Instead, it tore away the veil of misconceptions and opened the path for a giant health-care reclamation program for millions of sufferers of the disease.

Every alcoholic battling the disease should get on the knees for a moment every day and thank the medical profession for the most enlightened stand ever made for the disease-bearers who had been treated by many segments of society as everything from freaks to the mentally deranged. For years, society thought them incapable of being helped and not worthy of understanding.

Ironically, the alcoholic has thrust a tremendous burden on the medical field, which has cleared the path for rehabilitation and acceptance. I mean that every day the medical profession is challenged by the deceit, the lies, the chicanery of the drinking alcoholic trying to camouflage the disease from the very doctors who could provide a springboard for arresting the disease.

To understand the problems a doctor faces with an alcoholic patient, consider:

Only in a rare instance will the alcoholic admit to the doctor how much he drinks. In the early stages, the disease may not have affected vital organs to a degree that a doctor can quickly diagnose the problem. Then, too, if the doctor doesn't know the patient is a heavy drinker, it is unlikely he will find out, even from the spouse. They still, in most cases, fear the alcoholic and will not expose the problem to even a physician. One doctor told me: "It's like trying to get a family to admit they have a thief in their midst. Everyone clams up. Either out of fear of the alcoholic or because of the stigma attached if I find out."

Another doctor told me: "Strange as it seems, the medical profession is so often in the very worst position to discover the disease. There is no way to study the alcoholic's drinking patterns closely enough to know if the patient is indeed suffering from the disease. Not until an employer or family tells me he is hung up on the bottle, can I begin to get to the root of the problem. The alcoholic plays tricks with everyone—and the doctor is no exception. When I ask how much he drinks, he'll invariably say, 'Oh, maybe a couple before dinner.' There is no way I can look at him and tell him he is lying—unless I know."

Many psychiatrists are of tremendous help. And there are more in the field all the time who understand the vagaries and idiosyncrasies of the disease. Believe me, it is a tremendous challenge for even an able psychiatrist who has worked in the field of alcoholism to identify and categorize and understand the disease's ramifications. It can be a bewildering experience for the young psychiatrist who is not attuned to the gimmicks and ploys and deceit of the alcoholic.

The very fact that virtually all accredited alcoholic rehabilitation centers have capable psychiatrists on the treatment team proves how valuable they are. Once the psychiatrist knows the patient is an alcoholic, he can probe and stimulate and gain a tremendous rapport with the alcoholic. I have worked with many psychiatrists over the years. Their ability to get the patient talking is an art. Their understanding is a blessing. Their ability to diagnose learning difficulties is a great assistance and to observe the handiwork of the doctor medicating the guy so high he's an airplane to land in the group setting and causing the "mole" to come out of the ground and sit next to the high flyer is a miracle to behold. Then, too often, some psychiatrists concentrate too much on the personalities and the situations rather than the bottle. It is a combination of the bottle and the personality which join to create the alcoholic's problem.

To treat an alcoholic, a psychiatrist must be fully attuned with the latest information on the disease. He must be prepared for all the ploys of the patient. He must assume nothing. And he must believe that it is the liquor, as well as the disposition of the patient which generally caused the alcoholic his grief. Since we know the alcoholic is a chronic liar, cheat, and con man, the psychiatrist must deal and duel with a many-faceted character.

In the end, however, the psychiatrist will have such a glow of rewarding fulfillment it will make the challenge all worth-while. I had a psychiatrist, an old friend, tell me, "I can read and understand most human beings and see the causes of their plights quite readily. The scalawag alcoholic comes in so many disguises a psychiatrist must be part private eye himself to understand the man's affliction."

There is, also, a small percentile of doctors who are recovering alcoholics and seek desperately to retain their anonymity. They fear it might hurt their reputation. I can only say to them: I think if you share your affliction and your sobriety with any alcoholic patient, he will immediately feel you are a man to be trusted and perhaps have him become a friend as well as a doctor. This is a gratifying relationship. I can only urge alcoholic doctors to preach their joy of recovery to their patients. I am sure they will become a source of inspiration. There is nothing to be ashamed of. Conquering a terminal disease can only be considered a proud accomplishment. I can't believe in our enlightened world today, that you will feel any ostracization by your profession.

Examples:

The Pittsburgh attorney had hidden his alcoholism from his doctor for years. But one night, while suffering from ulcers after a prolonged drinking bout, he admitted to his doctor: "I've been lying, I've been playing games, Doc, but God, I need your help now."

The doctor had only suspected the attorney's problems. When confronted with them, he asked why the patient had never mentioned his drinking habit before and he was astounded at the answer: "I've told a few people I had problems with the booze, Doc, but the one person I couldn't tell was you. I know they say to confide in your doctor and minister. But I'm not that type. I could tell friends and they couldn't order me to stop. If I told you and you said I'd have to stop, it would have killed me. I'd have hated you the rest of my life."

* * *

A physician friend had treated Robert for a variety of illnesses over a 20-year period. Convinced Robert was drinking too much, he asked him some questions about his alcoholic consumption. Robert bounced up, insulted, cursed his long-time doctor friend and stormed out of the office.

He refused to let any of his family see the doctor again and branded him a "quack" to any who would listen. The doctor confided to me, "I'll never get involved in a man's drinking habits again." But the threat was an empty one. The challenge was tempting. The next time I met the doctor he announced joyfully he had helped out a dozen patients in treatment.

* * *

Another doctor I know is an alcoholic who has undergone treatment. But he guards so jealously his stature in the community and hospital that he has told no one. He told me, "I just don't want to go into it with patients. They'll discover I am one, too. It has to hurt my practice. You know, who wants a drunk doctor operating on him?"

My only comment: "I'd rather have a recovering alcoholic operate on me instead of a practicing one." Teachers, doctors, religious leaders all have a particularly difficult time believing that their illness will be understood by their peers—as does every other alcoholic.

* * *

I felt embarrassed for a young surgeon, a recovering alcoholic, who was joshed by his pal: "Jake, I'm glad you're an expert on gall-bladders, I sure as hell wouldn't want you on a brain transplant." Doctor Jake laughed but I knew he was hurt. It takes a brave person to be a recovering alcoholic. And it took a braver one to admit his temporary insanity in the first place. False pride is a mighty stumbling block for an alcoholic.

The biggest problem doctors have is the patient himself. He believes his drinking is one area in which a doctor cannot diagnose; one area he can protect. No x-ray is going to show the six martinis the night before. If it's high blood pressure, the alky can always say, "Oh, I was a little anxious getting here today in the traffic." Or, "I've been eating a little too much. I know I have to be careful."

He feels that the doctor will take his word—and will not pressure him even if he suspects the patient is drinking too much. I know one alcoholic who always told his doctor, "Just two high-balls every day. That can't be bad, Doc?" What could the doctor answer? He couldn't say he suspected the man was drinking at least 10 a day and the glow he carried that moment didn't come from a makeup kit.

* * *

Doctor Neil was a doctor with that extra sense of "reading" an alcoholic patient. I once asked him his secret:

"It's not the patient's body as much as his speech I listen to. Sometimes the alcoholic gives it away. One told me he had trouble sleeping and eventually I traced it back to nightly drinking bouts. Another told me he was nervous because of constant up-tight relations with his

41

wife. She gave me the clue that a bottle had come between them. Another told me that he was experiencing chest pains because of pressure at work. When I dug a little, I found that his boss was exerting pressure because he was late for work so often and that his tardiness was in direct relation to his alcoholic consumption.

"The problem with alcoholics is that you hate to go beyond the patients. In some families where I've treated other members for years I can get a close rapport. But many times I treat only the alcoholic. Then it's tough. It's almost like being a detective. I know there is something wrong with his health. Then I have to determine if there is something wrong with his stories. Sometimes it's impossible. Then I have to frighten him enough to get him into the hospital for evaluation or closer study."

* * *

This doctor is doing a brilliant service for his community and profession. Like Doctor James, he's a young doctor who gives four hours a week just to lecture alcoholic patients at a treatment center about the effect the disease has on their systems and about how they can accelerate their physical recovery. He tells me:

"I don't get paid for this—it's a work from the heart. These people have hidden their illnesses for years. But to see the glow of promise and hope in their eyes is a wonderful feeling. I just wish there was a way the doctors all over the world could detect this disease earlier. But I guess it's the strange nature of the disease. An alcoholic will blame any ache or pain on everything—but the bottle. It's very difficult to diagnose a patient who hides the true symptoms."

* * *

A psychiatrist told me he treated a fellow for three years and never suspected that drinking alcohol was at the root of all the man's problems. During the course of time, the man blamed his frigid wife, his arrogant boss, and his dope-ridden children for his nervousness and anxiety.

"Why yes, I had a drink now and then—trying to relax." The psychiatrist told me he actually advised a few drinks to ease the tension of his patient. It wasn't until the man had compiled a series of drunken driving convictions that the doctor discovered his patient was an alcoholic. Digging further into the problem, he discovered that most of his patient's trials were the direct result of his guarded drinking and his unwillingness to give up the bottle. The man conned and lied to the doctor for years. The doctor and counselor both look foolish unless they have behavior data from some source other than the patient. One had real insight as he said," A practicing alcoholic starts lying when his mouth opens."

VIEWPOINT

One of the most rewarding experiences for me to have in the field of alcoholism is to work with medical people who acknowledge that alcoholism is an illness and treat the patient as such. There is, however, the tendency too often for the doctor to pay little heed to the drinking the patient is doing. Instead, to make an effort to modify his emotions by giving him other drugs; hoping that new insights will be gained. However, the patient with alcoholic tendencies only gets worse.

The medical doctors and psychiatrists who recognize that alcoholism is a primary illness in itself insist that the drinking be stopped before anything else is considered. It is just amazing how much help can occur when the doctors recognize the drinking abuse of the patient and use the proper referral for this, such as alcohol counseling and information centers, treatment centers, and Alcoholics Anonymous.

I have been very fortunate in that from the time I began counselling alcoholics in 1958 at Willmar State Hospital, Willmar, Minnesota; then on at Heartview Foundation in Bismarck, North Dakota, and Mandan, North Dakota;

and now at Fountain Lake Treatment Center in Albert Lea, I had a good working relationship with the medical profession. These include medical doctors, psychologists, psychiatrists, fellow counselors, social workers, chaplains, nurses, aides, maintenance and administrative personnel, secretaries, food service workers, and the public in general. For this I will always be grateful.

Alcoholism is a multiple-faceted illness and it needs an honest, open relationship with people from all skills and walks of life to be of any value to the patient.

The doctor and the patient supposedly must have a close, honest relationship. Still, it can be difficult for doctors really to comprehend the intimacy between the alcoholic and his bottle. It is larger than life itself in some cases. The doctor rarely will learn the patient's true drinking habits from the patient. Consequently, he will be at a loss to recommend treatment.

Happily, many medical schools today are including special courses in recognizing and treating alcoholics. The more information the young doctor has in hand, the more likely he'll be to diagnose the alcoholic. He has to understand completely that this is the only disease he'll encounter where the patient is trying to dupe the doctor. It is a challenging problem for any young doctor.

The ones I have worked with in treatment centers are inspirations. They have learned to use intuition as deftly as they do their instruments. It is a joy to see the doctor, a man in whom most families put their trust, gain the confidence of the alcoholic. Nobody can make the impression on the alcoholic about the deadlines of his disease like a medical doctor. Nobody can hasten a patient into treatment quicker than a medical doctor letting the alcoholic know how devastating the damage can be to his body.

Once, however, the doctor and patient are working in the harmony of treatment, the medical man provides a stimulus for the recovering alcoholic which is exhilarating.

One of the tragedies I sense still permeating the air as it did in the 1950's is the weakness of not being willing to

44

cooperate with each other in fighting this insidious disease. Yet, the more open a person is to others' expertise, the better grounded we all are, personally and professionally.

Recently a large Midwestern city was scandalized by a feud among welfare and social and government agencies. Once a government agency declared they would not help in the alcoholic recovery program because alcoholism should be considered "willful misconduct." It is difficult to appreciate the fact that many people still feel that way about the disease today. Encouraging is the fact that most health insurance companies now pay for the treatment and recovery care of the alcoholic. A survey I made recently disclosed that 82 percent of our companies now give the alcoholic sick leave with pay for treatment.

It is a joy to see the doctor, in whom most families put their trust, gain the confidence of the alcoholic.

QUESTION:
WHAT DOES THE EXPRESSION "DRY DRUNK" MEAN?

SELVIG:

It means the condition of a recovering alcoholic who is not happy with his lot. Sobriety has not brought him the freedom of fulfillment he is hoping for. It is the irritating condition, resembling the one he was in when he would drink alcohol while suffering from the disease. He becomes agitated quickly. He feels frustrated. He feels inferior. He can have a variety of emotions—all bad in the "dry drunk."

He is quick to blame the other person when things go wrong. He will say such things as, "When I was drinking, I didn't worry about this." His nerves are like sandpaper. His ability to function is hamstrung. He feels hopelessly penned in. The chains of sobriety weigh heavily. He is up-tight with sobriety—but afraid to drink.

The "dry-drunk" alcoholic can be as equally frustrating to live with and as difficult to understand as when he was pouring down alcohol. He may be plagued by the despair he feels when he realizes the days he's lost through drinking. He usually dwells on "the good times" of the past—forgetting the problems they led to. In any Alcoholics Anonymous group of 10 men there will be two or three who will admit to experiencing "dry drunks," usually not more than twice a month. Ironically, it is usually these men who have prided themselves on giving up liquor themselves without the intervention of another party or without undergoing rehabilitation or recovery facilities. On one hand, they pride themselves that "I did it by myself—with no damn help." On the other hand, they probably still don't understand why they drank, the emotions surrounding their drinking, what feelings they should now experience and what sobriety should lead them to.

I am convinced that the "dry drunk," a serious depression in some instances, is far more prevalent among the alcoholics who have not been hospitalized or have not had the benefit of family counseling.

In the main, "dry drunk" alcoholics are people who haven't yet learned how to share their feelings with others. If an alcoholic will tell his AA group, loved ones or close friends that he is experiencing a difficult time and must talk to someone, he can generally "share himself" out of those tensions.

There is another moot point, too. The "dry drunk" alcoholic may have been a nervous, irritable, up-tight individual long before turning to alcohol. It's perhaps a bit caustic, but every time the subject of the "dry drunk"

46

comes up, I am reminded of what a dear old judge said to me: "If you have a drunken nut and remove the alcohol, you still may be left with the nut."

In this case, if you remove the "dry drunk's" belief that he feels rotten because he can't drink, you just might find a person who was always irritable and high strung. That could be his very nature. Blaming the alcohol may be just another bit of selfishness the alcoholic must overcome enroute to his recovery.

Personally, I feel the term "dry drunk" is overused and abused by a society which doesn't understand the alcoholic in the first place. The constant need of the alcoholic's critics to put a label on the behavior results in the degrading term. The accuser may be simply hostile toward the alcoholic or he could be parroting somebody else (Well, Sam calls it a "dry drunk"). Society must understand that a recovering alcoholic can have a bad day like anyone else. The term "dry drunk" is hitting below the belt. No human being trying to fight a potentially killing disease should have to have his behavior branded forever.

Examples:

Peter is so proud of his sobriety most of the time, particularly when he explains, "I simply walked away from my last beer at midnight in the Legion Hall. Nobody pressured me. But I just decided 'this is it.' " Fine. But Peter never really found out why he drank or where it was leading him or the extent of the danger to his health—physical or mental.

Now, when he is tempted as he sees friends consume alcohol at parties and sporting events, he becomes edgy and frustrated. He has not fully comprehended why he drank, the full consequences, the inner conflicts. Around the house he will become virtually intolerable for a week to ten days approximately every two months. He berates his wife for trying to keep him from having a good time and he continually reminisces about his escapades, particularly his amorous conquests, while drinking.

Peter still needs help. He will continue to have "dry drunks" until he is fulfilled by sobriety, but he won't be fulfilled until he can understand the disease and its many dimensions.

* * *

The robust former football hero usually goes into dry drunks after a reunion with his old college football peers. "I feel damn good when I first meet them. Then, when they start drinking beers, I tighten up inside and ask myself, 'Why me? Why me? What have I done to deserve this?' I quit thinking about how well things have been going and wish I could be funnier or act a little crazy or jump into their silly routine. I know I shouldn't. I get angry at myself for being an alky. I get mad at people who called it to my attention. I despair with my lot in life. I just feel like hell and get ornery."

Not uncommon. But the hope for the ex-jock could lie in longevity of his sobriety. As he becomes aware of his advantages and becomes more aware that the silly get-togethers of his ex-mates are so meaningless, he'll find the "dry drunks" becoming more rare.

It is perfectly normal that there are always times when the recovering alcoholic wishes he could drink with his friends. But these longings should arise no more often than with a man with a crippled hand who wishes he could play golf, or no more often than a one-armed man who wishes he were better on the dance floor. Growing up for the alcoholic means accepting that he has contracted a terminal disease—and beaten it. He will find serenity in that belief as the days go on.

"Dry drunk" is a condition that could be attached to the feelings of unrest, grouchiness, tension that just about all adults feel at one time or another. The alcoholic attaches a great significance to these feelings and takes them up with lack of liquor. The bottle was always a place into which he could crawl and hide until the bad feelings went away.

Now he realizes the guilt feelings of his drinks would be far more difficult to live with than the temporary "dry drunk." An AA friend of mine who admits to having dry drunks three or four times a year says, "I just bite the bullet and my lower lip. They wear off. I'm a little tough to live with but my family seems to know what is wrong. They sympathize. And I try to stay out of their way."

If the person were not an alky, they would simply say, he's jumpy or nervous today. The alcoholic, that sometime romantic individual which a goodly portion pictures themselves, must make a more dramatic connotation of his jangled nerves, and the truly unhappy alcoholic must gird himself for a dangerous period. His "blues" could result in a binge that might destroy him.

QUESTION:
ARE CERTAIN TYPES OF DRINK MORE LIKELY TO CAUSE ALCOHOLISM?

SELVIG:

The answer, of course, is no. Beer drinkers are notorious for saying when they reach the bottom of the barrel, "Well, one thing I'm not an alcoholic—I just drink beer." Naturally their appraisal is idiotic.

It doesn't matter if a man drinks straight gin, vodka, brandy, sour mash, wine or beer. As long as it contains alcohol, it will feed the disease. Beer-drinkers are perhaps the most stubborn because beer, through media advertising, has such a common connotation. It is the drink to have when bowling, watching football, baseball, basketball or at picnics. It is accepted almost universally as a natural wash. But it is as insidious as any liquor—perhaps more so. That's because the alcohol is taken in lesser quantities or mixed with other ingredients.

The beer drinker who is the alcoholic will have five or six beers, which are the equivalent of two or three martinis, depending on the strength of the beer. It just takes longer to reach the point of irrationality. The insanity of the alcoholic is just as threatening and real with beer as it is with gimlets or grasshoppers or scotch-on-the-rocks. Fully 30 percent of the alcoholics I have worked with were beer drinkers. That tells the story clearly.

Examples:

Hondo, as his pals called him, became an alcoholic at 30 and drank heavily for another decade. He began as a gin drinker and always contended that gin entered the bloodstream quicker than any other beverage.

When his wife asked him to quit his gin-with-a-twist favorite, he went to martinis, explaining that the vermouth would "soften" the impact of the drink. Naturally he staggered under the weight of martinis. Then came vodka, which Hondo was sure he could handle and which he was sure his wife could not smell. She didn't have to. He fell through their storm door one night with his mother-in-law sitting in the living room.

Next, Hondo tried Canadian whiskey. By then the blackouts were coming with more regularity. So, in desperation, he switched to wine—which he'd sip with cheese or crackers. The night he drove into a utility pole and killed a passenger, he explained he had "only" five or six glasses of wine. It matters not whether it's beer, wine or whiskey—all are lethal to the alcoholic. All are potential killers.

* * *

His name's Robert, a stately, personable gentleman who runs a respected restaurant in a Southern state. He son, Eddie, has had numerous problems with his alcoholism. The father refuses to believe Eddie is an alcoholic.

In the past two years, Eddie has smashed up two cars, has been arrested twice for drunken driving, ruined his marriage, disappeared for a week with $3,000 from the till, and still father Bob says he is not an alcoholic. Last time I spoke with Bob he said, "Eddie is going to be all right. I've got him off the margaritas. Just beer now. I don't tolerate anything stronger than beer. It's the cocktails—those damn fancy drinks—that he can't take."

Now mind you, the father has been around liquor most of his life. He is still convinced that the type of drink causes the problem. Eddie, in short order, will soon be again crashing cars, fighting, and disappearing—whether he is drinking mild beer or sipping wine. It's not the margaritas, it's the alcohol.

* * *

Most alcoholics try a variety of drinks—each one of which, they hope, will be the panacea for their plight; hoping against hope that one certain concoction will provide the elation and the fulfillment they seek while still enabling them to control their judgement and senses. They try to discover the drink they can handle with decorum and aplomb. It never happens. It's a fool's search. They deceive themselves for a while.

I know a man who said he really thought he found the answer—just four drinks a day: scotch and milk. He thought it would work so slowly and that the milk would be so beneficial to his body that he would remain in control and have a health stimulant as well! After four of his favorites he one day drove his car through a store front. "My God, they hit me worse than anything I ever drank!" he said from the hospital. Not worse—not better.

There is no easy drink. No governable alcoholic drink. No drink which enables the drinker to keep control, because the alcoholic mind and system seeks the level of alcohol which will maintain its high, its feeling of superiority and strength. If it takes three types of one drink or nine of another, the alcoholic will continue to try and quench the insatiable thirst—until he has become immobilized or cannot think reasonably.

It matters little if the alcohol content is heavy or light. If it is heavy, the alcoholic loses control and his mind borders on the insane a little more quickly. That's why you will see men who say, "I just have two martinis before steaks," invariably winding up with two or three more martinis or some other strong, quick-reacting drink after dinner. The body cries out for "more alcohol! more alcohol!" That is the terrible way with the alcoholic.

The insanity of the alcoholic is just as threatening and real with beer as it is with gimlets or grasshoppers or scotch-on-the-rocks. Fully 30 percent of the alcoholics I have worked with were beer drinkers. That tells the story clearly.

QUESTION:
IF ALCOHOL IS A DEPRESSANT, WHY DO SO MANY PEOPLE USE IT AS A PARTY STIMULANT?

SELVIG:

It is a depressant. In other words, the first two drinks do bring feelings of relaxation to most drinkers, a reduction of the inhibitions. We have pointed out the amazing personality change of the alcoholic: feeling confident, inspired, strong, intelligent, daring, and superior to others.

But every high is inevitably followed by a sag. The alcoholic's system craves more alcohol—so he sustains his drinking longer and harder than the non-alcoholic.

And the higher the rate of euphoria—the greater plunge when the alcohol consumption stops. Thus, while alcohol certainly is a depressant, the drinker nonetheless doesn't think about the low feeling—only the "good" feeling. He hopes that each new drinking experience will end differently—that the high will be retained.

His pursuit is useless. The highs become less effusive —the lows become longer and heavier. The roller coaster ride finally begins to go all downhill.

Listen to the words of an intelligent alcoholic on his search for the eternal Valhalla of high: "I think subconsciously I kept on drinking not for the reward of the good feeling—but to see if I might not conquer the inevitable low. I prayed for the day that the low would not come and I could keep the warm, fine glow. But it was not to be. And every alcoholic must realize that. If you don't know the price of the high is pain and sorrow and anger and internal despair, then you are an idiot. There is no way around it."

And another alcoholic who died in my arms said:

"If only I could have kept the good feeling. But where did it go?"

Examples:

Louis claimed he knew why pirates were so abusive —they drank rum and rum made them murderously mean. But the point with Louis was that the depressive effects of alcohol in his system far overrode the pleasant feelings of the drink.

On the way up, through four or five drinks, Louis was a fast-talking charmer. Suddenly, almost as if somebody had pushed a switch, he became argumentative, selective; a badgering, angry human being. He knew full well what to expect each time he drank. But he explained with embarrassment to me, "I thought each time maybe I wouldn't have that nasty feeling. I hoped the good feeling would stay. I even tried drinking alone in my hotel room watching a TV football game. But in the end I wound up smashing the set when my favorite team was beaten! Then I knew I couldn't control when or how the depressed feeling set in. It was like a shadow passing over me."

* * *

A tired young man named Dennis was a graduate student who suffered from a low thyroid condition. He seemed to lack pep and energy. He began drinking, hopeful it would give him the zest for life he so dearly sought. Lo, and behold, it did. For two years he worshipped at the temple of the cork—so happy he had found the elixir to spunk and spirit. He was a changed man—a night creature, partying and venturing far into the wee hours.

Gradually, however, the depressions after his drinking became acute. The sags were worse than normal and absolutely inevitable.

Alcoholism gripped him as if he were in a vise. As he tried to come off the horrible lows, he'd drink more than ever. And because he was drinking more, the lows became longer and drearier and he became a shaken hulk, sometimes as long as two and three days after his high had worn off.

So depressed was he that Dennis tried to cut his wrist, but as he explained weakly from a hospital bed: "I was too worn out to make even a good cut." But it gives you an idea of what a debilitating low can follow a high.

Of course, alcohol appears to be a stimulant, but only for a time. Then the depression. Sometimes it hits earlier, depending on the person and his health. If an alcoholic has another health problem, like Dennis, one which already is weakening the system, the low will be prone to last longer and with more wearing effects. And the longer the low, the more the remorse and guilt feelings which can utterly destroy an alcoholic.

* * *

The dear little widowed housewife decided to come back to work after her children had grown. But because she had been away from her occupation as a public relations person for hospitals, she was frightened by the prospect of returning to the sidewalks.

To bolster her fears she turned to alcohol in the morning, hoping that just a drink would enliven her spirits and infuse her personality with sparkle. But she gradually needed three or four drinks and then three or four more in the afternoon before her late rounds.

In the end, she became so dependent on alcohol she began keeping an open bottle in the car. Needless to say, Marcy, the housewife, could not make contacts with service groups with alcohol on her breath and her language jumbled, her points blurred. She lost her job and in despair retreated to her home and seclusion where she became a prime victim of alcoholism.

In her torment at not having been able to face the public again and ashamed of her efforts, Marcy sank lower and lower into fits of depression after short periods of alcohol high. An overdose of sleeping pills called attention to her plight. Her college children returned and with the aid of their family minister managed to get her into treatment.

She told me the classic story of how the victim of alcoholism keeps expecting the feeling of alcoholic elation to soar on indefinitely. The pain and the mystery of the disase are exemplified by the fact that, while the alcoholic is drinking, never does the thought enter his head of the repercussions to come.

The payment extracted is a horrible one—the kind that leads to emotional trauma, suicides, a complete loss of self-respect.

* * *

No depressive reaction is worse than the alcoholic who loses all moral values—winds up the next morning with a stranger in a room reeking of stale air, alcohol, and sweaty body odors. This abyss of depression is so severe, coupled with the remorse of marriage betrayal, that is has been known to bring on heart attacks and other physical damage. Yes, alcohol is very much a depressant, camouflaged by short, soaring highs which, ironically, blot out the thought of the inevitable drop.

At this point we see why alcoholism is so difficult to treat and why it is such a problem for the alcoholic to realize the scope of his disease—because it is a disease which camouflages its depression with the momentary elation so that the victim does not give a thought to the alternative of feeling normal or to pay heed to the coming, irrepressible agony of the low.

For instance, if a person were suffering from a serious skin malady and it worsened the more he drank orange juice, he might have a glassful and then say: "Oh, oh. That's enough. Another glass and it will hurt my skin." Or a person might have acute stomach pains after too much salt. He might sprinkle on a trifle and then, as the meal progressed, say, "I feel uncomfortable. I guess I better lay off any more salt."

But the alcoholic's mind is so mesmerized and anesthetized or paralyzed that common sense does not enter into it; only the elation of the moment, the magical escape from reality.

It is absolutely mentally and physically impossible for a confirmed alcoholic to stop drinking after three or four glasses of liquor and say, "Oh, I better not go on. I'm going to pay for this." That is why he is an alcoholic, the unpredictableness. The social drinker knows what is in store and may on occasion get "blasted." The alcoholic may know, but his mind is not capable of passing on the information to his body to quit. He is caught in a horrible, tightening vise.

Where but in alcoholism does a person aggravate and torment his body, torture himself, while unable to stop the very thing which is slowly killing him because he feels so good? Alcohol destroys the will and inclination to stop. Nowhere, but in the throes of this mysterious disease, does such a phenomenon occur.

I think I subconsciously kept on
drinking not for the reward of the good
feeling—but to see if I might not
conquer the inevitable low. I prayed for the
day that the low would not come and I could
keep the warm, fine glow. But it was not to be.

QUESTION:
WHAT FEELINGS SHOULD ALCOHOL CREATE?

SELVIG:

Excellent question. Rather than be a stimulant, which it appears to become for the alcoholic, it should be a relaxant. It should not unshackle all inhibitions—just untie gently a few nervous bonds.

For instance, over 25 percent of the adult population suffers from shyness. It can be a suffocating dilemma at social events. A drink or two should relieve the tension. The shy person should shed enough inhibitions to open conversations.

This is in no way the same as the mood changer or the personality transformation of the alcoholic. Just a light, balming, soothing effect. It goes back to my earlier explanation that a casual or social drinker should be as comfortable as the next person on two drinks and never more than three. He should want to be adequate—but never try to dominate or feel superior. Then he is infringing on the path to alcoholism.

In most people, the "little button" I refer to triggers them to quit after about two and one-half drinks.

Examples:

In a large Las Vegas entertainment arena seating over 1,500 people, all of the customers are given four highballs or cocktails with their ticket of admission. I was curious to see, after the show, what amount of the gratis liquor had been consumed. I made a close inspection and found that on the average a little more than one drink was still left at each place setting.

I asked two waitresses and they confirmed that only

about one person in eight drinks all four drinks—even though it is a part of the ticket "package." I think that is a typical national average. And you must remember these patrons were in a better mood and in more of a partying atmosphere than most drinkers.

* * *

It was $100 per plate athletic stag with all the drinks the crowd could handle in a swank Twin Cities restaurant. I checked with the owner after the affair since his cut was predicated on how many drinks were consumed. In the two-hour-long cocktail session preceding dinner, the average was a modest 2.4 drinks.

He was surprised and a little disappointed. "I thought all these big he-men would hammer themselves. But only a dozen or so had five drinks and a lot only one or two." Again, he was right on target. The alcoholic would like us to believe that everyone consumes mightily at social functions. But this is far from the truth. The alcoholic mind pretends everyone else is drinking as much and that his rate of consumption is normal when actually he is drinking twice as much as the others.

I carried my study into the sports arena since athletic fans are known as hard drinkers. I had heard that at certain college campuses the fans were "all stoned" by halftime. Although it is against the law to bring alcoholic beverages into the stadium, I was informed "they all do."

After the game, when the crowd had left, I made a spot check. Over 50,000 fans had been in the stands. I counted only 355 empty bottles under the benches. Since nobody likes to carry around an empty bottle, I had to assume most of those who drank from them left them behind.

At the rate, the crowd wasn't nearly as "stoned" as I had been led to believe. The truth is, figuring two to a bottle, only .012 percent found it necessary to add their own particular "feeling" to the fun of the colorful game.

The alcoholic would have us believe 99 percent were drinking because he and perhaps two others in the row were hitting the bottle. It is a common trait of the alcoholic to tell others, "Everyone was belting themselves out." It eases his conscience.

* * *

Mary is a sweet, small-town girl who came to the big city and became an instant success as an interior decorator. Her taste in color and fabrics was excellent. However, she tensed up when meeting people. She rarely met strangers in the small farming community where she had been raised.

Mary was inhibited. Tight. She found that two glasses of wine, while not changing her personality, enabled her to feel relaxed when meeting new friends and enjoying conversation. Through her increased social awareness, she began to loosen up in her work dealings. She still enjoys a glass or two of wine at social functions but has found that, with gaining more confidence, she can relate easily to her clientele. Mary is a social drinker. And it has been an aid.

The alcoholic can't stand the sipping drinker. "For God's sake, drink it or give it to me," he says.

Look out for the voluntary bartender. Many practicing alcoholics take over this role to keep track of the liquor supply. Make sure the amateur bartender isn't playing the role for his own "benefit."

"Whiskey, my friend, can turn a rumble into a thunderbolt; an orderly man into a frenzied fool. No potent changes a man's mask so quickly."
Anon.

QUESTION:
IS IT TRUE THAT A PRACTICING ALCOHOLIC'S DEATH IS THE WORST KIND?

SELVIG:

No question about it. It is the absolutely worst way to die. That's because the victim is leaving this world so alone. He may have a family and friends. But he feels so desperately alone that it is almost impossible to understand his remorse. His pride is gone. Take a man's pride away, they say, and you've left him a vacuum.

Well, the alcoholic has lost his pride. He's alone, riddled by remorse, no pride and nothing to look back upon. What kind of death can be worse? Forget the ailing body. It is the emotional scourge that really kills the alcoholic.

In those last throes of fighting for his life, he may suddenly realize that he gave in to his illness when he could have beaten it; that he's turned his back on all who loved him; and that he has left no legacy but failure.

That torment alone has sent many alcoholics to their graves long before their bodies stopped functioning. More alcoholics, I believe, die of broken hearts than bad livers.

Picture the scene of a man whose wife and four children left him long ago. He wound up in the gutter in a major city, dying of both heart and liver disease. He was only 56. I visited him in the last days and he grasped my hand while tears rolled down his cheeks.

"God, you're the only human being on the face of the earth who cares. Oh, God, Dick, this is hell. I couldn't wish this on my worst enemy! I could take the pain. But the thought I wasted my life and nobody cares; oh, God, what a way to go. Get out there and try to help the bums like me. It's the loneliness that kills. And the thought I threw away my health."

If it were true that a dying man's life flashes past him at the last moment, the alcoholic must go out in complete despair. For all he can remember is the times he disappointed his loved ones and his friends. He goes out a complete failure. It is not as if he left the world a poor man who died attempting to better himself. The dying alcoholic is ravaged not just by the physical complications but by the realization he gave the world nothing, he destroyed himself, he feels he let his God down and he has no one to share his last moments with.

It brings about indescribable anguish. The only freedom he faces from the bottle is ultimate death. And the death he suffers is slow and torturous since he usually faces it without a helping hand.

Examples:

The man had been a success but drank himself to a failure and after 25 years was lying on his deathbed. He leaned over to me and whispered, "Oh, what a helluva way to go. I gave it all away—my friends, health, family, God. I can't stand myself! I'm so afraid to die!"

I guess that sums it up. The dying alcoholic can't stand himself. Another lady of 55 years of age told me before passing away from a myriad of alcohol-induced ills, "I'm so sorry. I just couldn't stop. Oh, God, if I could only do it over again." The remorse of being a failure. It has to eat up the soul.

* * *

The man was only 35 years old, but after hallucinating for a week was near death when he came to his senses for a few moments.

"The worst," he wept, "is that I'm alone. I did it all to myself." And a week later I saw a rugged old fellow who had fought ill health and alcoholism for 30 years say, "I thought I could win. But nobody can beat the booze. What a terrible way to die."

61

The one common denominator among dying alcoholics: they feel so terribly alone. Oh, they can have a loved one standing nearby, but they know that through their own will and volition they have not only ruined their lives but disappointed their loved ones.

Actually, by being practicing alcoholics, they had lost the freedom to function. But in their sober moments they had choices. And they made the wrong ones.

The alcoholic knows he put himself on his deathbed as surely as if he plunged a dagger into his chest. That's a terrible reckoning. It is heart-rending to see the alcoholic on his deathbed. Few close relatives can even stand the sight. He is dying in despair. He is humiliated. He is tormented. He is without hope: how can he even gird himself to face a hereafter knowing he has thrown his life away?

He is as much a suicide as if he cut his own throat. He lies there, knowing he is a coward, and even more, having lost the respect of his associates. That has to be a mortal wound. One told me, "Look what I've done to myself."

* * *

On the other hand, let me tell you about a recovering alcoholic dying of cancer. He had only a week or so to live when I visited him. He, too, was down, naturally. Self-pity had set in. But I told him, "Joe, wouldn't it be hell to be in here for drinking? Think how miserable you'd be. Now you've got your family around you. You proved your guts by turning your back on the booze. Imagine how you'd feel if you were lying here, kicking the gong because you didn't quit drinking. You've got your sanity, and you're going out with people's respect. That's what means so much to your family."

He brightened up. He even laughed. And then he gripped my hand and said, "Dammit, you're right. I shouldn't complain. God, I couldn't stand myself if I were dying from booze."

* * *

A mother, broken-hearted by the death of her 40-year-old son through alcoholism, wiped away her tears and told me, "I would rather he'd have died from a policeman's bullet than this way. You can't believe the pain to a mother. What a terrible waste."

**More alcoholics, I believe,
die of broken hearts than
bad livers.**

QUESTION:
HOW MUCH COURAGE DOES IT TAKE TO QUIT DRINKING?

SELVIG:

Does it take courage to walk unarmed into a nest of bandits? Does it take courage to put down a cane after 30 years and walk unaided down a flight of steps? Does it take courage to say to close friends, "I'm suffering from a disease that could make me a social outcast?"

Oh, God, how it takes courage to quit drinking—even when you realize that you are saving your life by doing so!

It takes more courage than leaping into quicksand to save a child. For, in that action, you are doing something almost out of instinctive relexes. But to quit alcoholic drinking is to walk away from a support and a way of life you have known for years. It takes as much courage as it does for a farmer to move into the big city, knowing he can never return to the fields. It takes as much courage as leaving a steady job of 25 years to take a flyer in a profession you hardly know. It takes the courage of a Spartan warrior to quit. It take a strong man to pull apart the veil of a new world and say, "I am going forward—for better or for worse."

Put together the bravery of a combat soldier, a battling boxer, a politician starting a new party, a crusader in a foe's camp of thousands, and a man accepting a new life, sight unseen. Put together all of these and you have some idea of the courage it takes to give up alcohol—a force so strong it has dominated races and civilizations.

Tell a poet he doesn't dare to dream. Tell a historian he can never again look to the past. Tell a garage mechanic he can never again lift a wrench. The alcoholic who walks away from liquor is a man of right and strength and courage beyond imagination. You've heard smokers praised who quit the cigarette. But that is not the same. The cigarette was also a process which changes the feelings. It was a relaxer, not an energizer; a tranquilizer, a fantasizing force, all at once.

Put it this way. The alcoholic is suffering a pain—be it mental or physical or emotional. And he knows he can count on the alcohol to relieve him of his pain for an indefinite period; to make him a new person. Now he has to walk away from that pain-killer. He has to face today without a crutch, without support. He must suddenly become naked, vulnerable.

I have such a deep, abiding love and admiration for the recovering alcoholic. He is not a weakling. He is a person of fortitude and great strength. The alcoholic is to be admired above others who never had to fight the disease. For he is a man who has cast off a steel yoke and chains (which were forged in addictive servitude) so much more difficult to break than anyone can imagine.

Examples:

"Terrible Tuck" was a broad-shouldered, hard-hitting middleweight boxer. He was known as a fighter who would spot an opponent 10 pounds and carry the fight to his man in any ring because he was, as a sports writer put it, "a recklessly aggressive puncher, unafraid of man or animal; a throwback to the days when a

64

fighting man did his thing in saloons, alleys, or pits."

He had over 90 fights, many of them blood baths. None of them were easy. He was a preliminary fighter—a tribal horse. A man who tested potentially gifted young fighters.

He became a 10-drink-a-day alcoholic. When he quit he told me, "It was tougher than any fight I ever had. In the ring, I knew what was in front of me, was another fighter with two arms and two legs and a heart. When I went in to find sobriety I didn't know what I was encountering.

"I was never so frightened in my life. It was a new threat—a threat to the way I'd been living. Fighting in the ring was child's play compared to doing battle with my disease. There was nothing to it. Nothing to make me bleed. Oh, yes, I bled inside when I let them take my bottle away."

* * *

An outdoor guide told me his feelings. "I once rowed a flimsy raft across a stormy, churning river in a park to rescue some kids in a flood. I took that in stride. But giving up booze. I must have fought it for three years. I couldn't bear to think of giving up that bottle. It was my life-line.

"God, how I agonized! It was far greater torture to walk away from the bottle once and for all than I ever encountered on windy cliffs in the mountains, or in dangerous rapids. Those were things I could see and feel. I didn't know what to expect when I gave up drinking." The fear of the unknown is the most agonizing fear of all.

* * *

The little man had once been a driver for a robbery gang. He had served his sentence. In the course of his jail term he had been ripped up in prison knife fights. He had been assaulted by the homosexuals. He had been ridiculed and berated by bigger, tougher cons. But nothing he faced was comparable, he told me, to throwing away his beloved bottle.

"It was a nightmare. After I decided to quit, and before

I went to treatment, I would toss and roll all night in bed. I was lucky to sleep an hour. God, the thought of quitting once and for all nearly drove me crazy. Christ, I'd rather have faced a firing squad. That would be over quickly. I didn't know how long or how tough or if the treatment would kill me. Treatment turned out to be the roughest thing that happened to me in my whole life."

* * *

The soldier volunteered to go through a two-mile infiltration course in a Texas infantry camp. He told me: "The bombs would go off within feet of us. We crawled on our bellies and machine gun fire ripped over our heads, just inches above us. None of us really thought we'd come out alive. Well, when I quit drinking, that infiltration bit became child's play. My first week without a drink was such torture I would sit in my chair at night holding myself tightly with my own arms—to keep from shaking to pieces."

And the footballer (who once carried the ball for 44 times against a national championship foe) said: ". . . called the game a picnic compared to giving up the bottle."

* * *

A poet-friend who used to nearly starve between getting his works published, put it all on the line.

"I've faced deprivation and starvation. I've faced disappointment. I've faced family ridicule and I've faced cursing landlords. I've faced winter nights in unheated warehouses and I've faced days when I couldn't make my mind work enough to write a page of copy.

"But nothing in 40 years of battling to be a poet compared with giving up the bottle. God, to walk away from my old buddy into the unknown was almost too much to bear. Don't give me the trash that you rush in, hopefully thinking how great it is going to be when you are cleansed with your body and mind saved. Hell, I was only thinking. 'How can I do it? How can I live without my drink? How can I survive?' It was gruesome.

"Giving up drinking takes more courage than leaping out of a plane, I'm sure. I like to compare it with suicide. I'm sure giving up something you've loved has to be more difficult than shoving your head in an oven and giving up something like a life you can't stand."

The man who quit drinking has won the most difficult battle he may ever have to face in his life. Certainly the most frightening.

* * *

One of my best friends, a recovering alcoholic, met me one morning and said, "Dick, I dreamt last night that a guy had a gun pointed at me and said, 'Drink or I will shoot you.' Do you know what I told him? 'Shoot, you son of a bitch!'

To this man sobriety is the most important possession he has. It was worth the struggle. But he admitted: "You couldn't tell me a few years back it was worth it. Drunks, headaches—but I knew they'd go away. I knew the bottle was there and the good feeling would return. When I quit, hell, who knew what to expect? I just took my friends' word for it that it would be good, that things would start to go right. Quitting alcohol was as tough for me as it would be for a saint to give up his love for his God."

Here again is the irony of the disease. That which is so difficult to give up actually comes back as a bonus when the recovery begins. The patient has had to show such admirable strength and will that now he knows he can conquer whatever lies ahead. He knows he can face up to the world sober because he has proven his power by turning his back on the bottle.

The very strength which enables the alcoholic to give up the liquor, flows into his efforts at sobriety. I say the alcoholic is a person of awesome fortitude and inner power. To make that giant step takes the courage of an adventurer and the dedication of a Michelangelo.

These are the people to be admired and praised.

I have such a deep, abiding love
and admiration for the recovering
alcoholic. He is not a weakling.
He is a person of fortitude and
great strength. The alcoholic
is to be admired above
others who never had to fight
the disease.

QUESTION:
WHY DOES SOCIETY HAVE SUCH
DIFFICULTY UNDERSTANDING
ALCOHOLISM?

SELVIG:

Because society either tries to categorize alcoholism—or
tries to hide it. Let me explain: Society has the unhappy
faculty of trying to place "drunks" in various files. For instance, society thinks of the typical alcoholic as that vile
human wretch lying on the sidewalk Sunday morning, a
broken wine bottle at his elbow. That's Mr. Alcoholic to
the general public.

Then you have the laughable fellow who tells the dirty
joke at the party, pours his drink down the front of the
hostess's gown, and finally falls asleep with a potted
palm in his lap. And has his wife drive him home. He's
the "party drunk," no nemesis to society but just a Good
Time Charlie who can't handle the liquor at parties. Few
people call him an alcoholic.

And you have the suave, well-dressed professional
man. He can have his three-martini lunch, his three
scotches after a round of golf, and his three-drink night-
cap, but nobody in his circle would consider this suc-

cessful businessman an alcoholic. He is just part of the social circle and the fast-paced business world.

In other words, society has labeled the gutter bum an alcoholic, the heavy party guy as a "social drinker" who can't handle celebrations—and the businessman as a solid "controlled drinker." The truth is all of the them are alcoholics and perhaps the party fellow and the businessman are further advanced alcoholics than the poor transient on the sidewalk. He probably has consumed far less alcohol but because his body is in such a weak state due to hunger and privation, the wine has had a much more telling effect.

Few segments of society are prepared today to accept the fact that all the people suffer from the same type of disease. Few would dare categorize the board chairman or the country club president with some drinkers on Skid Row. But they are one and the same—sufferers of a terminal disease.

Now for what I call "the great coverup." That's the universal trait of families and loved ones and friends and business associates to protect alcoholics from "discovery." In any other form of illness, loved ones would be rushing the patient to a doctor or the hospital. Not so with alcoholics. Every one around them is tempted to hide the alcoholic's problem for fear it will cast a reflection on themselves.

Mothers do it, fathers do it, wives and husbands, bosses and social companions. Nobody wants to be the first to say, "I think Dave might be an alcoholic." Because most people feel vulnerable about some fault of their own. By pointing a finger, they are setting the stage for a reprisal from someone else ("You've got a problem, too, too much smoking"), and because they fear the loss of the alcoholic's love or friendship.

The result is a society which is prone to define alcoholism not so much by the effect on the sufferer as much as by the circles in which he travels. You have a society, still the greater share of which is fearful of itself absorbing some stigma of the alcoholic's discovery.

This great cover-up is everywhere. I've seen wives of

Alcoholics Anonymous members refuse to attend AA public functions for fear of being recognized. I've seen companies keep an alcoholic's treatment a secret. I've seen schools cover up for professors and teachers. And I've seen athletic teams cover up for coaches and players.

Between trying to label "drunks" good, bad or unharmful, and then hiding the problem because it fears repercussions, society has placed itself in a colossally vulnerable and foolish situation. It spends billions of dollars on experimentation to alleviate the pains of cancer, heart disease and blood disease, and it looks the other way from an illness which is one of the greatest and most expensive killers on the globe.

Examples:

I was going to church with a group of friends one Sunday morning and we came upon two derelicts, wine bottles in tow, struggling down the street.

"God, isn't that disgusting!" one of the church-goers exclaimed. "People like that should be put away—in jails or treatment centers. Common drunks. If they could only see themselves."

Later that afternoon the same group was watching a professional football game on television. The woman who had made the remarks about the drunks on the street was the hostess. Before the game was half way over, her husband had consumed three martinis. He not only was talking so loudly we couldn't hear the announcer, but he knocked over a tray of cheese and pickles. By the time the game was over he was snoring on the couch.

Never once did the woman see any connection between the bums on the street and her husband. I am sure he had drunk more alcohol in one afternoon than the street bums had put away all night.

* * *

I attended a meeting of a business group at a plush country club. The group had played golf in the afternoon.

70

At night, the drinking was heavy before the dinner and the subsequent speeches. The conversation grew louder, the jokes more off-color. Three of the men telephoned home to tell their wives the "business meeting" was more serious than they thought and that they wouldn't be home until very late.

Two of them proceeded to buy drinks for women at the bar. By the time we got around to the speeches, most of the group were on their fourth and fifth rounds.

The master of ceremonies turned to me and said, "We've got a hard-drinking, loud, aggressive group of men. But, by God, they're salesmen! Broke a two-state record last year. Oh, I suppose they overdo it a bit, but I'll never complain as long as they're producing."

A good case of a company official covering up several men who were headed for drinking problems because their sales record made them look good.

* * *

The coach, newspapers, and announcers all laughed about the football star's drinking. The general manager told me: "He's a wild one. Drinks a quart the day of a game. But I make sure it's good stuff. I don't care if he throws up on the sidelines, as long as he's on the field. He runs better drunk than the rest of my players sober." Shocking, but true. The case of society protecting and covering up a drunk because he was performing well from memory, made everyone look good, and was good copy.

A newspaper writer told me, "I think that kid's got a problem. But if I suggested it, the team'd run me out of town." And it might have.

* * *

The bartender knew the man could not navigate with more than three drinks. He knew he threw his money around and his memory failed after that many. But the bartender also knew he could pick up a healthy tip when the drinker got loose with his change. He would load his

71

drinks, keep him in conversation and eventually make a big kill in the tip department.

That is the ruthless kind of action which corrupts society when it comes to dealing with the alcoholic. There are many people who don't want to see him beat the disease. Others just don't want to believe he is anything more than a Good Time Charlie or heavy drinker.

That's why I say the alcoholic has to have a good-sized soul to encompass his own hope and fend off the problems he encounters from a society which can't bear to believe that one out of seven of its drinking loved ones and friends has a serious health problem.

I've had hundreds of recovering alcoholics tell me: "God, Dick, if somebody around me only knew my problem years earlier."

* * *

Well, many people probably did—and chose to ignore or cover it up. Many others considered the circle in which the alcoholic traveled and concluded he certainly was no bum—alcoholics are the ones in gutters.

**It spends billions of dollars on
experimentation to alleviate
the pains of cancer, heart
disease and blood diseases, and it
looks the other way from an
illness which is one of the
greatest and most expensive
killers on the globe.**

VIEWPOINT

Is alcoholism an illness or a disease of shame?

The greatest problem the alcoholic, family members, friends and other associates have to face is whether they believe alcoholism is an illness or not. Society often defines alcoholism as an illness long before the practicing or recovering alcoholic does. That's why the recovering alcoholic may be prone to threaten that he will drink again. He has not fully accepted the fact he has a terminal illness—and perhaps many of his loved ones have not either.

At the same time, so many non-alcoholic family members, friends and business associates say to the recovering alcoholic: "You are doing so well, I am so proud of you.

"What has happened to you could happen to anyone of the rest of us. Seeing you doing something about your problems is a real inspiration for me. You are a better person now than you have ever been." That approach is so helpful. The alcoholic whose family is aware of his great stuggle can only help his recovery by building up his sense of pride, which usually has been destroyed by his disease.

If the alcoholic can't accept these statements and feel good about himself, he is still fighting the illness concept.

Highly respected Marty Mann, founder of the National Council on Alcoholism, so aptly puts it:

"It is no shame to be an alcoholic but it is a shame to do nothing about it, once the alcoholic is aware of it."

It is even a greater shame to let a recovering alcoholic threaten or coerce his family and friends into giving into his whims when he says he'll return to alcohol if his wishes are not met.

There are strong-willed alcoholics who must be looked in the eye and told directly, "Go ahead, drink, damn you, but next time you recover alone!" There are the more timid who should be approached differently. "John, I can't stop you from drinking. But wouldn't it be a shame to waste all those wonderful days of your recovery for a drink that can only bring misery again?"

It can be a delicate matter. Or it can just be a barrage of words, the recovering alcoholic shouting off his frustrations and knowing that the threat of returning to alcohol is a dagger to his loved ones—a dagger he knows would eventually be turned on himself.

The Alcoholics Anonymous people tell the story of the two friends discussing their friend, Bill, as he lay in the funeral parlor. "How did he happen to die?" one asked the other. And the reply: "He died from drinking. But his wife didn't think drinking was that serious." The other asked again, "She never suggested Alcoholics Anonymous?" And the other replied: "She said he wasn't that bad."

The recovering alcoholic may find himself in a situation where, if his family is not convinced of the seriousness of the disease, his threats will fall on deaf ears. Then in self-defiance, the alcoholic may return to the bottle.

That is why I urge family treatment. If the alcoholic's family is not aware of the perils of the disease, he is alone, bobbing on a sea of self-destruction.

But the man who has been through a raging forest fire and goes back to leaving his campfires glowing, needs help beyond alcoholic treatment. He is a masochist, bent on tormenting himself and everyone around him.

That is why I urge family treatment.
If the alcoholic's family
is not aware of the perils of the
disease, he is alone, bobbing on
a sea of self-destruction.

PART II

CHARACTERISTICS
OF THE
ALCOHOLIC

QUESTION:
WHO CAN BECOME AN ALCOHOLIC?

SELVIG:

The answer was best supplied at a seminar I was holding. This was one of my first questions. None of the adults seemed to have the answer so I turned to one of the children who happened to be at the proceedings. "What are the two kinds of people who can become alcoholics, son?" I asked the eight-year-old.

The child replied readily, **"Men and women."** Of course, he was right.

Any human being who drinks alcohol may become an alcoholic. The disease strikes indiscriminately. It spares neither young nor old, rich nor poor. It strikes in mansions and ghetto hovels. It strikes in small towns and large cities. It is the most frightening disease on earth because it is the most misunderstood. No one is safe. No one can gain immunity with a shot from a needle. It can not be stopped by a quarantine or antiseptic ward. A plague can be stopped by proper medication and medicine. **Alcoholism is extremely difficult to control.**

It is completely ruthless. It can attack youth at an early age—and retired citizens hoping to live out a peaceful, fulfilling life. It can attack important public servants and great artists. It is a disease of such epic proportions it has wiped out empires and crumbled dynasties and even brought into play the powerful wrath of God.

Is is particularly dangerous, because unlike an epidemic—where perhaps a rat-infested atmosphere can be wiped out—there is no germ source to be eliminated. There is no spawning ground to obliterate. And no individual to be vaccinated to prevent the disease from spreading.

It is insidious like no other disease because it comes from within; the growth is a feeling tumor, like a giant, invisible infection eating into the body, soul, and mind. Its implications are so far-reaching that the disease not only can maim and end the lives of its victims—but do irreparable harm to the millions with whom they come in contact.

The irony of alcoholism is that there are millions trying to catch the disease!

The only requirements for membership in the huge alcoholic club are:

(1) a human being;

(2) an alcoholic drink; and

(3) the resulting feelings from the drink.

The potential alcoholic gets a feeling of fulfillment, complete freedom, and complete acceptance almost from the start of his drinking. The alcoholic believes that while he is drinking he has life "all figured out." Soon the feeling of superior intelligence disappears and the alcoholic is left with an emptiness which is almost unbearable.

I walked into a plush lobby of a major hotel to meet three persons who would soon join me for treatment of alcoholism. Let us consider them for a moment.

The one well-groomed, middle-aged man sat fingering a Girard-Perregaux wrist watch. He wore a Calvin Klein sports jacket and radiated success. He was a department store president. He had lived with vast amounts of money.

Next to him sat a frail, small woman, perhaps 40 years of age. The dimpled fresh face could have belonged to your favorite neighbor or babysitter. But look closely. She appeared washed but not clean. There was drabness where the luster should have been. She had trouble holding things. The small hands felt cold at first grasp and trembled ever so slightly.

And across from her sat a rangy-looking youth. He was tall even by today's athletic standards—perhaps six feet five. His dark hair charmed his face in shaggy disorder. He was perhaps 25 years old. His color was good but there was a slight twitch to his right cheek. His foot kicked nervously into the carpet.

Nobody, at first glance, could appear much more normal. They were all alcoholics, in advanced stage.

The well-to-do executive tells me quietly, "I'm in terrible shape. At the age of 55 everything is falling apart —my home, my family, the business. Hell, Dick, you've got to help. I can't beat the bottle alone."

The woman's story is cut from the same cloth. "I'm afraid I'm going out of my mind. I'm a professor's wife. Just when life should be easy it's become terribly hard. Dick, I need help. I'm drinking over a quart a day."

The young man is an athlete. He's a professional basketball player. His coach has sent him to seek advice before his career is ruined. I have nothing to compare his figures with but when he says, "I'm down nearly 10 points a game," I presume the worst. "I can't sleep nights. I'm drinking more and the pressure of the game is getting to me. Help me, Dick, or I'll be a bum before I'm 30."

It is everywhere—the danger of the disease of alcoholism. It is in the schools and the churches and the brokerage houses. It is often camouflaged by the pace of today's society which won't slow enough to recognize the symptoms.

And don't just look in the gutter. It is in the exclusive clubs and in the PTA membership. The killer is so subtle that even loved ones fear to ask—for they aren't sure. The alcoholic himself isn't sure. That's why he fights for every day and every drink with a passion.

Because the disease is so misunderstood and carries such a blemish in many parts of our society, people do not want to examine it too closely. It might be lurking in their own family. For years when I brought up the word "alcoholic," the response I'd get would invariably be: "I know what you mean, Dick—I've seen those drunks in the gutter. Disgusting."

Nobody wanted to believe that the alcoholic was the humorous Mr. Jones next door, the delightful hostess at the church bazaar, or the high school principal.

Examples:

Last year an estimated $39 billion was lost by industry in the United States alone through loss of production and man-hours by the effects of alcoholism.

One out of every three broken marriages and divorces is caused by an alcoholic. Five Presidents of the United States have been alcoholics. Nearly half the tragic auto accidents are caused by drivers in various stages of alcoholism. Nearly half of the job positions lost in this country every year are caused by the disease. In some cases, as much as one-fifth of a hospital population will be treated for alcoholism and its repercussions.

Every alcoholic's disease affects the lives of at least six others on a national average and many influence the lives of hundreds of thousands of people in the case of vital public officials called upon to make key important decisions with alcoholic minds. Alcohol has ended or shortened the career of many brilliant artists, depriving the world of their gifts. One of the nation's most illustrious retirement centers is fighting the highest percentage of alcoholism ever tabulated in a populous Western metropolis. One out of every two homes in this country has association with an alcoholic.

And we all know armies have been virtually destroyed from within by the dread disease.

Today, an estimated 10,000,000 Americans fight the disease and at least another 100 million alcoholics populate the vast reaches of the globe.

* * *

There is no doubt that alcoholism strikes everywhere—men and women of all classes, all backgrounds. At one group session I attended a few years ago, there were included: a judge from Vancouver, a teaching nun from Missouri, a scholar from New York, a banker from Detroit, a newspaper man from Detroit, a housewife from Seattle, an insurance executive from Fargo, a painter from St. Paul, and a woman secretary from Iowa City.

This mixture gives some idea of the ramifications and

diversity of the disease. The nun told me she would drive 60–100 miles to secure a bottle to protect her reputation and that of the convent.

The judge said, "I've seen it all and you'd think I'd have learned. I've sentenced over 500 alcoholics for law violations—yet the disease claimed me, even after I saw all the trouble it caused others."

The banker said, "It is ruining my life—and my family's. Nobody can believe the hold it had and how fast it was wasting my life. Fighting alcoholism is like fighting a vapor." And the housewife confided, "Ten years ago if you said I'd be in a treatment center with alcoholism, I'd have said you were crazy. But here I am. How or when it happened I don't know. But I was powerless to fight it."

* * *

The cross-section waylaid every day by the disease is mind-boggling. In one afternoon I welcomed a race driver, farmer, Army captain, politician, detective, doctor's wife, and used car salesman to our facility.

That's what I mean when I say it can strike anyone—the best student or the worst liar, the most gifted musician or the flop of the class, the football hero—or the skinny beach bum. This is because it's a rare thing—a mind disease, fostered by the people it afflicts. Man or woman—no one is safe.

Don't let anyone tell you that big men can "handle" their booze. Or that little people are affected more quickly. It is the brain which becomes paralyzed or unstable. It is the brain, virtually the same size in all of us, which sends out the messages the liquor conjures up. It is the absorption qualities of the sensitivity system which dictate the effect of the alcohol.

Respectable people are leveled just as frequently as those in lower social strata. Alcoholism is not a respectable illness for it brings out the worst in us. But it claims respectable people with astonishing regularity.

The prime reason why alcoholism is such a hidden problem is because it is a behavioral problem. It is a powerful conveyor of guilt, remorse and self-hate, all repressed to such a degree that the feelings are crying to burst out and rage against loved ones. Yet it is often gallantly camouflaged under the disguise of verbosity, personality, and aggression.

"What are the two kinds of people who can become alcoholics, son?" I asked the eight-year-old. The child replied readily, "Men and women."

VIEWPOINT

It is essential to recovery for the alcoholic to have brought to his attention the way he has carried on when drinking. "I don't know what happened" is the way the alcoholic vainly tries to handle what transpired. An alcoholic has a built-in "forgetter" but it is completely unsuccessful to alleviate the pain, anguish, or the question of "what did I do last night?"

To hide from the alcoholic what he did while drinking is cruel, for he will imagine he was much worse than he was or go to the other extreme, and think he was not so bad. The diseased needs to know the past or he is certain to repeat it in the future. A person's life is made up of the past, present, and anticipated future.

Remember, the present is a product of the past and if we know anything today, and we certainly do, it is due to our past experiences. Sometimes in the blacked-out portions of a drinking bout good was accomplished and we need to hear about that as well. Many times the eyes of the alcoholic can only see with the help of others. This is true of all people, alcoholics and non-alcoholics.

I have heard many people say, "To bring out the behavior of the alcoholic when drinking is degrading the alcoholic." This is far from the truth. An alcoholic needs to know what he has done or else corrections and improved relationships are impossible. The only way I can feel close to any one is when mutual sharing takes place. Not a degrading or embarrassing or critical honesty but a NAKED honesty where the alcoholic's life is like an open book and he is willing to talk about the torn pages.

Aside from the fact that alcoholism claims two kinds of people—men and women—it numbers among its victims three kinds of intellects: (1) the brilliant; (2) the average and (3) the below-average. No one segment has a claim to numerical superiority in the ranks of the alcoholics. A bank president told me, "I drink to relieve the tension of my decisions." He must have had a multitude of decisions for he consumed nearly a quart of scotch a day.

A beloved old bootblack told me while shining my shoes, "Man, being out in this weather really hurts mah bones. But I got a nice little jug of Old Granddad over there in mah pick-up. It gets me through the day."

Alcoholism plays no favorites when it attacks the confidence syndrome. With equal abandon it hits those who appear to have loads of confidence (I can do anything if I set my mind to it); those with some confidence (I think I can handle the situation if everything breaks right); and those with little or no confidence (The world's against me. I never get a break and I never will).

It attacks all types of physical specimens. I know a midget who goes through two pints a day. I know a wrestler who is benumbed by four beers after every bout. I know a former welterweight fighter who nearly died after four scotches.

Remember, alcoholism is caused by what it originally does for the drinker and not what it does to him. Background or breeding has absolutely no bearing on his sensations. Call it the "original sin of alcoholism," there is no explanation. Only the fact that certain people "feel better" with more drinks. They may not act or think better—but they "feel better" to themselves.

It is so ignomatic yet startlingly true that the longer an

alcoholic is sober the earlier he finds that he became an alcoholic.

"All the armies of the earth do not destroy so many of the human race nor alienate so much property as drunkenness."
Sir Francis Bacon

QUESTION:
IS ALCOHOLISM INHERITED?

SELVIG:

Only the sensitivity to alcohol. Let's put it this way. In a family of six children where the grandparents are non-drinkers, why is it that one or two or three of the children will become alcoholics? That doesn't make much of a strong case for inheritance of the susceptibility of the disease. No more than the fact that in many cases where both parents are alcoholic does it stand that the children are all alcoholic.

In one family I know where the parents have both been committed, one of seven children drinks alcohol. But the fact remains: the alcoholic does have a sensitivity for alcohol. This means it has become a major source of fulfillment for him. If the alcoholic did not have that sensitivity, how could so many, in fact almost all alcoholics, tell you exactly when they had their first drink?

I tell people who ask about heredity that an alcoholic no more inherits this sensitivity than he'd inherit the ability to play second base or play the flute in the school band. Let me give another illustration. I checked into the background of one alcoholic who insisted he inherited his "drinking ability." Well, of his closest 38 relatives on both his mother's and father's side, there was not one other instance of an alcoholic. By the same token, another family produced four non-drinking members of the clergy and two alcoholics.

What do I mean by sensitivity?

Let me cite the gentleman who told me of his first drink, down to the minute details of his surroundings. His recollections are vivid. He can remember it all because of his extreme "sensitivity" to alcohol—the kind of sensitivity that many times only one of a large family feels.

He explains the situation of his first drink:

"I was 39 years old and it was midsummer in a bar in Minnesota. The time was 9:30 p.m. and it was a cloudy night. The wind must have been 12 or 13 miles an hour out of the Northwest with gusts up to 20. I had been to a baseball game and the temperature was 75 degrees. The barometer I noticed was 29.35 and rising. It hadn't rained for two days. The humidity was about 40 percent. I had a double gin and tonic. The fulfillment and freedom and the complete acceptance I received were tremendous. My first drink! It was like a spiritual experience. The creator and I were one. It was good. So good."

Most alcoholics can relate the circumstances of their first strong drink with astounding accuracy. The acute awareness and fulfillment of that initial joust with alcohol has to be extremely vivid and poignant to the alcoholic. Rarely can a non-alcoholic recall his first strong drink, I have discovered. Sensitivity to the alcohol, that is the key. Whether or not that sensitivity is inherited is a moot point for speculation. (No more, I feel, than the ability to catch a ball sets some children in a family aside from brothers and sisters.)

Examples:

A brilliant student in law, Tony, was one of four sons of a judge. He had the most talent, the quickest mind. However, he ruined a promising career by drinking profusely, finally being barred from the court. The Judge always asked, "How could it happen to Tony? He was the brightest boy. And nobody in our family, going back 80 years, was an alcoholic.''

All well and good, but Tony had a sensitivity to alcohol. He felt a compelling need.

At first, the two drinks gave him courage. The third gave him verbal glibness. The fourth turned him into a bully. And the fifth made him intolerable. His sensitivity to alcohol was so acute he died of an ailing pancreas at the age of 37 after a long drinking bout. Nothing in Tony's family lineage pointed to his eventual demise from the disease.

*   *   *

A nice young mother named Mabel had three children, a beautiful home in Chicago and an adoring husband. She was brought up a strict Baptist and did not have her first drink until she was 33.

''Then a compulsion came over me. I couldn't quit drinking. I even made excuses to get up in the middle of the night and do some ironing or some other housework and kept hidden bottles of wine in various places around my home. Eventually it cost me my home, children and husband.''

Mabel had never been exposed to drinking in her home. None of her relatives or ancestors for three generations were drinkers. Yet she had an insatiable compulsion in the mid-stages of her adult life to consume vast quantities of liquor because, as she explained, ''It gave me a feeling of warmth and well-being I never enjoyed before.''

She wound up taking treatment in four rehabilitation centers but, sad to say, could not shake the disease which destroyed her at 42. She will die a lonely and forsaken alcoholic in her forties. (Everyone doesn't recover from this illness.) There was absolutely no clue in her family's past to indicate she would inherit vulnerability to this disease.

*   *   *

The accountant named Jerry was a Kansas City civic

leader. His Irish father made him take an abstinence pledge on the altar of his Catholic Church where he was an altar boy. None of his family drank. At the age of 40, for no apparent reason, Jerry began—small amounts at first and then into heavy three-day binges which resulted in blackouts and hallucinations.

For five years he fought the disease. Today he is a recovering alcoholic, living again with respect from his family and the citizenry. He has no explanation for the compulsion of fulfillment he felt in alcohol. Jerry simply had a powerful urge. There was absolutely nothing in his background or heredity to indicate he would be a problem drinker.

I tell people who ask about heredity that an alcoholic no more inherits this sensitivity than he'd inherit the ability to play second base or play the flute in the school band.

QUESTION:
DOES THE NUMBER OF DRINKS DETERMINE IF A PERSON BECOMES AN ALCOHOLIC?

SELVIG:

Absolutely not. There is no measuring stick for an alcoholic. There is a relatively small number of what we call "heavy users" who can consume six to eight drinks and never vary their drinking pattern. They don't disturb the tranquillity of their homes or labors or sleep. However, they never consume more than a particular amount.

The alcoholic never has enough although any alcoholic consumption is actually too much. It's not how much you drink that determines whether you're an alcoholic or not but what it does to you. There are alcoholics who, after two cocktails, cannot find their car. There are alcoholics who, after three scotch and sodas, forget where they live and will launch a four-day drunk.

Alcoholics can be spree drinkers who drink only five or six times a year during holidays but in that period can smash their car, kill a pedestrian, run away with a strange woman, or lose a life-long profession.

No truer statement about an alcoholic has ever been made than this: One drink is too many—and a thousand not enough. The alcoholic can lose reason and lose his freedom to function with anywhere from one to ten drinks. Usually the total depends on his emotional state and the contents of his stomach.

Examples:

Louise drinks only at Christmas time. She contends the sentiment of the season affects her. She does not see any problem. Yet, in one holiday period she lost her job, fell down a flight of stairs, fractured both legs, and drank herself into a stupor in her apartment. During this binge, her cigarette set her bed aflame and she was critically burned. She has no more than six to eight drinks daily during the two-week Christmas season, but is an alcoholic, desperately needing help.

* * *

Phil is a 35-year-old railroad engineer. Once every two or three weeks he visits his in-laws in a small town. He is antagonistic towards them and drinks heavily the day preceding the visit and during the visit. He claims that he drinks only to ease his tensions and become a better conversationalist. But invariably he winds up in arguments with his in-laws and on occasion throws an ash tray through a window.

These temperamental sessions and drinking bouts go

on only the two or three days twice a month, during which Phil visits his wife's relatives. But they cause heated family hassles and the day that Phil returns to work he is moody, irritable, and slow-reacting. Phil is an alcoholic.

* * *

The sweet old gent everyone calls Uncle Edward tells us he drinks only on St. Patrick's day, on the Fourth of July, his birthday, his anniversary of his army discharge, Ash Wednesday, the day before Easter, and two or three other special occasions.

Uncle Edward is 68 years old and sensible most of the time. What he doesn't tell you is that on one Easter morning he demolished his garage. He conveniently forgets that during a wonderful St. Patrick's Day party he pushed an old friend through a glass door, injuring him to the extent of 146 stitches. He won't admit that on the last birthday party for him, thrown by neighbors, he dove into two feet of water in a wading pool, suffered a broken collarbone and missed six days of work. Uncle Edward picks his spots. But he has a severe case of alcoholism.

* * *

The pretty girl down the street named Eleanor is just 16 years old. She rarely drinks according to her parents. According to her friends she drinks only "when it's a dead party." But she has missed 11 days of school by being indisposed after beer busts. She became violently ill at the last two school formals, vomiting in the rest rooms. She says she only "experiments"—but has been sick a dozen times the last year after consuming liquor. Her work in school has fallen off a grade in every course. Nobody appears concerned. But Eleanor is an alcoholic.

* * *

The serious-minded Doreen, a devout Catholic, used to pledge never to drink during Lent, out of respect to her family's tradition. Then, that one fateful night, she had two Lenten drinks with friends and decided to go bowling. She dropped a ball, crushing her foot, culminating in a $7,500 operation which wiped out her bank account. To this day she blames the ball, her friends, the alleys. She refuses to look at herself and say that without the two drinks in Lent, she would not have been injured. She could be an alcoholic. The symptoms are there.

* * *

And there was old Ben, a blind man. He took pride in his seeing eye dog. One night on a rare occasion Ben came home in the arms of John Barleycorn and his faithful dog bit him in the ass with great authority. The canine therapist had told him in no uncertain terms, "I've had enough of your infantile behavior." Ben was not a steady drinker. He imbibed only infrequently. But the dog knew it. He was telling him those few drinks could mean a serious problem to the bodily health of the blind man.

* * *

Joshua is a captain at a prime military academy. He has jurisdiction over 150 youngsters. He admits to a "mild drinking problem." What he has told only his intimates is that one night after four or five wines, he became so unstrung, that in correcting the tests of his pupils he made grave errors.

The grades he meted out were inconsistent and caused his young minions serious mental anguish. He says it won't happen again; that he will cut down to just a couple of drinks when he is correcting tests. While Joshua is not a consistent drinker, he is an alcoholic. Because when he drinks he loses control, loses judgement, and is unwittingly hurting others.

"The first mint julep is a warm promise. The second is a tender caress . . . the third is a serious mistake. . . ."
An old Kentucky Derby drinking rule

QUESTION:
WHAT CHARACTER FAULTS ARE CAUSED BY THE "ALCOHOLIC MIND"?

SELVIG:

Many. Procrastination is a very grave weakness. Lying is a profound problem. Selfishness rears its ugly head continually. Impatience can be an excruciating affliction. Nervousness is rampant. You name it. The gamut of mental and spiritual despair is run by the alcoholic.

No alcoholic is afflicted with just one of these tormenting problems. He usually embodies all of them. Throw in loss of integrity. Then arises vanity and rudeness. Soon you have a completely unbearable character. I return to selfishness. It is always evident.

Thankfully all his weaknesses usually don't rear themselves all at one time or he could disturb people on all sides. But every day one of his bad habits or wayward conclusions have to cause distraction and problems for somebody with whom he comes in contact.

Examples:

I recently had lunch with a major labor leader in California. He is an alcoholic. He did not became a success in business and life until he was 47 years of age and recovering from the disease. I asked him what the difference was between himself as a drunk and as a recovering alcoholic.

He pinpointed procrastination—the putting off of necessary duties. "I would know what had to be done to be a success—what events I had to make transpire. But like all alcoholics all I did was daydream and talk. I had no initiative or force of will. When I quit drinking and my mind could focus on my life, the first thing I felt bad about was the time I had wasted in procrastination. No more did I say, 'Tomorrow I'll try that.' I did it now."

That's what bogs down the alcoholic. Putting things off. Living a fantasy. Not going out and—making things happen. That's the difference between failure and success.

An author told me the same thing about procrastination. He said that while he was suffering from alcoholism, he was lucky if he wrote a book every three years. Since recovering, he has written four books in less than two years.

"Now I turn out better writing—far superior books," he explains. "When I drank, I had to drive myself to work two or three hours a week. My concentration was virtually gone. Now I can work steadily for six or seven days at a time. It's like a new life. Writing is fun again."

* * *

Another problem is lying, which is almost second nature to the alcoholic. It is part of his protection, as natural to him as a pheasant's colors in camouflage. Part mask. Part defense. Lying is a basic feature of the alcoholic. No alcoholic can harbor the disease without lying.

The easiest thing in the world, almost instinctive, is for the alcoholic to tell his wife the next morning, "Yes, I was late—but I only had a couple of drinks. We spent most of the night joshing over coffee."

It is instinctive. "Yes, honey, I stopped off with the boys. Just a beer. You know how it is." The "is" is three or four beers. Time is of no essence. The clock stops for the alcoholic. "Gosh, it is 1:30, sir. My watch must not be working. I'm sorry—it won't happen again."

At the doctor's office, the five or six drinks invariably became one or two. In self-defense against scorn, the alcoholic carries his lies even to his bartender. "Geez, bartender, got a lousy head today. Must be catching a cold. Make it a good one. For medicinal purposes only, heh, heh." You've heard it a thousand times.

Lie to the wife. Lie to the boss. Lie to the doctor. Lie to the bartender. Where do the lies stop—the confessional?

Not always. Listen to Arthur: "I used to figure the one place I could square myself around was the confessional. Then one day the priest asked, 'Do you drink much?' Instinctively I answered, 'Just now and then after a golf match, Father.'

"I took the absolution but it bugged me. I couldn't walk up for communion at Mass the next morning."

Drinking alcohol is almost based on the lie because in effect we are lying to ourselves. We are telling ourselves we need the drink, that the drink will change everything, make the world rosy, improve our lot, make us more acceptable, make us feel better.

When you can lie to yourself you can lie to anyone. A patient of mine told me he figured he lied between 50 and 60 times a day—just to protect his habit and his reputation. Ironically, lies catch up, contradict each other and are the quickest way of ruining a reputation. Most people can tolerate a drunk. I know of few who can tolerate a liar. I like Abraham Lincoln's version of why we are not successful liars. He said we don't have a good enough memory to succeed in it.

Let's take selfishness. I know a businessman who has kept acquaintances waiting at lunch time for his arrival almost daily for years. The reason: He stops at a favorite bar to have two quickies enroute to the restaurant where his friends meet. He wants to feel really "good" when he arrives, full of optimism and charisma. But he invariably keeps his business associates waiting from 20 to 45 minutes. Their time is their most valuable commodity. But he thinks only of himself. The man is selfish because he's an alcoholic.

*　*　*

The alcoholic can be so untrustworthy. I knew a man who cost his insurance clients hundreds of thousands of dollars by faulty moves and finally destroyed a 70-year-old family business by his alcoholic nature. He simply would take trips, buy cars and leisure homes he could not afford with the insurance payments. It eventually caught up to him and today he is in jail, getting out only to attend classes at a treatment center. He told me, "I blew everything and a lot of my clients' good money simply because when I was drinking I wanted to own the world, be a big man, to show off to my friends. I was a compulsive drinker—and a compulsive spender. My mind just went crazy as the alcohol got to my brain."

* * *

I think that there isn't a frailty in human nature that isn't at one time or another encompassed in the alcoholic's makeup.

For instance, I knew a respected gentleman who confided to me that despite his position as a pillar in society, that when he drank to excess he was capable of almost any heinous act. They ranged from sexual perversion to larceny. "My whole nature changed. I wasn't the same person. I thought nothing of picking somebody else's money off the bar. Or cheating at golf. Or hiding away with a female companion of any type. Or pulling a shady business deal. It was just like my conscience quit operating. When I hit that certain point with liquor, I actually became evil. It's hard to believe."

Not so hard to believe, sir. Alcohol not only can drive our moral inhibitions below ground but can obliterate our sense of reason. The man, who in an alcoholic rage beat his dog to death, told me it will bother him for the rest of his life. The woman who whipped her two-year-old within an inch of his life told the judge: "I can't tell you why. I was drinking, I guess."

Every sordid aspect of our nature, the mean streaks hidden from the public, comes out with a vengeance when many alcoholics drink. It's as the old Oriental proverb says, "The drink of potency oftentimes lets the leopard out of the cage. And the leopard turns on the creature who unleashed it, devouring the giver of freedom."

VIEWPOINT

I find one of the most difficult aspects in treating the alcoholic is to get him to believe that he is much more like other people than different from them. Each person has his unique area in which he excels. Most of us are experts on some subject and ignorant on others. The bright individual finds out the secret and the skills of the other's success and tries to emulate him. The dreg sits back and says, "Bill had all the breaks in life. He's so damn lucky." One tragedy with the practicing alcoholic is that liquor has raised such havoc with his mind that he is unable to remember or recognize the amount of talent he may have had before contacting his disease. This is an area, of course, where friends can be so important.

The alcoholic has four inventories he must take of himself:

(1) What was he like before he contacted alcoholism?

(2) What was he like while drinking alcohol?

(3) What was he like when he had sobriety?

(4) What is he today?

To do this the alcoholic should use the following fact-finder which works as a mirror to reflect personality assets and defects and makes him aware of his true value. For the alcoholic:

I. PERSONALITY DEFECTS:

1. Write down a list of attitudes and defects that I don't like in others.

2. Who or what irritates or bugs me from the first time I can remember or right now? (Example: My relationship with my dad, mother, brother, sister, spouse, etc. This also might include circumstances and events as well as people.)

3. Selfishness: Me first, concern with one's own welfare at the expense of others, if need be. (Example: I don't want to go to the picnic today, but plan on staying at home and resting. I had a tough week on the job. Family's opinions and desires not important.)

4. Envy: Begrudging another's success. (Example: The neighbor gets a new car and I have a great need to reply: "He gets all of the breaks as his dad helped him.")

5. False Pride: Great big adorable me. (Example: Did I ever make a mistake and get called on it?

What was my reaction to this blot on my character? Why did it irritate me so?)

6. Intolerance: My way is the right way without looking at the other person's point of view. (Example: Other people might have a different religious preference or are of a different nationality. Do I feel superior to them and unconcerned how they feel?)

7. Impatience: Waiting in a hurry. (Example: Do I get upset over the fact the wife or husband is about five minutes late for our scheduled get-together?)

8. Resentment: Strong feelings against a person I once loved, feelings that they would not do to me what they did if they really loved me. However, they did. (Example: The former friend who said to me, "Gee, Charley, you sure aren't the guy you used to be.")

9. Self Pity: Poor me; unlimited compassion for myself. (Example: "No one understands me.")

10. Feelings Easily Hurt: So touchy. (Example: I was expecting to be called on at the meeting and was prepared for it but the Master of Ceremonies failed to call on me, or I met a friend on the street and he did not respond to my big, "Hello.")

11. Dishonesty: Treating the truth rather lightly. (Example: Am I letting the wife know about the extra bonus check I got and am I loyal to her or do I have a secret love affair to stimulate myself?)

12. Procrastination: Easy does it to the extent it is never done. (Example: No need to hurry with the leaky faucet or the baby's broken toy as I can always fix them tomorrow.)

13. Perfectionistic Striving: When I do it, it has to be done right. (Example: Do I expect more of myself than the boss or the average worker?)

14. Fear: Scared of failure or afraid I will not impress another person. (Example: Does the fact I might not get the promotion prevent me from applying for the new position I am qualified for?)

15. Alibis: Reasons with an accompanying big IF. (Example: I would do fine, if people would leave me alone and mind their own business.)

II. PERSONALITY ASSETS

There are a great number of things you can be very thankful for and proud of that constitute assets. So often these factors are taken for granted and thereby never allowed the privilege of growth. For example, as guides:

1. I have good physical and mental health opportunities.
2. I have many friends if I allow them a chance to be such.
3. Many hidden talents lie within me; some are known and others are not recognized.
4. I know right from wrong, and I want to do right.
5. I want to be kind to others rather than hurtful.
6. I have a high degree of sensitivity. If channeled properly, it allows me to do for others what many overlook.
7. I am a good worker if "on the ball."
8. I have done many things of which I am proud.
9. I respect people who display truth and fair play.

Congratulations! You are embarking on a new way of life, displaying courage to look at yourself and your shortcomings as well as your good points. Fold these sheets and put them away. Don't reread them. Remember, it won't be perfect, and we are seeking progress, not perfection. However, if new insights come to you, jot them down at the bottom of the page with no concern as to where they fit.

"Intoxicating drinks have produced evils more deadly than . . . all those caused to mankind by the great historic scourges of war, famine, and pestilence combined."
William E. Gladstone

QUESTION:
ARE CERTAIN RACES
OR RELIGIOUS TYPES
MORE PREDISPOSED TO BECOMING
ALCOHOLICS?

SELVIG:

I don't believe they are. For years we have heard the statement that certain races are more susceptible to drinking and alcoholism, that it was "a part of their nature."

When I moved into the rehabilitation field it was a popular theory that people of Irish Catholic descent were characterized by alcoholism. So were Indians—because they had such a short period of exposure to alcohol and had built up little tolerance. The French also were supposedly easy victims to the disease, and the Scandinavians and the Russians.

I had heard that those with a Jewish background rarely became alcoholics. And I heard that most Latins and people of Italian extraction rarely were alcoholics because wine was used as a basic fundamental part of the meal from the time they were children. Their tolerance was invulnerable.

Well, I tell you after treating thousands that these are questionable theories. The Irish don't become alcoholics because they were victims of hundreds of years of tyrannies at the hand of oppressors. The French don't drink because they are "light-hearted and light-headed" people. The Scandinavians don't drink more because "they have to keep the blood flowing in the cold climates." And the Russians, because they love to dance and sing, are no more predisposed to the disease than any others.

On the other hand, I've treated many Jewish alcoholics—even though the argument that alcohol is such a strong religious symbol you don't find it abused.

The need for fulfillment through alcohol in Irish, Swedes, Germans, French, Italians, and Indians goes back to the individual searching for a feeling of superiority or "better feelings." We have treated many priests and wives of many ministers. You absolutely cannot categorize who becomes the alcoholic and what ratio relates to what race.

I can go to awesome St. Patrick's Cathedral in New York and find many people with hangovers. I can find the same number in the cathedrals in Hamburg or in a synagogue in Miami, in the Protestant churches in England. I can find packed Alcoholics Anonymous groups in Phoenix, New Orleans, Duluth, Charlotte, London, Berlin, Paris, Rome, and Madrid. Russia, they say, is having a terrible problem with alcoholism. But no more of a problem, I suspect, than the state of Kansas.

The Irish have a great reputation as heavy drinkers—but you will hear of countless Irish who took the pledge of abstinence at an early age and have never touched a drop. The Indians on reservations have a high rate of alcoholism because drinking has become one of their rare forms of social activity. They drink because on some reservations it has become accepted as the primary social function. But no more than at any country club.

You will find as high a rate of alcoholism at a swank resort as you will at an Indian reservation. But because the country club and resort set has the money to purchase privacy, their disease is not publicly exposed. But it is there and in the same proportion as on farms, reservations, and industrial compounds.

Examples:

In one counseling class of 12 people I had two Scandinavians, a priest, an orthodox Jew, an Indian, an Italian, a Pole, an Irishman, a German, a French doctor, and a Canadian attorney of Scotch-Welsh ancestry. It was as diversified a group as you could find in North America.

There was absolutely no relationship that I could detect among their races and religions. They had come from completely different backgrounds, but all had identical needs: to lose themselves in the elevative qualities of alcohol and to seek a fulfillment of their worth in the bottle. It was strictly emotional—strictly a personal thing, not engineered or suggested by racial idiosyncracies or tendencies.

They all felt a particular need and were searching for fulfillment through alcohol. They had nothing in common from the standpoint of racial backgrounds. They had everything in common when it came to the disease. Alcohol gave all of them a feeling of fulfillment, complete and unabating.

* * *

His name was O'Brien and he explained to me, "With my name you can understand why I drink. It's kinda expected of us in our little town—almost all Irish. We all drink and laugh a lot and cry a lot."

I didn't dispute the gentleman. But I checked into his background and town. He was the only member of his family who consumed alcohol to excess. He was the only acknowledged alcoholic in his block. He was the only member of his Knights of Columbus group to get out of line at parties. And he was the only person thrown out of his favorite Irish saloon in the past year for disturbing the peace. O'Brien had no pressure on him to become an alcoholic, other than his sensitivity to the disease. It wasn't his bloodline. It was his emotional and sense line.

* * *

The French Foreign Legion, portrayed in films and books for years as a rowdy drinking organization, had the reputation for being able to consume more alcohol and for containing more alcoholics and lost souls than any fighting force in history. Yet its record is second to none in battles fought valiantly and successfully. There is no way such a force could be a degenerative drinking crew, immersed in the swill of the grog and yet able to perform with such discipline. Just another myth perpetuated in story and legend.

* * *

I know an Italian family with three alcoholics. I knew a French family with not a drinker in the family of 11 children. I know six Irish Catholic priests who never drink anything stronger than the wine of the Mass. I know two ministers who are confirmed and rehabilitated alcoholics, now working as counselors. Six of my acquaintances are successful Jewish businessmen with the help of treatment and Alcoholics Anonymous programs.

"The sight of a drunkard is a better sermon against that vice than the best that was ever preached on the subject"
George Saville

QUESTION:
WHAT IS THE DIFFERENCE BETWEEN A SOCIAL DRINKER AND AN ALCOHOLIC?

SELVIG:

When the social drinker consumes alcohol he feels as good as the next person. The alcoholic drinks and feels superior to the others.

The social drinker has one, two or perhaps three drinks to relieve a few inhibitions and act more relaxed in conversation and on the dance floor. The alcoholic wants enough liquor to give him such a "high" and feeling of confidence that he becomes an expert in conversation and a teacher of dance.

The social drinker has an "invisible button" which turns off after a few drinks. He may become tired. Or logy. At a certain point, alcohol intake does nothing for him. He rarely becomes an alcoholic. But the alcoholic's system demands more liquor the more he drinks. He must dominate the scene. His personality changes—and he welcomes the change. He is not content to be an integral part of the group, unobtrusive, but lucid; warm but not volatile. The alcoholic wants to be noticed, wants to dominate conversations, wants to be heard and become the center of attention. He is not fulfilled being merely one of the party. He wants to be the party.

Examples:

Tom is a robust but generally quiet engineer. However, inwardly he feels inferior, particularly on social occasions. He is balding, paunchy, and his clothes never seem to fit. To make sure he feels "good and relaxed" by the time he gets to the party, Tom has a couple of "booster" shots at home, complaining to his wife, "You know these parties—they never make a decent drink."

What Tom really wants is to come in feeling more relaxed than the rest and then consume enough quickly at the party to get a big jump in enthusiasm and stimulated conversation. After two hours of partying when the rest of the people are in a mellow, relaxed and controlled mood, Tom is roaring from one end of the gathering to the other. He is pouring out jokes, talking a shade too loud and firmly convinced he is the life of the party. Tom, by this time, has consumed seven drinks. The others, an average of two to three. The rest are social drinkers. Tom is an alcoholic.

* * *

The holiday social function of the plant for the foremen and foreladies is held at the country club. Julia and her boyfriend attend. She is an employee. Before attending, Julia insists they stop for a drink enroute. At the party she slips away to the bar area where she knows other male employees will offer to buy her a drink.

She makes a point of this each time she excuses herself to go to the rest room. Her boyfriend complains he is being left alone. "Nonsense," Julia smiles, "I just like to mingle with the people I work with. They're such good sports and we never get to talk at work." But Julia is crying for alcohol.

Until she has had the drinks, she is inhibited and feels shut out. With the added alcohol she feels prettier and more intelligent. No longer the little bossy employee who is a demanding taskmaster on the job, infinitely fastidious and wound up tight with dedication, but a lady hopelessly lost in the main stream of social proprieties.

The truth is, Julia doesn't like herself unless she is drinking. The alcohol infuses her with confidence. It changes her whole feeling. She hasn't missed work to this point, but Julia will. She is an alcoholic.

* * *

Mel, a very quiet fellow, imbibes liquor and continues to withdraw physically from social functions where internally he is feeling like the outgoing bear and lover. He is envisioning himself as the life of the party but is still in a withdrawn physical state. He is an alcoholic. But some people externalize freedom and others do it internally. He imagines himself dancing with the prettiest girl, singing on the stage, dominating the conversation. But he is imagining it all. He's in an alcoholic fantasy. I call them the "inner glows." They are going through the motions inside themselves. They are a sad lot. You see them by the thousands on bar stools all over the world.

* * *

The whole softball team makes it a ritual to consume four or five beers apiece after the game—win or lose. Teddy, the rugged third baseman, is the spark of the team. He chatters incessantly during the game. He makes the biggest plays—and biggest booboos. He loves the spontaneity of the action, the noise of the onlookers, but mostly the glow from within.

Before the game, Teddy has had three or four

"bumps," as he calls them, in his car—straight shots of gin. During the game, he sips two or three beers. Enroute to the post-game sortee he has another two or three bumps from his car flask. At the beer post-mortem, he enjoys three or four more beers.

"Where'd he get that spirit?" "How does Teddy keep up that line?" "How can Teddy go all night like a whirlwind?" all his teammates ask. Easy. Teddy's going on an alcohol hyper.

He's pumped the adrenalin with four to five times the alcohol the others have consumed with their few beers. At this time in life, Teddy is strong, able, a funster. Later the doldrums will set in. Teddy, you see, is just not the fun guy on the team. He is an alcoholic. The rest of his teammates are social drinkers. Alcohol does too much for Teddy.

* * *

[Selvig]

"I'm my own best example. I had confidence in many areas but in college I desperately sought the friendship of a pretty girl. But I was too bashful to call her on the phone. At a party one night, I wanted to ask her to dance —but I didn't have the nerve. I didn't think I danced that well. I always wanted to be the first to lead a song—but I never thought I had a voice. And I never had the confidence to start out first.

"Well, at this party, I went into the washroom. I had a couple of straight whiskeys out of a pint I bought that afternoon. After an hour of admiring the girl and consuming four or five drinks I walked up, put my arm around her waist, put my cheek next to hers and whispered, 'Hey, beautiful—let's swing our bodies.'

"She accepted and I gave her a spin on the floor which dazzled me and left her breathless. Later that night, I jumped up on the stage, grabbed a megaphone from the songster for the evening and sang for the troops. I couldn't believe my own courage. I shouted out the song loud and clear and became a hit with the crowd.

'Hey, this is easy,' I thought to myself. Just a couple

drinks. God, if they can make me this kind of a swash-buckler, they've got to help in every way. I was on my way to being a record-breaking alcoholic. I once hyped myself before I pitched a baseball game. And I lost.

"I used alcohol for virtually every phase of my life, fig-uring it sharpened my senses. It certainly gave me brav-ery I never knew I possessed. But at the finish, I lost a college education. I lost my friends. I got only laughs and finger-pointing from the girls. I was an alcoholic. The others were social drinkers."

* * *

In a fine home in a manicured neighborhood, hostess Marie entertains regularly. She is regarded highly for her charm, beauty and graciousness. Before each party she plies herself with four or five brandies and fortifies herself with four or more during the course of the party.

She has an inner glow, her friends say. She sparkles, others contend. A natural hostess, others say.

Marie is an alcoholic, hoping to keep her drinking se-cret—and knowing she could never face her guests with-out being heavily laced with the spirits. She is not a social drinker. She is an alcoholic who needs liquor to gain ful-fillment. In time it will wreck her health, mentally and physically.

* * *

Watch any sporting crowd. The champs and ladies who insist the game is never as good without a thermos of liquor to "warm the chills" or "make that damn, lousy band sound better" or "enable me to put up with that stinkin' coach" generally are alcoholics. They plan for their outings. The games are no mere events to be en-joyed. They provide the excuse for a planned drinking rit-ual. They are the sets on which the deadly drama is played. A bartender in the Chicago stadium told me that each night between 50 and 60 customers didn't know who won the hockey game when it was over. Twin Cities police had to patrol the soccer games in Minnesota be-cause the pre-game parking lot parties got out of hand so badly that only half the young fans were even attending the games. They preferred to stay and drink and party. I know a friend whose five-man party spent three days at a Notre Dame game every year, most of it spent drinking. He admitted to me that more than once they never got to the game after driving more than 500 miles.

The Kentucky Derby is a stage where you can catch alcoholics in a dazzling array. Look at the consumption of the tall, inviting mint juleps. I once counted 11 empty glasses strewn next to an unconscious visitor.

At the exact moment they are playing *My Old Kentucky Home* before the great moments of the race, you can see thousands consuming liquor at the bars all over the acreage without a thought being given to the classic thoroughbreds.

It is the same at baseball games where so many of my acquaintances admittedly go to sip the cool beer, away from family complaints.

All of this may seem like innocent fun at a glance. Believe me, hordes of the nation's sporting crowd are using the games as an excuse to drink. It's not because the game gets better or the bands sound sweeter. It's simply because they need the fulfillment alcohol brings. They would get the same high and glows at home, in the garage, on the lawn or on a piano bench. But the game affords them a legitimate excuse. Generally, the fan can attend the game unshackled by spouse or critic.

I would say a good share of any sporting event's cheers are sent up for the spirit in the bottle—not that shown by the players.

The alcoholic wants to be noticed, wants to dominate conversations, wants to be heard and become the center of attention. He is not fulfilled being merely one of the party. He wants to be the party.

QUESTION:
WHEN IS THE SO-CALLED "HEAVY DRINKER" AN ACTUAL ALCOHOLIC?

SELVIG:

When he begins to have more than the ordinary number of drinks he usually consumes. And when he gets into trouble with his drinking. And when he refuses or is unable to quit or control his drinking.

Usually the added drinks and trouble are almost simultaneous. Ironically, a heavy drinker might go on for many years, consuming his seven or eight drinks a day and actually suffering few repercussions. His particular system is attuned to handling the alcoholic excesses. He may even manage to sleep well, stay in control of his family obligations, and maintain his job security.

Then one day, almost imperceptibly, the heavy drinker has one or two more drinks than his norm. Suddenly, he is having three or four or five drinks more per day. He has now become an alcoholic. He no longer is free to make the decision for himself how many drinks he will have. Rather, he can no longer make the decision to quit drinking.

He has lost will power and control. At this point he crosses over from a heavy drinker to an alcoholic, completely addicted. Two out of every three so-called heavy drinkers I've known eventually become alcoholics. He is a rare exception who can continue to drink steadily without the alcohol changing his life pattern and dominating his will. Those that don't become alcoholics may suffer physical damage as the result of daily consumption.

Examples:

Big Ed prided himself in being the finest over-the-road truck driver in North America. That's what he told his cohorts. He said he never missed a day's work in eight years. And that was true. He also said he never had a hangover—and could eat a hearty breakfast after a night of drinking. That also was true.

Then, slowly, Ed began to consume that extra beer or extra scotch during his lay-overs. Few could notice the change at first—except close associates who saw Ed become irritable with his long-time partner. Suddenly, Ed wanted to stop in the afternoon for a quickie.

"God-damn road is beginning to bore me," he'd explain. And then he wanted that extra hour's sleep in the morning, after tossing and turning most of the night.

His partner, Bill, saw the change and mentioned it to Big Ed. He only laughed and roared, "Never worry about Big Ed! He can handle all the booze God created."

In six months his nerves were shot. A short while later, Big Ed ran his rig into a ditch in a fog. His co-driver was killed and Ed spent six months in the hospital. He lost his driver's license. Nobody knows what prompted the change—almost overnight from a heavy drinker to an alcoholic.

* * *

The college football coach was a veteran. He had led grid teams for 31 years. He told me, "I used to have six to seven drinks a day spread out before practice, after practice, on recruiting trips—at press gatherings and alumni dinners. But it wasn't until I was 59 years old that I had an extra three or four while waiting for the plane. I don't even remember getting off the plane. I came home and was terribly sick.

"I thought that would end it. But the next week I went overboard again. And the next weekend, too. My wife complained. I laughed it off. In three months I was drinking a quart a day and couldn't stop. I told myself it was silly. I could discipline myself.

"I went back to my old six and seven-drink routine. But it only lasted for a week. Our team was upset in a game and I went on a complete binge again. Somewhere along the line I wasn't controlling the alcohol. It was controlling me."

* * *

The lady we call Lucille came to me with a story that was so improbable it could only be fact. She used to drink six Alexanders a day—two at a sitting between lunch and bedtime. She was a manager of a lady's wear outlet and for 11 years had continued her pattern. She was a spinster.

Then one morning she awoke in a strange hotel room, next to a strange man—and, unbelievable as it seems, in a strange city and a strange state! All she remembered was saying, "I'll try just one more drink. That's over my quota." It happened in a hotel bar in her hometown. From that point on, she had blacked out.

The sad story is that the emotional jolt of meeting a new consort and traveling to a strange place was such a delicious thrill compared to her tedious existence, Lucille tried the extra drink time and again—hoping each one would turn her into Cinderella. The drink only turned her into an alcoholic. Although asking whether she courted the disease or it attacked her is like asking which came first—the chicken or the egg?

"Call things by their right name. Ask for a 'Glass of brandy and water.' That is the current but not the appropriate name. Ask for a 'Glass of liquid fire and distilled damnation.' "
Robert Hall

QUESTION:
WHAT IS A SNEAK DRINKER?

SELVIG:

Just what the name implies—an alcoholic who tries to hide his disease. Oh, they are the most devious people on the face of the earth. It is entertaining, I am sorry to admit, to hear sneak drinkers tell where they hide their alcohol. They are inventive, almost ingenious in the manner in which they feed their "secret" guilt.

We must understand that the bottle is their most prized possession. A bottle means more to an alcoholic than his family, employers or friends. It is his key to the freedom of fulfillment he thinks he has when he is drinking. He will not share the fulfillment with anyone. The world becomes a sinister threat to him. Everywhere he sees threats—the ministers, doctors, bosses, children.

The alcoholic becomes so devious that he himself can often not remember where he stashed his liquor. The sneak drinker gets a vicarious thrill of believing he's hoodwinked a wife or friend as much as he enjoys the drink.

Drinks have been hidden in everything from Ray Milland's light shade in *Lost Weekend* to vacuum cleaner bags and woodpiles. The sneak drinker tries to hide his affliction. But rarely does he fool a close observer.

I know a farmer who hid two cases of liquor every three months in various spots on his farm. Sick of his sneak drinking, his wife took only a few days to find his treasure and destroy his supply. There is no greater emotional upheaval for an alcoholic than to find he has not duped his family or friends. It brings a sense of shame and degradation to him which can be crippling emotionally. It can also turn him into a raging tyrant. ("I'll show you!")

Examples:

For years, a neighbor of mine named Fred hid his liquor supply among the bottles of paint remover and kerosene and lawn mower fuel in his garage. He knew his wife rarely entered this area and certainly would not suspect him since he had poured the liquor out of the bottle into an old handyman container. Fred wasn't discovered until a neighbor happened to be helping him clean his garage and knocked the container with the alcohol onto the floor, where it shattered. The heavy aroma of booze was all over the scene.

Fred was mortified and tried to explain to his friend that he kept a bottle of liquor there to cut the dirt and grease on his car windows. The neighbor, I'm sure, didn't buy Fred's story and I know the shame had an effect on him. He told me later he never asked the neighbor to his house again. And he began hiding the alcohol behind the furnace, where it was discovered by a repairman who pulled the bottle out and gave it to Fred's wife, Fred told me while taking treatment, "I had six perfect hiding places and every damn one was found out. It's like a alky is harassed by a million bloodhounds. There were spies everywhere."

* * *

Mildred kept her liquor with her cleaning detergents. When she was doing the laundry or ironing, she had a supply close at hand. She was the happiest ironing housewife in Wisconsin. She never complained about doing her household chores.

But one day, in a drunken stupor, she burned her hand horribly with the iron. Her hiding place was discovered. If the alcoholic keeps at his sneak tricks long enough he is either discovered by someone else or calls attention to himself by being involved in an accident or making a terrible blunder.

* * *

"Ingenious," I said. Yes. Larry at the country club kept

111

his supply in a hollow shaft of a driving wood. His friend, Mike, kept his in a hair tonic bottle. And they used to laugh over Billy who had a bowling ball drilled out to accommodate a pint of liquid refreshment. I know a baseball pitcher who used to hide a small thin flask in the inside of his baseball glove and could suck down enough liquor to make himself tipsy by the seventh inning. I don't believe anyone ever suspected him but he screamed at a teammate who tried to take his glove home with him after the game.

The people who come into treatment centers would test the skills of the finest hound dogs and private eyes. They've carried in "supplies" in the heels of long-stemmed slippers, in hot water bottles, in phony camera cases, and in hollowed-out books.

One of the most ingenious was an insurance executive. He would put his liquor supply in the container which held the window wiper wash under his car hood. He had a small tube attached to come out under his dash. He carried paper cups and could fill them quickly and dispose of them just as quickly. Another fellow hid a small bottle in his radio. It remained undetected until his wife knocked the radio off a table onto the floor. Vases, laundry chutes, and even heavy shrubs are natural hiding places. With the alcoholic, it becomes a deadly serious game, a challenge.

* * *

Sometimes the sneak drinker will employ the help of a confederate. A millionaire Minneapolis businessman had his favorite restaurant where the bar happened to be only a few feet from the men's room. His keyed-in bartender always had a pair of triples under the bar, waiting for Mr. Rich Blood to make his move.

He would always sit with his wife in another section of the bar. As soon as Mr. Rich Blood headed toward the rest room, the bartender would have a powerhouse drink sitting on the bar. Mr. Rich would swoop it up and in no lost motion make it to the rest room to hastily consume the liquor. Then out again and, with a quick pivot, he'd pour another down the hatch and be back seated at his table in less than five minutes. His wife found out when the bartender became drunk and told a friend of hers. A sneak drinker will always find another outlet until he is either too tired, too embarrassed, or too sick to cover his tracks.

"Drunkenness is nothing else but voluntary madness."
Lucius Annaeus Seneca

QUESTION:
WHAT ABOUT THE ALCOHOLICS WHO SEEMINGLY CAN NAVIGATE AND PERFORM WITHOUT LOSS OF EFFECTIVENESS?

SELVIG:

The strange phenomena may be attributed to the subconscious mind, the unconscious mind or muscle memory as psychiatrists, psychologists and other medical experts speak of.

A perfect example is entertainers, many of whom are alcoholics. They become adapted to the routine. Generally, they sing the same songs and dance the same steps and tell the same jokes for months at a time. As long as they keep that routine or thoroughly learn a new one, their reflexes and responses can be almost programmed.

Oh, they may slur a few words in their speech or miss a step or flatten a note, but they get by because they retain 90 percent of the moves and right notes. It's a case of repetition.

I have seen politicians give the same speech so often that, even inebriated, they function fairly well. It's almost a case of putting a nickel in the doll and watching it operate. However, when the alcoholic performer has to be innovative or creative or even put down a heckler with an extemporaneous slam, he may be in trouble. And certainly from the high rate of family problems, divorces, broken contracts, and wasted lives of entertainers, we can assume the alcoholic ones have many more problems with their liquor consumption than performing in front of the footlights.

It is relatively unimportant whether the subconscious mind or body is responsible if it happens continually—another strange facet of a bewildering disease.

Examples:

The man had a high-wire act in a small circus and performed brilliantly for years. Gradually, then, fear crept into his mind after 30 years of performing. He began to drink and soon was a diseased alcoholic. In his mind he created the picture of a man more daring than ever, a young, vibrant performer.

On this particular day in a small town, it was dusty and windy but he insisted on going through with his act without a net. He was caught in a gust and tried to cling to the wire as he fell. His reflexes, dulled by what friends told me were six or seven pre-show shots, could not respond in time. Where his feet had been steady, his hands had lost their coordination. He fell, and was crippled for life. He died of alcoholism, however.

* * *

Famed baseball manager Casey Stengel used to relate a story about one of his veteran players who was known to play with an alcoholic high a good deal of the time. But his memory, reflexes, and eyesight were so sharp he was still a valuable addition to the lineup.

In one particular game, the man hit a two-run double in the second inning and a two-run triple in the sixth and a homerun in the ninth. In the 11th inning with the score tied and the bases loaded, he struck out on three pitches. "What do you think happened?" Casey was asked. And the humorous old warhorse answered: "Simple. He just sobered up."

* * *

The boxer was a master of his craft when he was younger. He told me, "Dick, I could be drunk and beat most of the bums around." He was attacked by alcoholism in his late 20's.

In a particularly gruelling fight he would resort to brandy shots between rounds—not uncommon for some fighters. In one fight, set for 12 rounds, his routine of jabs and split-second timing of his right crosses, were so routinely patterned he held a wide lead going into the sixth round. But his legs were tiring.

He poured in the brandy between the next three rounds. By the 10th round the liquor had given him a daring high and he came out punching, turning from boxer to slugger. The false bravado was fatal to his chances. He was knocked out in the 11th round of a fight he might have easily won.

* * *

I remember the race-car driver—famed at Indianapolis. He was known as a party boy at night. But with shakes or a hangover, he was a veritable machine at the wheel in a race. He used to say, "I could drink forever and still drive a straight line 500 yards without swerving an inch."

He raced with hangovers for 102 performances all over the world. He was killed at the wheel of his sports car after drinking for four hours when he lost control at 50 miles an hour and hit a tree.

* * *

Too often the alcoholic believes he is performing perfectly when it is evident to the bystander he has lost touch with reality. I remember an attorney telling me that he believed his reflexes and mind were so sharp and toned so well he could drink all day and still perform at his peak in the court room.

On this particular day, Jack had three martinis at noon and was scheduled for a summation of his case in defense of a young man charged with manslaughter in a car accident. During the course of his summation he sensed that the alcohol had betrayed him. He stumbled, lost his train of thought. Afterwards, he overhead a juror mutter to another: "That attorney sounded like he was high."

Jack's client lost the case and had to serve three years in jail. The attorney cursed himself for months. He finally, because of this case, submitted himself for treatment.

His words were interesting: "I began to wonder how many other times alcohol had betrayed me and I had betrayed my client. The disease not only wrecks you inside but gives you false impressions. I lost judgment."

Nobody can ever be certain, entertainer or professional, just when the alcohol wil smash down the muscle memory reflex. It can happen in a matter of seconds, again providing insight into the insidious and frightening ways of the disease.

It is relatively unimportant whether the subconscious mind or body is responsible if it happens continually—another strange facet of a bewildering disease.

QUESTION:
IS A "DRINKER" THE SAME AS AN ALCOHOLIC?

SELVIG:

All alcoholics are drinkers but not all drinkers are alcoholics. I am a recovering alcoholic. But I'm still a drinker. I consume on an average of 10 to 12 cans of warm pop daily. When a man gives up alcohol, he does not necessarily give up drinking. And I mean he can be a "drinker" of coffee, pop, orange juice—you name it. Drinking is a habit which is almost compulsive with millions.

There is nothing wrong with drinking as long as the physical system doesn't react against the consumption of too much of one beverage. It is perfectly natural for many people to have a drink in their hand; to lift it to the lips. It gives a sense of fulfillment, too. It could go back to the baby at its mother's breast, seeking the nipple for security and contentment.

The touch of liquid to the lips is a very real need for many of us. It is not fair to brand as strange a person who feels the compulsion to have a drink of some kind of beverage in the hand and the good feeling derived from the liquid passing the lips and going down the throat. Millions of people have a very real need for a drink of liquid—be it water, juice, malts or milk. Aren't we all drinkers to some extent?

I know successful people in all fields who almost incessantly have a drink in their hand. They should never have the stigma attached to them of being strange. Drinking is completely natural and harmless to most drinkers. I never tell a recovering alcoholic to forsake a drink. Most of them, too, are natural drinkers who need a glass in

117

hand, liquid flowing over the lips. I encourage them to try pop, coffee, or other liquids.

Examples:

I had a landlord who drank 22 cups of coffee a day, by his count. It might have made him a shade irritable. Perhaps the caffeine was not good for his body. But as I always told Andy, "You're not hurting anyone with that coffee. You're not ruining your mind. You're not tearing up the house. You're not punching your wife or your boss or driving off the road. Godspeed. Have another coffee. One thing at a time. In later years, his doctor ordered him to cut down on his coffee drinking as the caffeine was harmful to his physical being. They are experts on our physical condition. It pays to listen to them, but, ironically, we don't follow their orders too well, do we?

* * *

I had a college professor who continually held a cup of tea in his hand. One day we asked him how many teas he consumed during classes. He said, "Only one. I guess I just feel more confident with a cup in my hand." He had the need to feel something in his hand. I have had cigarette smokers tell me the same thing. Others say the feeling of a pipe between the lips gives them an aura of wellbeing.

"Sippers" I call the ones who can sip on root beer or soda pop by the hour. But if the liquid is not causing them stomach problems, what is wrong with their drinking? Absolutely nothing.

A psychiatrist friend of mine told me that there is a definite need in perhaps one out of every three people to hold a glass of liquid and take it between the lips at short periods of time. It supplies relaxation.

In many cases it eases tension. I find in my case a definite need to supply my system almost continually with warm diet pop. I can't take cold liquids. I have to ask the waitress or the fountain girl if the beverage is warm. It usually draws a startled look or a smirk. But invariably they comply with my request. It hits the spot—warm pop, believe it or not. My doctor told me cold drinks are injurious to the lungs.

I would be as much at a loss if my pop were not obtainable as I was when I searched for liquor on a holiday while suffering from alcoholism. I don't consider myself a freak, although I take good-humored needling from my friends. I simply love to drink. I see no harm in it.

* * *

Look around you. You will find at work, at play, at parties, at discussion groups, people who must be holding or consuming a drink of some type. They are no more social outcasts than the smokers who must suck or hold something, or the cigar-chewers, or the nail-pickers or the nose-scratchers. In fact, I'll bet the next time you are at a meeting or public occasion of any type that if you scan the crowd around you quickly you will not see a person without some small idosyncrasy.

That goes for the leg-swingers, head scratchers, finger tappers or gum chewers. I believe they are nature's little cushion of resiliency against the pressures of everyday living, that little safety valve for human emotions. It is that movement, that action, that drink, that scratch which provides normal insulation against common pressures. It is not until the caffeine drives the drinker up the wall or prevents sleep, or the nail biter draws blood or the finger tapper disturbs a library full of people that he has a problem.

QUESTION:
DO HOLIDAYS—LIKE CHRISTMAS AND EASTER—AFFECT ALCOHOLICS?

SELVIG:

It has been reported that more murders take place on Christmas Eve, more horrible domestic fracases on holidays than at other times during the year. A high percentage are alcohol-related.

I had a patient who drank only on six holidays. But they cost him his family and every penny he had. Again, it goes back to looking for an excuse. It is a known fact that holidays can trigger grave misfortunes for the alcoholic—and that is natural if you analyze that he is exposed to more drinking, more parties and more celebrations in these periods than during the normal course of activities.

The key here is that alcoholics get drunk during holidays in front of more people than ordinary, are exposed to more situations and social provocations to drink. A man can be a silent drinker for 300 straight days and then his company throws an office party and he drinks —but this time in front of many who have never before seen him unstable. Consequently, they assume, quite normally, that the holidays add to his drinking ills. Holidays call more attention to the alcoholic because many times he is on public display. The ailing alcoholic needs no excuse to drink, although he may use the holiday period in defense of his actions. It is a convenient atmosphere. The celebrations are there. Good fellowship abounds. He need not hide his addiction.

Examples:

Joe used to tell everyone that he got deplorably drunk during Christmas for two reasons—the sentimental music and the memory that his boyhood had been poor and Christmas never was a time for presents, family reunions and good meals as was the case in his friends' homes. But a counselor dug deeply into his past and found that his boyhood was as normal as most; true, the family had little money but offered great love and Christmas was a time of devotion and a profession of deep religious beliefs.

Joe wasn't the recipient of expensive gifts but the family exchanged modest ones. But Joe wanted to drink at any time and found Christmas an ideal time to explain his outlandish behavior. As for the sentimental songs, the more the alcoholic drinks, the more sentimental they sound. It is the remorse coming out of his soul. Or conscience.

A song of inspiration to the non-alcoholic becomes a sad song of expression to the alcoholic. Play *Yankee Doodle Dandy* into a drunk's ear and he'll make it a funeral dirge.

* * *

Lydia was a lovely lady who claimed that she only drank a little more at birthday parties, weddings and anniversaries. Those were the occasions she drank more in public—when the three or four drinks were unnoticed and she had a feeling of temporary freedom. (Nobody cares because others are busy drinking, too.) No longer did her alcoholism seem like a sin. But the truth is, Lydia, a fashionable spinster, was an alcoholic for years, consuming eight to ten drinks daily.

Holidays afforded her the chance to drink openly. It was a soothing balm for her conscience and spirit. Sadly, Lydia died from alcohol and its complications at the age of 59. Her friends only said, "Gosh, Lydia wasn't that much of a drinker. Only a few during special occasions." She would have liked that.

* * *

And Mollie the waitress was a fresh young divorcee who seemed to get a charge out of life. She poured me

121

coffee for years, always regaling us with stories of her bar during the holidays. She liked the Fourth of July —and admitted that when she felt patriotic and visited fireworks displays, something inside her turned her into a drinking dervish.

When her illness was detected, she told me that as a young girl her first exposure to beer and heavy drinking were Fourth of July celebrations in her small hometown. She conjured up feelings of youthful vigor and good times past during the Fourth.

But the Fourth only triggered more serious repercussions. If it wasn't the Fourth, it was homecoming football games or reunions. Always something to bring back memories of the past.

This was her way of dealing with her problem—and making it palatable. If she told herself she drank to bring back past glories, past happy memories, what could be bad with the drinking? But it was no more heavy during Fourth of July celebrations. Mollie was a free-wheeling alcoholic who, when she realized that she was using myriads of excuses to drink, finally recovered and was able to see how ridiculous her affinity to the Fourth of July really was.

Excuses. Excuses. The alcoholic finds them everywhere. The holidays give him that many more. It is sad, too. I have known three people who lost their jobs by making fools out of themselves at office Christmas parties.

One employer told me he quit office parties because of so many problems: husbands taking out secretaries; a man falling through a plate glass door; car accidents enroute home. An employer said, "I can't believe that all the people who get out of line at Christmas parties are alcoholics. It's just a fling, I guess."

Perhaps he is only speaking wishfully. I have a hunch that the ones causing the problems were alcoholics, again being exposed to public view. The social drinker will rarely tolerate liquor long enough to cause damage to himself or others. Occasionally a neophyte who is not used to testing his capacity will drink himself under the table or over a bumper. But, generally speaking, the person creating noise, havoc and headaches is an alcoholic—on display for perhaps the first time to his fellow employees.

Too often people say, "Don't play that sad song. It makes me drink." What they are really saying is, "I hope to God they play that sad song. It gives me a chance to pour down another." Same with holidays. The alcoholic loves them. He plans for them. His pre-drink strategy is drawn up, perhaps subconsciously, days, weeks, even months ahead of the holiday celebrations. He uses them, with liquor, in his eternal search for fulfillment. They give him reason. But if they were not there, he would find other reasons to drink, although his insatiable drive needs none.

I asked a police officer why so many homicides and why the violence on Christmas Eve and other holidays. He pointed out that liquor was greatly responsible for the violence—but that alcoholics were not the likely law breakers. "They are drinking enough so their families know what to expect," he said.

"But it's the one I call the 'amateur drinkers' who can't handle the stuff and are unused to its potency that explode and cause the trouble. The wife of an alcoholic knows what to expect, how to gauge the drunk. The wife of a neophyte drunk has no barometer on what he'll do. He can turn into a killer."

QUESTION:
WHAT ARE BLACKOUTS AND HOW SERIOUS ARE THEY?

SELVIG:

Very real and so serious, blackouts are like playing Russian roulette—with three bullets in the six chambers. Science and medicine once frowned on the excuse that a

123

person could act for hours without ever remembering a single occurrence.

The first time a murder defendant used that defense it was called the "cause." "Preposterous" and "asinine" were some of the charges hurled against the defense. Now, all of science is willing to accept the fact: alcoholic blackouts are common. Most alcoholics will admit to blackouts in some degree—ranging from a few minutes to, in some serious cases, days.

Blackouts mean simply that the alcoholic performs and is conscious, but has lost all recall of what he did. The alcohol apparently paralyzes the memory cells, almost like an anesthetic. The victim of a blackout is as out of it as if he were hit on the head by a blunt instrument and collapsed unconscious.

Amazing feats have been accomplished in the throes of a blackout without the alcoholic remembering a thing. Blackouts can be caused by a tremendous drinking spree, or in the acute cases, after only a few drinks. Today, most judges and courts of law will accept the blackout as a fact of life; not necessarily an excuse for criminal behavior but certainly a valid argument that the accused was not conscious of any criminal act of which he may have been guilty. The brain simply cannot register the actions of the blackout victim. It is a terrifying experience and usually signals acute alcoholism.

I was told many years ago by an informed doctor that a blackout was nature's way of warning you that the chemical you were using was detrimental to your health. There are alcoholic experts who believe that 90 percent of the alcoholics suffer from blackouts. Frankly, I have not met one alcoholic in over 20,000 cases who did not eventually admit to suffering at least one blackout to some degree. That could be as minor as forgetting to pay the check or forgetting an errand for the family to driving over 200 miles and not remembering the trip. I have known hundreds of alcoholics who told me the most hectic minute of their lives was getting up and looking out in the driveway to see if they had driven their cars home!

Examples:

The man entered his home, covered with blood. His young daughter screamed, "Daddy! Daddy! You're all bloody!"

Until that moment, early on a fall evening, the alcoholic was unaware of his condition. However, his nose had been broken, he had a fractured rib, two broken knuckles, cuts around both eyes, a chipped tooth, and his clothes were torn and dirty. He obviously had been in a savage fight—a long, gruelling fight in which he or the combatant might have been killed.

Yet this man told me he had absolutely no recall of any argument, who he might have fought, where, or the outcome! When he recovered, he was so curious he ran an ad in the personal columns of the paper asking for information of anyone having seen or heard of a fight that particular night. A stranger called and, without giving his name, described the donnybrook.

It had happened in a near-empty parking lot. The alcoholic was told by the witness that it was he who prompted the fight, calling his eventual antagonist in the lot vile names and threatening to beat him for parking his car too close to the alcoholic's. It was the drunk who threw the first punch. The other man began fighting in self-defense and then, losing his temper, smashed the drunk into the pavement and repeatedly beat him about the head.

A witness and another bystander stopped the fight and helped the alcoholic into his car. He apparently drove home 16 miles on freeways without even recalling he entered the car or where the fight occurred. He told me: "It was a nightmare. I might have killed somebody or been killed. Later, I wanted to find out who I fought with. I was going to give him a $100 bill and thank him for saving my life." The victim entered a treatment center shortly after the blackout brawl.

* * *

My neighbor was a martini drinker. He confided in me

125

that often after four or five drinks after a round of golf he would drive 30 miles in heavy traffic to a favorite restaurant. Many times, he explained, he did not remember driving home. He would leap out of the bed the next morning, praying his car was in the garage. It usually was.

But another blackout victim told me he couldn't find where he parked his car many nights and in one week lost his automobile three times. It was a standing joke with the police officer on his downtown beat. "Which way should we go tonight, Mr Jones?" the officer would ask. The blackout completely blotted out his memory.

I know of another case where a man drove his speedboat 52 miles, finally ran out of gas and floated for three hours before finally, waking from the blackout, only to discover he was lost on his own lake. His frantic family had sent out patrol boats in a desperate search. He had evidently navigated heavily trafficked waters in the dark without a problem.

I have heard of cases of people who drove as far as 200 miles, came out of the blackout in strange territory and couldn't believe they accomplished the trip without incident. Others have had terrible wrecks, fights, family explosions and after one particularly violent blackout, the victim attacked three police on a busy corner. He was given a mental test before being put in jail. Nobody could believe he was in the throes of an alcoholic blackout.

* * *

A particularly severe blackout victim spent four days of wandering in six states. After drinking heavily one afternoon, he boarded a plane for Seattle. Somehow, he wound up in Las Vegas. He also wound up with a strange woman from his home town whom he didn't even remember meeting. She was as married as he was.

His wife, meanwhile, had notified authorities. Before the soul-shattering affair was over, he had lost his wife, two children, home, and most of his bank account. By the way, the woman he had picked up stayed in Vegas with another stranger. The same man, sad to say, eventually suffered hallucinations and died at his own hands three months after his divorce.

The body is amazing—and blackouts prove the capabilities of the marvelous God-made machine. The instincts apparently prevail over the mind. The reactions in driving and eating and walking and talking are so ingrained they superimpose the conscience.

As a good friend of mine said, the blackout not only freezes the will and recollection, it turns the soul to stone. Another, and perhaps most terrifying aspect of the disease: the blackout suffocates the conscience.

A blackout was nature's way of
warning you that the chemical
you were using was detrimental
to your health.

QUESTION:
IS IT TRUE AN ALCOHOLIC LOVES HIS BOTTLE MORE THAN ANYTHING ELSE IN LIFE?

SELVIG:

Most assuredly. The bottle is the most important thing in the alcoholic's life. More important than wife or children? Of course. That's why so many alcoholics lose their families. They have a choice—the bottle or their family. Far too often, they choose the bottle.

It is certainly more important to the alcoholic than his job; otherwise he wouldn't jeopardize his profession with drinking bouts. It is more important than his health—or he would readily understand his system cannot take the abuse. It is more important than his financial status or so many alcoholics wouldn't be penniless, having spent small fortunes or large ones on liquor and in pursuit of the false fulfillment.

It is more important than social status or so many would not have made fools of themselves in public. Plagued with the disease, the alcoholic will lie, cheat, and sometimes kill for his right to his bottle. He spends every waking moment thinking about the next drink. He rearranges family and work schedules to permit drinking time.

Examples:

Big Marvin was a secret alcoholic drinker for years. One night Marvin tore up his lady friend's apartment, knocked her unconscious with a picture frame, and was taken to a drunk tank in a nearby town. He was not charged with any criminal offense, but police warned him he had to stay in the dreadful place until he would agree to treatment.

"Aw hell, let me die you SOB's!" Marvin shouted. The next morning a friend heard from the drunk's beaten girl friend. He drove 67 miles through a snowstorm to see Marvin, who was whipped mentally and physically from his drinking ordeal and the strain of having been picked up by the police.

The friend, an alcoholic, said: "Marv, you're too young to wreck your life. I want you to go into a hospital rehab program. I know in time you can be a new man."

Marvin fought the idea for two more dreadful days in the tank. He finally relented. After treatment he surfaced as a solid individual. Today, two years after going into the tank, Marv makes inspirational speeches at Alcoholics Anonymous rallies and has become a leading citizen in youth programs. He married his girl and gives his friend credit in public for "saving my life." No friend becomes closer to you than the alcoholic whose life you've saved.

* * *

They dared me to walk up to a friend who had torn up

his home on Christmas Day, smashed the tree, and frightened the children. He had a club in his hand when he greeted me at the door with this warning: "Don't give me this alcoholic shit! You're all alike—God damned reformers!"

I told him I frankly didn't give a damn if he saved himself or not—but that I wasn't going to let him frighten his nice family. I took the club away, poured him coffee, and let him take a nap.

When he awoke, I took him by the arm, led him to a car where three of his friends were waiting, all of them giving up their holiday to save his life. The alky reluctantly let us drive him to a rehab center.

He still fought against confinement for three days, gradually giving in. After six months of sobriety, he threw a party for us that was almost extravagant. We didn't expect any material show of gratitude, but he presented each of us gifts with tears in his eyes: "God bless you. You're all saints in my book."

I didn't have dry eyes either. You can't believe the feeling of fulfillment and well-being when you help an alcoholic find peace with himself.

You wouldn't walk away from a wounded dog. But too many of us take the easy path when it comes time to confront our friends with the stark realization they have a disease which is killing them. There is no need to apologize for trying to help save a friend's life.

The drink dictates the alcoholic's life. And he believes that he loves every second of the domination. Nothing in this world is guarded more jealously than the bottle of an alcoholic. That is why the disease has such a treacherous nature. The alcoholic fights to preserve his right to suffer the illness—at the expense of everything else in his life. Evil fully overcomes good in the life of the alcoholic.

His sense of reason is so dramatically damaged that his love becomes the bottle. It is his passion. It becomes an obsession. It becomes his God. The sober layman cannot begin to comprehend what the bottle means to the alcoholic. It is his life-blood, his only true companion, his only release from turmoil, imaginary or real.

Never underestimate the power of the bottle to the alcoholic. It is all-powerful to him, the nectar of the gods. He will go to almost any length to protect his drinking opportunity. He has been known to kill for it. He is capable of turning on friends and family in savage rage to protect his supply of liquor.

* * *

I sat at a poker game one night when a man leaned over to his acquaintance who was losing heavily.

"Jeb, if you don't quit drinking, you'll lose your home." And Jeb replied while grinning like the Cheshire cat, "Hell, what's wrong with that? I'll take the booze over that God-damn hunk of brick."

At the moment, he meant every word. It mattered not that his wife and children used the house as their only foundation of permanency.

* * *

I have heard the alcoholic shout, "To hell with my union dues—pass the bourbon, honey." He means every word he says. It's the insanity of the alcoholic mind. I know a woman who was a terrible gambler when she drank. Yet she could not resist the alcohol while playing away her vacations at Las Vegas' gambling casinos. She lost almost everything she had. But she refused to quit drinking when she gambled because she explained to me, "When I gamble and drink, the thrills are so great it's unbelievable. I feel like the richest, most daring person alive."

She didn't care to just gamble. She had to have the drink even though it could mean financial ruin. This is a pure case of an alcoholic loving the bottle more than money—a common occurrence.

* * *

The story of Ned is difficult to believe, but shockingly true. He was a pillar of the community and a leader in church activities. Ned would take up the collection at church, sing in the choir and greet new parishioners after services. He also was the town's top insurance agent and ran an office based on integrity.

Still the bottle meant more to him than his reputation. As he began to consume alcohol heavily, his life style changed. He joined a country club, had delusions of grandeur and put a smart pontoon boat on the river—the better for drinking parties and to get away for long afternoon liquor sessions.

As money began to flow through his hand, Ned actually turned to forgery on clients' premium loans with banks. He was also caught taking money from the church collection! In two years, the alcoholism ruined a reputation which Ned had built up over a 30-year period. He was sentenced to a year in jail and his business was ruined. The last time I heard from him he was trying to start a new life alone. He had lost his family as well as his position and reputation.

* * *

We know that more than half the broken marriages today are shattered because of lust for alcohol. A particularly grief-stricken case is that of Tommy, the school teacher. His best friend tried to console his wife and tried through all means of communication to help Tommy, who would go on six-hour benders in his basement as soon as he returned home from school.

He became abusive to his family. At 9 or 10 p.m., he would fall into a drunken stupor and sleep in his clothes until morning. His friend, a bachelor buddy of years standing, fell in love with Tom's wife. She fought the liaison but was in such need of sympathy she finally shared her loneliness with the best friend. He courted her openly, telling Tom what he was doing.

Tom's sad but candid reply: "Go to hell. She's yours. Just lemme alone." The wife divorced the drunk, received custody of their three children, and married Tom's one-time best friend. This case, I believe, proves clearly that too often love of alcohol for the alcoholic is greater even than his love of family, a terrible truism.

131

I am convinced that no man can share his love of the bottle with anything else in his life. I've known race horse connoisseurs who loved their thoroughbreds. But they would miss a race to continue drinking in the clubhouse. I know golfers who have missed matches or played dreadfully because they preferred to imbibe. I've known executives who have blown major accounts because a drinking session cost them appointments.

The alcoholic will sacrifice absolutely everything in life to drink. It is such a consuming disease that it lays waste great realities. It supplies a temporary gratification which utterly destroys reason and responsibility. It's a disease so encompassing it cost kingdoms and castles, loves and life.

QUESTION:
WHAT ABOUT THE FIVE-DRINK "HAPPY HOUR" COUPLES?

SELVIG:

They are asking for trouble. It's a shame that you see so much of this five o'clock habit in so many upper middle class homes. I would estimate close to a million couples in this country indulge in what they call the "happy hour." I call it the "playing with fire" period.

You will see this so often in homes where the children are raised and the couple has a secure way of life. There is no drive now for security. The future seems serene enough. The husband has settled into his niche. The wife no longer has to impress the neighbors or the relatives. Now they turn to alcohol to either stimulate conversation or make their lives more interesting, or to make the time pass more quickly, or, as some have told me, to make them more tolerable of their mates.

The husband and wife who think they can "drink to-gether and stay together" are playing a dangerous game. The two-person pattern asks for trouble. They are accomplices for each other. They are playing with dyna-mite.

It is true that the home-drinking sessions may not cause automobile accidents or cost jobs or even destroy family relationships. Still it is a tremendous health hazard at a time in life when alcohol can wipe out constructive hours for people whose experience and success should be helping and supplying inspiration to service, commu-nity, and civic groups.

Worse yet, the happy hour can also turn into a horror hour when they lose respect for each other. Drink has a way of alienating even the closest of companions. The tongue may become a launching pad for insults. The lack of respect liquor can produce may torment the other. In-hibitions crumble with respect. Primarily, it is a great waste of vitality and spirit and will. Anything that is waste is a loss.

Examples:

Martin and Milly are a delightful couple who retired in their early 60s to build a lovely home on a lake-site near the Canadian border. They always enjoyed mild happy hours with two martinis but now with time hanging heavy, a scarcity of neighbors and television static snowing the screen, they have become five- and six-martini drink-ers.

You ask what harm it can cause in a compatible couple at this age. In three years I saw a couple who shared a warmth for years begin to bicker and needle, to pick and argue at the slightest provocation. Previously their chil-dren and grandchildren would visit for days at a time. Suddenly the children made excuses.

One son told me, "I can't take that drinking and bicker-ing. They get at each other's throats. They used to be fun. Now they're bores—retelling the same stories, the same jokes, forgetting what they said two hours earlier. It's disgusting. Even the grandchildren can't stand them."

* * *

Todd and Gert have a lovely little guest ranch near Mesa, Arizona. At one time they booked solidly for five and six months at a time. Then they went from the two or three cocktail predinner social hour to a prolonged affair starting at 4 p.m. and continuing through mealtime until bedtime.

What I noticed on my last trip to their hostelry was the agitation between them after a few drinks. From a fun time it turned to a period of complaints, each blaming the other for minor problems during the day.

The guests were not spared. On one occasion the usually hospitable Gert told a guest, "God damn it, we can do without your complaining about the room. If you don't like it, get the hell out—and take your lousy snot-nosed kids with you!"

I found out that this situation was common and that rentals had dropped nearly 50 percent in two years. Now the former love birds were not only agitating each other but, as the drinks wore off or the nerves became frayed, were turning their inner torments on the guests. It is just a matter of time before Todd and Gert, now obsessed by alcohol and terribly diseased, ruin their business, their health, and their relationship. The happy hour becomes their horror hour.

* * *

The quiet retirement neighborhood with the lovely $90,000 homes and manicured lawns is a nest of happy-hour alcoholics, most of them contaminated by the disease in their sixties—when they could be enjoying gracious, hobby-filled days.

Dan told me that the custom now in the plush little neighborhood is to have two drinks before golf in the morning at 11 a.m. Then after golf, a couple more. Then

134

a nap and three or four drinks more before dinner, tapering off with sociable drinks late in the evening.

He admitted to (along with his wife) drinking nine or ten glasses a day. "But we don't have any trouble. Nobody drives. Nobody goes out giving somebody trouble. We just sit and drink quietly and have a few laughs."

Well, it won't last. The quiet will soon be shattered by raging temper tantrums. The good, friendly neighbors of today will become the "SOB's who cheat on the course" or "the damn fools who never water their yard" in the next two or three years. Violence could even rear its ugly form.

* * *

Many middle-aged or retired couples who begin happy-houring the time away don't realize that their experience and skills and adaptability could be such an asset to youth groups and planning commissions. Political parties need their knowhow. But laziness is the ideal spawning ground for alcoholism. Idleness breeds the disease.

It is one of the rising threats to American society as elderly join the retired roles every year. It is a shame to have to admit it, but the retirement communities are drinking more liquor and there is a faster growing rate of alcoholics in their midst than in any other social strata of our civilization! It is apparent that getting older doesn't necessarily make us smarter; only more susceptible in many cases.

The retired great-grandmother put it this way to me: "Too often we feel all we have left are a few years—so what if we drink them away. We aren't hurting anyone."

Oh yes, my dear, you are hurting your children, costing the world your experiences and leadership—and most of all, destroying your own faith in yourself and giving up your pride.

You can wind up the most forlorn figure in your family in just a matter of years. If there is anything sadder than a young drunk, it is an old drunk.

For 45 years Nel and David were inseparable and a delight for their children and grandchildren. They built a small retirement home on a lake in northern Wisconsin. They began their casual 5 p.m. drinking bouts before dinner. Gradually, the drinking began at 4 and then 3 p.m. I met David one day when he was agitated and tired.

"Got problems with Nel. Dammit, we're starting to fight like cats and dogs. I don't know what's wrong with her. Must be old age. I told her the other night, let's sell the house and split. We can't get along anymore. She's a damn crab."

I sought out Nel. I heard almost a duplicate of Dave's story. "He's so darn nippy. Nothing I do is right."

I inquired when the problems usually started.

"Oh, we'll have a few drinks and he'll bring up something that happened 30 years ago. Or he'll complain about the meal. Then at night before bed we usually get into another hassle about bills or the lawn or who should do what. I can't understand it."

I could. I sought them out and explained that I felt the liquor was getting to them; that the pleasant highs were followed by quick drops which affected the personality and emotions. Just as so many people get pugnacious after a few drinks, Nel and David are bickering away a life-full of happiness.

They agreed to get off the drinks for a trial period. A month later they said things were working out wonderfully. Same old pals and lovers. It was the happy hour. It had turned into the hate hour. Liquor will do that, at any age.

**Worse yet, the happy hour can
also turn into a horror hour
when they lose respect for
each other.**

QUESTION:
ARE ALCOHOLICS ALWAYS LONERS OR NON-SHARERS?

SELVIG:

Alcoholics are more like other people than different from other people. By that I mean they don't have the corner on the market for loneliness or introverted personalities. Some have exuberance and reservoirs of confidence, the same as some alcoholics are large people, small, fat, slender. They are not necessarily slower or more brilliant.

There are callous alcoholics and weak ones and tough ones and bashful ones. There is no way you can walk up and stamp an alcoholic "loner" or "secretive." Some are spiritually orientated. Others question a Greater Power.

I have known alcoholics who in sharing tests were proven to be mental recluses. And I've known as many who graded excellent on sharing.

It is not true an alcoholic is a loner just because you see many heavy drinkers sitting by themselves in dark bars or because so many wives drink in the secrecy of their homes. Just as many gregarious alcoholics congregate at country clubs, at lodge meetings, at civic affairs and at sports events. What they have in common is not loneliness, only a tremendous dependence on the bottle which gives them a feeling of elation—to change their personality.

It is true, as we often have heard, that people are lonely because they build walls instead of bridges. The alcoholic's "wall" is the one built on the temporary euphoria of his drink. He may not guard it with sullenness or insults—but it is there. He doesn't want the stranger or

137

the loved one to probe that invisible wall of elation. He wants to pretend it will always be there. He wants to pretend he can shut out troubles and harangue; anything distasteful to his feelings of elation and superiority.

That doesn't mean he is a glump. He can protect that wall with a vibrant personality, even if it is brought into play solely by the alcohol. He can be charming, persuasive, cunning, exciting, tender, and gregarious.

But don't make the mistake of asking him why he is what he is. The wall is there to shut out the investigative or soulful overtures of his associates. In that way the alcoholic is a person hidden in the recesses of alcoholic guilt, but certainly not a loner.

Oh, there are loners from the cradle. There are people who can't communicate with society. Some of these drink alcohol to lose their inhibitions. But these drinkers are basically loners trying to change that detriment to their personalities. The real loner does not even want alcohol to betray his actual feelings of despair. He doesn't trust the alcohol or what it will do to his basic tendencies.

As for non-sharing, many alcoholics have this fault in one particular area: they don't share the guilt of their alcoholism. Since they love the bottle more than any other worldly possession, even to the exclusion of loved ones, they certainly won't share and expose their dependence on the liquor.

By the same token, if you mean "sharing" to impart their philosophy, their theories, their ideas for change, their ability to convey their beliefs, alcoholics can manage with the best of society. You need only to look to the many politicians, born leaders, who can share their dedication and inspiration—but are concealing their alcoholic disease.

Examples:

The 34-year-old wife is reticent, unwilling to talk about her inner turmoil or that of the family. She seeks solitude. She drinks late at night. In a party, she will invariably be the one in the corner of the room, rarely speaking.

138

Her husband is an alcoholic—but of a completely different vein—outspoken, loud, the life of the party. He is even willing to tell anyone who listens that he has problems with his liquor; that he has to stop or that he'll lose his driver's license. He examines his relationship with his wife, children, and in-laws.

The two, on the surface, could not be more different. But underneath they both are seeking a new personality development through liquor. He is not really as confident as he appears. He recognizes his shortcomings, which is good, but believes drink makes him as expert in all fields, which is bad.

The wife doesn't know how to come out of her shell. But the more she drinks, the less she is aware of her social and personality shortcomings. She wishes to become an extrovert. But who can really identify these people as loners or not? All of us are a combination of introvert and extrovert, the shy and the volatile; with circumstances and various consumptions of liquor the mood in us changes continually. Highs become lows and lows become highs.

* * *

Alfred is a welder who confided in me in treatment that he was always dubbed a loner in school and work. He said that he felt it was because his family rarely conversed. His mother was mute. The father spoke through sign language. The children did, too, as they conversed with the mother.

Words became almost unnecessary. It was a family of actions—not words. Alfred told me that he got in the habit of not asking and felt that his communications via verbal exchanges were not acceptable in most cases—that he sounded coarse and could not put his correct meaning in the right words.

He said he lived with the tag "loner" for years. Gradually he began to drink so that when he did speak, he did not care if his pronunciations were correct or what the reaction was to those who listened. In other words, he was not really a loner. He sought desperately to mingle but not until he drank alcohol did he have the courage to open his mouth.

This is a case of a man who became an alcoholic to change his personality but who normally was not a loner. His body cried out for friendship.

* * *

At a dinner one night at a major sports event I looked closely at the four most important people at the podium. Two were polished speakers. Two begged off with short explanations that they weren't qualified to talk because of lack of eloquence. All four were alcoholics. Two of them had been our patients. Two others soon would be.

I knew that the one talented speaker would consume four or five martinis before a speech. He told me, "I ordinarily tighten up in crowds and I have to drink to loosen me up and give me the courage to face an audience."

The other of the gifted speaking pair was a natural who usually could speak long and eloquently on most subjects without a drink—but still was never quite sure of himself. He eventually turned to the bottle to reinforce his confidence. Of the two quiet men, one could be absolutely brilliant in a quiet conversation in a corner. He, too, did not need the alcohol to embellish stories and regale captive listeners. But he hated to appear in public and drank heavily before moving to the head table.

The other quiet man was a true loner who experienced bitter pangs trying to communicate and admitted that even three or four alcoholic drinks did nothing for him. But he could drink himself into a stupor, sitting alone, pretending in his fantasies that he was making brilliant speeches.

See what I mean? Four alcoholics—two natural talkers, one quiet, one loud, one at ease, one a true loner. The alcoholic can find a reason to drink, whether he be more subdued or more gregarious. You can't brand an alcoholic by how much he talks or how many people you see with him.

* * *

I recall a man about town who was always the center of discussion. Call him a loner and suddenly he would appear to host a dozen friends at a fine restaurant. Call him a show boat or party man and he would virtually disappear underground for weeks. Call him a spendthrift and he'd leave you with the check. Call him a tight-wad and he'd pick up the round. Inconsistency became his constant. He was an alcoholic, of course, and explained to me in treatment: "I wanted to be a little bit of everybody else. I drank heavily and would become a man about town. I'd go into a 'dry' and didn't care if I met a soul. I was always wishing I were somebody else and I'd try to capture their personalities with my alcohol. The subsequent letdown would nearly destroy me.

"I found out you can't drink your way to being Mr. Great Guy. That comes from working and learning and consistency. The alcohol changed my personality. But in the end I never knew the real me. Now when I'm sober, I'm comfortable. I'm not a wild spender, I'm not a tight-wad. I'm rather an ordinary guy but I am enjoying me."

* * *

The young singer told me, "I sing better when I drink. I'm naturally shy and without the booze my throat has a tendency to tighten up."

I told him either to get out of the business or seek help with some expert, who through breath or relaxation exercises might help. If he thought at the age of 20 he could rely on alcohol to make him a great entertainer, he would be a physical wreck by 30.

**Alcoholics are more like other
people than different from
other people.**

QUESTION:
IS THERE SUCH A THING AS AN ALCOHOLIC PERSONALITY?

SELVIG:

There is the alcoholic personality which is universal. We are not speaking now of types of personalities which demand liquor. We are speaking only of the kind of alcoholic personality the bearer takes on after consuming the alcohol for a period of time in which trouble appears.

The alcoholic personality must also be defined from what goes on behind the exterior pattern of change. Behind the change is the lonely, lost, confused, irresponsible, undependable person, usually with little faith in a Higher Power, others or himself, filled with guilt, remorse, and self-hate and an abnormal need to control people, events, and circumstances.

Conning the deceptive front and the constant problems in the background, the "alcoholic personality" is one which can be diverse; at times appealing, at times frustrating; at times almost unbearable to the beholder.

In the end, the "alcoholic personality" is one which can literally destroy its carrier. It's unnoticed by the afflicted or the affected.

There is absolutely no basis on which to theorize that certain personalities are more addicted to alcohol than others. That has been proven false. But the one constant in their approach is that they seek change.

Once plunged into the course· of constant change, then the detriments of selfishness, greed, despair, anger, humiliation, loneliness, and self-hate and self-pity all combine in a morass so complex and so damaging that treatment is needed.

Examples:

Norma was a personal secretary whose drinking personality took on widely different aspects. She could be the coquette of the office party. She could be the super-sophisticated snob of the opera set. She could be the floozie at the pot-luck supper or the misty-eyed goodie girl at a church bazaar.

Always she could hide her drinking personality from view. She was master of personality disguises, but only after four or five heavy drinks.

Sober, she was a rather ordinary individual who camouflaged her alcoholic idiosyncrasies in a methodical, but highly efficient approach to her work. But to peg Norma's "alcoholic personality" would be virtually impossible, as she was very deceptive.

She was a bizarre array of people after drinking and she had an acute awareness to be able to tune herself in, almost make the perfect clone, for each occasion. She rarely moved from one event to another in the same crowd, thus shielding her many facets of personality.

She was a natural-born actress. Unfortunately, she had to drink heavily to play her roles. She play-acted for 15 years on the strength of the liquor until her health betrayed her charms and forced her into a treatment center for three months. She returned to her position but unfortunately could not stand being just plain Norma, a girl of one personality—her own. She died from drink at the age of 56. The loss of the effect from liquor overwhelmed her.

* * *

The airlines pilot was handsome, endowed with a large salary, a bevy of admiring females in tow and a bright future. Between flights, he became a heavy drinker and eventually an alcoholic.

His personality change after drinking was explosive. He turned from a gentlemanly, quiet, warm individual into a boisterous rogue, intent on shoving, bragging, pushing, ordering, insulting his friends and acquaintances.

I saw him snap into his new posture after just two drinks in a chic restaurant and berate a waitress unmercifully. He turned on his date and in a matter of minutes had her in tears. He suffered from "Alcohol Toxicity" insanity when drinking.

Shortly after I left, I heard he was asked to leave and wound up punching a waiter. This man absolutely was two different persons—one when drinking, one when sober. Before he was through he had lost his flying job and the last I saw of him he was working at a menial task in a post office. I wonder if he ever realized the damage his alcoholic personality had caused.

* * *

Then there was Peter, a brilliant lecturer in college, headed for a top position on the staff. But as alcoholism overtook him, he retreated into a basement bar in his own home. He would drink for four or five hours daily —and the toll on him was dreadful.

Peter lost his ability to communicate or to understand as the liquor paralyzed his mind. Nobody could speak to him during these alcoholic sojourns—and he lost touch with his wife and family.

Peter told me, when he eventually wound up at a treatment center, that he really never could believe anyone would want to hear him speak. He didn't consider himself that much an expert in his field—poetry. He wanted to crawl into a hole at the conclusion of classes. His alcoholic personality was that of the stupefied mummy, who saw nothing, heard nothing, could not talk.

I have never seen such a change take place in a man —from a teacher of magnificent capabilities to the rummy you might expect to see in a soup line or in the gutter. The drinking personality can be frighteningly menacing in a matter of minutes. It can turn a charming personality to stone. It can make a pipsqueak think like a brute and a brute behave like a pipsqueak.

* * *

The strange case of Dennis the cop tells a perfect story

of the alcoholic's split personality! He was afraid of his job so he overreacted to his authority. During the case he was obtrusive, a dictatorial police officer even his peers had trouble understanding, authoritative, loud, abusive. He was capable of carrying this aggressiveness over to his home life, but his wife actually preferred his drinking personality so she supplied him with three or four drinks after he had been on the beat. Then he would turn from the bully into a sentimental slob. He would sing songs with his children, play games, reminisce about his childhood and finally fall off into a heavy sleep!

Sadly, the wife helped fulfill his alcoholic tendencies until he was two different people. The sorry part of this situation is that the drunk was actually more affectionate, more understanding and more easy to live with than the sober man. His wife did not want him to change his drinking habits. When his health finally gave way we had more trouble with her than with him. He was "sweet" but failed to come to work. After he recovered, he took intensive family counseling and psychiatric treatment. The last I heard he was a happy, sober cop, had changed his ways and was a delight at home.

One of the biggest problems of the counselor many times is getting a mate's cooperation when she or he prefers the alcoholic personality to the real one. These are rare cases but they prove that sometimes we blame alcohol for a very unattractive personality which was there long before alcoholism.

QUESTION:
DOES ALCOHOL PLAY A MAJOR ROLE IN THE LIVES OF CONVICTS?

SELVIG:

I can only answer what a close and trusted former convict says. Mike Burns served over 13 years for everything from bank robbery to assault with a deadly weapon. He is now working with young addicts in a half-way house. Listen to Mike:

"Of course, alcoholism is prevalent among convicts. I would say that over 60 percent are alcoholics and a goodly number are druggers. Let's put it bluntly: do you think a man in his right mind would walk into a bank or store and put a loaded gun on another human being and risk becoming a murderer? Or risk having somebody shoot him in the back—if he wasn't on some kind of 'high'?

"Hell, I couldn't remember half the jobs I pulled until I sobered up and was told about them. God, I was no swashbuckling, quick-shooting Robin Hood. Nor are any of them. Most of them are poor addicts suffering a disease, the kind of disease which can turn a man with criminal inclinations into one. The booze gives him the courage. It wrecks his common sense. It gives him false bravado.

"And what hurts me is to go back and visit my many friends in jail and see that the authorities are not getting at the root of the problem. They are trying to turn them back into honest citizens and ignoring the fact that most of them are addicts.

"I've seen guards and other prison officials smuggle drugs and alcohol in to the prisoner thinking they were making life easier for them. My God! They were just perpetuating their problems. And when they get out they continue to drink, lose their judgment and common sense and turn right back to the criminal thinking which put them behind bars before."

Another con named Pat, who now is working with alcoholic youngsters, agreed with Burns completely:

"I could have gone back to jail a fifth and sixth and seventh time on forgery and assault charges over and over if I didn't quit the bottle with the help of an Alcoholics Anonymous group in the jail the last time. But too often peer pressure in the prison keeps the man who genuinely wants treatment or help away from it. The cons can be rotten about a guy who wants to go straight. They figure he is a threat to them."

Wherever Burns goes today he preaches his philosophy: get to the root of the convicts' problems, which generally are alcohol and drugs. Burns says:

"I turned my life around because an official who cared told me, 'Mike, you are two different people. When you're not drinking, you are kind, considerate and a helluva worker. When you're drinking, you turn savage. You're two different people.' I finally got the message —or I'd be rotting in jail today. I had to be a four-time loser before good people helped me discover what really ailed me. The bottle on my lips put the gun in my hand."

Examples:

"Fast Freddie" they called the little Italian waiter in a Chicago restaurant. He was extremely popular with the customers. The host called him "the quickest waiter in the Windy City." He got big tips and had the cream of society requesting his tables.

But in the after-hour clubs from 3 a.m. to 6 a.m., another Freddie emerged. As he sipped the aromatic wines his head would fill with visions of riches and success and he would whisper to friends: "I'm fed up waiting on society snobs. I'll get my own bundle and spit in their faces."

Gradually he organized a small ring of thieves who would strike the homes of wealthy, vacationing people

—the very ones whose conversations Freddy would overhear at his tables. When he heard a group planning a night out at the club, his ring would hit the vacant home.

It wasn't until his ring had committed over 200 robberies and stolen over $300,000 worth of valuables that he was caught. His explanation was so simple, yet so complex: "I was a happy guy until I started to drink. I don't know what happened then. I'd get illusions of grandeur. I could hardly wait to get back at the very people who were making me a nice living with their tips. When I was sober I couldn't believe I was doing this. But I got in too deep."

The happy ending here is that the very people whom Freddie's ring robbed went to the authorities, pleading his case and proving he was the victim of his own alcoholic web. A sympathetic judge intervened and after a light sentence, Freddie underwent treatment. Today, thanks to benefactors who saw the good in him, he has made complete restitution, owns his own restaurant, and is a complete success.

He says: "Nobody can imagine what the power of the drink can do. It can change your mind from thinking rationally to something so far different you are not the same person. I never got any fun out of the alcohol. All it did was make me unhappy and bitter."

* * *

The lovely shoplifter named Irene could have fooled a majority of the people forever. Her behavior as a computer firm analyst was impeccable. Irene was a leader in the company's social strata. She was a college graduate. She laughed easily and displayed an enormous capacity for work. She also loved bacardis. Not a particularly strong drink, nonetheless the accumulative effect of four or five after work on a daily basis turned Irene into something a witch doctor would have a difficult time understanding.

She became a skilled shoplifter, if there is an admirable trait in the sordid profession. She told me that she would steal scarves and gloves and moved into watches and jewelry in suburban department stores after work. She became so adept that one night she "lifted" over $1,200 in goods from a total of three stores for the "sheer thrill of it." She didn't need the goods. But the drinks made her a daredevil.

"The police could not believe I was a thrill thief," she said after being caught taking, of all things, a dresser lamp, concealed inside her expensive leopard-skin coat. "After four or five drinks in a nice place I get an uncontrollable urge to rush out and challenge the world. Stealing seemed the place to be. I would rove all over the suburban areas, looking for busy stores with liftable items.

After hearing her story, the judge told her: "Miss, you're not a thief—but you're something worse: a very sick alcoholic. If you can get it under control in the next six months, I'll suspend your sentence." Horrified and hurt, her dignity shattered, Irene was a willing and exceptional recovery patient. Her firm gave her back her old job and now she helps rehabilitate recovering alcoholics in the firm.

"It was so strange," she told me. "One minute I was a respectable professional woman. The next, a shoplifter, taking things I didn't even want. I had absolutely no control over my actions after five drinks." Every night, she told me, she prays to her God, thanking him that he didn't put a weapon in her hand or that she wasn't shot running from a robbery.

One of the first basic qualities liquor removes from the alcoholic's mind is his judgment and common sense. Then it plays on his fantasies. Then it can initiate drive or response actions, an irrepressible mobility force. In his condition, the human being is almost incapable of restraining his own actions.

That is why you'll see a suddenly complacent man leap from his seat and attack someone he thinks has done him wrong. Or turn and scream at his wife, berating her in public.

It is particularly a kind of dangerous compulsion, which uncontrolled and running rampant, can lead many people to prison. Only compassionate, intelligent judges and prison officials can understand a victim of this explosive action. That person needs recovery treatment—not jail. But an addict must still be responsible for his behavior to society.

* * *

Selvig: I was the instigator of violence the night I ripped up a VFW club which I was working in, shattering bottles, and running out good customers. It happened to me in a matter of seconds. A giant compulsion, coming over me like a black cloud after five or six strong drinks, turned me from the host into a raging, screaming, dangerous force in a savage rage.

I was fortunate nobody was hit by flying glass. I was more fortunate authorities recognized me not as a criminal—but a drunk. Joe Jacobson, Willmar's Chief of Police in 1949, sensed my insanity was caused by alcohol. I was a drunk in dire need of help. I will be forever grateful to him for his understanding.

The paroled convict climbed into the car of a waiting friend and before his companion could say a word, the parolee looked at him and said: "Now that I'm free of prison I've got to free myself of another prison—the booze that put me behind bars. Until I am free of the booze I am not a free man."
Unnamed

QUESTION:
ARE MANY ARTISTIC AND CREATIVE GENIUSES ALCOHOLICS?

SELVIG:

A famous author once said he believed so many playwrights and authors were alcoholics because (in order to believe that you could create a story in your imagination which thousands would want to read) it required a gigantic ego—and many authors drank to give them that ego.

I say, nonsense. The reason the public thinks so many creative geniuses are alcoholics is simply because any of their problems with excess or success are so highly publicized. They are so vulnerable to media exploitation that the number of them suffering from alcoholism seems extremely high.

The same can be said for newspapermen, who have been long pictured as traditionally hard-drinking characters by the cinema.

Yet, in one newspaper editorial office of a metropolitan daily, I counted only seven alcoholics out of 84 on the staff. That hardly seems like an overwhelming number, despite the fact a psychiatric study claims newspaper people are under a higher degree of tension than any other professional field.

It goes back to the earlier statement that certain people have a sensitivity to liquor and they can be found everywhere. In other words, there is absolutely no reason to believe that painters, sculptors, writers, artists of any nature, are driven to drink any more than other workmen and other types of professionals.

You will find as many alcoholics in factories as you will behind typewriters, as many alcoholics in blue collar jobs as in white, as many in proportion in sports as you will in the clergy. Certain glamorous fields as the arts simply receive more exposure in the media. The problems of these people are exposed to scrutiny. They are the subjects of much rumor and publicity, so we naturally assume they have more hangups. There is a certain mystique about a famed author or painter who, disillusioned about life, drinks himself to death. He will invariably have tons of biographers researching his life, whereas if he died a quiet death in the arms of his children, it would hardly create a stir.

I am certain as many plumbers have gone mad as artists like Van Gogh. But what is romantic about a plumber?

Examples:

In one counseling group at a treatment center we had 10 people. Three of the patients were from a group we don't ordinarily associate with alcoholism. I am speaking of farmers. Generally, if you drove down a highway, you'd expect the tranquility of the rolling farmland to preclude any problems with alcoholism. No so. Today's farmer is plagued by the disease. I can point to many ranchers, farmers, men of the soil, who are continually bedeviled by the bottle. They are as far away from creative art work as they can possibly be, but they are miserable as they suffer from the disease.

Their problem is even more acute because of their isolation. One farmer told me, "I buried a case of whisky every month at different spots on my 400-acre spread. I had markings. This went on for nearly a dozen years before my wife knew I was drinking heavily. I had to fall off the tractor and lie unconscious for three hours before she discovered me and got down to my problem."

What made this farmer an alcoholic? He claimed loneliness, being by himself for hours on end on the tractor. And he made a point: today's super enclosed tractor cabs with their earphones and subtle undulations created more tension in his system and a greater need for escape from his work than when he was out in the air and sun in his old-fashioned tractor. He drank alcohol and it fulfilled his needs—this is why he became an alcoholic.

* * *

The artist I knew studied in Paris, painted in New England, vacationed in Mexico and drank everywhere. He was analyzing the case of the painter and liquor one night: "You just think you're painting better on booze. You just hallucinate—but it isn't the true scene and color you're getting. You only think so. It's like a musician on a high. The music sounds better to him—not necessarily the public. The artist who thinks he can paint and drink alcohol is only kidding himself."

This man, Lowell, admitted that he had been drinking from his teens and that his artistic profession had done nothing to hyper his alcoholic cravings. "I've been an alcoholic since I was 16. It is just fortunate that I created some good things on canvas before my hands began shaking when I was 25. I went from a potentially great artist to a 25-bucker, meaning that's about what I get for lousy landscapes in cheap resort areas."

I think it is entirely true that often young artists conjure up the picture of a successful painter with a jug of wine at his side, relaxing on a South Sea beach under warm sunlight. These are silly, immature thoughts; like the writer I knew who always wore old sneakers, hung a battered cigarette from his lips, sucked a pint of gin, and hammered an old typewriter because that was his idea of what an author should look like.

* * *

Nobody can create better with a hangover. I am reminded of the golfing friend who was addicted to martinis. He was taught that his biggest problem was relaxing. So he began drinking two or three gin fizzes before he teed off.

This was done on the assumption he would relax more, hit a freer, easier shot. The second time he tried his routine, he missed the ball completely. The third time he had three muffs in six shots. He quickly gave up.

153

Relaxing and losing your coordination by drinking are two different things. The golfer hasn't been made who can drink while he plays and play as well as normal. The same with the writer. I know a writer who wrote a miserable book while drinking. He explained that it gave him more freedom of thought, a better imagination. But the book lacked cohesion. He wrote another book, while not drinking, and it turned out to be a best-seller.

One needs to learn that the ability that seems to appear after a couple of drinks is there without the booze. Booze just makes one less critical of how he does, bad or good. We need to learn to relax without using alcohol.

Traditionally, through the years the writers, artists, musicians have been portrayed as sensitive people bedeviled by alcohol, drugs, lost loves and heartbreak in their careers. I think they often paint this picture of themselves, perhaps searching for a little public empathy or hoping to be known as wayward a character to match those in their works.

We all know of the battle of Stephen Foster with alcohol and that of F. Scott Fitzgerald. But if they hadn't written *My Old Kentucky Home* and *The Last Tycoon* would anyone have known or cared? Think of the thousands of engineers, teachers and dentists who were and are alcoholics but whose plight is never immortalized in legends. Because the few brilliant ones attract so much attention, so much more is written and spoken about their personal battles. Their fame propagates their failings.

Checking over a list of patients over a period of two years, I discovered only about four percent affiliated with the arts. Hardly enough to construe that artists are notorious as practitioners of alcoholic consumption.

QUESTION:
WHY ARE HOUSEWIVES PRIME VICTIMS OF ALCOHOLISM?

SELVIG:

Many acquire a feeling of having been neglected. Again it is a matter of wanting to change their "feelings." They drink alcohol, hoping to make their lot seem more worthy; hoping perhaps to gain a little attention from husbands they feel are neglecting them; hoping to create fantasies of lovers and princes.

I particularly find that wives of men in helping professions such as professors and doctors and teachers are susceptible to the inroads of alcoholism. I think that is because their husbands are so actively involved with other people they feel themselves being shoved into the background, not intentionally. It's just that it happens that way.

So many times I've heard wives say, "At first we were helpmates. Now he's spending most of his time with his profession. The children are grown. I feel empty and alone." They become Mrs. Benjamin—wife of a successful man. It is frequently observed that wives of successful men become the most prevalent heavy users of alcohol. They feel frustrated, set aside. The husband gets the public attention. They get the scenes behind the glory —running a house, raising children, providing the family base.

Often that isn't enough. And the most grating part is, that usually these wives were bright, successful people on their own accord before they married. That's part of the mutual attraction between themselves and their successful husbands which radiated the spark of love. Then, as the husband moved into the busy swirl of his skyrocketing career, the wife was left in the lake.

I've seen so many bitter, lonely wives turn to alcohol that I feel it constitutes a major national health problem. Of course, not all become alcoholics—only those whose sensitivity to alcohol has been aroused. But the problem is growing. In her loneliness, in her belief that she is forsaken and lost, the wife finds what little joy she can in the bottle. With it she relives in her mind happier days. She pretends that she is important again. She pretends that it is she the children look up to.

She satiates a great need for respect and honor and worth in alcohol. In the end, however, the illusion of her importance and value is diminished as the bottle's attrition takes its toll. She becomes a diseased body risking her life for a few momentary feelings of worth. But these will be followed by worse pangs of regret. I tell the wife who feels forlorn to take up new hobbies, get into the public sphere herself, join clubs and force herself to push forward and regain her faith in her own worth.

If she must take a job, take one. Any new change is better than turning to the bottle. It only cripples.

I have heard sociologists say that with nearly half of today's wives working, they fear that the woman on the job may be a prime victim of alcoholism. I don't agree. I say the wife left in the home is the one primarily in danger. She has the time. She has the inclination. She has the privacy. And in most homes, she has easy access to the family's liquor supply or she has the availability of neighborhood bars and restaurants.

No factor contributes more to starting a person toward heavy drinking and eventual alcoholism than the loss of self-worth. The housewife who was an attractive, vivacious person early in her marriage can begin to feel old, tired and useless. It is easy for her to trade the pain of self-pity and the pangs of alcohol's momentary fulfillment. It's a bad trade—but it's very tempting.

Examples:

Rosemary was a pretty girl, vivacious, leader of her

class. She married a successful engineer who spent as many as three months away from home building bridges and dams. He gave her the $200,000 mansion, country club membership, three beautiful children and two servants. He didn't give her time or respect or himself.

She began drinking at the club. Then she would follow up with drinks at home before the children returned from school. She drank herself into stupors and eventually couldn't eat with the children. In dire search for her identity she became a dissipated alcoholic.

The chain reaction was withering. In time, one daughter became an alcoholic, seeking attention from her mother and trying to call attention to both of their problems. The son became a drug addict, secretly hoping his father would give the family the attention it deserved.

It wasn't until both children were thrown out of school and Rosemary collapsed on the steps of the country club that the father realized he had given his family nothing but material gains. He cried in my arms: "What have I done?"

I didn't brand him with the stigma that he had created three addicts. He didn't put the bottles or pills in their hands. I only said, just ask me what you can do and I'll tell you. He saved the family, all of them joining me in a two-month family-orientated treatment. Oh, yes, the scars are there. But perhaps it was worth the suffering. The father knows he must be more than a wage-earner. The wife knows the bottle leads to only more suffering.

* * *

Eleanor had a husband who was too popular with too many people. He was the constant flirt. He would pinch the neighbors' wives at parties. He would take the office girls home from parties. He had a dozen flings in their first 10 years of marriage.

His actions drove Eleanor into silent drinking, alone in their own small basement bar. She ran up liquor bills which were called to his attention by delayed payments. By the time the errant husband had discovered his wife's alcoholism, the situation was virtually beyond repair. The wife's crisis became a near tragedy when she locked two of her youngsters in their rooms while she went to the basement to drink. A lighted cigarette in the upstairs bathroom set fire to a waste basket and soon the upper portion of the house was filled with smoke.

The little children had presence enough to break a window and call for help. Neighbors rescued them and discovered the mother half asleep in the basement. The husband was forced into drastic action. After treatment and counseling the wife was advised to seek a divorce. The last time we saw her she was healthy and had remarried. She had no problem with alcohol in this marriage.

Escape. That's what housewives seek. And too often, they turn to the bottle instead of a counselor who might suggest new activities. I know of one lovely wife who became a drunken shame and eventually in her frustration tried to commit suicide. Fortunately she was saved in treatment. But over 7,000 wives in this country every year, caught in unhappy home circumstances much like those I've given, have taken their lives—feeling rejected. Many of them I have to believe were alcoholics as well as distraught individuals.

The disease can prompt insane thinking. And what makes it so terrifyingly dangerous is the fact that those early days of drink make the victim feel elated, as if the wife has found a new friend. She talks to the alcohol, makes it her mate. She worships at the shrine of its potency—because it has changed her feeling of being a lonely, lost, misunderstood house fixture to that which she envisions being as a lovely lady, cherished spouse and family inspiration. Too often the busy husband overlooks the symptoms. He is just happy he hasn't a nagging wife in the house. He doesn't suspect she has a terminal disease, encouraged perhaps by his lack of interest and attention.

Here you might think that I contradict myself. Earlier I mentioned that nobody can make you drink and no circumstance should arouse an appetite for alcohol with the well-balanced person. But in the case of the housewife who for years has not sought or enjoyed outside activities and has not kept up with her husband intellectually, I feel a deep sympathy. I think she definitely tries to escape her humdrum existence with alcohol, never meaning to harm anyone else.

She is to be pitied and helped and sympathized with. She is caught in a social sphere over which she has no control. Turning to liquor is not the answer. But perhaps being out of touch with counselors and therapists and improvement and study groups she does not know which way to turn. Television constantly tells her to take a drink, so it will make her feel better.

I've seen so many bitter, lonely wives turn to alcohol that I feel it constitutes a major national health problem. Of course, not all become alcoholics—only those whose sensitivity to alcohol has been aroused. But the problem is growing.

VIEWPOINT

One of the major tragedies today are the countless alcoholic housewives who will never receive treatment or will receive it too late. It is so much more difficult to detect alcoholism hidden in the home. And so many husbands are unaware of the problem. I know a woman who would get up in the middle of the night to do the family ironing, telling her husband she couldn't sleep. She would consume half a bottle of alcohol while she ironed until dawn. Another sought out an alcoholic friend nearby. They would drink during the afternoons, telling their families they had a bridge party.

It is so difficult to penetrate the camouflage of an alcoholic wife. Her perfume can cover odors. If she has a drunk sleep coming on she can collapse and explain it as a headache or that she is just taking a little nap. Young children may sense a change in personality and feeling, but are not sure. Older children usually are so busy they don't have time to study their mother's behavior patterns.

A sociologist told me recently that he believed behind one out of every six doors in an upper middleclass neighborhood resided an alcoholic wife. I have no reason to doubt him.

And for those of some means, the situations in which one can drink alcohol are provided almost constantly by our leisure world. I know a woman who would consume six drinks at her bowling league on Mondays, six or seven more at indoor golf lessons on Thursdays and then attended two lunches a week at the country club where it was customary to sit drinking a good hour before lunch and continue into the afternoon. On top of that she belonged to a children's charity group of 14 women and they were all heavy drinkers who met once a month.

At no time did her husband so much as suspect she had a problem. He, too, was busy with his drinks at lunch, at the club, after business meetings. It became a part of their natural environment.

Again the insidiousness of the disease. It attacks under the guise of entertainment. The woman says, "I'm expected to drink with the others at these social functions." The man says, "It's all a part of the business world." Suddenly one out of five of all these people has become an alcoholic—the one with that certain sensitivity. The one with no shutoff "button."

Another sad commentary on women's drinking in the home and in social circles is that so little is demanded of them to produce, as in the job capacity, that virtually their only activity is drinking—consequently they deteriorate so much more quickly.

The woman fights even a more difficult road in rehabilitation, too. That's because society still places far more shame and stigma on the alcoholic woman than the man.

So often you've probably heard it said: "What a party

last night. Bob sure was flying high. But hey, his wife Betty didn't look good, did she? I guess she can't handle the stuff.''

So the woman drinking in the home has a very difficult situation. Most of society still doesn't understand her. People who could help rarely know. Only a shattering family experience usually jolts the housewife alcoholic into life-saving action.

It is so much more difficult to detect alcoholism hidden in the home. And so many husbands are unaware of the problem.

QUESTION:
HOW DO CHILDREN GET STARTED TOWARD ALCOHOLISM?

SELVIG:

A combination of factors. Let's start with accessibility. Many parents have the habit of leaving excess liquor where children can get their hands on it. Children are prone to experiment. That's how they learn. Doing something he's not supposed to do is a thrill—a sensation to the youngster. He may not be sure he likes the feel until he tries again. The taste of alcohol is unappetizing to most youngsters.

I have seen many cases of 12- to 14-year-old drinkers who tried liquor only because it was availabe—a challenge like an apple tree.

[There is the case of peer pressure so great in high school as well as in our society generally.] ''Ah, come on,

Billy, don't be a nerd. Have a beer. Everybody else is."
My experience tells me two out of every three high school
youngsters at least try a drink. And in many schools,
many students drink steadily. If you don't drink, in many
crowds you are an outcast. The youngsters in these
crowds are told by leaders, "If you don't drink, you don't
belong." One needs to make an individual decision
whether to drink or not. There are alcohol drinking
groups and non-alcohol groups. One should be able to
think and speak for oneself and make an individual
choice.

So, we have availability and the experiments of youth
and peer pressure. Then there is another angle. The
child observes relief from watching his parents. First, he
hears his mother or father say, "God, I've had a terrible
day at the office. Let's have a drink, honey." That seems
to infer that to drink alcohol will soothe the tensions of the
day, eliminate problems, make the body and mind feel
better. The young person sees that alcohol, as in the
case of the pill-taker, has some magic potion, some balm
that eradicates the troubles of life.

I was deeply interested when I heard a particular well-
regarded Midwest high school had a reputation for heavy
drinking. A father of two sons who he said were "headed
for alcoholism just like me" had what he thought was the
answer: "It's a drinking class that the youngsters come
from. Good, high-income, intellectual families who always seem to have a reason for a drink. It became my
way of life. It's hard for me to criticize my sons. I went to
the same school and we drank, too."

Availability and the fact that many parents are either
alcoholics themselves or frequent consumers and have
alcohol in the home, or do not frown on youngsters drinking because they did, too, help contribute to the youngster's addiction.

Examples:

He was only 11 years old but Terry told me he had
been drinking for three years. I asked him why he

started. His young frankness was refreshing and frightening: "Mom and Dad were always fighting. Except when they had a drink. I figured the stuff made them feel good. It would feel good for me, too." He admitted getting frightfully sick two or three times and found out he could drink only what amounted to six or seven ounces. He said his parents never discovered the missing liquor since they had large quantities.

Little Terry tried gin but decided on bourbon. "I would drink when they were away. Sometimes I would take a drink before I went to school. And after school one day, I had five of my friends over to the house to drink. Finally, the other parents found out and told mine."

Terry was fortunate he was found out. He responded beautifully to help. One of his little friends, however, went back to drinking and had to undergo treatment for some time before he recovered.

But the idea that alcohol makes everybody feel good is the prime thought running through many children's heads. Yet they must experience these feelings when drinking to have a problem with it.

* * *

Little Margie was just 14 but said that at first she believed alcohol could do wonders. She would keep a bottle out of the cases her folks would order and hide it in her closet. She would drink when she was lonely and enjoyed the fantasies she could create in her mind from the effects of the alcohol. She usually drank near bedtime and her habit went unnoticed for nearly a year. It was only when her school work fell off abruptly that an investigation pointed to alcohol as the cause.

* * *

Sidney was a 15-year-old alcoholic who could not resist peer pressure. Let him tell it as he related it to me:

"You have no idea of the peer pressure. All your friends start out drinking. Maybe half continue. But that half that drink seem to be the fun guys and girls you want to chum with. Their parties are always better. Getting liquor is no problem. Always there's older brothers around or kids can swipe it at home. You just do more crazy things with alcohol.

"Like I rode on the roofs of guys' cars or went swimming without any trunks—stuff like that. Or at a football game our crowd always had the crazy cheers. Just seems the drinkers had all the big laughs and the best-looking girls.

"I got more confidence when I drank. I had more fun and was braver. That's it."

And why did Sidney eventually give it up?

"I ran the car through our garage door. My parents knew I drank a little but that night I was swacked. That was it. They made me come in and get treatment. I hope I don't have to go back to the same school. If I don't drink, I lose all my friends." After treatment, returnees should plainly and honestly state, "I can't handle liquor as I have been in treatment;" this usually ends the pressure. Where the youth gets the heat from other users (who are also too young to use legally) is that his former associates are afraid he'll "narc" or squeal to others where they get the supply. His sensible remark is, "I've got enough trouble staying sober myself and what you do is your business. The stuff is poison to me. That's what I know."

Statistics tell us there are 800,000 students in this country's high school today feeling peer pressure to drink alcohol. Half of them, if they are particularly sensitive to the alcohol and get unrestrained highs, will become alcoholics! Hopefully, the other half will get sick or their "off button" will tell them the alcohol doesn't agree with their systems.

Alcoholism respects no age. We have heard of cases where seven-year-olds were well into addiction. Children drink for the thrill. It's like lighting the first match, or climbing the first ladder.

A solid number of them are put in a position with fellow students of being afraid to quit; or actually liking their drinking personality better than their own. This generally happens with the more shy student. Others emulate their parents. Children copy how their parents talk, walk, act. Why wouldn't they copy how and what they drink?

* * *

A boy named Todd told of a disheartening story but one happening daily—and in greater numbers. The case of where older people actually invited him to drink. He was 12 when his parents offered him wine. His mother actually told him one day, "Todd, you're cuter and nicer when you have a little drink." I've known parents who encouraged a 13-year-old daughter to have a cocktail so she wouldn't be so shy. I've heard of dads offering their sons drinks out of their flasks at football games. "That's the way, son—now you're a man." Unfortunately many parents, particularly dads, think of their sons as "men" when they can drink with them. None of them seems to realize the devastating effects that may lurk down the road. One out of six or seven fathers will be actually turning his children over to the hands of a killer unknowingly.

There is nothing sadder on the face of the earth than a young addict. I have been asked repeatedly what I think about the lowering of the legal age to drink in many states to 18 years. I say it just makes available legally that much earlier the alcohol which will contaminate the people whose genes are sensitized to the liquor. In other words, it is this simple: the lowering of the drinking age just means there will be that many more alcoholics legally drinking that much sooner. Liquor is tricky and so easily mishandled by youth, who appear to do things to excess. Alcohol is dangerous at any age but more so with youth.

"But I want my children to know how to drink," so many parents have told me. Nonsense. What they really should say is, "I want my children to know about alcohol." There is a vast difference. There is nothing wrong, in fact, it is absolutely essential, that we explain to our children about sex and alcohol. Schools need instruction in it. The youngsters should learn that one out of five or six cannot control their freedom to turn down drinks once they have started. They should be enlightened to know when it is dangerous to change feelings, how and when liquor can be handled by the physical system—and what it does mentally.

But the problem here is basic: most schools don't have instruction and most parents don't give instruction because it is still basically a mysterious disease, the most misunderstood in the world. I only hope this book gets into the hands of young people who can study the dangers and ramifications of early drinking.

It's impossible to teach a person sensitive to alcohol how to drink successfully. The cemeteries in our nation are living proof of this fallacy.

"The little boy looked up at the idol of his life and asked: 'Father, does that stuff you drink out of the bottle make you feel good?' And the father looked down at his son and answered: 'Sometimes.' "
Anon

QUESTION:
IF A CHILD GETS SICK FROM DRINKING, IS HE LESS LIKELY TO BECOME AN ALCOHOLIC?

SELVIG:

It varies. I'm not an allergist but in my clinical experiences we find that most children who become violently ill from alcohol have little desire to return to the bottle. I am speaking now of children in the important formative years between 11 and 15. There is an indelible revulsion stamped on young people who drink too much and become ill.

It is a little like smoking. If a child becomes nauseous from smoking at an early age, chances are he will turn away from cigarettes. This is a natural reaction.

However, young people at a later stage know that vomiting and headaches and the horrible symptoms of acute drinking sickness are only temporary. They soon learn there is medicine readily available to settle their stomachs, soothe their heads, stop the throbbing. But in the early teen mind, the violence of overdrinking can leave a wretched memory which follows the child to and through adulthood.

I don't recommend it, but there are parents who force a child caught drinking to consume enough to get violently ill. It's a harsh way to teach a lesson—but it appears to work for some.

I was called in to talk to a group of young girls at a junior high school and I asked them about the prevalence of drink—how many had tried it, who had gotten sick. I found that almost half the group had experimented with alcohol. About one-fourth of these said they had become sick.

Questioning the ones who had become violently ill, I found that all but one said they did not care to ever try alcohol again. The one girl put it this way: "I might try it again in two or three years. Just to see if I can take it by then."

But in many ways children are far brighter than adults and show more maturity. The alcoholic will suffer headaches, upset stomach, shakes and flushed complexion and rush out to have another bout with the dog which bit him. The youngster who said, "I can't see why I'd ever be dumb enough to try alcohol again after throwing up all over the bathroom floor," made much more sense.

But the irony of alcoholism is that the adult body, after having repelled the alcohol earlier, will welcome the return bout hours later. I knew a friend who suffered the dry heaves in a saloon parking lot for nearly an hour each morning—on the way to a half dozen triple scotches. I know another young man who would walk out in the alley and regurgitate for an hour, walk back into the bar, and continue drinking.

The fools, the alcoholics be.

But, in general, a young teen-ager who suffers the pangs of tremors and total distress while consuming one of his first drinks, may shy away from alcohol for years, sometimes for a lifetime. Youthful pictures oftentimes are the most vivid in our lives: the sand castles, the first date—the first revulsion of liquor.

Examples:

Nancy told me she was caught drinking at age 11 and her mother said, "I want you to finish the pint." She did and was so revolted that she vomited for nearly an hour. Then came the "dry heaves." She told me that she didn't touch a drink again until she had light wine at her wedding. Chalk one up for an early experience.

* * *

Betty Lou, however, told me she was sick for two days after her high school prom. But on the third day she decided that nothing could make her feel worse and friends introduced her to something resembling a silver fizz —containing egg whites and milk. It made her feel great and a little lightheaded. She eventually became a completely depraved alcoholic.

* * *

It happened at a high school prom. Rosemary brought a bottle of brandy and consumed nearly a third of a quart, mixed with Coke. Trudy consumed perhaps another fourth, also mixed with Coke. Melody had a little, too. Before the end of the night, Rosemary was violently ill in the parking lot. Her escort rushed her to the hospital, not sure if it was the alcohol or something even more serious. The traumatic experience of having to undergo emergency treatment and then facing her folks turned Rosemary so against alcohol she became almost an enraged animal if any of her friends even mentioned liquor. Apparently she will not take a drop again.

* * *

Trudy had a rather pleasant evening. But she became ill upon arriving home. Her parents were not in and she passed out on the living room floor. Her parents found her at 5 a.m. and proceeded to reprimand her. She was shoved into the shower with all her clothes on and mistreated verbally. Trudy turned against her parents, whom she blamed for not being understanding. She drank again regularly. "Just to show the old SOB's," she told me when I admitted her for treatment when she was 22 years old.

Here was a case where the parents had a perfect time to point out clearly and without malice the effects of alcohol. Instead, their unbridled anger created a severe breach in child-parent relations.

The third girl at the prom, Melody, didn't like the giddy feeling of lightheadedness she got from just a little alcohol. She vowed then and there never to take more than a drink or two again. "It turns me off. I like to know what I'm doing," she told her friends.

There you have it. Anything is possible after an early-age drinking experience.

**Youthful pictures oftentimes
are the most vivid in our lives:
the sand castles, the first date
—the first revulsion of liquor.**

QUESTION:
DO SOME ALCOHOLICS ACTUALLY ENJOY ALCOHOL FOR THE TASTE?

SELVIG:

If a person drinks for taste, then one or two glasses of an alcoholic beverage should suffice. I don't care how reputable the heavy drinker is, if he claims he is drinking only for taste, he is a liar, voluntary or involuntary. He would like to believe that. And he would love you to believe that. But regardless of how adamant he is, the heavy drinker is looking for the effect, not to satiate the taste buds.

In the first place, the taste of alcohol is not that pleasant. There are fancy rum concoctions in South Seas recipes replete with a fruit salad in the cup that tastes delicious on warm days. But they are filling. The person who would want to consume four or five of them would be so uncomfortable he couldn't look at another Pink Virgin or Firey Volcano for a month.

Many alcoholics, in fact, are so turned off or sickened by the taste of alcohol they continue to change brands and tastes. It is not uncommon for the alcoholic to switch from daiquiris to martinis and from martinis to stingers and from stingers to grasshoppers. Ask him if he loves the taste of alcohol, why he continues to switch drinks? There is no explanation other than he is searching for that high feeling while trying to comfort his rebellious taste buds.

I know of a few who will go to their deathbeds saying they sought the taste only. Isn't that ridiculous? I may like ice cream but I won't eat it until I get chilblains. I may love rare steaks but after eating them for a week I won't want to see one for a spell. If it were merely taste, the alcoholic's body would soon tire of the sameness. No, the alcoholic who says he drinks for the raw taste of alcohol and delights in it, is asking you not to believe he is an addict. And he's hoping you'll just think he's got a "freak" appetite and is a real he-man.

Ask this man two hours and five drinks after as he stumbles over chairs and pours his drink in your lap if he's still after the taste. He wouldn't know then if alcohol tasted like red peppers or rotten tomatoes. And he could care less as long as he was enjoying his terrible glow.

The ones that use the "taste" pitch are alcoholics who have a great need to attribute their problem solely to a physical allergy.

Examples:

Well-groomed Greg runs a fine restaurant. He told me, "I have a couple with the customers. Mostly because I like the taste, really. And it gives me a good appetite."

The same man, who was recovering two years later, told me confidentially, "What an idiot I was. I could always eat a horse; the drinks just made me feel that I was more friendly to the people. I needed that 'feeling.' The taste? Hell, I really couldn't stand it. That's why I drank so fast. What I really love is the taste of ice cream."

* * *

And Russ, a bond salesman, had much the same confession:

"It used to be a conversation piece—saying I drank for the taste. I don't believe a man in the world does. I tolerated the taste only for what the feeling would do to me in a matter of minutes."

* * *

And a newspaper friend of mine told me about drinking

Irish whiskey toasts with a former Lord Mayor of Dublin during a good-will venture to this country. The Mayor saluted with the "finest Irish whiskey made"—served straight in water cups. My newspaper friend and one of the other guests professed before the luncheon that they loved the taste of Irish whiskey—forget the effect.

Well, after two full glasses, the journalist was coughing and his stomach was burning. He had to excuse himself and regurgitate in the rest room.

His friend tried to wash down the straight whiskey with coffee and he, too, wound up in the men's room. Never again, my newspaper acquaintance said, did he boast that he liked the taste of whiskey. At the showdown, he was proven an outright liar.

* * *

Women often say, "Oh, I love the taste of a grasshopper." That is harmless banter and I'm sure the Polynesian and exotic drinks that are served everywhere today certainly titillate the taste buds. But you rarely hear the ladies say, "It's the liquor taste I love."

No, they praise the mix, the fruit, the whipped cream, all the adventurous morsels decorating the cocktail. They mean what they say. But the lady who has four Pink Virgins at one sitting isn't pouring them down for the taste. She wants that glow. She's the one who might have problems.

VIEWPOINT

So often the sober alcoholic feels so guilty about taking a drink he must manufacture a reason. His reasoning can range from the sad to the laughable. I asked a farmer who was the perfect example of the "alibi system" why he drank. He said he couldn't stand living with his mother. I asked him why he didn't leave her. He looked down sheepishly, grinned and answered, "I never thought of that."

We all have alibi systems built in to some degree. The pitcher whose outfielder drops the ball looks at him in disgust, blaming the faulty support. The outfielder looks at his glove, blaming the glove. The team loses and the entire bunch blames the ump for not calling the game when it rained for five minutes in the fourth inning.

Certainly some songs bring back memories—and many times sorrows. They provide flashbacks to our earlier years. It is normal to feel a little tinge of sadness or perhaps they supply a fleeting glimpse of our glory years. But the alcoholic is not content to listen to sweet music. He must sentimentalize it, proving to his companions he has a warm heart and tortured soul.

"I'll drink to the good old days," he tells himself. "I was younger, better, had my hair, and the girls adored me. Where has it gone? Damn that song. Bring me another drink." And then as the evening wears on and the song's been on six times, he shouts to the waitress, "Turn off that God damn song. It's driving me nuts." Insanity has taken over his mind. He has used the song to get to a planned point of intoxication, exactly where he wanted to be. The song was his alibi. If anyone doubted his sanity and the reason he drank, the song explained it all.

The alcoholic doesn't need a rendition of *Away in the Manger* or *White Christmas* to make him sad enough to drink. He's been planning this holiday spree for months. It is the perfect alibi season. His friends and relatives know he can't stand that sentimental music. He's got them all fooled now. The alcoholic plays games like this continually.

I have to recall the way an alcoholic can shift blame or find excuses under any circumstances. The drunk wandered out of the bar and collided with a sober man bringing his grandfather clock in for repairs. The collision sent the man and clock sprawling, a hundred parts rolling and flopping into the gutter.

The clock-carrier looked up in disgust and asked, "What's a drunk like you doing on the sidewalk?"

The drunk, angered too, snarled back, "Why the hell don't you wear a watch like the rest of us?"

If a person drinks for taste, then one or two glasses of an alcoholic beverage should suffice. I don't care how reputable the heavy drinker is, if he claims he is drinking only for taste, he is a liar, voluntary or involuntary.

PART III

FAMILY AND FRIENDS OF THE ALCOHOLIC

QUESTION:
DO ALCOHOLICS USUALLY HAVE ACCOMPLICES?

SELVIG:

For every alcoholic drinking today there is an accomplice who helps him continue these self-destructive patterns. One of the most important treatment processes is to find out who this person is, and if possible, if he can be brought in as a part of the patient's treatment. Strangely, the accomplice often is not aware he is contributing to a killing disease.

The accomplice handles the alcoholic in one of three ways:

(1) He over-responds with extreme hostility towards the alcoholic. This further supports the alcoholic's theory, "Anybody would drink when you have a family or friends like that."

(2) The next type of accomplice is the overly sympathetic "poor you" breed. Mothers fall into this category continuously, "You poor boy, who were the nasty people who got you drunk?" The alcoholic thrives on this kind of accomplice.

(3) The third is the friend or relative who takes the alcoholic off the hook financially or otherwise. If he is arrested for DWI, the accomplice says, "Don't worry, Fred, I'll take care of everything. I've got a good lawyer and we'll get you before the right judge." And you've heard of the worst type of all—the "friend" who makes it financially possible for the alcoholic to continue to buy liquor. Without funds, he'd at least be slowed down. This accomplice actually is paving the alcoholic's road to ruin.

There is a frightening aspect to the role of accomplice or enabler, too. That is the accomplice conjured up in the imagination of the alcoholic.

I had a wife say to me, "I just know I'm the accomplice. I enable Tim to drink because when I threaten to leave him, I never follow through. I lose my courage. I wouldn't be an accomplice to Tim's drinking if I were firm with my threat."

"Nonsense," I told her. "Tim would make you an imaginary accomplice if you were the Blessed Virgin." If she left, he'd just drink more and say, "I had a disloyal wife who walked out on me." If she stays, he'll say, "That woman's driving me crazy. I've got to drink."

The poor wife can't win. In this case she can only hope a strong friend steps in. Rather than destroy her own life, it would be better to join Al-Anon or some Alcoholics Anonymous-related group and proceed to live as independently as she possibly can. **HOWEVER, DON'T LET THE ALCOHOLIC GO UNTREATED.**

This imaginary accomplice whom alcoholics build up in their insane thinking is every bit as real to them as the friend with the money, the adoring mother, and the weak wife.

Examples:

She was the typical widowed Italian mother of a big brood. Her youngest, Jamie, seemed to be the favorite. He was in trouble from the fifth grade on, fighting, chasing the wrong girls and drinking heavily in high school.

His brother tried to tell the mother that Jamie was headed for problems, but Mom wouldn't hear of it. "Jamie's a good boy—as good as the rest of you. He just gets in with the wrong companions."

When he'd come home drunk and sick, she'd nurse him and feed him broth. He could do no harm. Not even when, at the age of 20, he shot a policeman and was given 10 years in jail. On the way to jail she hugged him and cried, "Jamie, promise me you'll give up the evil companions." No accomplice ever did more to harm a son—even if it was love which fanned the flames.

* * *

I know a large family in which the father has been on

tipsy street for 25 years. The entire family knows he's an alcoholic of the sorriest kind—usually out of work, out of money and out of resistance. But nobody dares tell mom or the other brothers that father needs help.

"He's a good man—true and loyal," they say. Even at parties they laugh at his stumbling, bumbling tactics, his loud, coarse jokes and insulting demeanor. Nobody dares say anything to the head of the family—or to anyone in the family. Pop is the grand old guy—the grand old drunk. Nobody seems to care. Pop will die in loneliness and torment of his own volition but with a tremendous push from his dear family.

* * *

The nurse is full of compassion. She works in a jail. She is so sorry for the convicts whom she believes need to be upgraded and uplifted. I know for a fact she has sneaked dope and liquor into the cells to brighten the prisoners' lives.

An ex-convict and alcoholic who knows the situation says, "Nearly 60 percent of those men are alcoholics or addicts of some type. She is doing them a great injustice to get their pills and liquor. She is an accomplice of the worst kind—and she has no idea she's killing them." The former convict points out that most prisoners need help to leave alcohol and pills alone.

* * *

I know a hockey coach who has an alcoholic scoring star. He makes sure the hero has a jug of good Canadian whiskey after a top performance. I asked him why he'd ply an alcoholic with liquor.

"It does him good. He gets up tight for the game and the liquor relaxes him. It isn't hurting."

The coach-accomplice actually is selfish, fighting to hold his own job at the expense of a man who needs help—not goals.

* * *

The alcoholic finds an accomplice anywhere. I know a

friendly bartender, a man with honest empathy toward the alcoholics who frequent his bar. He says, "I know how it must feel when they're short and they need that drink. Sure, I pour them some free beer, but only the good customers." He is handing poison to a dying man —and can't see it.

The wife who says, "Fred likes a drink now and then and gets a little drunk every now and then," almost seems to relish her husband's problem. Others hide it in secrecy but still supply the alcoholic with liquor so they won't make the drunk angry.

Some families are frightened. Others are weak. Some are intimidated. Others don't care. The alcoholic can find an excuse in all types of accomplices. But he needs at least one, even an image.

It need not be a friend. It can be a boss he thinks browbeats him. It can be a youngster who runs and hides and cries and makes him feel bad. It can be the minister who tells him, "You've got to pull yourself together," turning him against church and God. The alcoholic can make an accomplice where none exists. But if the accomplice figure emerges in his mind, it's all he needs.

So often I've heard the alcoholic say, "It's the damn young people. The country is going all to hell with those hippies and yippies. If I didn't drink, I'd never be able to stand them." Imaginary young people are his accomplices—as real as if they stopped by the bar and bought him a year's liquor supply.

I know a former gambler who blames "crooked" athletes for his financial destruction. "The damn quarterbacks who throw the games," or "Those lousy umps who are bought off," or "Those two-bit basketball players juggling the score." The world of sports stars are against him. They are his accomplices. He curses them but accepts them readily.

That is how far the unreliability of the alcoholic mind can go. Insanity? Of course. The alcoholic is as insane when he is inebriated as the poor souls in the mental hospitals catching imaginary butterflies.

The sad part of the imaginary accomplice is that he has absolutely no control over his role. The real accomplice has, but too frequently isn't aware of it. Another dazzling vagary of the strange disease!

**DON'T LET THE ALCOHOLIC
GO UNTREATED.**

QUESTION:
HOW DO YOU TELL AN ALCOHOLIC HE NEEDS HELP?

SELVIG:

A friend can walk up to the alcoholic's home and say:

"I'm concerned about your drinking problem, Roy. You can toss me out if you like, but I want to help you. I think I understand what you're going through."

The wife must put aside all threats. She must act: "Harry, we have one of two choices to solve our problems. Either you or I are going to leave, or you must be evaluated in an alcoholic treatment center. And you must decide what it is going to be—immediately." However, have an ace in the hole such as commitment if the alcoholic says he will leave.

Or the family doctor must say: "Tom, you've got health problems brought on by heavy drinking. I think you are an alcoholic. I want you to talk to friends of mine at a treatment center. Your health is at stake."

Or the family minister may say: "Bill, I believe you have an alcoholic problem. To keep your family together I suggest we get in touch immediately with some help. I have people who will help."

Diplomacy has cost too many lives. Eventually some-body from the family has to confront the alcoholic. The friend who does so is as big a hero as the man who dives into a raging river to save a child or the man who throws an old lady out of the path of a runaway auto. You're fortunate if you have one of them. A team approach is needed here. This is sometimes called "the confrontation."

Hints and innuendoes are fine—but in the end, for the one who cares, the alcoholic must be approached as the footballer would say, nose to nose. The friend must be strong enough to be prepared for a rebuff.

I've known alcoholics who screamed and threw their friends out of the house. I've known some who threatened them with weapons. I knew a man who took a knife to his friend who tried to intervene and save his life.

However, in six cases out of 10, the alcoholic is waiting for someone to take an interest. In the other 40 percent of the overtures, half the time the alcoholic will come around as his problems mount. Among the other half, (20 percent), the alcoholic eventually has to be forced into rehabilitation by the law or have some family member commit him.

It takes a brave person to confront a friend who is an alcoholic. Perhaps for years the wife has tried vainly to get her spouse to accept help. He knows her threats are idle. The friend who helps save the alcoholic's life finds his reward in a feeling of goodwill second to none this planet has to offer.

Look the alcoholic in the eyes. Don't look down on him or apologize, either, for being there. Remember you are inviting him to partake of the finest feast in the world—sobriety and sanity. You have nothing to be ashamed of. You are the soldier, fighting for a cause.

It may take three or four or a dozen calls. But you eventually will be rewarded. The neutral party or friend can generally accomplish a great deal more than a member of the family where long-standing jealousies and feuds and inter-family squabbles have made the alcoholic suspicious. The friend who approaches the sick man need not be an alcoholic himself, although sometimes a past comrade in drink has more rapport.

I prefer that the team approach the alcoholic, rather than one person such as the wife, doctor, or minister, although any one might be the effective instrument.

But the wife generally has fought the problem for years and has threatened so many times the alcoholic will presume, "Just more threats. She doesn't have the guts to put me away. She loves me too much. It'd embarrass her too much."

Of the doctor, the alcoholic might say, "I'll find another doctor. Hell, I've been drinking for 20 years. If it was going to hurt my health, it'd have happened before." He may rationalize until he is struck down by the illness.

As for the kindly man of the cloth, the alcoholic may say, "Why doesn't he keep his nose out of my business. I contribute to his damn collection. He's got no right telling me how to handle my affairs."

But the friend of good standing has the inside track. He may have been there himself. He may be a life-long hunting companion. He is genuine. The alcoholic knows he has no devious designs. The good friend is a man to trust. When he tells you the problem, you'd better believe.

Fortunately, there are thousands of good friends doing this service every day. They are the life guards in alcoholism.

Examples:

The path of the intervening friend can be filled with booby traps. People have been killed trying to help alcoholic friends solve their problems. Police term alcoholic domestic problems the most dangerous on their dockets.

I recall the story of a friend who called upon an alcoholic who was in the midst of a terrible temper tantrum. He came at the insistence of the wife. Before the explosion was over, the intervening friend had been cut horribly about the face with a jagged bottle. Finally, in desperation, he had to smash the alcoholic's head with a vase, nearly splitting his skull to quiet him.

Both were bloody messes. After the alcoholic's ordeal and subsequent treatment, it was three years before he forgave the friend for coming to his home at his own wife's call. When he did, he swore undying devotion. Once the alcoholic is well and his mind again welcomes sanity, he generally becomes closer than ever to his friend who took the time to help. Sometimes the friend even risks his own life to save the alcoholic's life. Ordinarily, however, the bewildered, lonely, alcoholic is no more violent than patients with other illnesses. He is always ashamed of his behavior and sometimes even docile.

* * *

Generally the alcoholic welcomes the man who says, "I come as a friend to help. I invite you to partake in sobriety with me. Let's try this together." Usually the alcoholic—whose need is so obvious—is throwing out his hands for aid.

It is the wise and true friend who sees his plight and offers him comfort and hope. There may be some embarrassment about the situation but the intervening friend, I'm sure, is given a spiritual strength to handle the task. The rewards are an intangible feeling of accomplishment. Remember, there is no such thing as a voluntary alcoholic, giving himself up freely for treatment. The friend must be the alcoholic's guide and inspiration.

The friend of good standing has the inside track. He may have been there himself. The alcoholic knows he has no devious designs. The good friend is a man to trust. When he tells you the problem, you'd better believe.

VIEWPOINT

I believe in a solid campaign to bring the recovering alcoholic back to a strong position in the community and in his home. It is based on support, confrontation, encouragement, and hope. Let's analyze these vital phases:

Support—Bring to the attention of the ailing drinker the fact that he has an asset, too. "You're a strong businessman, Art, so why not use the strength for good and not for evil." In other words, too often we are guilty of removing all self-esteem from the alcoholic. I suggest we look at his strong points.

Confrontation—When we approach the alcoholic, be firm when we present the dangers of continued alcoholism. Be realistic but candid. "If this problem of yours goes on, you'll wind up with a bad heart or liver or possibly even in jail. You don't want to ruin your health or your family's name."

The innermost cry of the practicing alcoholic seeking recovery is: "You must show me how I act when I'm drinking if I am to get well".

Keeping the past withheld makes one of two feelings occur in the sorely wounded practicing alcoholic. He feels: "I'm not so bad after all." or "Boy, I must have been bad as they are afraid to tell me about myself."

Both feelings have a tendency to lead to further intoxication.

Encouragement—"You've got a lot of friends who are interested in your welfare. Without the bottle you've got the kind of personality that friends admire. When the liquor isn't talking, everyone is on your side."

Hope—"Why not try to get back on the right path, Art? It's not that tough. It's rewarding. How about coming with me to a treatment center? It's a tough fight, but one you can win. We're winning the battle every day. There are people all over waiting to help. The best part is that treatment doesn't take long, and the result can be good for you. At one time AA was the only known successful way for alcoholics to get well but with the modern approach, it's sensible to go to treatment first and then to AA. One can learn in a treatment program what would take years to learn in AA.

The friend confronting the alcoholic must keep one fact paramount: He is trying to take something away from the alcoholic—the bottle. It is pride and passion. The friend must substitute something in its place. He begins by substituting support, friendship, praise, encouragement, and hope. He must be prepared for the anger that usually results, temporarily in most cases.

If the alcoholic is not accorded an alternative to the bottle, the friend's approach becomes an act of hostility. If subsequent support is not forthcoming, the confrontation becomes cruel and disillusioning.

While the confronter is taking a big chance that there will be an emotional upheaval, it is far better to come one day early than one day too late.

QUESTION:
HOW DO YOU TELL A 20-YEAR-OLD ALCOHOLIC HE CAN NEVER AGAIN HAVE A DRINK OF ALCOHOL?

SELVIG:

I don't. I stress not taking a drink of alcohol today. Never more than 24 hours and oftentimes less. A minute by minute decision in some cases.

Just like you'd tell his dad, "If you go back to the bottle, son, it could be curtains. You don't want to be a rehab center retread, do you? You don't want to ruin a good young mind. Of course, it's not that easy to go to all the parties you have ahead of you and not have an alcoholic drink. But being 'the same' as all the other drinkers isn't the answer. You can have fun and relax and know what's going on much more with a soft drink. You

186

need not quit drinking but just change what you drink.

"Remember, the rest of these people may not have the disease. Only one in seven or eight does. But you do. It's a terminal disease. You can arrest it and become a fine, healthy young man—a real success. Or you can give in and become a bum, a broken spirit, insane from the booze.

"It takes courage. But in place of looking at the dark side, aren't you damn fortunate that you discovered this thing before you were 40 years of age and out of your mind? You should be so happy for yourself. Just remember, one day at a time."

Certainly, I was stunned and shaken when I found out at 28 I could never safely drink alcohol again. But a buddy pointed out how lucky I was that I hadn't killed anyone with my car—or really gotten in a serious jam.

The young person will say to himself, "God, why me?" But as he adjusts to the wondrous world of sobriety, he will see so many exciting things to do—so much world to conquer. Lord, how wondrous he'll feel! It's so true; the birds do chirp louder; the air does smell sweeter; the wind does blow more freshly and the sky does look bluer to the alcoholic who is recovering.

The young alcoholic will feel a sense of rapport with other young recovering friends which he never had with his drinking peers. He will soon be convinced that he can be happier, more successful, more popular sober than he was a sodden drunk. The longer he is sober, the more the realization of his happiness will abound.

Young people are intelligent today. They can communicate. They can listen. They can understand. Never sell them short. A 20-year-old, in the face of a health problem, can be more mature and understanding than the middle-aged.

Examples:

The old parochial school building is called "Team House." And it's all the name implies. It is the home base for 400 young addicts—all of whom have more than their addiction in common: they have been in trouble with the law. The law turns them over for hospital and treatment center care. When they are healthy, they are accepted at Team House.

Now mind you, the average age is 19—the kind of young people we are talking about. They come from all walks of life. They embrace all religions and backgrounds and races.

Every year more than 800 young people go through Team House—and the rate of sobriety three years later is a healthy 72 percent. But the big thing is that these youngsters must first face the reality that never can they successfully take drugs or alcohol. Their counselors tell me that once the shock has worn off they then ask: "But what can we do to have fun?" And they are orientated into music, sports, crafts, jobs, friendships.

One young man told me, "I never knew anything about playing on a team or anything about sports until I got here. Geeze, if I knew about this five years ago I'd never have gotten hooked."

A young girl was showing me her trophy won in a tug-o-war. "It's the first thing I ever got for anything. It makes me feel worth-while. I can make it without drinks now. I have many other things to keep me busy."

Team House officials have found out that a good share of the addicts never had exposure to sports, friendships, dances—the kind of sharing and cameraderie that makes them a whole person.

I have to feel that any young person, once he gets his feet back on the ground, will find the "highs" for scoring a winning goal or basket or forming a little singing group or learning a new dance far surpass anything they've ever experienced before. The rate of recovery attests to the validity of this theory.

* * *

He was a scrawny little boy who explained that he got hooked on drugs at the age of 11. At 14, he was in trouble with juvenile authorities. At 17, he was a hardened offender, with a record for stolen cars and purses and muggings, all aimed at securing money for his habit. His last chance before winding up a hardened criminal was to get treatment and then come into a half-way house to re-establish his role in society. For a month he was in the doldrums and seriously considered running away. But then a peer told him, "Hey, we need somebody to decorate the gym for the dance."

Henry pitched in and was amazed to find that he had artistic talents and a way with colors he never suspected. "I got into art, took painting and sculpturing and now I'm in school, studying for an art degree," he explains. Henry adds: "I'm convinced most kids get into booze and other drugs because they don't feel accepted by regular people or don't feel they have anything to contribute or get in with a crowd that's not tuned in on fun activities. I found everybody's got something to give. If a young addict finds that out, the new challenge takes his mind right off the pills and shots and bottle."

* * *

It has been said that loneliness is the chief cause for drinking in young people—real or imagined. I had to hold back the tears when I attended a party for six-month sobriety winners at a youth center. They cheered each other. They hugged. They shared. They loved. They talked freely of their problems.

One girl's parents in the audience radiated wealth—furs and jewels. Another boy's mother was on hand from the ghetto. Another youngster's dad had just come back from a jail sentence. A prominent athlete's daughter was in the midst of the celebration. Sharing. Togetherness. Call it what you like. But it's the mingling of people.

It's the abolishment of loneliness. Get to the tough alcoholic or other drug addict and tell him, "When you come out of this, you won't be lonely anymore—you'll have the best of new friends." He'll respond.

* * *

And get them with the half-way crowd and in the AA groups. They'll find a far more exciting life than they ever believed possible. But you can't take away the bottle and the hypodermic and give nothing in its place. The last open AA group I met with before working on this book had a meeting with over 600 on hand to receive pins for various lengths of sobriety. I felt so good— because there were over 400 young people under 30 years of age on hand. You might think that would be discouraging because it indicates a growing number of young alcoholics. But you should have seen the radiant faces. One particular instant I was struck when a 17-year-old boy received his pin and on the way back to his seat was embraced in the aisle by an older man heading toward the rostrum to receive a three-year sober citation. They held each other while the man next to me whispered, "A year ago that same man, who is one of our juvenile judges, had to sentence that boy to a detention home for three months. Now they both share the freedom of sobriety."

This is where it's at really. Youth. Fortunately, the young generation is perhaps more aware of the dangers of addiction than past generations. Their response to AA and recovery has been wondrous. Never fear leveling with youth.

The young alcoholic will feel a sense of rapport with other young recovering friends which he never had with his drinking peers. He will soon be convinced that he can be happier, more successful, more popular sober than he was a sodden drunk. The longer he is sober, the more the realization of his happiness will abound.

QUESTION:
CAN PEOPLE DRIVE OTHERS TO DRINK LIQUOR?

SELVIG:

Not unless the alcoholic is looking for an excuse. I have never seen anyone put a bottle to somebody's throat, hold a gun at his head and order, "Drink!" I have heard alcoholics by the thousands explain, "I couldn't take her complaints any longer. She drove me to drink." Or "I'm a golfer and after a lousy game, I just had to start drinking." Or "I began drinking to forget that dirty bastard of a partner of mine who ruined our business." Or "I drink because the damn neighbors were always reporting our dog."

I've heard it all. The alcoholic will find an excuse anywhere if he wants to drink. I've known alcoholics who drank because it rained, because it was too hot, because they'd lost their job—or because they were promoted.

I've seen them go on binges because they won a bet or a prize—or because they had a sick child. The excuse: "I was so happy I had to have a drink to celebrate." Or, "I was so down with all the bills and sickness I just had to hit the bottle to make it a little easier." The alcoholic is an excuse manufacturer of the most brilliant kind. Any excuse will do—senseless or not. But the excuse is absolutely real to the alcoholic.

I knew another who went on a two-week binge and wound up in the jail hospital because his wife left him. The alcoholic is so sick that he sees any trouble or even any holiday or celebration as a legitimate excuse. Yes, it is legitimate in his eyes. He doesn't need another person to "drive him to drink." Any circumstance may be used by an alcoholic as a reason for imbibing.

Examples:

Timothy would plan his drunk for St. Patrick's Day with the excuse, "I'm Irish. The Irish have to drink to celebrate a great Saint and for getting rid of those damn English scoundrels." But Timothy also used his birthday as a reason. "It's a sad day. I used a little whiskey to blot out the thought of getting older."

He loved his anniversary. "Mary's a helluva wife. I could drink all week to our marriage." So it went. There were, I counted one time, exactly 18 days during the year when Tim thought it a vital necessity for getting drunk—and at least another 30 days when he got drunk thinking about the good days coming up. He was what I call a "celebrant drunk." He only got zilched on days when there was something good to commemorate and in Tim's eyes there were no bad ones; not until his liver was eaten up and he drank to kill the pain of his failing health and because his beautiful Mary left him to drink himself to ruin.

* * *

The "Old Warhorse," friends used to call her. Cantankerous, lively, buxom, officious, loud. A real character was Lillian. She ran a chili house in Chicago and used to say, "I drank for only one reason. Business is so damn poor that if I didn't drink I'd never come back in the morning and hang up the 'Open' sign."

She had a built-in excuse. Business would never get better in the poor neighborhood where she operated. She wouldn't leave if she could.

She was an alcoholic and the mediocre business and the grind gave her a built-in excuse. That's perfectly logical in the mind of an alcoholic.

* * *

Like Nathaniel, a garbage man. "I hate my job so much but I keep at it. It's steady. And I get away early enough every day to have a few bumps before I get home." He couldn't quit his run if he had to ride down the alley with his head in the garbage. He loved the excuse it afforded him in his insane thinking.

It's so easy to say, "My wife drove me to drink." Wives are constantly there. But it's a savage, repetitious business, this alcoholism. The wife sees the husband deteriorating, sees him lose control of himself, his job. She sees him lose control of the children.

He, in turn, seeking an excuse to continue drinking, uses her reprimands and criticism as a perfect excuse. "She's on me continually," is what you'll hear the alcoholic say.

In truth, he's on the bottle continually and it becomes the moot point of which happened first—the drinking and the chastisement or vice versa. I have to believe in most cases the alcoholism brought on the castigation.

* * *

I know a poor soul who uses as an excuse the unhappy combination of the alcoholic disease and an addiction to gambling. He drinks when he wins and drinks when he loses and gambles for just one reason: to supply himself an unending series of excuses to drink.

It is not humorous. It is deadly serious. The alcoholic, in that vain search for fulfillment, to feel better than the next man, has to soothe his conscience by telling himself he has a perfectly legitimate reason for drinking. The truth is nobody ever drove another person to drink. The person who wanted to drink only wanted an excuse to clear his unstable mind.

The little boy helped his drunken father up the stairs and then, with tears streaming down his face, he asked: "Daddy, can't I help you stop drinking? I'll do anything." The father wept, too. There was nothing his little boy could do. There was nothing anyone could do. It was up to the father. And he only hoped he was strong enough.
Anon

QUESTION:
CAN AN ALCOHOLIC RECOVER WITHOUT A SPOUSE'S HELP?

SELVIG:

It can be accomplished, but it's very difficult. Sobriety is a pact between the alcoholic, some other person—and a Supreme Being. It is of great support if the other person or persons are family members. Family counseling is such an important part of rehabilitation today.

In the clinics where I have worked, a great deal of time is devoted to making the spouse aware of the alcoholic's problems. The many strange phases of the disease also are amplified. The spouse is taught to help support the alcoholic and to share in the joys of the recovery.

It is not always easy. I don't believe today that more than 50 percent of the spouses really accept the fact that alcoholism is a disease. Many have been so emotionally bruised by long years of hardship with the alcoholic they have built up a huge reservoir of resentment.

"I'll always hate that man for what he has done to me and the family," is a common threat in family counseling. It is not until the spouse is aware that the disease is responsible for the other's anger and irresponsibility that the husband or wife can begin to understand and help.

I was present at the reunion of a rehabilitation center group in a large civic auditorium. Only about one-third of the wives were there. I questioned many alcoholics who showed up and most of them said the same thing: "My wife tries to understand, but getting her out in public is a problem. I know she resents me. She can't fully understand."

It may take years for the spouses to fully comprehend the effects of alcoholism and how the alcoholic is helpless in the disease's grasp. In the homes where a spouse is willing to try to forget past trials, where the spouse is so pleased that the loved one is recovering, the joys are a thousandfold. The alcoholic—who must force his recovery on a spouse who is ridden with suspicion and torn with memories and doesn't share or trust—has a very difficult time.

Examples:

The man owned four night clubs and was independently wealthy. But every two or three months he would disappear on a drunk, raiding his cash registers and safes. Three other brothers owned minor shares of his business and kept blaming Jason for being a good guy but a lush who can't be depended on. He became their fall guy, the one on whom they could blame everything that went wrong.

They had his wife feeling the same way. In desperation a neighbor brought him to me for help. In three weeks, Jason began to grasp the fundamentals of alcoholism. Soon he almost bubbled with joy over the discovery that the longevity of sobriety could bring a fulfillment he had never experienced even on his wildest drinking escapades.

I was certain he would recover. I invited his wife and brothers to take part in the family counseling. Instead of throwing open their arms and welcoming him back to the world of sobriety and congratulating him for his efforts, they came up with the same refrain: "Well, it probably won't last. Remember the last time in 1968? When he laid off the booze for a year and came back and took $10,000 out of the business only to lose it gambling?"

His wife threw in the same doubts. "I'd like to believe it—but I know you'll be back on the booze in six weeks. You just can't keep your word; you're a weak man." The wife left after two days. The brothers disappeared the same night they arrived. Jason struggled desperately for help—someone with whom he could share his problem

195

and whatever success he might attain in sobriety. Nobody was there.

I had to give up treatment when he left abruptly one night with only a week to go in his recovery course. Not once in a four-week period did any brothers or his wife even call. Last I heard he was back on his wild two- and three-day escapades. I am convinced that not only did no one in the family trust him, but that no one really wanted him to recover for fear they would lose their "fall guy." Many times a recovering alcoholic meets a stone wall like this.

* * *

Then there was Judy, the alcoholic wife who once put her small son in the hospital, having beaten him while drinking. The husband refused to let her forget that incident. "I wish I could believe in you but you were an animal that night. How could you be so savage." He tormented her about something she could not even remember. The husband refused to believe that Judy had absolutely no control over herself; that she was insane, when her brain was ravaged by alcohol. All the husband saw was a person he felt was capable of great bodily harm.

He forgot that any of us is capable of destroying another when our mind is sick. And the alcoholic's mind, when drinking, is more sick than anyone can imagine. It is an insane mind, incapable of normal thinking. In months to come, Judy would finally convince her husband that she was a tender, warm person who could never have harmed their child if she not had been under the influence of alcohol.

* * *

Tony was a direct contrast. His wife always said, "It's the damn bottle, Tony, it's not you talking." She had a comprehension far greater than many medical men. She knew the bottle turned her spouse into a different person. No transformation is as distressing as the one created by alcohol. A spouse must learn that.

Tony's wife joined his Alcoholics Anonymous group's

auxiliary. The women didn't sit around and burden each other with what had transgressed. They planned picnics, theater parties, a splendid social schedule. They knew that their husbands' disease was a thing of the past and that the recovering alcoholic is as healthy as a man who has just had a cyst removed from his arm.

They knew that instead of a bodily growth, alcohol had attacked the minds. Tony's wife told me, "We both share the joys of his sobriety. It's a new world for him. And a new world for me. Anyone who wants to dwell on the past only harms the recovering alcoholic. He needs strength to fight his disease. Constantly dwelling on the past would do great harm."

* * *

But there are vindictive spouses everywhere. They either wait for the alcoholic to become edgy so they can shout, "See—I knew you would always think like a drunk!" Or they throw up old escapades like, "I'll bet you'd still like to see that floozie you used to smooch with at the bar."

No greater torture is man forced to endure than the alcoholic who is constantly reminded of his past. The spouse, like Tony's wife, who says, "It's cause to celebrate—the rest of our lives," is the sharing companion an alcoholic needs. Too often spouses forget the recovering alcoholic has just narrowly escaped death. They can't comprehend that he has suffered the remorse of the damned and must take each day in stride—never looking back.

I remember what the great old black baseball pitcher Satchell Paige used to say when they asked him to what he attributed his success. "I never look behind me. Something might be gaining on me." That's the answer to a spouse's role in the treatment of the recovering alcoholic. Don't constantly bring up the past. Talk only of today. Many wives can't understand the disease. It is ironic that thousands of wives live and suffer with alcoholics during their terrible throes of drunkenness and then can't adjust to or believe in the recovering mate. In many cases divorces occur after the spouse has recovered, all because the husband or wife can't appreciate a near miracle which has occurred.

Too many wives remain too secretive about the disease. I can understand a certain need for anonymity. That is natural. But some women harbor a gnawing resentment for years for their husbands. Instead of joyously declaring, "We're accomplishing wonderful things together," they turn bitter and sour. "Why did it have to happen to me? God, how I hate to have a husband who's a drunk." I have no sympathy for these people.

On the cross, Jesus Christ absolved a murderer. Can't we find it in our hearts to absolve a person who through perhaps no fault of his own has contracted a terminal disease? Its not a self inflicted illness but one which occurs due to a sensitivity to alcohol that the potential drinker is not aware of. The remark a son gave to his dad and mother about his alcoholism is so true, "Dad and mother, do you think I would have ever taken a drink if I knew it would cause the trouble it has caused us?" Of course not!

In the homes where a spouse is willing to try to forget past trials, where the spouse is so pleased that the loved one is recovering, the joys are a thousandfold.

QUESTION:
WHAT EFFECT DOES A DIVORCE HAVE ON AN ALCOHOLIC'S BEHAVIOR?

SELVIG:

Very little while he's in his alcoholic stupor. The threat of a divorce might help put the alcoholic in a treatment center. The divorce itself will only add to his remorse or relief. The more remorse, the more likely he will try to bury it under another cascade of alcohol. He might feel relieved and drink because of this.

You must understand that the person who walks away from an alcoholic spouse is leaving a sick and dying spouse. There is no way an alcoholic's spouse can aid in the recovery and save his life by leaving. Don't misunderstand me. I am not urging a spouse to stay on with an alcoholic and lose her health or her sanity. I had a wife tell me, "I tried everyting for 20 years. But no more. Threats did no good. Counseling did no good. He's ruined my life and the children's. I am getting a divorce before I go crazy."

This woman tried everything. But rather than try to help an alcoholic with a divorce, which has no little effect, I would urge young wives to seek counsel as soon as possible once they're sure the husband is an alcoholic. If this fails, then bring up the subject of separation or divorce. Likewise for men. Today over 30,000 divorces a year are granted because the wife is an alcoholic and refuses treatment. An alarming point to consider is that among divorces due to or related to alcoholism, 90% are men from alcoholic wives and only 10% are wives from alcoholic husbands.

Rather than have a shock effect on the alcoholic, too often the divorced spouse who walks away serves only as a greater force of "accomplice" in the alcoholic's eyes. He drinks more to rid his mind of a loved one who (he believes) has proven to be untrue.

Too often, on the heels of a divorce, the alcoholic winds up in the hospital or on the deathbed. I have known hundreds of cases where well-meaning wives thought if they "walked out" on the husband, it would cure his ailment. No, it just makes him that much more bitter and resentful. He now drinks to erase another memory of another person he thinks has caused him harm. His life becomes more forsaken, his role more desperate, his drinking heavier.

Examples:

Vivian told me, "I did what any good, loving wife would do. I got a divorce to shock my husband into seeing that his illness was killing not only him but me." She was distraught a year later when her husband died because of a diseased liver.

* * *

A very attractive woman in her 40's, Norma, said she had taken all she could. She divorced her husband although admitting to everyone she loved him dearly and hoped some day he'd come to his senses, dry out and then perhaps they could get together again.

In treatment two years later, her husband was heading for recovery but he said: "I never want to see that bitch again! She walked out on me when I needed her most. It was a young woman of 20 who gave me the will to live. Norma hated my drinking and I wound up hating Norma."

The same alcoholic recovered his health, but never sought out Norma again. He married the 20-year-old who had given him inspiration.

* * *

There is the case of Ramona who divorced Frank and

said: "This will change him. I know he loves me. The divorce will bring him to his senses and I'll bet we're back together again in two years."

She was heartbroken two years later to learn that Frank had arrested his alcoholism and explained: "I guess there wasn't that much love there after all. I disciplined myself—alone. At first I used her as an accomplice. Anyway, I got into treatment because of fellow workers and I feel wonderful. I have no feeling toward Ramona. No hate or vindictiveness—I just want to forget her."

* * *

There are cases where the divorce shock treatment will turn the alcoholic around and he will make every effort to regain the love of his former wife and perhaps even culminate his recovery with another marriage to the same woman.

That happened to a fellow named Knox, who needed five years after the divorce to recover and another three years to recover his wife. It was a beautiful story with an ending which would have done justice to a Hollywood script. Unfortunately, only a few divorces caused by alcoholism find the recovering patient seeking out and winding up again with his spouse.

In the major share of divorces, the alcoholic develops a sense of antagonism towards his divorced spouse which is so great that he accelerates his drinking pattern and usually winds up in the gutter. And ironically, of all the divorced wives or spouses of alcoholics I have interviewed over the years, the vast majority had hoped for recovery of the alcoholic and for another liaison with the original spouse.

Strangely, another goodly portion again married alcoholics—something which makes me believe there is an innate sense in some people which cries out to help those more weak than themselves. Many women married to alcoholics will remarry exactly the same type of diseased persons—perpetually hoping to save the next ill spouse. And chances are if their methods failed to get the first alcoholic spouse into treatment, they will fail again a second or even third time.

I personally feel no person should divorce a practicing alcoholic without first getting him or her into treatment where withdrawal and sobriety should result and at that time discuss it out in the open. [Don't threaten the alcoholic but promise him and state only what you will do. If one says, "one drink and we are through," then follow it through but don't say it if you don't mean it.] The manipulation and maneuvering game has gone on too long as it is.

You must understand that the person who walks away from an alcoholic spouse is leaving a sick and dying spouse.

QUESTION:
IS A MOVE OR CHANGE OF SCENERY LIKELY TO HELP AN ALCOHOLIC?

SELVIG:

No more than a move helps save a tottering marriage. No more than a move will bring inspiration to a ne'er-do-well wage earner, or will make a youngster a better student.

I've had dozens of wives say to me: "Mr. Selvig, maybe all we need is a change. To get Bill's mind on something else. New friends, a new house, a new job."

No. The truth is the alcoholic has a disease. He no more can rid himself of that disease in a different climate or atmosphere than a person with diabetes can shed the disease by moving from California to Florida.

Human beings have a penchant for believing a change of scenery can mean a change of character. That's a ridiculous assumption. It's the copout, the run-away theory. Too often we've heard of people moving and making new starts. But this is a disease. You don't make a "new start" on a disease. It grows worse daily, regardless of the environment or with whom we mingle.

Bring in a new crowd. The liquor is still available. While liquor is available, the alcoholic will drink. If he says, "I need a change of scenery," all he is saying is, "I'm tired of drinking with the same cronies," or "My boss is wise to me—I'd better look for another job." I know of no case among the thousands I've helped treat where a move or switch in jobs or surroundings staved off the alcoholic's inevitable pursuit of the bottle. The wrong person always comes along—the alcoholic.

Examples:

Theodore sold his wife on the idea that an engineer can gain a job anywhere, that his profession was always in demand. He also sold her on the idea that a family should move to enrich its life. It needs to move to sophisticate the children, he insisted.

His slogan became the theory on which the home life was based: "Every place becomes a bore after five years—keep moving, keep exciting." Exciting? Ridiculous. The man was constantly hoping that somewhere, someone, somehow, something would happen to help his alcoholic state. His wife suspected he had problems. She never realized his desperate search for someone to give him a strong enough hand on which he could lean for help.

She was too weak. The children didn't dare interfere. Father was God. He persisted in his lonely search for help. In his vain trek he lost four jobs, disappointed many friends and always moved on, fearing discovery on one hand—and hoping for help on the other.

At the age of 50, after half a dozen moves from all parts of the country, he collapsed in a small Montana town where his health betrayed him. By then, he had lost his family who tired of the nomadic life. He died outside a saloon among strangers. Never in his travels did he find contentment or help. A proud man, the change in scenery only left him broken—a lonely shell.

*　*　*

Gloria was a dance instructor who kept saying, "If I could just find the right spot." What she wanted was a dance studio which would permit her to teach under the influence of drink. She moved from New York: "It was too competitive and hard on my nerves." She moved from Omaha: "There wasn't enough exposure to metropolitan traveling troups." She moved from Denver: "The Western clientele didn't appreciate my style of dancing."

She eventually wound up in Hollywood, in a third-rate studio. She was fired the fifth day. Fortunately, she came to her senses when the dance studio manager saw possibilities in her and realized she was suffering from alcoholism. But she had traveled 4,000 miles and made a myriad of stops before realizing that it wasn't the scene or the people or the climate. It was herself. Her story has been repeated many thousands of times.

*　*　*

I never knew a harder or more consistent drinker who maintained his job by traveling than Chuck, a travel tour guide. He was a cunning fellow. He took a different tour every two months. Among the strangers he was gregarious and full of life.

Chuck knew the best restaurants and the finest hotel bars and always a goodly portion of his traveling tour were happy to accompany him. It wasn't until the tour was over that perhaps they realized he had not been a very good tour guide—except to the night spots when the sun went down.

He would consume two goodly shots early in the morning, have two cocktails at lunch with his group, and drink late at night with the hangers-on. Because he was constantly with new faces and covering new territory, he managed to keep his position for several years.

In his case, traveling preserved his vocation for a period. But it was an "enabling" job. The job was his accomplice and eventually the liquor and his disease ravaged his body. Again, the change of scenery was of no help—only a shroud to hide his fatal weakness. Chuck, too, died at a young age from alcoholism. Because of his travels and new companions, nobody was able to study him long enough to realize how serious his problem was.

The truth is the alcoholic has a disease. He no more can rid himself of that disease in a different climate or atmosphere than a person with diabetes can shed the disease by moving from California to Florida.

VIEWPOINT

One of the prime assets of the Alcoholics Anonymous program is the step asking the recovering alcoholic to make restitution or at least go to those he has injured by his overindulgence during his disease. It is a vital part of recovery, helping cleanse the conscience, and restore integrity and dignity to the alcoholic.

That is why I am so against the idea of moving away and making a "clean start," as former convicts are so often tempted to do. Too many times the runner will not return to the "battlefield." His recovery is not as complete as it might be if he had stayed on and fought his war in the trenches with his antagonists and loved ones looking on.

A recovering alcoholic told me the one sore spot in his

life was that he never got back to the old home town to show his sobriety and make restitution for hurts before his acquaintances and friends, for they had either died or moved away themselves. "It always will pain me to think that so many of my old neighbors never knew I cleaned up my act," he said. "I admire much more the man who stays in the place where he created his problems and completes his recovery on his home grounds. It may hurt a little more while he's going through his recovery but in the end, he has to be happier than the alcoholic who ran."

The man who stands his ground will find that people around him will turn from detractors to admirers over night. Nothing is forgotten more quickly than yesterday's old newspaper and yesterday's old drunk. Life tends to wash away the past, that part of the past which was distasteful. In the case of the recovering alcoholic, he is always amazed that people will change from critics to admirers in a matter of months. It is invariably true that people admire the fallen who rise to their feet to walk again.

In fact, a beautiful dogma for success in the alcoholic's life might be: the alcoholic is admired who gets up one more time than the number of times he has fallen down.

I remember a young man named Lee telling me while I was a municipal judge, "Just give me the chance to get out of town, your honor. I have friends in Denver. Suspend my sentence and let me go and try to start over out West." I told him, "Lee, the air is thinner in Denver and liquor is just as strong. It'll be as rough on you there as here." But he insisted and I let him go. I heard six months later that he had fallen out of the third story window of a Denver apartment and was crippled for life.

It is so difficult for the alcoholic to accept the fact that his disease comes from within. It isn't put on him by the atmospheric conditions, the winds, the change in temperature, or the scenery. The man who has that sensitivity for alcohol in New York will have it in San Francisco. The man who changes from being a carpenter to a mechanic or to a painter will still be harassed from the irrepressible desire inside to change his feelings regardless of his vocation or new job.

They say San Francisco is said to be a city of drunks and deviates and derelicts. Perhaps it is true many of them have moved Westward and eventually come to the Pacific barrier. But they have found no comfort in the beauty of their surroundings. They have found no substitute for their alcoholic sensitivity or their character defects simply because they are with others of their own.

In fact, the alcoholic or any addict who runs and continually strives to get away from his family and work and health problems and places, will go down hill faster physically and mentally in a new locale. Because the remorse he suffers when he finds out that the world isn't responsible for his disease, that he is the victim regardless of where he settles, only adds fuel to his pangs of frustration and plight.

"The difference between the practicing alcoholic and recovering alcoholic is very basic: The recovering alcoholic gets up one more time."
Selvig

QUESTION:
WHAT'S THE VALUE OF AL-ANON AND OTHER SUPPORT GROUPS?

SELVIG:

It depends greatly on the philosophy of the group. The majority offer tremendous support to spouses. Some of these programs teach the spouse or relative of the alcoholic to live his or her own life—with independence and freedom which the alcoholic should not be able to penetrate and ruin. I don't completely buy that philosophy. All systems aimed at helping an alcoholic should be aimed at helping him quit drinking and live a better life with his family if at all possible as well as improve the life of the non-alcoholic family members.

If the wife says, "Let John have the bottle, but it is not going to ruin my life," she is doing nothing constructive to help him end his drinking or arrest the disease. If she gets an understanding of the disease from her group and learns ways she might bring the alcoholic to a recovery program, splendid.

But too often, I've heard women say, "Well, it's in his lap now. My group is teaching me to live my own life."

A family partner has no right to that line of independence. If your love is caught up in the hell of a terminal disease, he needs your support, confrontation, encouragement, and hope, as difficult as any of the four are to give.

It is not easy to live with an alcoholic. Neither is it easy to live with a cancer patient or spouse suffering from a serious heart ailment. They take time.

The stricken ones can be short of temper, unruly, difficult to manage, hard to please. The alcoholic is the same way. But you don't run to a group which tells you to "let the cancer patient live his own life. You have yours to think about."

That's nonsensical—and cruel. I know the alcoholic can be a wife-beater, spendthrift, chaser, harasser of children. But I also know that he needs a spouse to help him meet his problem head-to-head.

One auxiliary group stresses "complete detachment." This "detachment" will bring about the very changes we are powerless to make. I sincerely doubt that.

Now for the positive action groups, many of which are Al-Anon people, working beautifully hand-in-hand with AA.

The wives certainly gain a better feeling for themselves. But they attend meetings to study the disease, then recharge their emotional batteries and move back into the family force to help their alcoholic loved ones get straightened out. It's not a case of "let the alcoholic shift for himself and show him he's not going to ruin the whole family." Instead, they fill themselves with spiritual and emotional strength to gird for difficult days ahead.

I know an Al-Anon member who says: "There is a very real presence of God at our meeting. We use the AA Twelve Steps to become stronger and better people, more able to cope with the alcoholic we love. It gives us a fresh approach. Like AA, we gain from each other. Sharing helps. To talk over our problems helps. It is a wonderful way of life."

Al-Anon groups like these which don't stress independence but direct their energies toward creating hope and strength and will and edification in the spouses and relatives of the alcoholic are a tremendous source of help to the recovery program. These teams are growing in numbers daily.

One should join an Al-Anon group to help the loved ones of alcoholics help themselves and in so doing give them the strength to become more free to function as individuals; therefore more helpful to the alcoholic.

I fully realize the drain on the constitution of an alcoholic's loved one. But I am sympathetic toward the alcoholic's cause as I feel he must have strong support from his loved ones and or friends to help him survive.

Examples:

After 15 years of abuse, arguments, and unpredictability, June joined a group which promises release from her worries—for the moment. She would learn how to live her own life, without being beaten down by her husband's alcoholic outbursts and whims. She was told to forget about his drinking, to quit harassing him, and to go her own way. She was told to get out with her own friends, get out of the house, and show her single independence again.

Well, her husband became so upset over her new interests, he went on a two-day drunk and wound up smashing the car through the window of a store, injuring himself critically. He said, "When she kept leaving me, I didn't think she cared anymore." Now, on the one hand, that is the typical alcoholic's excuse for another drink. On the other hand, if he had killed himself, how would the wife have felt?

* * *

The young wife named Nancy ran a dance studio. Believing her husband to be an alcoholic, she joined an Al-Anon group and her peers told her to "go your own way." She did. Getting back with her old girlfriends, she began doing most of her socializing with them.

When her husband asked why, she replied: "I don't need you when you're drinking. I'd rather go with the girls." Hurt, rejected, he went out with his old crowd and in six months they were divorced. Perhaps they wouldn't have made it anyway. But I see them both now and they are sad. Her independence didn't jar him into sobriety. It only drove them further apart.

"The trouble with trying to quit drinking is those terrible sharing groups where you feel so bad that when you come out you need a drink to steady your nerves. And after the drink you wish to God you listened to what was said at the meeting.
Anonymous drunk

QUESTION:
ARE CHILDREN OF ALCOHOLIC PARENTS MORE LIKELY TO BECOME DISEASED?

SELVIG:

Yes. It goes back to a very basic premise: We are the products of our environment. I know that I've stated earlier that I don't believe heredity can be held responsible for alcoholism.

But let's talk about atmosphere and environment. If young people are constantly exposed to alcohol and their parents' drinking habits, it becomes a way of life. It's more accessible than in the home of the non-alcoholic, so there is that much more reason to drink. The more drinkers the more alcoholics, simply by percentage.

With liquor available, with no control from the parents and with the mother or father or both actually fostering alcoholic consumption, the children of these people are bound to be a higher percentage of alcoholics. That doesn't mean they've inherited any more sensitivity than the next person. It means that just by being exposed to alcohol at an early age, those with sensitivity have a far higher chance of acquiring the habit more rapidly.

For instance, there are more opium users in Hong Kong because the drug is there in abundance. There are more race drivers developed in Indiana and California because in these areas young people are exposed to the sport much more often. Likewise, Canada produced more exceptional hockey players because it is the national sport and the children are exposed to it virtually from the cradle.

The same with alcohol. If it is there and used frequently in the home, it becomes not a thing of repulsion or a threat. It is a social stimulus. If both parents drink, they are saying in fact: "We like drinking alcohol. It is a way of life with us. You children are in the family—it is part of our way of life. Feel free to join us." They may not actually say it in those words but their actions express that opinion.

Examples:

A ruggedly handsome young man named Nick told me that out of six children in his family, three resisted drinking with the alcoholic parents. But it became easier to drink than to put up with the loud, raucous partying. Alcoholic sensitivity appeared in two of the original three non-drinkers.

They might never had been victims if they hadn't begun drinking regularly almost in self-defense. "They couldn't sleep or study with the parties going on so they joined rather than fight," Nick explained.

* * *

The case of Carole was obvious to any layman. She hated the taste but said, "My folks urged me to keep trying different drinks until I found one I liked.

"I came across some fruit juice concoction. I drank just to be a part of the crazy household. I hated the feeling of a hangover and dizzy spells I'd get. Yet, I felt a feeling of fulfillment also. But eventually I drank so much that I became stupefied a good deal of the time. Nobody cared. In fact, my parents urged me on. They loved to have me drink with them. Eventually all I wanted to do was drink.

"And imagine, I hated the taste of the stuff at the start! I hated myself for giving in. Now I'm recovering and I resent the years I spent drinking. I understand my parents, but I may have some resentment there, too. I'm trying to fight it."

* * *

And what about sisters Beth and Nancy? Neither could even stand the odor of alcohol. Their alcoholic parents told the sisters that they'd have to learn to drink to get along in the family—that everybody drank. So they began putting small amounts of alcohol into the girls' chocolate, soft drinks, fruit juices.

Eventually they not only acquired a taste, but became heavy drinkers who needed two or three shots for breakfast! Alcoholism had arrived, so cunning, baffling, and powerful as it is.

"The child's heart curseth deeper in the darkness than a strong man's in its wrath."
Elizabeth Barret Browning

QUESTION:
SHOULD PARENTS BE HELD RESPONSIBLE FOR ALCOHOLIC TEENAGERS?

SELVIG:

Absolutely not. Parents have an abnormal tendency to blame themselves for everything that goes wrong with their children. Remember, none of us were born with the credentials to be parents.

We become mothers and fathers via the act of sexual intercourse. Suddenly we are parents. We stumble and fumble, but most of us try to do our best. In the case of alcoholic children, we must remember that they acquire alcoholism in spite of us. Not because of us.

No parent should ever hold himself responsible for a child of his becoming an alcoholic. If I had known I'd be putting genes of alcoholic sensitivity into my children, one of whom would eventually become an alcoholic, I'd have had a vasectomy at 19. The greatest gift parents can give their children is the parents' own integrity. And then provide them with an example of love and sharing and hope, mixed with honest doses of discipline.

Parenthood is a first for all of us. And we all make mistakes. Compound our mistakes with the fact that every child is different in temperament, emotion, and drives, and no parent can expect to be all things to each child.

And no adult, except perhaps the ones who force alcohol on children or expect to party with them, should be made to feel responsible for the offspring being attacked by alcoholism. No more than they should take bows for Johnny's great broken-field runs in football or Susie's tennis accomplishments.

You don't hear a parent say, "I'm a flop—my boy never made the football team." And I hate to hear any young alcoholic say, "Blame it onto the genes. Blame it on the parents. They made me—and I've turned out to be a rummy."

The weak-backed offspring who wants to blame his parents for his drinking problem is simply looking for that accomplice we talked about earlier—the fall guy. The parents of an alcoholic are no more responsible for his disease than the parents of John Dillinger or the parents of Bluebeard are for the infamous exploits of their sons.

* * *

I will be perfectly candid. I was a recovering alcoholic—sober for nine years—before I became a parent, yet I had a son, Johnny, who became a known alcoholic at the age of 16. This despite the fact that I spent a good deal of time with him and we were very close and shared recreational outlets like hunting and fishing. In other words, I knew him well.

I don't hold myself responsible for Johnny's addiction. And I don't attempt to crawl into a hole, pull the earth over me and hide his problem. I simply said, "Johnny, let me help you get out of this rat race. You have too fine a mind and body to ruin them at this age. Don't snuff out your potential to live a real, meaningful life. Stay in bed with the helluva hangover you've got and we'll see what we can do."

I was flattered when Johnny said, "Whatever you say

dad." He went to Heartview Foundation, where I worked. That was five years ago. Johnny has sobriety and now writes music for young addicts, his lyrics reflecting the problems they face and the happiness they can find when they get the bottle out of their life. Just think, today he has five years of sobriety at the age of 21.

I could have looked at his plight and looked at myself and accused myself of being the worst failure in the world. Here I was out working with recovering alcoholics while my own son was stricken with the disease. I looked at his experience, sorry as it was, as a growing experience for both of us. He said he got his first drink from a neighbor girl at the age of 12 and felt, "Wow," like I did in 1939.

The real parental fool is the one who blames himself and then refuses to learn from the experience. Every day has to be treated as new, a new learning experience for the parent. The shock of discovering a young alcoholic in your family can be unnerving. But be thankful the disease was discovered at an early age and then plunge yourself into the recovery program with as much enthusiasm as you can muster. You will, I promise, come out of it a better, more tolerant, understanding person. You know my son has a right to be an alcoholic as I did. Every one of us has the right to suffer from an illness, even if it is alcoholism.

* * *

The grandest parents I ever knew (perfect examples of hard work, honesty, family time well spent) had three alcoholics in a family of six children. The mother told me, "At first I was heart-broken. But then I looked at the three children who were addicted and I said, 'How can I hold myself responsible?' I studied their problem and came to the conclusion there was nothing in our family life that turned those three into alcoholics except their own susceptibility to the disease. I loved them as much as ever and tried to help.

"Two of them are recovering and told me, 'Mother, it wasn't the family. We just had to have liquor. Nothing you did made us drink. It was what liquor did for us. It was our choosing. But now we can see how much we hurt you.' "

* * *

Alcoholics have come from the most solid and traditionally orientated homes in the land. I know a minister, a beautiful man of charity and good works, who had four children. One became a bank robber. Another an addict. A third was married four times. The fourth is a bishop. Now how do you explain that? Or try to pin it on the upbringing.

* * *

In another home, the parents devoted nearly half their married lives to helping addicts of all types. They had wealth and built a half-way home for young people on the way back.

While they were doing this, one son became an alcoholic and the other became a pill addict. The alcoholic told me, "I did it for attention." I told him he was a damn fool; that his parents weren't ignoring him—only trying to help the less fortunate.

In the end, he didn't drink because of his parents, he admitted. It was actually for "new thrills." He had everything money could buy but the excitement of the liquor highs, the unpredictability of his actions when he was drinking made life more exciting.

"I drank a jug on a plateau of Mount Everest when the sun was sinking—what a sensation," he explained. That sensation had nothing to do with his parents who were working in public service and spending hours with young people in need of help.

* * *

The ruse that parents cause alcoholism is greatly abused. Take the insurance executive who in therapy claimed he drank because he hated his father. It turned out that the only grievance he carried against his father

216

was that, as a six-year-old on the farm, he had been sent away to an aunt to board during the winter so that he might attend a better school.

His loving father felt the little schoolhouse near the farm did not offer enough of a challenge or the kind of background his son needed to pursue higher learning. When he finally got his hate out in the open and analyzed why he blamed his father for his drinking, it sounded so outlandish the man was apologetic. He dropped to his knees in my office and cried. The truth was his system needed alcohol; he sought the change in personality—the feel of the high. He was not at ease in his insurance business until he had a "good high."

Parents in general do what they think is best. There is no foolproof book or theory for raising children, who themselves are as varied as the sizes of leaves in a forest. Remember, children become alcoholics in spite of their parents—not because of them. The only requisite for membership is to drink and get the feeling of complete self-acceptance and fulfillment that all of us seek. Unfortunately, the feeling is only momentary. And the price we pay is devastating.

"Childhood has no forebodings; but then it is soothed by no memories of outlived sorrow."
George Eliot

VIEWPOINT

I feel that each and every one of us alive today is a model, an idol, or an example that someone looks up to. Yes, an inspiration. Many times I think that I have failed as a parent. I have to ask myself: are you playing it straight with them, are you involved with them, and when is the last time you told them "I love you"? Here is a poem by an unknown author.

217

TO ANY LITTLE BOY'S FATHER

THERE ARE LITTLE EYES UPON YOU AND THEY
ARE WATCHING NIGHT AND DAY;
THERE ARE LITTLE EARS THAT QUICKLY
TAKE IN EVERYTHING YOU SAY.

THERE ARE LITTLE HANDS ALL EAGER TO DO
EVERYTHING YOU DO;
AND A LITTLE BOY WHO IS DREAMING OF THE
DAY HE'LL BE LIKE YOU

THERE IS A WIDE-EYED LITTLE FELLOW WHO
BELIEVES YOU ARE ALWAYS RIGHT;
AND HIS EYES ARE ALWAYS OPEN AND HE
WATCHES DAY AND NIGHT

YOU ARE SETTING AN EXAMPLE IN EACH
KINDNESS THAT YOU DO;
FOR THE LITTLE BOY WHO IS WAITING TO
GROW UP TO BE LIKE YOU.

Call it sentimentality, but to cope with alcoholics and learn to love them over the years for their very faults takes some sentimentalism. I see parents broken-hearted because they believe they have fostered lost, alcoholic children. I see children blaming parents for no reason. I see parents completely oblivious to the disease as they offer alcohol to children in their home. I see children lie to parents so that they might succumb to peer pressure. I see parents blame other children for their own children's problems.

What I'm getting at is that whether the child is twelve years old or twenty-two years old, alcoholism is a disease to be fought by every member of the family, regardless of which member is directly afflicted.

And here is the irony of it all: the tears and trials and sleepless nights of the parents and the indiscretions and suffering of the children eventually can be blended in treatment, analyzed, wiped out and new life started which not only enhances the diseased, but makes the entire family more emotionally mature.

I had a father tell me, "I had guilt about my son's drinking and alcoholic behavior for years. During treatment I finally began to understand what made him tick. I learned about his doubts and tears and inner turmoil. I would never have known my son if I hadn't joined him in family treatment."

A mother told me, "My two daughters nearly broke my heart when they became drunks. In treatment everything came out. They did have resentments against my harsh discipline. They blamed me for insulting their dates and criticizing their friends. In the end, I felt I had to remake myself, too. I had as many hangups as my daughters."

I see this every day: parents blaming themselves because somewhere in one of their children is a sensitivity to alcohol over which they had absolutely no control. And for every recovering alcoholic generally I can count two reborn parents. They learn about their own weaknesses and their own images through the eyes of the alcoholic and others. I have seen alcoholics literally save families which were coming apart at the seams and were not even aware of the problems in their own households.

That is why I will continue to pressure parents who refuse to join their children in treatment—and my experience proves that about one in four families are either too busy or not close enough to the alcoholic or too embarrassed to join the afflicted in treatment. That is a figure which must be eradicated by knowledge of the disease and the ability of society to recognize it not as a black mark against parenthood—but simply as a disease to be fought in a candid, open fashion.

QUESTION:
HOW DO CHILDREN REACT TO RECOVERING ALCOHOLICS?

SELVIG:

Beautifully. The experience can be so rewarding it is almost like watching a miracle before your eyes. Nobody suffers as much at the hands of an alcoholic as children.

Imagine, from the time they are toddlers they emulate the parents—patterning themselves after the way dad talks or mother walks. Suddenly one or the other of the parents, or both, refuse to return that child's adoration and love. The parent snaps at the child for no reason, or becomes silly at a party, embarrassing the youngster. As the child grows older he not only becomes disappointed and hurt—but begins to spawn a deadly resentment; one which could be harbored all his life. He is ashamed to bring other children to the home for fear his alcoholic parent will make a scene.

He is frightened of physical abuse. He knows he will be rejected if it is at a time when the alcoholic is drinking. And even greater, as he grows older, he cannot count on that parent. A child lives by the dependability of his parents.

He is continually disappointed. If he can't depend on the parent, who can be depended on? Children of alcoholics tend to distrust most adults—teachers, coaches, employers, the clergy. Thus it may take the recovering alcoholic a year or two years to generate the feeling of trust, and it comes in a direct ratio to the dependability an alcoholic shows during his recovery.

Actually, the recovering alcoholic tends to be not only dependable but almost exacting in his efforts to make appointments, as if he were trying to make up for all the lost dates and time that are in his wake.

Once the child knows the alcoholic parent will be there, will listen, will share and understand, the relationship is gratifying. In fact, I have found that the parent-child relationship between recovering alcoholics and their children may be superior to others—for, to recover, the alcoholic has had to learn to share, to describe his feelings, to talk honestly of his family trials. How many non-alcoholics can make that claim in their relationship with their children? Oh, there are a few exceptional cases where the drunken adult will have bribed the child's affection with money or tickets. "My daddy was more fun when he was drinking," a little eight-year-old told me. "He always gave me things." But this appealing aspect of the disease is virtually nonexistent in teenagers, who want a solidity and consistency from their parents.

The greatest attribute the recovering alcoholic has going for him is his ability to now share his feelings and to discuss life with his offspring. He has hit rock bottom. His experiences are invaluable to the child. And since no alcoholic can be completely recovered until he can talk readily of his disease and share easily, the children get an added plus in easy communication with their parents.

Yes, the long, tortuous road to recovery brings a bonus of sharing and getting along with children which many healthy households do not have.

There is little room for resentment since a child's natural outlook is enthusiastic. He tends to forget the troubled past and lives for today—just as the recovering alcoholic must. Children and recovering alcoholics share a great deal in common: mainly the vigorous attack each day, using the past and building a backlog of healthy experience for the future. The recovering alcoholic has proven his resiliency—the same kind with which God endows every little boy and girl.

Examples:

It wasn't until a counseling confrontation in a treatment center that Judy and her dad leveled with each other. She was 17 years old at the time. With hurt in her eyes, her voice breaking, she described to him the accusations he had made to her during his drinking bouts, the times he had called her a "whore" and "no good, God-damn tramp," when she had been out a few minutes late.

Her father could hardly believe his ears—although he did not deny it. Another son said his dad "punched me around alot—and hit me on the head" during his drinking bouts. Then one said he grew to hate his dad.

Both fathers, during their recovery process, made a point to explain that they were out of their minds with alcoholic insanity and did not know what they were doing. Later, both parents told me they had made great strides in rapport with their children—and they actually now felt closer to them than at any time in their lives.

* * *

A teen-age daughter who told me at one time, "I want to kill my dad for slapping my mother around," became so proud of him that she wrote a theme in high school on "My Dad—the Alcoholic" which brought her an A and which was discussed in two class sessions.

When her other classmates found out her father was a recovering alcoholic, several of them came to her, telling about their own alcoholic parents and asking advice.

On two occasions, she brought home classmates and she and her father sat with them and tried to help them with their plight. "My dad's a big man around the gang," the daughter told me. "He can talk about things most of the other parents can't or won't. He can understand my friends who are having dope and alcohol problems. They trust him because he's one of them. He knows about troubles because he's been through so many."

* * *

Another sample is the seven-year-old twins who were

222

having sleeping problems and had to be on sedation while family quarrels over alcoholism prevailed. Once the mother began to recover, the youngsters became bright and happy—and almost miraculously, their grades improved in all subjects.

No matter how small the child, he senses something is wrong when one or both parents are tormented by alcohol. Sometimes he will blame himself. Even the family dog will sense something strange in the atmosphere when there is an alcoholic in the house. But children can be ruined by the sense of insecurity at a time when they need it most.

There are very few incidents I can recall when the recovering alcoholic didn't make giant strides in his relationship with his children. Sometimes it can happen almost immediately. Other times the children hold back, wanting him to prove himself. That can be a time of anxiety and sometimes resentment for the alcoholic who wants instant acceptance. But I tell him, "It took you 15 years to get in this spot—you can't retrieve it in 15 days."

Most recovering alcoholics know that the misery they have wreaked on their family will not be obliterated by their vow not to drink. Generally, a family needs that year, sometimes two or three years, to really tune in once again—to rid itself of guilt waves and to count on the alcoholic again. A recovering alcoholic needs to prove himself. Trust is earned and not inherited. But you can't blame children who have been frustrated for years for not adjusting overnight.

* * *

One of the toughest cases surrounded a 20-year-old daughter who vowed never to marry because "you can't trust men—my dad taught me that."

It was even more difficult when the father, upon attaining sobriety, divorced the mother. The daughter left home, devoting her time to cars and dog shows while never forming a close friendship with a member of the opposite sex.

One day I told Mike, "I know you're afraid to contact

her in person. Well, don't call her, but do write her. You might be surprised.''

"She'll ignore me," he said sadly. I convinced him to try—he was risking only a 15-cent stamp.

Two weeks later I saw Mike and he could hardly wait to tell me the news: "I wrote Trish and in three days I had back a beautiful letter. We met for lunch. It was a little stiff at first but in the end we embraced and she told me, 'Dad, I learned to love you again today.' " It had been six or seven years since they had really talked. A year after that meeting, Trish was dating boys.

* * *

Children have a tendency to blame themselves for family problems such as divorce. But alcoholism can damage the child, also, mainly because he doesn't understand its vagaries and mysteries. All he knows is that something's wrong with dad—or mom. He isn't sure what. He thinks they may be angry with him. And when they disappoint him, he loses self-worth.

A little boy of eight years told me, "I guess daddy hates me. That's why he drinks."

You can understand, then, that when suddenly the problem drinker is clean and he wants to pick up as if nothing had happened, he must be patient. And the children must be told that they should give dad a little time to get used to his own sobriety. That mutual respect will start many times in family treatment.

But in the end, I can recall few families that didn't draw closer together. Most of the time the families of alcoholics eventually turn out to be a closely-knit team. Dad, because he's been at the bottom of the barrel and seen hell, can understand tribulations in the children. He can talk openly about festering emotional wounds and bad habits. He becomes more than a father—he becomes an experienced sharer with those he loves. Over the years, the children will grow to respect him even more for showing the courage to whip a terrible illness.

* * *

A co-ed daughter of a recovering alcoholic told me, "I love my dad even more because he proved he could fight and conquer a terrible disease. I see so many parents of my friends who won't admit it or won't try to help themselves. The child of an alcoholic can grow up terribly warped."

* * *

And the mayor of a town in North Dakota told me, "I owe everything I have to my father—an alcoholic. When he recovered, he could guide me better than the parents who never experienced the trauma and troubles he did. I could not argue with his experience. And he was never afraid to tackle any problem. Nothing could be worse than what he went through."

Once the child knows the alcoholic parent will be there, will listen, will share and understand, the relationship is gratifying. In fact, I have found that the parent-child relationship between recovering alcoholics and their children may be superior to others—for, to recover, the alcoholic has had to learn to share, to describe his feelings, to talk honestly of his family trials.

QUESTION:
HOW CAN A YOUNG WOMAN TELL IF HER BOYFRIEND HAS ALCOHOLIC TENDENCIES?

SELVIG:

Very simply, although she may not want to believe her discovery. If he calls on her and says, "Sorry I'm late—just stopped for a quickie at the club," or if he suggests while leaving for a social gathering, "It's still a little early. Let's stop for a drink along the way;" or if he says about a restaurant: "It's nice, but the drinks are terrible. Weaker than bus-stop tea."

Then the young lady had better cast a wary eye. In the first place, if her boyfriend needs a picker-upper before coming to her home, he is saying in reality, "I need a little courage to date this girl," or "This won't make me so shy—it'll loosen my tongue." If he says these things to himself, he very well could be on the road to alcoholism—because he is trying to change his true identity, hide his true personality.

When a boy sincerely cares for a girl, he wants her to know his true self. He doesn't want to mask his shyness or his ineptitudes or his lack of dance rhythm of his little awkward habits. He wants her to get to know him as he is normally. And when a date has already analyzed the strength of drinks served in various eating spots, it tells something, too. Ordinarily, a social drinker could care less if the drink is potent or not. He'd prefer not to have a loaded drink. It will make him uncomfortable.

The alcoholic seeks out bars and bartenders who load the drink with "bombs." He needs and craves alcoholic potency. And if a date has to have that extra drink before the party, he is saying, "I need to be hyped—I want that high before we get there so I'll feel better than the rest of the people."

That's alcoholic thinking. Any girl who sees these traits in a date should beware—or at least expect problems if she continues to see the young man.

The beauty of young love is getting to know the other person. Sharing. It is impossible for a girl to share with a young man who is not himself after a few drinks. There is nothing wrong with enjoying a couple drinks themselves during the course of the evening to stimulate conversation, take the edge off of shyness, and foster discovery in one another by removing a few natural inhibitions.

But the girl must beware of the young man who drinks enough to drastically change his personality.

The boy who feels he must drink before he picks up his date, or have strong drinks during the date, or insists that he is more interesting only after several drinks, is looking for that euphoria. He is not a good risk. The more girls discover this while dating, the more stable marriages.

I've had so many wives tell me, "Oh, how I wish I had seen the telltale signs when we went together. I remember now, how Frank used to like to stop on the way to a party to make sure he'd feel 'really good' when we got there. Or how he'd explain, 'I can't stand Mary's parties. She serves lousy drinks.'" Just being with the girl of his choice should be enough of a "good feeling" for the normal male. Beyond that he is searching for a synthetic glow, the consistent search of which can trigger alcoholism.

There is something in the boy's personality a girl must study carefully. So many young women have told me that they fell for the boy with the glib tongue, imagination and sparkle in his demeanor—only to find out it was the alcohol which supplied that radiance. The best answer is to make sure that a good deal of the charm the boy exudes isn't coming from a bottle. Invite him to a sports event or a social gathering where no alcohol is served to truly study his behavior. If you can enjoy each other's company for hours without alcohol, you can take a sound inventory of the young man.

Examples:

A college junior named Julia fell deeply in love with Larry, a pharmacy major. She enjoyed what she described as his "bubbly" personality. In other words, as Julia said, "He radiated charm from the minute he'd pick me up. Compared to the rest of my boyfriends, he had so much more spark and was so much more fun. I knew he drank a little liquor but he never seemed to be out of line.

"Then, one day I was at his folks' house for Sunday dinner. There was no alcohol. It didn't seem like the same Larry. He was so edgy and uptight and said very little. I thought he was just a little tense with me meeting his parents, you know. But it turned out that wasn't it. He needed to drink to get in a fun mood."

She found that out when his fraternity friend told her, "If you two ever settle down, I hope you like to drink a lot. Larry can't get going until he has a belt."

The shocking news so dismayed Julia that she made further investigations and found out that Larry kept a bottle in his desk in his fraternity room. She found out he'd been arrested twice for driving while intoxicated. Brokenhearted, she resolved never again to date a boy who seemed too effusive, too volatile.

* * *

Pretty Pam is a stewardess who picked up an old friendship with the boy down the block. They thoroughly enjoyed so many of the same things together. She thought nothing of it when Jerry spiked his coffee at a chilly football game. The wind was cold. She paid little attention when he spiked his non-alcoholic punch at a friend's wedding. Lots of the young people were doing it, and Pam actually saw nothing wrong when Jerry carried a flask to the barbecues down at the beach. A lot of them were doing it.

But she was a little shocked to see him "chuggalug" every last drop right from the flask as the evening wore on. When he said, "God, Pam, this sauce makes everything seem so great," she should have been warned.

Still she continued to see him, became engaged and it wasn't until a shower, just six days before the wedding, that she came to realize how dependent Jerry was on the bottle.

He collapsed in a drunken stupor on the doorstep of the house at which he was picking her up after the shower. Embarrassed in front of her friends, she sought counsel from her minister. He advised her to put off the wedding, although all arrangements had been made.

The shock of the wedding postponement sent Jerry off on a four-day drunk and verified her fears. His mother finally told her that Jerry had a liquor problem for five years. He wound up getting treatment but Julia married another man—a sober one.

* * *

The story told by Mike is typical of an alcoholic dating a girl. Listen:

"I would get through work about 7 p.m. at the post office. If I had a date with Roxanne at 9 o'clock, I'd always stop and fortify myself with three or four belts. I loved the girl. We got along great. But I just felt more confidence when I walked up to the door with a little glow on. I felt more comfortable with her.

"I knew I was wrong. I knew if we got married, I couldn't keep up the charade—of being a very positive guy when I was not drinking. I wasn't. I felt that I had to have the drink to be positive. She thought I was a strong-willed leader. In reality, I was usually on the uprise of a liquor high.

"Eventually, I took myself out of her life before I could do any damage. My alcoholic mind didn't ruin all judgment."

Think of what might have happened in a marriage where the one partner comes in needing to feel 'loaded.'

QUESTION:
SHOULD A RECOVERING ALCOHOLIC CONFESS INDISCRETIONS TO HIS MATE?

SELVIG:

The most difficult problem in rehabilitation to many alcoholics is confessing to their wives that they were unfaithful during their drinking escapades. One told me, "I can do anything but that."

Yet, we know that to make amends means to put our past on the table and examine it. That is one of the most rewarding steps in recovery. But many alcoholics will say, "God, my wife can put up with anything but infidelity. If I tell her, I lose her."

I have studied many cases like this. It is a difficult decision—but I would advise the alcoholic to make a clean breast of it; to tell the wife about his indiscretions. If you cannot be completely honest in confessing adultery, you really never had a valued, pliable relationship. The recovering alcoholic will always feel he's hiding something. He will always have that inferior feeling in the presence of his wife.

It is not an easy choice. But the alcoholic must remember that the damage isn't done when he's confessing to his wife; the damage was done when he chased the other woman. Also, the exposed lover is less likely to be tempted to do it again once the painful issue has been brought out.

The wife, if she is reasonable, will try to believe her husband was insane with liquor when he was unfaithful. It is never an easy time. Many marriages have cooled for months, sometimes years, after the confession. If it's any relief to the hurt wife, the alcoholic feels worse about it than she does.

But sobriety is based on making amends, being honest and sharing. If you can't share your indiscretion, even if it makes your loved one miserable for a time, you are being unfaithful again—this time to yourself.

It has been said that love grows and lust wastes. The injured partner must understand that alcoholics in their insanity have killed, maimed, broken the law and harassed the public. If the wife or husband doesn't understand that the lust was a mating of insane frenzies rather than true love, the spouse does not really understand the disease.

It can be an emotionally disturbing decision. But no recovering alcholic can live with pent-up guilt anymore than he can live contentedly knowing he has cheated a business acquaintance. To ignore a guilt with someone you live, can destroy the very foundation on which recovery is based—sharing. The name of the other person is not important. Many tricky alcoholics will name the other party and then sit back and relax while the mate directs her anger at the other woman. This is one of the greatest examples of manipulation to emanate from the alcoholic.

Examples:

Dashing Nels would make amends about anything —but never confess his unfaithfulness over a two-month span in his drinking days. His wife, Catherine, suspected but never pushed him. Nels had a terribly difficult time with recovery. It wasn't until his third trip to the treatment center that he told me, "It's killing me. I can't confess to Catherine—and I can't live with myself if I don't."

I told Catherine he had a difficult time, that there was something he wanted to tell her but his pride wouldn't let him. She astounded me by saying, "I suppose it's about that woman. I've known for years. I would have brought it up if I thought it would help Nels."

I think most wives feel that way, too, understanding

that a man becomes a different breed under the influence of alcohol. When Nels found out her feelings, they discussed his indiscretion. Afterwards, he was a new man and well on his way to recovery.

* * *

In the case of Laura, it didn't turn out that way. While recovering, she diplomatically brought up an affair she had with a taxi driver in a night of despair. It was a lonesome, weakened woman, out of her mind with the tortures of alcohol who succumbed to the brief romance.

She tried to explain it to her husband. He screamed in anguish and eventually walked out on her. Family counseling almost provided the answer—but the husband was so difficult to reach and with so little understanding, Laura gave up.

I thought her philosophy was excellent: "I'm fighting for my life. At this time I'm in no position to fight for a husband, too. Some day it may work out. But right now I take that one day at a time.

"Of course, it's a blow when a husband brands you for an indiscretion you didn't even have to tell him about. But I'm comfortable with myself. That's the important thing right now. My sobriety depended upon my naked honesty with him."

* * *

I thought Jennifer's heart would break when her husband confessed about not one but two women he had affairs with during his alcoholic haze.

"How could he do this to me?" she cried. "The one thing I thought we had was loyalty."

I pointed out something to her: "The man was sick. Sick mentally. Under those circumstances people have committed robberies, murders, beaten children. You can't believe it was something your husband, under sober circumstances, would have done. If you can, or can't handle it, it's your decision."

She understood. But it didn't come easily. It was painfully slow. One day, a year later, she said, "Thanks, Dick, for the talk. I was ready to walk out. Now it's all out in the open. And I've got the finest man in the world."

It takes a large heart in a good spouse to try to overlook transgressions. But all of us are guilty of hurting someone else some time in some way. To err is human. To forgive is divine. The alcoholic makes more, due to his illness which brings out the worst in him. However, he is responsible for his behavior.

Sometimes it will take a third party. In fact, it seems that this is the most comfortable way. The act of unfaithfulness is so difficult to talk about. Yet, it is the very sharing of the intimate aspects which makes recovery a worthwhile venture. If you can't tell your loved ones everything, if you have to hide the most minute secret, it can come back to haunt the recovering drinker and cause his loss of sobriety.

There are those who hold secrets, refuse confessions and survive. But theirs is not a happy sobriety nor a happy relationship with their family because it lacks integrity.

It is not an easy choice. But the alcoholic must remember that the damage isn't done when he's confessing to his wife; the damage was done when he chased the other woman.

VIEWPOINT

It is impossible to say that becoming sick early from drinking means you will never be an alcoholic. For myself, I became violently ill from cigars when I was a little tyke and knew I would never smoke them again. But I want to share something.

I started smoking cigarettes with a passion when I started drinking alcohol the summer of 1939 and continued to use them with little judgment but to excess until the summer of 1964. I knew that the best way to quit cigarettes was to smoke a pipe. For I hated pipes. Although I almost burned up trying to learn to smoke the pipe, I got to enjoy it. So, then, as a last resort, I decided I would smoke cigars since I hated them, but again the same thing occurred: I began to enjoy the cigars.

Tapering off was as successful here as it was with the liquor—to no avail. I was an addictive smoker. I warn youngsters: Don't challenge the bottle. It is so cunningly destructive, not even the strongest will power can manipulate against it—if once the sensitivity to that "warm glow" feeling is roused. I have seen strong men challenge the bottle. You know the kind.

"I'll drink any softie here under the table and still outrun all you guys to the flagpole in the morning." That kind of talk crumbles in face of the alcohol's potency; the many-pronged assault the intoxicant can make. Too often youths who say they just want to show they can whip the bottle, wind up sickening testimony to the fact that nobody alive can whip alcohol on a head-to-head basis. It will level the weight-lifter and the stevedore with the same lethal effect it has on the 125-pound librarian.

Augustine said that "the confession of evil works is but the beginning of good works."

That is why I so firmly want to recommend the sharing among spouses over past indiscretions attributable to alcoholism. Lord, we make ten thousand mistakes or more in our lifetime. Adultery by a drunk should not be considered any more heinous than a decade of insults, lies, or erratic behavior, but it is for the mate as it's a very personal thing. Really, is it not the singular debased action which requires as much strength to confess as the maze of faults created by an alcoholic's utter selfishness and inability to see the hurt he is causing.

We must have to live with the fact, too, that the alcohol's influence on optic nerves has resulted in many wrong marriages, and after the married pair look clearly at each other through sober eyes, they may find they were incompatible. This is a difficult decision, but the bright light in a dark situation is that at least a life has been saved.

QUESTION:
DOES AN ALCOHOLIC'S FAMILY NEED HELP?

SELVIG:

Yes, without any question. Let's put it this way: All the character defects of the alcoholic rub off on his family. His loneliness separates the usual family rapport. His secretiveness alienates family members. His shame will not permit him to share with his loved ones. The bottle has been his constant companion for years. Faced with the shame and insecurity and lack of trust of the alcoholic, his family many times goes into a shell—almost in self-defense. The family, once it is rebuffed by the alcoholic, has a strong impulse to divert its life elsewhere.

So often the family feels responsible for the alcoholic's drinking. He has used them so often and blamed them so readily that many times upon self-examination, the family may even begin to agree with the alcoholic. Now the family faces two grim situations: its own blame and the repudiation of its love by the alcoholic. The family suffers a deep hurt and many times a guilt as deep as the alcoholic's.

The loneliness that makes the alcoholic so confused and lost envelops the family. The family will ordinarily strive and sacrifice to repair the breach. But after many years, the efforts by the family have failed so often that the breach widens into an insurmountable chasm.

What really happens is that the alcoholic is not only imprisoned with his own disease but the family is imprisoned in its own particular type of cell block. It is thoroughly ashamed of the alcoholic member and many times retreats from society and outside help. It prefers to bury the tragedy or dilemma rather than face it openly. Only one out of ten families will ever open up the can of worms. Society has put such a stigma on alcoholism that families fear for their reputation and that of coming generations.

Families try to maintain the love for the alcoholic but many times their trust is so misplaced that they doubt their own worth. They doubt their ability to help and this impedes their freedom to function.

In other words, the disease usually spreads like wildfire through the family and even the most understanding mother or father begins to blame oneself for spawning such a disease and even to question one's own sanity. Wives become as mentally upset and distraught as the alcoholic's behavior is insane. Brothers and sisters fear their own worth and doubt their own motives. The disease also causes the family members to become dishonest. They begin to lie and make excuses for the alcoholic. They use a network of cover-ups and only, ironically, when once-healthy family members become ill or emotionally beaten, does the truth too infrequently come out. The alcoholic many times is not exposed and his disease not treated until he has jeopardized the health and welfare of many other members of the family.

The alcoholic is sick from a terminal disease caused by a drug. The alcoholic's family is riddled by pain and broken hearts and anguish, and many times thoroughly shattered. I have seen one alcoholic virtually destroy a warm, closely-knit family of nine members.

Now back to the basic question of help. Certainly a recovering alcoholic's family needs time to adjust as the patient. But I have never felt it was as difficult for a family normally to regroup as it was for an alcoholic to recover. As I have pointed out before, the joy and relief of having the lost sheep back in the fold, can more quickly obliterate the years of mental suffering than could be expected. It is truly a miracle of the program.

But the family will have many adjustments that first year or two of recovery. I urge the entire family of the alcoholic to work in unison with the rehabilitation counselor. The maintenance program is so important. This is a great time for the spouse to join Al-Anon and experience the joy and tremors of family rehabilitation with others in the same situation.

It will take time. The family must learn to trust again. The family must learn to work and live and love together again. The trust takes time—so does the loving. This is where the time element is so important. The new union takes weeks, months—sometimes years.

To be honest, there are times when love and trust cannot be rebuilt. The family may have been too shaken by the disease. There are times when a family discovers that it cannot again function normally even with the return to sobriety by the diseased person. It is better for these people to dissolve their relationship before they destroy one another.

Examples:

Laura was a lovely 52-year-old matron who suffered through a husband's indiscretions for over a dozen years. It was liquor, late hours, women, and financial problems. When husband Tom finally recovered, she had so divested herself of trust for him she told me, "I really don't care now if he comes home. I'm happy for him, but I don't think I can ever again feel that close. I'll always look into his eyes and see reflections of other women."

All I told her was, "Give it some time. You've spent many years keeping the home together." I told Tom, "Don't expect trust overnight. Treat her like you were wooing her again. Try a new romance. Don't push. See what happens."

In six months she told me, "Things are a little better. He's really a different person. He's kind of like the boy I dated 30 years ago. He's considerate and gentle. It's like being courted over again."

Tom said, "I have times fighting myself against rushing her off her feet. I'm impatient. I want to tell her, 'Dammit, I've suffered, too.' But I contain myself. I just try to be patient."

He found out that patience was the key reaction. By not being overly aggressive or demanding too much, he enabled Laura to gradually regain her trust. She finally told me 18 months later, "We've made it. And be sure, Dick, to tell other wives and husbands not to rush it. Trust comes from acts of love. And acts of love don't come overnight."

* * *

Gennie was a bright young 19-year-old and Sara was her younger sister. Gennie was so happy to have her mother back in the recovering fold, she could hardly wait to excuse her for past indiscretions, lies, and vile family squabbles. But Sara needed more time. She had grave encounters with her mother which shook the walls. She told me three months after her mother returned home from the rehabilitation center, "I don't give a damn if that woman ever gets healthy. I hate her. She ruined five years of my life and embarrassed me among my friends. She's an animal. I'll always hate her!"

Sara moved out and lives with six working girls in an apartment. Her mother takes her to lunch once a month. Sara told me recently, "I guess mother had her own reasons and her own problems. I'm just beginning to learn what she's really like. I still don't feel completely at ease. But it may come. I pray it does."

Prayer and faith. Bringing the "superior power" into the healing process is so important.

* * *

Take, however, the case of Neal, the affluent insurance executive. His wife was an alcoholic for a decade. He raised three daughters. The wife returned home, hopeful that her recovery would trigger an instant affirmative response from Neal. Just the opposite happened. Neal told me he found his wife's temperament and personality incompatible with his. He felt even more tensions arising when she began recovering. This might seem strange, but this is how he explained it:

"For over a decade, I remained blind to the fact we

were corroding our marriage with a violent clash of personalities, ambitions, and desires. I blamed it all on drink and when I nursed her I would always say that things will get better if she ever stops drinking. And now, sober, we can talk it out rationally. We're just two different kinds of people headed in two different directions. As we've grown up, we've grown apart."

That is sad. They have divorced but still see each other occasionally. The little girls, no longer torn by dissent and bitter battles in the home, are growing up with an awareness and maturity that is beautiful to see. One of them told me, "The time we spend with Daddy is great. And so is the time we spend with Mommie. We can see they are two different kinds of people. We love them both. We know they both love us. We still have great parents even though they are living apart."

* * *

There is the case of a large family where the father earned the love and respect of his wife and two children again. But three other children are still cold and aloof. One girl has vowed never to marry because, "I don't want to wind up with a problem like mother's." But the father tells me he'll keep trying to win back the estranged children's faith.

"I don't blame them. Maybe in time we'll all grow enough to share our feelings. Right now that's impossible, it seems. But I have faith. I'll keep trying to get their love back some way, some day."

**Certainly a recovering
alcoholic's family needs time
to adjust as the patient. But I
have never felt it was as
difficult for a family normally to
regroup as it was for an
alcoholic to recover.**

239

VIEWPOINT

I firmly believe too many people talk too much about the publicized generation gap—the inability of youth and adults to communicate. Frankly, I believe it is vastly over-exaggerated. If there is a gap, it's the adults' fault. I have yet to find a youngster who, when interested in a subject, was not thoroughly pleased to be included in adult's conversation. We older folks once were young and the young have never been older. We create the generation gap. Let's not forget what we were like when we were young.

The trouble with most adults is we talk down to the youth. We don't ask enough questions of what's going on in their world. We presume we know. I tell parents that's ridiculous. The changing times have swept by most parents. They have no idea of the tempo, resourcefulness, intelligence and resilience of today's well-traveled youth group as compared to our days of youth.

True, we have a greater edge on experience. But they have experience, too, in a youthful society of which we are usually vastly unaware until a family problem such as a young addict erupts in our midst. Then we scurry to the counselor and ask: "Why our children?" And halfway through the counselor's explanation of why the youngsters might become involved, suddenly it dawns on the parents that they haven't had any idea of what was going on in their children's society.

To me, the ideal half-way or recovery group for alcoholics would be made up of one-third youngsters 20 years or younger, another third from 20 years of age to 45 years, and the other third over 45, including a few senior citizens.

The young ones will learn some valuable facts about life, which only the experienced 50-year-old can deliver. But he must just state them. Never preach. Or threaten.

For instance, I heard a 50-year-old car salesman capture the imagination of a 15-year-old boy in treatment, explaining the various facets of trades and styles of cars which sold best and why. The boy, in turn, enraptured the older man, explaining to him what young people liked and looked for in automobiles. They spent many enjoyable hours exchanging information; the older man never talking down—but seeking out the youth's opinions which were considerable and noteworthy.

At the same time, the mid-aged group can extend immediacy to life's problems and tribulations. The young people see the problems alcohol can cause with marriage, how it affects families and friends and business acquaintances.

All the time the young group, because of its vitality and enthusiasm and ability to bounce back, can give the older patients a new concept of determination and willingness to fight. I've seen more young people inspire older ones·than veterans inspire the young.

Never have qualms as to whether a young person can accept his alcoholism. Chances are he will gain your admiration with his ability to straighten up and face society in the eye with a big smile and bounce to his step.

Today, the young alcoholic finds a rewarding experience in Alcoholics Anonymous. This is reflected in the fact that the membership of members under the age of 30 has doubled in the last three years. Young alcoholics tell me they find a serenity of mind and an enjoyment of sharing which they cannot find anywhere else.

PART IV

THE
RECOVERING
ALCOHOLIC

QUESTION:
CAN AN ALCOHOLIC DRY OUT FOR A PERIOD AND RESUME SOCIAL DRINKING?

SELVIG:

Absolutely not. Remember I told you earlier this is a terminal illness. A fatal one. An alcoholic can stay sober from six months to six years but when he resumes, the disease attacks with a vengeance more awesomely destructive than before.

It's much more emotional than physical. The alcoholic who resumes drinking is smashing his most prized possession—his sobriety; his freedom to function; his ability to maintain a sane mind. Nothing is that important. When he goes back to drinking, his conscience grips him with such pangs of remorse that his ability to tolerate even a small amount of alcohol is broken.

He's frightened because he again is isolating himself —the most depressing state known to man. When he drinks he destroys his faith. The emotional repercussions of losing faith in himself, losing his cherished freedom to function, losing the confidence of all his loved ones and friends, is so unbearable the alcoholic who restarts drinking (even after a 10-year dry period) will be miserable within hours.

His dissipation will be much more frightening and quicker than before. There are theories that physically, with the passing of time, the aloholic's resistance diminishes in direct relation to his age. I believe it is all psychological—all emotional. He may be as strong physically as a blacksmith or Russian weight-lifter, but the knowledge that he is now destroying himself, after having regained his self-respect, is as certain death as putting a gun to his head.

The alcoholic who tries to drink again mentally kills himself, another victim of the disease. The old adage is time-worn but so true: for an alcoholic, one drink is too many—and a thousand not enough.

One of the most startling stories along these lines took place in a large Midwestern treatment center where the head of the institution for 12 years, and an arrested alcoholic for 23 years, went off the wagon during a Christmas Eve party. He confided to me later: "I couldn't believe a man like myself who had preached and worked in alcoholic treatment for all these years could believe he could handle a drink. But I did. I challenged it. One glass of wine at a festive occasion? What's wrong with that? It would be one and only one. God! Four days later I wound up in my car in a snowbank 50 miles from my home."

His quickie spree cost him his position, naturally. He's starting back at the bottom of the ladder. His learning experience: "The power of the drink is still overwhelming for me. No alcoholic can afford the luxury or the thrill of one sip. Until the alcoholic learns that, he has learned nothing."

Examples:

A car salesman friend named Chuck refrains from alcohol for periods of five and six months. Each time he comes back to the bottle, he says confidently, "This time I'll have only two a day." And then quickly adds, "I'm in top shape. Work out at the Y every week, swim two miles a week. I'm able to handle the stuff now."

The true facts: The first time, after a prolonged period of sobriety, that Chuck tried his two-drink-per-day special formula, he crashed up his car to the tune of $800 in a golf course parking lot. That was the third day he was on his two-a-day plan. The next time, a year later, he tried again, and wound up with a bar-maid floozy in a motel room, where his wife's friend spotted his car. The witness reported his indiscretion to his wife, breaking up his home.

Next time around, a good 18 months later, he had two drinks and wound up in a bar fracas where a patron hit him over the head with a bottle, blinding one eye and giving him permanent dizziness.

In the space of three years, Chuck's well-thought-out course of conservative drinking after long periods of training and abstinence had cost him his marriage, career, and health. He finally admitted, "I don't know about others, but for me it gets worse each time out."

* * *

The trim little housewife was proud that she could quit drinking every three months for what she called "my conditioning period." But the fourth time around, the drinking became so troublesome, she severed a finger in the kitchen with a knife, hit the dog with a baseball bat, and threw her husband's favorite putter into the ash can. This prompted her family to request she enter a treatment center, which she did dutifully.

After six weeks of out-patient treatment, she quit drinking for three years, to the joy of her offspring and husband. Then, at a New Year's Eve party at her home, she said to her husband, "Honey, I've been a good little girl. Just one drink." He requested that she did not drink, but Helen insisted. Before the night was over, after just three drinks, she had fallen down the family room stairs with a tray of drinks, cutting her wrist for 22 stitches, and fracturing her knee cap.

"It hit me like a bolt of lightning," she explained. "I thought after all that time I could handle a couple of drinks—but everything just went out from under me." That inclued her pride in regaining family stature and her God-given free will.

* * *

Tony was a produce man, up early, delivering vegetables at 5 a.m. He loved the outdoors, the smell of his fresh produce and the chance to meet people. He knew he was an alcoholic. After counseling with family and a priest, he entered treatment for nearly three months. He couldn't believe that an alcoholic had to give up alcohol for life if he were to survive.

He, too, decided one little drink was not going to hurt. His wife, sensing more problems, asked him to leave the house. He promptly continued his drinking in a neighborhood bar, vowing, "to show them all old Tony can handle his drinks." Later that night he was virtually poured into his car. And shortly after midnight he was walking, for no apparent reason, on the highway when he was struck and killed by a passing truck.

Tony had learned the hard way the lesson so many alcoholics won't accept: you can never take up drinking once you have quit. Emotionally, the terrible inner vacuum alcoholic drinking creates for the diseased is so earth-shattering that only an alcoholic will ever experience it. You can only imagine the terrible loneliness a Tony or Chuck feels before they have begun to drink again. No elation or happiness. Only the crushing weight, knowing they have let everyone down—and mainly themselves.

* * *

I spent several hours questioning a patient of mine who had been dry for eight years and four months and then suddenly, in minutes, was turned into an uncontrollable drunk once more. He said: "It was terrible—like a nightmare I couldn't control. One day I was dry. The next thing I knew I was at a VFW club chatting with friends. I don't even remember the first drink. But in two hours I was sick, almost paralyzed. They had to take me home. I couldn't think straight until noon the next day."

What had this man quit doing or begun to do during his sobriety that might have led to a sudden, uncontrollable urge to take a drink? I found out among other things:

    1. He had discontinued praying to his God for strength.

2. He had quit reading his Alcoholics Anonymous literature.

3. He had quit going to AA meetings.

4. He had quit sharing his feelings with his wife.

5. He believed he was "cured" for good and needed no follow-up support program.

It goes back to the principle of the sober alcoholic: it can't be done alone. The man or woman who begins drinking again after a long period of sobriety is one who always quits sharing his arrested disease with others. It is so powerful, this disease, that unless all of sobriety's weapons are brought into play almost continually, the patient can become afflicted in a matter of months or even days. That is why so many AA members swear, "Show me a man or woman who misses two meetings in a row and I'll show you somebody heading for trouble."

The alcoholic who tries to drink
again mentally kills himself,
another victim of the disease. The old
adage is time worn but so true: for an
alcoholic, one drink is too many—
and a thousand not enough.

QUESTION:
CAN A RECOVERING ALCOHOLIC RETURN TO NORMAL ACTIVITIES?

SELVIG:

Absolutely. In fact, in approximately three fourths of the recovering cases in which I have come in contact in the last 20 years, the recovering alcoholic becomes more productive, improves his family life by many degrees, and is accepted back into the community with open arms.

In nearly half the cases I have seen, the alcoholic becomes an actual leader in community and work affairs. He is trusted more. The fact he has accepted his illness and, in many cases, has been completey open about it, endears him to his associates.

There is something about humanity that when one member shares his problem openly, others flock to him —many times for advice and counsel. He or she has become a person who's "been through it."

It is the only disease in the world where a person can become a better human being, more energetic, quicker-thinking, and can improve his personality traits by recovering—another miracle in the long line of miracles associated with alcoholism.

Unlike so many diseases which leave the body scarred and maimed and crippled, the joyous part of the alcoholic recovery is that the person invariably comes out feeling comfortable with himself, a complete person who can "live with himself." There are rare cases, true, where the long attrition of drink has dulled memories, done irreparable brain damage, and left hemmorrhages and burned-out tissue and only parts of stomachs in its wake. But if given early enough, alcoholism treatment shores up the body, improves the spirit, improves the attitude and sends the recovering alcoholic out into the world more sure of himself, certainly with a much clearer picture of where he is going and what he expects when he gets there. Rarely does the recovering alcoholic have an identity crisis.

Examples:

My friend Jim never earned more than $17,000 a year as a tire salesman in a major firm. He traveled and drank between calls and eventually his drinking went up and his calls went down. After recovery treatment he went back to his old job. He not only made 25 percent more calls, but initiated new sales campaigns and slogans.

His personality, once shaky and uptight, proved to be a gregarious, honest attribute. In two years, he was earning $25,000 a year and was next in line for a key regional position.

Jim told me: "Dick, I couldn't believe life was so different when I sobered up. I actually can't wait to get going in the morning. If I get a turndown, the 'no' that used to send me off on a drinking spree, I offer to take the guy to lunch. Half the time I wind up selling him after the initial turndown. People can't seem to get over the fact they can be liked even after they say 'no.' It's a whole different world."

* * *

Johnny was a young, handsome bartender who drank himself out of a dozen jobs in 10 years and eventually wound up stealing petty cash for his disease. When recovered, he was welcomed back to a club which hired nothing but recovering alcoholics. His ambition and casual friendliness and openness made him a good person for the job.

Within five years he was made the club manager. In seven years, the owner installed him in his own place. Johnny told me, "The greatest thing that ever happened to me was getting the disease. It made me a much better person. I don't recommend that as the answer to getting ahead," Johnny laughs, "but in my case it 'cleaned up' my mind. I got to see myself for what I really was. I learned about alcohol. Hell, I'd been a bartender for years and really knew nothing about booze—or alcoholics."

* * *

She was a private secretary for a major advertising firm in St. Louis. And Joyce hated to come back from the rehab hospital stay to take her old job. "What'll they think of me?" she asked.

I told her, "Go back with a smile, and tell the truth—be yourself. You'll be amazed what happens." She called a year later and was bubbling over the phone. "It's so won-

251

derful, you can't believe it. I've got a big raise. I'm entrusted with very vital work. I'm on the 'in' with the executive's family and three of them have asked me to help them with personal problems—much like mine. I'm so happy, I can hardly talk." Oh yes, Joyce. I can believe it.

Most times the recovering alcoholic finds that the people around him are amazed by the fact he has been open, admitted his weakness, and sought help. I doubt if there is a handful of people in the world impervious to help.

* * *

And Dick was a promoter who had wonderful dreams over his potent Stingers but couldn't put them together when the pieces needed fitting. He was a promoter who had six straight heavy losers when I first encountered him.

After recovery, he found his imagination still intact, but now his follow-up talents were also working. He staged two big rock concerts which were superb successes. He staged three sports events that were winners. After a dozen successes he called and could hardly contain himself.

Dick explains: "When I was boozing I thought I needed the Stingers to hatch ideas. I worked promotions out in my mind perfectly when I was drinking. When I sobered up, the ideas either didn't make sense or I couldn't put them together. I know a dozen promoters who are sharp and heady. If they'd quit drinking they could separate fact from fantasy. That's where a recovering alcoholic has an actual edge. He knows what it's like to emerge from a stupor. And he knows what it takes to make things actually happen. I'm thankful for the experience—although it's a helluva disease. And it rips you up to admit you need help."

Everywhere I look I see recovering alcoholics making huge successes of themselves. Some are not meant to be big winners in business. But invariably they find a fulfillment with their families and whatever menial jobs they have which gives them far greater contentment than the eternal search inside the bottle. Among my patients who became successes are three bank presidents, an advertising executive, and two professors who are now college presidents.

The real danger for a person who has a drinking problem is to quit a job without first giving it a whirl with sobriety and a program of recovery to aid him. Stan, an insurance agent, said he hated his job and was going to quit it. However, he decided to give it one more chance sober. Six months later he called and said he had been promoted to district manager of the company. Too often a recovering alcoholic fears going back to his place of employment. He need not. Usually he's treated with respect and succeeds where he failed before.

**It is the only disease in the
world where a person can
become a better human being . . . by
recovering.**

QUESTION:
DOESN'T A RECOVERING ALCOHOLIC
RUN INTO A SOCIAL STIGMA?

SELVIG:

Of course. That's human reaction. More than half the world is still uninformed or misinformed on alcoholism. Many millions still think the alcoholic is the bum in the gutter under the elevated or the pan-handler they meet in parking lots Sunday mornings after church.

A large segment feels alcoholism is a terrible stigma. Families hide it. It's the skeleton in the closet. It is so misunderstood in some cases—it has caused the deaths by heartbreak and the breakdowns of many parents and wives and husbands of alcoholics. On an average, six people will be vitally affected by an alcoholic. That means friends, families, employers, police. Nearly one-third of alcoholics' wives and husbands will refuse to discuss their spouse's disease!

Alcoholics Anonymous has probably been so successful because it provides the anonymity so many alcoholics and the sponsors seek. I find one out of four employers are suspicious or uninformed about alcoholics. Actually employers and wives and husbands and friends need courses in the illness almost as much as the alcoholic. I can walk in and guarantee any employer who is hiring a recovering alcoholic that he is getting a solid citizen, perhaps better than the next, as an employee. I have great faith in recovering alcoholics—and when I tell major firms that an alcoholic may be as good or better than the next man they hire, they sit up and take notice.

Alcoholism has been such a drain on business that companies today listen, search, and hope to conquer the disease. I also guarantee the recovering alcoholic that if he goes looking for a stigmatic attachment with a chip on his shoulder that he will find it.

But it is getting easier. The world is more willing to listen and talk about and try to comprehend the disease today far more than it was 10 years ago. Where it was a horrible, not-to-be-talked-about social sore 40 or 50 years ago, today in intelligent, sophisticated societies, it is taken for what it really is: a dangerous disease to be arrested, one that probably makes the patient a better person than he was. There still is a massive enlightening program needed. With thousands of articles being printed and aired, with the subject so prevalent in high schools and colleges, let us hope, convinced the next generations will wipe out the stigma and replace it with solid, structural knowledge of a common disease, one which is being fought successfully every day.

There will always be that mother-in-law or old aunt who will turn her head and close her eyes when the discussion comes up. But more and more they are becoming rareties. More and more the world is seaching to solve the mysteries of alcoholism—perhaps, because of its prevalence or because it hits home so often. But I think mainly because it is such a waste and the young people today are concerned with wastes—be it food, land or people.

Examples:

The boss told me he'd rehire Sam, the alcoholic, if he promised never to take another drink. I said that was foolish. "Do you promise me you'll never catch another cold? Or have another headache?" I asked him. He grinned.

Then I said, "I will guarantee you that Sam is a hell-of-a-gifted employee who has fought long and hard to beat a terminal illness. If somebody came back from cancer or heart treatments you'd take him back, wouldn't you?" The boss admitted he would. "Then take back Sam. He's had a disease. He's recovering today. Nobody can guarantee it won't strike again. But with God's help and a friend like you can be, he can lick it, and stay well. You can thank yourself for hiring a top employee." The boss rehired Sam, who eventually became his right-hand assistant.

* * *

The young man had been treated for liquor and drugs and his addiction had taken two years to combat. Now he was still shaky and needed friends. His old gang, now all successful businessmen, turned their backs on him. His indiscretions and publicity attendant to them had turned off his onetime friends. Now he was more alone than ever. But he joined a half-way house where he met a college professor and people of the art world. They, too, were fighting the social stigma.

Together they formed a bond which the man told me has rekindled his faith in human nature. They share. Ironically, some of his old pals now are going through the problems of liquor and drugs and call him for help. He has not turned his back. He now has more friends than ever.

The point I make is this: if you can't get back in with the so-called gang; forget it. They aren't what you want or need. There are many places where you can seek out other recovering alcoholics on common ground and form bonds more meaningful than any you have ever known.

* * *

A friend of mine was desperately anxious over the reception his high-toned, successful country club group of golfing friends would give him. He and his wife invited four couples over for dinner after his two months of treatment. He served wine and cheese before dinner and everyone, he noticed, seemed up-tight and tense. When they saw he was not ill at ease with them drinking, the situation grew more relaxed.

After dinner, George, the alcoholic, smiled and asked his friends, "Aren't you going to ask me about my treatment? I'm dying to tell someone. Even though I have no scars to show." They laughed. The conversation grew in depth and scope. Before the evening was over, two of his companions asked about advice for their children who had drinking problems. Another wife confided she thought she might be an alcoholic—and asked how she would know.

George became the pillar of the group and the friendships are far more meaningful now. "We used to talk about jobs, vacations, dogs, and boats. Now we dig deep. We talk about ourselves, our problems, and what help we can be to each other. It's beautiful."

Sometimes the recovering alcoholic won't share as much as he should. He must come across the line. He must make himself vulnerable to the extent that others feel at ease.

* * *

I have a newspaper friend who returned from treatment and wrote a column about his alcoholism. He said,

256

"Well, here goes—nobody may ever speak to me again." After the column, he was shocked. He received more than a dozen letters from prominent people informing him of their own battle with the illness and thanking him for having the courage to put his fight in public print.

One businessman asked him to join a Monday lunch group which met to discuss the disease. They were all recovering alcoholics. Much to his surprise, the columnist found that out of the Monday group, one was a state senator, two were doctors, another was a bank president, another an insurance company manager, and another the vice-president of a major airlines.

But the truth is, only a particular segment of the population feels at ease with known alcoholics or talking about the disease. Mainly, I'm convinced, because they are so ill-informed and are so fearful of saying the wrong thing. The first thing a lady asked me when she heard I was an alcoholic was: "I didn't even know you were ever on skid row." It's best to laugh. I just said, "Almost—but not quite."

Alcoholics themselves sometimes can be blamed for the stigma. A major treatment center held a reunion in a metropolis recently, renting out a large civic center for what it hoped would be a gathering of thousands. The crowd was sparse. The director of the reunion made it a point to find out why more alcoholics didn't come to the Sunday afternoon event. He was stunned to find that many of the alcoholics' wives did not feel at ease about being out in the "broad daylight" with their husbands at such an affair. And a tremendous number of alcoholics themselves said they didn't want to attend such a function in such a public building during the daylight hours. He was amazed. I could have suspected as much. A large group of alcoholics do as much to attach stigma to the disease as that part of the uninformed society which goes only on whispers and second-hand hearsay. When we were drunk, we didn't worry about our anonymity. Why jump into a garbage can and hide when we recover? Let's help individuals when the case appears in front of us. Where would we be if others had not aided us and instead had turned their backs to us?

I have great faith in recovering alcoholics—and when I tell major firms that an alcoholic may be as good or better than the next man they hire, they sit up and take notice.

VIEWPOINT

I don't buy the recovering alcoholic's pet excuse that his return to drink was "just a slip." I don't buy their shrug of the shoulders, straight-ahead stare and words, "God, I don't know why." Of course, they know why and, of course, it's not just a slip.

They have been preparing for the breakdown in their resistance for many days, perhaps weeks, sometimes months, and even years. At the bottom of every alcoholic is the great, unrelenting desire to "see if I can hold one again—if really, maybe I'm not an alcoholic." That challenge is there. I admit it.

But the alcoholic who turns his back on the facts given him through thousands of factual cases, through his dedicated AA group, and through histories of people just like himself, is looking for that breakthrough. Likewise, no recovering alcoholic can maintain control of the disease without continual sharing with his AA group or family and his God. The man who is going to have that "little slip" is paving the way. He is planning his drunk. Oh, he may not honestly believe that he will have trouble with a drink or two. Subconsciously he knows a drink would be a grave mistake.

It is no slip and he knows why. He has set the stage. He has talked himself into believing he can regain his old feeling of elation—at the same time controlling his sensitivity. That is nonsense, of course. But rational thinking is unknown to the alcoholic who wants "just one more fling." That is sadly true even though his sobriety may have brought him comfort, respect and returned his health.

Again—the deadlines of the disease. No other disease tempts a man to dare its lethal options. The cancer patient whose disease is arrested certainly wouldn't begin eating bananas if they caused the cancer cells to take hold of his body again. The man with a benign brain tumor wouldn't take up boxing if they told him his head could stand no blows. But the alcoholic, with a terminal disease, so often wants "one more chance to make sure the diagnosis is right," even if it winds up maiming or killing him.

As for society causing agitation for the alcoholic, I'm reminded of a waitress who was serving drinks to a group of men at a business meeting. She came to a neighbor and said undiplomatically, "Well, Dick, being an alcoholic, I know you don't want a drink." Used to this kind of verbalizing, Dick retorted: "Geeze, Marge, I bet nobody here knows that you're a sex deviate, huh?' Marge rushed away in tears. It was not a kind cut. But there's a lesson to be learned here for all alcoholics: everyone has some secret or something in their nature they prefer to keep unknown. Being an alcoholic is not a badge of honor. But no worse than many afflictions or habits all of us share.

No recovering alcoholic can maintain control of the disease without continual sharing with his AA group or family and his God.

QUESTION:
CAN A RECOVERING ALCOHOLIC BE EXPOSED TO LIQUOR?

SELVIG:

It depends entirely on the individual; I've seen some who generated a serious anxiety. They should not have to be exposed to alcohol. I've seen others so sure and solid in their sobriety that they could work in a wine distillery and never be tempted.

I have questioned over 2,000 recovering alcoholics about this. I find that about 40 percent are completely at ease around alcohol. Another 20 percent say they can handle certain situations. Another 40 percent admit to suffering difficult anxieties the kind that make it troublesome to function well in their surroundings when exposed to liquor. These people should not have to be asked to risk their state of fulfillment and contentment in atmospheres where liquor is served.

The same goes for the home. About half of the recovering alcoholics I have questioned can live with alcohol in the home, for the convenience of their wives or other members of the family. They entertain. Many of them are perfectly capable of pouring alcohol without suffering any jitters or uncomfortable feelings.

Now let's suppose the alcoholic is not sure enough of his feelings to let his family use alcoholic beverages in the house or drink them with him when they are out to dinner. He should explain the situation, sharing all his feelings. If they feel compelled to drink after he shared his feelings and doubt, they should be permitted to. He is actually showing a selfish side by demanding they adhere to his wishes because of his disease; the same as it would be selfish for a person who can't use salt to forbid its use at the family table.

However, I find most families who have suffered with the alcoholic will voluntarily remove liquor from the house if it affects the alcoholic's comfort.

This is a purely personal decision which, when made, should be explained to people with whom the recovering alcoholic may eat or drink. It is not fair to ask the world to quit drinking because alcoholics feel anxieties toward the serving of liquor. That is nonsense. There is no need for a recovering alcoholic to stay away from a restaurant where liquor is served unless it unnerves him. Most other liquor drinkers could care less if he is drinking. They are concerned only with themselves. I've never heard yet of a case where anyone put a shotgun to the head of an alcoholic and forced him to tipple.

Examples:

The man named Edward has a wife who likes two martinis before dinner and sips a brandy after. He told her when he recovered, "Esther, you can have your drinks. I'm the alcoholic. It's not fair to dictate to you." She offered to quit. He insisted she continue. But after three months of watching her routine and seeing her attitude embellished by her nightly quota, Edward began to seethe inside, again asking, "Why me?"

Rather than return to drink or change his decision, he did the intelligent thing: "Dear, do you mind if I take a jog around the block while you're having your drinks? I'll feel a little more comfortable." He insisted, despite her pleas that she would desist. After dinner, he retired to the billiard room to stroke a few balls while Esther had her brandy. He laughs about the arrangement. "While Esther drinks, I get in my training. I'm getting in great condition and becoming a helluva pool player. I feel she deserves a little relaxation."

Not a bad way, if a bit unorthodox, to handle a situation that could be trying. There are many ways to handle a potentially touchy area.

* * *

Broad-shouldered Henry was an outdoor writer for a metropolitan paper who used to say, "You can't be a fisherman or hunter without being a heavy drinker. Everybody drinks." Well, Henry found himself in a police station, locked up and his health nearly gone. After recovering through three months of treatment, he admitted he hated to think about going back with his hunting and fishing cronies—not to mention the long cocktail press parties and resort wingdings that took up much of the weekends.

Particularly, Henry hated to think about the opening of the fishing season and the governor's party when all the celebrities imbibed and partied for a full weekend. I told him. "Listen to the chatter, laugh a little, joke like you always do, and carry a 7-Up or Coke or Tab in a glass with ice cubes. Nobody'll even notice." I never heard of anyone at a fishing opening twisting another guy's arm to drink. They're all too busy belting themselves blind.

Well, Hank went to the party, poured down cokes and other soft drinks, listened to the silly chatter, and reported back to me on Monday. "Hell, I fished better than anyone there. I wrote tons of good stuff. Nobody even noticed if I was drinking and I never got sick or fell out of the boat. And best yet, I can remember every damn word I heard."

Too often the recovering alcoholic feels the other drinkers will castigate him. Most of them won't even notice he's not drinking. When I drank, I didn't care if someone else ate a peanut butter sandwich or juggled a can of worms. As long as the drinker has his alcohol he could care less about what or how much you're consuming.

* * *

The matter of wine parties at the neighbor's house or wine being served at the table during a major meal can be a trifle embarrassing. A salesman named Dave tells me he lifts the wine glass to his lips so as not to start a discussion or embarrass his hostess. He puts it down and nobody in seven years has asked him why he didn't finish the wine. Presumably he doesn't like wine.

Four out of every 10 adults do not care for wine with their meals. Another friend of mine merely switches glasses with his wife when she finishes her wine and she sips on his. If wine and cheese are given you, it's easy to set down the wine and nibble the cheese. No hostess will insist you drink. Remember, you might have an upset stomach or be allergic to wine.

They may ask if you'd care for another beverage. Then you can merely ask for a soft drink. The alcoholic is all too often prepared to be embarrassed. That's ridiculous and the more he moves about, the more he understands it.

Nobody is forced to smoke at a party. Nobody is forced to chew gum. Turning down a drink is no more offensive to a hostess than turning down a cigarette or potatoes because you are on a diet.

This is an area where the alcoholic can't, on many occasions, take the counselor's word for his acceptance back into society. He thinks everybody is noticing that he doesn't drink. Ironically, he forgets completely that people noticed his heavy drinking far more than they will ever notice his abstinence. Experience remains the most profound of teachers—the alcoholic learns quickly. A recovering alcoholic with 20 years of sobriety returned to the bartending trade he knew as a youth and said with a wink, "Liquor is to be served but not to be drunk by me." Nobody has ever questioned him.

* * *

A socialite who entertains often and is a recovering alcoholic said he actually likes to take a stand at his recreation room bar. "I enjoy the parties so much. I dispense a good drink but I don't overwhelm anyone. I like to see the social drinkers begin to get the conversational buzz on. I still picture myself going overboard on the night I blew my nose on our new drapes. Disgusting, embarrassing moments like those make me happy to realize that today I can be a part of any party anywhere and not be a disgrace. Nobody wanted me then. Now I'm invited out all the time. And when I pour the drinks, I make damn certain that no poor devil who is on his way to an embarrassing drunk will get any more from me. I know his wife will be thanking me in her heart."

> About half of the recovering
> alcoholics I have questioned
> can live with alcohol in the
> home, for the convenience of
> their wives or other members
> of the family. They entertain.
> Many of them are perfectly
> capable of pouring alcohol
> without suffering any jitters or
> uncomfortable feelings.

QUESTION:
WOULD YOU RECOMMEND A ROMANCE BETWEEN TWO RECOVERING ALCOHOLICS?

SELVIG:

Absolutely not. On the surface it seems like a splendid idea—helpmates who can lift each other up, lend moral support and comfort to each other and understand each other's illness. But I've seen too many romances between alcoholics which were shattering disappointments.

In the first place, the one with the good feeling doesn't tend to lift the low one up to his level. Rather, it works the other way around. The alcoholic at low ebb tends to bring the other down. What you have here is more than a man-woman relationship. You've got two potentially vulnerable individuals. It's like the blind leading the blind. Instead of helping each other get well and maintain sobriety, too often they help each other get drunk.

The person who is recovering and is unmarried too often is feeling the pangs of loneliness and has such fears about this condition he takes up too quickly with a girl he thinks is understanding of his disease. This could be another addict. But he is not ready to offer strength —only a character which is trying to rebuild itself and is not yet strong enough to support another addict. The addict on his way back faces enough temptations and must concentrate enough of his strength on his disease not to have to worry about a romance in which the other also is trying to combat the disease. From the hundreds of cases I've reviewed in which alcoholics take up romantically, I have perceived a very grave danger. Under no circumstances would I recommend a relationship which ironically seems so natural to many.

One common statement heard by would-be romantics in treatment is, "But this is a platonic relationship." My response to that is: "Platonic, all right, play for one of you and tonic for the other." The success ratio of treatment romances is so low that it must be classified as a serious risk. I doubt if more than 10 percent of these romances will survive. Definitely high-risk odds.

Examples:

Susan was a counselor in a rehabilitation hospital and Jed, a truck driver by occupation, was a patient. They were both young and attractive. Susan felt great empathy for Jed because she was a recovering alcoholic with six months of sobriety. He was handsome and robust and told her, "With your inspiration I can make it. Together we can help everyone else who has problems."

She came to me for advice. I spoke against the match. Unfortunately, the physical attraction was too great and they were married. Both went into counseling. Susan was better educated than Jed and moved ahead in the counseling field while he bogged down. Irritable, losing his self-worth, he began to argue and harangue. Gradually he had attacks of depression which grew worse.

Torn between her career and love, Susan lost her courage to fight back and her will to remain sober. In the end, both returned to us for treatment. They dated again, but returned time and again until they finally separated. Jed is now in a mental hospital. Susan, getting over the tragic affair, has returned to counseling.

She put it this way: "When you are recovering and beginning to get well, you want to feel close to someone who understands. Then when the cold, hard world of reality pops back into your life, it begins to be an effort—not for yourself but for both of you to understand each other's problems. Resentment comes in. Then self-pity. Remorse. And you are on your way back to the bottle. It's not a healthy situation. I had to find out the hard way."

* * *

I remember being in a discussion with a fellow named Art, a young student who was bright in many ways. He and his girl friend, Dottie, had drunk themselves into the disease as juniors in college. She was having trouble with her rehabilitation and had moved away from her parents. They frowned on Art, claiming he had led their daughter down the primrose path.

His argument: "I got her started on this thing. I have to stick by her." My opinion: you both owe it to yourselves to get back on solid ground and forget the past; to keep conjuring up the past will only make the effort of sobriety more difficult.

Still they eloped. The last I heard she was again hospitalized and he had lost two jobs and was heading for a nervous breakdown. Perhaps Art was influential in exposing Dottie to the disease, but just because he was salving a troubled conscience was no reason to risk his own sobriety in a romance of addicts which had from the beginning very little chance to succeed.

* * *

"We can pull together. Two people can be stronger than one." I've heard that statement by addict lovers like

Judy and Tom. Both were young, bright and seemingly recovering. But Judy wanted children. Tom wanted to wait. Just a little tension.

He wanted to move to another city. She wanted to stay close to her relatives. More tension. Secretly, both began drinking, lightly at first and then more heavily. When they found out about the other's slipping back into diseased ways, they berated each other. Both became more interested in the other's problem than in their own. They forgot their own vulnerabilities in an admirable show of love, but with miserable results. They simply could not stand the day's high-pressure tensions.

It has been said the alcoholic must guard against overwork, undersleep, loss of temper and excessive tensions. They fell far short in all areas. They again sought fulfillment in the bottle—not each other. Sad to say, that happens with regularity in romances of two addicts. The strength of one can be dissipated by the inadequacies of the other.

Sexual attraction, the pledge of loyalty, the devotion to one another are all beautiful offshoots of romance. Unfortunately, the recovering alcoholic must guard jealously his battle for sobriety. It is sad but true that two cannot battle as effectively as one when both are suffering from the disease. There are no germs. But feelings of remorse and guilt and loneliness are as contagious as any germ in the universe.

* * *

Nicole was pretty, vulnerable and a 26-year-old interior decorator. Stan was a musician of sorts. Both were patients of mine. They knew the rules of the center: no romances on the grounds. Just a week before Nicole was to leave she was found in a compromising situation with Stan. Both were thrown out of the clinic. You might say it was harsh treatment. But examples have to be set and rules enforced strictly if a treatment center is to function. The expulsion was a shock to both parties. Nicole kept a steady pace, however, joined AA and today is a successful businesswoman. Stan rejoined a band, turned to cocaine, and today is a derelict.

Nicole told me several years later, "Best thing that ever happened to me was that expulsion from the treatment center. Suddenly it dawned on me that I was finding just solace for my loneliness in Stan; we would have destroyed each other if we had continued the romance."

On the surface, it looks like a storybook ending: two alcoholics recover and live together happily ever after. But this disease is an uncompromising one. The alcoholic must jealously guard his sobriety. He has no time to worry about moods and tensions created in the marriage. Oh, he can handle problems. I don't mean that. I mean that the inner striving of the alcoholic leaves no room to play games emotionally with another addict in the same household. Instead of giving each other strength, too often the addict lovers are caught up in a maelstrom of emotions and moods and actually devour each other. In the AA group, the addicts share and build equally. In marriage or romance, too often one must give too much too often to the other. Instead of sharing relationship, it becomes one of sacrifice. That's where an alcoholic can lose his will to remain sober.

One common statement heard by would-be romantics in treatment is, "But this is a platonic relationship." My response to that is: "Platonic, all right, play for one of you and tonic for the other." The success ratio of treatment romances is so low that it must be classified as a serious risk.

QUESTION:
MUST AN ALCOHOLIC HAVE A RELIGION
TO AID RECOVERY?

SELVIG:

No. But it certainly does help. An alcoholic must have a power greater than himself to turn to in his recovery.

Look at it this way: when he is drinking, the alcoholic has a power greater than himself in the bottle. It dominates him. Consequently, when he recovers, he must have a power greater than himself to take the place of that which the bottle occupied. That only stands to reason.

The new power greater than the individual can be an organized religion which has been a tremendous source of strength to the recovering alcoholic. It is easier for someone with an organized religion to turn to the new power. If one was raised in a spiritual home, that spiritual belief is usually retained.

But the power to supplant that of the bottle can be many different forces to different individuals. I've worked with North American Indians who called that power "Mother Nature." They got their unseen strength from the woods, trees, wind, and earth. The unseen power which the alcoholic must have can be his belief and trust in Buddha, Mohammed, or any spirit and supernatural being in which he believes.

The trouble with all too many alcoholics is that they take themselves too seriously—and the unseen power of God not seriously enough. The agnostic may be at a disadvantage unless he can console himself that there is a force in the universe stronger than himself and put faith in it. The atheist simply has to put his faith in something outside himself—perhaps in other people.

The man who has some religion or even believes in a power greater than himself has a triumvirate of support—himself, God, and other men.

No alcoholic can recover doing it by himself. Exactly 100 percent of those I've known who have tried are either still practicing alcoholics, miserably sober—or are dead.

For an alcoholic to just quit on his own is so remote that I deem it virtually impossible.

There have been alcoholics who dared brave recovery by simply putting themselves in the hands of their almighty power. I don't believe that's a satisfactory answer. Before they can begin to recover, there are steps to be taken—tangible steps. Certainly a grace may come from the Supreme Being of the alcoholic, but that grace is to give strength so that the mission of recovery may be completed. That grace does not supply the recovery.

Look at it this way: a young boy may want to become a ballplayer—and pray to his Supreme Being that he succeeds. He may get the grace to give him desire and dedication. But he must practice. He must go out on the field and play and learn the fundamentals.

Whatever God or Power we pray to will give us inner strength. Then we must take this strength and turn it into practical application. You don't get a job by just praying for it. You must go out and fit yourself for it and then apply. You don't become an author by saying prayers. You must write and make mistakes and write again.

The beautiful thing about this is that I have known men and women who were never close to their God, who never prayed and who never gave a thought to superior forces. Then they became afflicted with alcoholism. Suddenly, as recovery loomed in sight, they became enlightened and aware of their Supreme Being.

It mattered not that they were not brought up in the Catholic, Jewish, Protestant, or Buddhist faiths. It mattered only that they prayed for strength and were given it by a power greater than themselves.

I have never known a recovering alcoholic who didn't believe strongly in some Superior Being. Without that belief the recovery work is only a facade. The strength doesn't come from the treatment. It comes from the Superior Being through the alcoholic.

Examples:

The middle-aged accountant named Rudy had not been to church since he was 11. His parents died in an auto crash. He grew up feeling "every man for himself." God was something or someone that nobody saw, a figment of the imagination, a fantasy. God never came down and grabbed you and said, "I've got a job for you." And He never slipped an extra roll of bills into your pocket.

It was easy to drop the habit of saying prayers. How does a nothing hold your attention? When Rudy was being treated, a minister told him to relax. Rudy was worried about his ability to discipline himself. "You try," the minister said, "and God will give you the strength to make the 'try' work. Watch and see."

Rudy took his recovery a day at a time. Just before falling asleep at night he found himself saying, without anyone suggesting it, "Thanks, God. Another day." Gradually, he faced the days with optimism and courage. He told me a year after his recovery began, "There is something big and wonderful and mysterious out there. I don't know what it is, but I talk to it all the time."

The "Thing out there" has made Rudy's recovery a reality and will continue to supply him with the will to discipline himself.

* * *

No greater expression of a recovering alcoholic's faith is that which says, "Let go. Let God."

That's exactly what Edna said she did. Edna hated clerics, or what she called, "the unbending autocrats of the inflexible Church." She hated organized religion. She hated preachers, faith-people, evangelists.

"Religion simply doesn't understand or give a damn about the everyday struggle of the everyday people," she said for years.

While seeking recovery, Edna became friends with one of our Indian patients. He worshipped what he called his "Sky God," something up there that controlled the winds.

"He blows freedom to us—he blows in on the winds down here to give us many choices and many chances," he would say.

Edna became fascinated. She didn't call her new discovery God or a Super Being or even The Man Upstairs. She did call him Mr. Motion—with a wink and a grin. "Mr. Motion" became the wind which blew her strength, confidence, new faith in herself.

I don't know if Edna ever went back to an organized religion. But three years after her recovery she told me, "I still have my 'Mr. Motion.' It may sound corny or trite but there is 'something' which blows power and strength into my very being. I don't have to preach about it—or pray to it. But it is there. Something is blowing great courage into my system. I'm glad I met that Indian boy. I don't know if our God is the same thing, but I have a faith in something other than myself; something which does help."

* * *

There is the case of the priest who was a terribly troubled man. He made a disgrace of himself at a funeral in the small town where he was a pastor. The conservative old German element never let him forget it nor did it forgive him. He confessed to me that he was torn between his great love of his God and the horrible thought: "What if God doesn't care about me? What if I am really not wanted in His flock? What if I am an outcast?"

He groped with that turmoil for years, pouring in alcohol to ease his pain and his conscience. "The God I knew was a tough, stern God. If I committed an unworthy act or committed that sin, I fully expected a bolt of lightning to strike me down."

During his recovery, he began to feel that God was a compassionate, wonderful friend. I told him, "Get on your knees, look up, and say, 'Hey, Jesus; this is your pal, Steve. Give me a break today, eh? I don't need the booze when I have Your help.' "

I'm sure at first he thought I was sacrilegious, but a year later at a reunion he told me that he conversed with a new-found friend—a God of warmth and compassion, a God who dearly loved his alcoholic children.

I told him God had to love us dearly—as there are so many of us drunks. The priest found out that whatever Supreme Being guides and inspires and helps us, thinks no less of us because of our disease than he does an ill child or crippled old woman.

Oh God, oh Supreme Being, oh Master of the Wind. I don't care who the alcoholic speaks to. He must have someone. It helps so much to receive that hidden power from the unknown source. Truly, the alcoholic can recover much quicker, become much healthier with the aid of the Supernatural Power. Speaking to that Supreme Being, for the alcoholic, becomes as natural as breathing.

No alcoholic can recover doing it by himself. Exactly 100 percent of those who have tried are either still practicing alcoholics, miserably sober— or are dead. For an alcoholic to just quit on his own is so remote that I deem it virtually impossible.

QUESTION:
CAN A RECOVERING ALCOHOLIC TAKE WINE AT COMMUNION?

SELVIG:

I must give two answers. Yes and No. I take it. I take it because I believe I am not drinking wine but the blood of Christ. I am firmly convinced that there is no way Christ is going to permit his blood to ruin my sobriety; not when he's given me such strength to attain it. It is such a warming experience for me. I will never refuse it.

On the other hand, I know priests and ministers who will not touch communion wine—and many will replace the wine in the chalice with grape juice. It is purely a personal decision and I respect every alcoholic's opinion. It all depends on how the alcoholic approaches the communion. If he says, "I have vowed never to let liquor pass my lips" and it would be a matter of anxiety, he should under no circumstance risk drinking it. The person to whom a drink of communion wine would cause tension or worry should absolutely refrain.

Out of 400 recovered alcoholics whom I questioned on the matter, about 50 percent said they do not touch communion wine. Some worry about it; others freely accept the wine.

There is the crux of the decision. If you come to church thinking about drinking the wine and worrying about it, you are not fully prepared to receive it. The mystical transformation may not be enough to guarantee some alcoholics' sobriety if they become upset emotionally over the prospect. I will never try to talk anyone into taking communion wine.

Examples:

A minister told me he worried so much about taking the wine that he nearly had a nervous breakdown. It became an obsession. I told him under no circumstance to drink the wine. A priest told me the same thing. But a lovely old gentleman (who was recovering at the age of 72) told me, "God won't let me be a drunk again." His words were beautiful.

* * *

A 25-year-old law student told me he consumed less than half an ounce of wine at service and a sudden, compulsive feeling for more swept over him. He rushed out of church and consumed two quarts of wine during that Sunday, winding up in the hospital on Monday, with tremors and chills and horrible nausea.

I questioned him intensely. We both came to the conclusion he was not taking communion properly and perhaps he should refrain. He was still waiting for an excuse to drink. He simply used the church service as an excuse for an off day and felt he could blame God for his indiscretion. The alcoholic who has not had a true recovery may be waiting for a situation such as communion to break his sobriety.

* * *

I've known many drunks who used the old saw, "Jesus made wine at the Cana wedding feast. He must have OK'd drinking." They forget it was the religious custom to drink wine with the meals at occasions of celebration. It was no more intended for Jesus to provide drunks with alcohol than it would have been if he made another pot of coffee or tea in today's society.

The communion wine certainly is not enough to start a treatment-oriented alcoholic drinking unless he has not recovered after all—and is searching for a trigger to start his drinking once more.

The people I have questioned about drinking altar wine

say, "It's ridiculous to believe I'll get drunk over taking communion." The person who is tempted is desperately looking for the way out. A healthy, recovering alcoholic should harbor no fear.

But I respect those who have decided that liquor of any type will not enter their mouth. That's the resolution to which they must be true. I'm sure Christ understands.

I will never argue with the man who says, "When I stopped drinking alcohol I stopped—I made no concessions." Never ask that kind of strong-willed, discipline-recovering alcoholic to take wine at communion. For most alcoholics the struggle has been hard and difficult. No need to risk their treasured sobriety in a place of salvation.

That would be pure folly and contempt for what the House of the Lord stands for. Christ would never be an aid to a mockery of a man's dedication and faith.

The church is the Lord's house. If your hostess is not concerned and understanding when you turn down wine at her dinner table, our God certainly is all-comprehending and fully admires the alcoholic's pledge to sobriety. For those to whom the wine is the Lord's blood, I'm sure they will encounter no trouble. For those who doubt the strength of their sobriety, I'm sure God understands and basks joyously in the reflection of their devotion to their health and sanity.

A lovely old gentlemen (who was recovering at the age of 72) told me, "God won't let me be a drunk again." His words were beautiful.

VIEWPOINT

I remember a question a friend asked me in the early days of my recovery: "Have you found Jesus yet?" I was

276

still not aware of the role that a belief in a Superior Being played in fighting the disease and I answered flippantly, "Is Jesus lost again?"

It was two years later at a baseball game when I sought out the same friend and whispered to him between innings, "Hey, Fred, I've found Jesus, He's with me every second." The friend held my hand in his and smiled, "You've found out, Dick, you can't do it alone." I knew what he meant.

For me, Jesus is a very real person. I'll drop down on my knees in the morning, look up to the sky and ask: "Jesus, help me to handle today, old friend." He's no ghostlike apparition. He's real to me. Real man. He's alive. He strengthens me every day. Oh, not in words or messages. But in the feelings I get. His spirit becomes mine.

I know a brilliant woman professor who says her feelings come through the stars. Another alcoholic says her source of strength is particular Saints on particular feasts and religious days. Another prays to the spirit of his ancestors. And there are the nature worshippers. I ridicule none. To those who believe, whatever the source of their strength is their God.

They may not call their source of strength God. They may never have imagined what their Superior Being is or even if it is a being. They only know something outside their own body is generating an amazing force and strength to aid their recovery. That object, as mystifying as it may be, is so real the alcoholic feeds on it and cannot recover without the power of its presence in his person.

This is not deep religious philosophy. It is as simple as a child looking out in the dark of night and saying, "I don't know who is out there—but whoever you are, be my friend. Help me."

Many recovering alcoholics have a deeply ingrained antagonism against their God, brought on by inner feelings of guilt. For instance, a bitter man told me, "Hell, God gave me a freedom of will. If I chose to drink, why can't I blame God?" Another was even more adamant. "If God is all-good and compassionate, why would he let me suffer like this?'' They contradicted themselves, naturally. Another anti-God alcoholic said, ''I prayed to God for years to make me a success. He didn't. That's why I started to drink.''

The alcoholic has a natural inclination to put the blame on someone else. God's the easiest to blame. He or It is not there to talk back, to remind the alcoholic that his will power was what crumbled and that he didn't see a need for intervention or strength of will from his God when he was drinking.

God and spouses are the patsies for more alcoholics than any other commodities on the planet.

As an old French priest used to tell me, ''The drunk never blames the devil. That's his companion in drink.''

I feel that recovering alcoholics, more than most people, get very close to their God. Just question them about their experiences. Ask them where they get the inner force to obliterate the temptation of alcohol. Ask them where they get that glow which seems to permeate their bodies and give them that gift of happy anticipation every day they get out of bed.

It comes from something unseen ''out there.'' I call it Jesus. You may call it something else. It doesn't matter. It works for the alcoholic.

And when I have a bad day and things go wrong, I look upward and ask, ''Hey, Jesus, what happened today? I didn't need all those tests. Or did I? Maybe I did. I came through them, didn't I? That must mean you really were with me. I didn't have a drink. Thanks for giving me that perseverance. I love you, Jesus. You're a great guy.'' He's the greatest human being who ever lived, in my opinion. He's an example of ''one man with courage is the majority.''

I'll tell you something else. Recovering alcoholics aren't afraid to talk about their faith. The other night at an Alcoholics Anonymous meeting a well-dressed businessman said, ''I was up tight early this week and for three days everything went wrong. I fought with my wife and the kids and at work. Suddenly it dawned on me; I wasn't 'talking' to my Lord. When I did, everything simply turned around and began to go smoothly again."

Recovering alcoholics learn to share religious experiences. Many are people who haven't been near a church for years. That isn't the important thing. The important thing is they are seeking out the power of God, they are asking for His help. And He never refuses.

Even more important, they know they need it. One of the great differences in the practicing alcoholic and the recovering alcoholic is that the drinker feels, in his omnipotence, that he does not need a God. He is bigger than the Superior Being.

It is almost a foregone conclusion that the practicing alcoholic belives either he is bigger than his faith or he has been alienated from it.

I love what the recovering alcoholic said on the anniversary of his first year of recovery when he received his AA pin:

"I wish I could give it to my God. He helped me and so did all of the alcoholics and non-alcoholics and I was a part of it too.

It was Abraham Lincoln who put it so strongly:

"I have been driven many, many times to fall on my knees and pray because of an overwhelming conviction I had nowhere else to go."

If a man of Lincoln's magnitude can rely on a "Greater Power," it is easy to understand why this communication with our God is so important to the alcoholic.

I know he hears me. You see, faith is everything. Without faith in himself, his fellowman, and a Superior Power, the alcoholic has no chance.

QUESTION:
IS IT TRUE A SENSE OF HUMOR IS A MUST FOR A RECOVERING ALCOHOLIC?

SELVIG:

Heavens, yes! Without the capacity to laugh at himself and his illness, the alcoholic will have a difficult time with recovery. This is another of the wondrous, yet strange, ironies of the disease.

Who can laugh with anger? Who can laugh over a kidney transplant or a heart bypass? Yet, the alcoholic is told to see the humor in his situation if he is to have a 50-50 chance at recovery. The reason is very simple: the alcoholic suffers from such remorse and has so many pains of regret and tortures himself so much over what has transpired that if he didn't have a sense of humor, he'd quickly dig a grave for himself.

Oh yes, I have seen countless alcoholics die of heartbreak and remorse, cursing themselves. The alcoholic must see the bright side—and certainly every alcoholic need only look at some of his sillier moments, his dizzy doings, to regain a smile. I don't say the alcoholic has to go out publicly retelling the pathetic, twisted episodes of his drinking dilemmas. He can do it on the inside.

The day he misplaced his wallet and didn't dare tell the wife must bring an inward grin. And so must remembering the day he sneaked off to the liquor store and the car wouldn't start when he came out. How about the day he fell over the dog in the entryway with his mother-in-law sitting in the living room?

Then there was the day he tore up his check instead of the stub. Or the day he forgot the name of the guest he was to introduce at the speaker's rostrum. How about the night he got in a cop car, mistaking it for a cab? There was the day he came home with his neighbor's groceries.

All little, curious momentoes of the drinking past. The alcoholic must be able to say to himself, "Hell, there were some laughs—some good times. It wasn't all tears and hangovers."

If he thinks it was all bad, all dirty, all dishearteningly fruitless, he will become a person who beats himself out of sobriety. There are only two streets the alcoholic can live on—Gratitude Street or Grumble Street. He can't relive the past but can change his attitude about it.

It is best to laugh at yesterday—even if it's under his breath or quietly to himself. There's never been an alcoholic who didn't provide a laugh during his insane days.

I recall confronting a fellow for laughing during a lecture I was giving many years ago. "Hey, back there, there's nothing very funny about this. This is serious business," I said.

The fellow looked at me, wiped off his smile and frowned: "Serious business, eh? I'll tell you how serious it is. I've just lost my job, my family, and my house. Buddy, that's serious. But if I couldn't laugh, I'd be in the nut ward—not here."

I never reprimanded an alcoholic for laughing again. The very resiliency which makes a man laugh when the black chips are piled so high against him provides the cushion which enables him to surge back.

Examples:

Charlie was so down-trodden over his alcoholism that he hated to face his wife. During their first confrontation at the hospital, I suggested to her that what he needed most was a laugh. She said it would be difficult but somehow she managed to bring up a day when hubby was painting the house trim. He had a few bumps or more and suddenly lost his balance.

The bright green trim landed all over his white paint clothes, all over the white veneer of the house, all over the picture windows. He landed with a crash on the grass, his one foot immersed in the paint can. He stripped down to his underwear in the garage and then rushed up to the door. She was in the shower and the doors accidently had been locked. The neighbor lady ran into her house and a little child screamed. The alcoholic and his wife were nearly hysterical as the story wore on. I found myself laughing, too. It was a therapy that did Charlie more good than any session that day. He found that even the wife he had maligned and disappointed over the years could still see some humor at his drunken antics. Even through the tears.

* * *

Marty couldn't smile about his past, even if you tickled him with a feather and read *Playboy* jokes to him all night. He was so downcast that he needed a reprieve from his torment. I asked two of his old golfing cronies to visit him.

In a few minutes they were uproarious with laughter over Marty's booze and golf problems. They reminded him of the day his golf cart got stuck on a sprinkling mechanism, hung itself up while he was drenched with water as onlookers at the first tee tittered in glee. There was the day he spent too much time in the clubhouse, leaving his partners waiting. They replaced his ball with a fake one and when he swung, he nearly lost his arms from the sockets as he hit the tissue ball. They entertained themselves for two hours with stories of his ineptness when he had been drinking, like the day he got in the ladies shower by mistake.

It was a session which seemed to turn Marty around. I told him, ''Us drunks weren't all ornery. Sometimes we were clowns. Sometimes we were comedians who kept the world around us laughing. So much we have done is humorous. We must learn to smile again—inside, privately.'' Marty got the idea. He loosened up. He began to laugh again. He hasn't had a drink in eight years.

* * *

I can grin over dozens of instances in my youth when

the drink of the foolish made me a laughing stock. Like the day I volunteered to pitch in a relief role with the bases loaded and a slugger at the plate. I had been nipping behind the dugout at the water cooler. I threw what I thought was the perfect screwball and the pellet was last seen, I swear, in a holding pattern over the adjacent county.

One time my friend in the church choir sang so loudly and so far off key that two old spinsters came up to the director during services and asked that he be put out of the church. There was the time I ripped my trousers before the prom and had a pal clamp on a safety pin and then it opened and I screamed in pain while sitting next to a pretty girl. She thought I was a lunatic. Oh, it goes on and on.

* * *

I remember a young Indian girl of 20, already a mother twice, divorced, left to shift for herself. She fought dope and liquor. She was downcast. "What the hell do I have to live for?" she frequently asked.

I told her, "You have your two beautiful babies and yourself. God made no garbage. You must have had some fun in life. Sit down and tell me the last funny thing you can remember."

She told me how her husband tried a venison steak she made after they were married. And, tipsy as she was, she put sugar in place of salt on the meat. He spit the food all over the room and accused her of trying to poison him.

She told of shooting an arrow at a deer and hitting her brother-in-law in the rear instead. He had on a fur cap and she thought he was an animal. As she talked, she laughed. I told her episodes in my life. She left the treatment center two months later, a very substantial human being.

At her farewell address to her group I remember well what she said: "I can face myself now. I can remember the bad things—and the good things. I can remember the funny things especially. I'm going out and stand in the sunshine again and laugh. Hear that, Dick Selvig—laugh!" I embraced her and said: "Smile and the gang smiles with you—cry and you cry alone." It was an oldie, but she accepted it—with a big, sweet grin. She made a little pact with me. We agreed she'd "grab a grin" a day.

* * *

The alcoholic, ironically, can be very humorous when he doesn't realize it. When he tries to force humor, he usually stumbles all over himself. He loses his awareness. What he thinks is funny, likely is not. But the alcoholic who has turned serious episodes into laughters —because he lost his balance or made an embarrassing mistake, or became a ploy in public—may have been a source of genuine good-natured amusement to his friends. Generally, they will tell him about it.

* * *

I recall a dignified friend and practicing alcoholic who defecated one night in a musician's sousaphone during an intermission behind stage. It certainly wasn't funny to the musician. But as the story was told over the years, it became a constant source of amusement to the drunk and his friends. When he recovered and I reminded him of his "big night," he actually blushed. Then he regained his composure and asked, "Do you suppose I should find the fellow and make restitution?" I told him I don't think the musician would appreciate it and that his AA group, I'm sure, would forgive him if he never brought up the matter again.

* * *

I had a friend who jumped on a stranger's horse during a hunter-jumper show. The frightened animal raced off and the drunk fell off while the crowd roared. The poor fellow didn't even remember it the next day. But somebody brought him a picture. Now, as a sober member of society, he attends horse shows, has two children in the saddle, and is delighted if somebody asks to see the pictures of his flight and plight.

There are times when it is too embarrassing to bring up a drunk's silly actions. I remember one time I tried joking with an old friend who was in treatment. "The only kind of wagon this guy was ever on was a paddy wagon," I told the nurse. Bill didn't think that was funny. I never joked with him again. But the day he was released he dropped by my office.

"Hey, Dick, did you hear about the time I was put in charge of the food supplies for our hunting trip up to Canada? When we got there and opened the trunk, all I had brought were two loaves of bread and two cases of booze!"

I knew he could make it.

The alcoholic must be able to say to himself, "Hell, there were some laughs—some good times. It wasn't all tears and hangovers."

QUESTION:
DO OLD DRINKING COMPANIONS EXERT PEER PRESSURE ON THE RECOVERING ALCOHOLIC?

SELVIG:

An overemphasized notion. A cop out. I've never in 30 years of sobriety had one old drinking pal say, "Come on, Dick, let's have one for old times sake." Don't get me wrong. It can happen. But it is highly improbable.

The recovering alcoholics I talk to tell me almost in

unison that this is one of their most astounding revelations in sobriety—how few old friends ever try to get them to drink. I think the reason is so basically simple: If the other man is a drinker, he is interested only in himself.

Remember, I've emphasized that the alcoholic or hard drinker is a very selfish person, zealously guarding his right to the bottle. He really doesn't give a damn if you drink or not. Just don't deprive him of his.

Most recovering alcoholics tell me they order soft drinks or coffee in the presence of old drinking companions and nobody really cares. The old "drinking buddy" is just that—a pal in drinking alcohol. He doesn't really care about the recovering alcoholic's sobriety. He doesn't want to hear about his own problem. He simply wants to be left alone to drink.

Secretly, most other afflicted alcoholics look with admiration at the recovering ones of their breed. Occasionally, they will resent them. Only once in a great while will they try to talk the recovering alcoholic into a drink because they are usually too embarrassed to let the dry friend know their need. And by this time, he is the dominant force. They are much more likely to soft-peddle their own consumption.

This peer pressure is something alcoholics who are fighting sobriety use as one of their myriad excuses. The old pals in their drinking fraternity again become the accomplices. But the truth is the very selfish nature of the alcoholic does not permit him to exert influence in general on another member of his group. That takes too much energy away from the task at hand—consuming and becoming a consummate expert. It destroys the drunk's concentration to have to try to exert influence over a non-drinker.

"What's the use?" he'll ask himself. "I can't worry about him. If he can or can't drink, that's his problem."

Whenever a recovering alcoholic asks me about what kind of peer pressure he need expect, I look him in the eye and ask this question and seek an honest answer: "When you were drinking, did you ever care if the people around you were drinking? Did you have a need to co-erce the non-drinker?"

I've never heard anything but a "no" answer. Of course not. The alcoholic drinker is concentrating so much on his own attainment of that special feeling he could care less if his companion had a coke, highball, or milk.

Only when a recovering alcoholic goes into a bar and looks down his nose at the drinkers or tries to crusade when they are imbibing is he transgressing and disturbing them. Nobody wants a lecture at a bar. Nobody deserves one in that setting. In that scene, the alcoholic is on his own turf. The crusader belongs somewhere else.

Examples:

The husky iron-worker named Zack was the first of his group of a dozen hard-working buddies to accept treatment. He had some qualms about going into the little saloon near the plant, a virtual Friday night obligation and ritual. He told me his palms sweat that first week back. After a couple of minutes of good-natured kidding about "good old simon-pure Zack has come to save his por' old drunken buddies," the conversation never came back to his sobriety.

He ordered a soft drink and within minutes his pals were enjoying the conversational gamut from pro football to boxing. He noted shrewdly that after two or three drinks none of them cared if he shoveled down apple pie or hot peppers. They were too immersed in their own highs.

It is typical of the response an alcoholic gets. Still he must conquer legitimate fears. He can't remember being with his buddies when he wasn't consuming liquor. He doesn't know if he can take their joking. He tries, too hard sometimes, to still be the "regular guy." That can be dangerous if his recovery is not secure.

* * *

Ed is a publicity man. His advertising firm is constantly staging cocktail parties to introduce new promoters, ventures, and products. Drinking is almost second nature—and 90 percent of the drinkers are using alcohol.

"It's that buzz of conversation that I feared. Occasionally I bar-tended and I knew how the conversational pitch went from quiet and low key at first to a buzz that grew to an almost roar in an hour or so. With everybody talking, everybody interrupting, everybody trying to tell their own joke."

Ed said his body was soaked with perspiration and his legs felt weak the first time he attended a cocktail party of this type after his recovery.

"But I was amazed. As the crowd grew alcoholic in tone, I was sharp. I was only one of a handful who heard everything I wanted to hear—who got my points across. I was thrilled when the manager asked me to make an information presentation. And I was proud when he said, 'I know that Ed can get the point across since he's one of the few not drinking his head off."

"It didn't seem to offend anyone, my sobriety. From that point on I could hardly wait for business cocktail parties. I had a super advantage being able to hear everything and speak clearly and to the point. I wondered how much I'd missed all those alcoholic years." The big thing was that nobody resented Ed. In fact, his group was happy it had a sober spokesman and an articulate representative.

* * *

Theresa ran a temporary help company and had six women salespeople under her. Every Friday afternoon the seven of them would relax in a cozy bar near the office at four p.m. For two hours they'd drink and chat about the week's progress and problems.

Theresa said she felt because of this little drinking session that she had great rapport with her employees. Coming back after six weeks of rehabilitation, she admitted, "I was frightened to death. How would they react? Would they still confide in me? Would I still be one of them? Frankly, I figured this as the end of the line for me."

Theresa was amazed that when she ordered a diet pop that not one head turned nor did one of her girls make a remark. They seemed as relaxed as ever. But she noticed one difference: They confided in her even more! She couldn't understand that until I told her that her sobriety had won her even more trust. Nobody can be quite sure of the alcoholic—what he heard or what he will say. But with a sober confidante, they know that generally he will not betray their secrets.

"I became even closer to myself by not drinking. I made it a point, however, not to reprimand them or try to force my sobriety on them. That, I knew, they would resent." Good thinking. Too often the recovered alcoholic dons saints' robes and tries to reform the world. Nothing can do more to harm the example of sobriety. Sobriety sets its example, quietly, effectively, and subtly.

* * *

The backyard bar-b-que was a place, though, to torment Lon. A neighborhood leader, a block spokesman, suddenly he would be the only non-drinker at the 20-person neighborhood spring pig feed.

"God, how I hoped that day would never come," Lon admitted to me. "I simply couldn't believe that I, Lon, the big, loud talker who used to say I could drink the whole block under the table, would be the quiet little sober nobody. But God, what happened—I couldn't believe it!"

What happened was this: "Two of the families came over to the house later on and sat until 3 o'clock in the morning asking me questions. They were particularly concerned over a neighbor's brother and over one of their own children.

"As they left the house, one of the men leaned over and whispered to me, 'Lon, I think I've got a problem with the sauce; could you help me sometime?' I felt like a king."

This is what recovering alcoholics are going to find repeatedly: The old alcoholic drinking buddies or just the solid friends are so admiring of the alcoholic for taking steps to arrest his illness that they seek him out for counsel and help. He has shared with them by admitting his problem and by facing it. Now they feel they can share their problems with him. He becomes a much bigger person. Nobody wants to shove a bottle down his throat. That isn't human nature. Even the old lushes don't want to try and force a drink. They are just happy having one in their own hands.

**The alcoholic or hard drinker
is a very selfish person,
zealously guarding his right to the
bottle. He really doesn't give a
damn if you drink or not. Just
don't deprive him of his.**

QUESTION:
HOW IMPORTANT IS ALCOHOLICS ANONYMOUS IN RECOVERY?

SELVIG:

Nothing is more important than AA to the recovering alcoholic. Here is the most beautiful recovery program in the world. It could well be a philosophy of life for everyone, whatever their beliefs.

Its twelve steps are so profound that if a person lived by its creed, he would be a success immediately. By that I mean he would have complete freedom to function. This is a program where the alcoholic becomes **well** again.

Step One I call admitting the loss of freedom. [Going

on to other steps, I put them in my own words.] Admitting that liquor is a problem. Admitting we need others' help to succeed. Knowing ourselves better. Sharing with others.

The most difficult step, I think—is learning to grow up, and I mean that for adults of any age. Then, asking for help from others. Then, making a list of those we've harmed with our disease. Then, a solemn pledge to make restitution.

Now look at ourselves with a personal inventory. Then get on our knees and ask our Superior Being in our own words to help us.

Finally, gain the freedom to function, to help others.

There is something magical or miraculous, if you will, about the steps. Each may have his own version or interpretation of just what they mean and how to carry them out. But they add up to a magnificent force—powerful and awesome in its potential to generate rejuvenation of the body and mind and spirit. Every day I see transformations in human nature moulded and inspired by the AA concepts which virtually defy explanation.

But one element stands out—the sharing and the giving.

You give of yourself. As you give to others, you receive back strength and hope and spirit from them. It is no place for a man or woman who is hiding from themselves. In fact, I don't believe a human being has been born who can play a charade or mask his true self with the members of his AA group. Before AA, I say, the alcoholic bends his elbow. With the help of AA the alcoholic bends his knee.

And oh, the love that pours forth from an AA group! I have seen hard men of the beady eye and concrete conscience come away from their first AA meeting with tears in their eyes. I have seen life-long liars pour out the bitterness and hostility and anger of their systems before their AA group, laying bare their innermost secrets.

There is nothing like this Society of Salvation. The only profits reaped are the dividends of saving man from himself. It is an order of change so profound that founder Bill Wilson once said, "A blinding light shown in my dark room to lead me to help—and to inspire me to help others."

Another member told me, "I see miracles performed before me in my AA meeting every night; people being saved through love—not criticism or castigation. It is the work of a Master Creator."

Getting back to the sharing and massive exchange of love, I recall the story of the little boy looking at the Grand Canyon. He pulled away from his mother and raced to the edge. She called for him to return. Angered, he shouted, "I hate you, mother! I hate you, mother!" The vast echos of the Canyon returned his words of anger a hundredfold. Frightened, he began to cry and retreat to his mother's waiting arms.

"What does it mean?" the bewildered child asked. His mother led him to the canyon's edge once more, this time holding his hand. She wiped his tears and bade him shout out, "I love you, mother! I love you, mother!" And the canyon's echos answered him in loud booming richochets of sound, "I love you, mother! I love you, mother!"

Again, perplexed and frightened, the little boy repeated his question. "What does it mean, mother?"

She answered: "It just means, little son, that whatever you give out in this life returns manyfold. If you give out hate, you receive hate manyfold. And if you give out love, it comes back a hundredfold."

That's the way it is with AA. If an alcoholic gives out his love, shares himself with 20 other members, his love is returned twentyfold.

Nobody asks anything in AA but hopes the alcoholic will be honest with himself and with the group.

The burden of an alcoholic's recovering is shared by many. I haven't met many recovering alcoholics who could find sobriety without their AA group. Bill Wilson and Dr. Bob Smith may have founded the amazing organization. But I'm sure a Superior Being had a mighty hand in it.

Examples:

Ross, a big game hunter, a man about town, the very essence of the hard-drinking sportsman, was leery about joining AA. "Weak men leaning on each other—like little old ladies in a sewing circle," he once said.

After his rehabilitation program, he joined a group in his neighborhood. He was amazed. There was Tom, the rugged filling station operator. There was Bill, the best damn bowler on the South Side. There was Pat, his own accountant—the guy with the trigger-quick mind. There was Neil who used to be a football star in their college days. And there was Sam. God! Sam was the president of one of the top banks in the city.

The obvious point Ross couldn't digest was that so many of what he thought would be weaklings were in reality the strongest men in town—people he admired; forward, successful in business, and certainly not pipsqueaks. That's AA. The weakest person is strong enough to be there—for it takes the lion's courage I spoke of to walk into a club based on helping diseased people. It takes grit and determination to say to others, "I have a terrible weakness—I can't recover without your help."

After you have made that declaration you wind up in a family which is yours through thick and thin, through hazards, setbacks, disappointments, problems of all types. And should you fail, they are there to pick you up. No debt owed.

The weakest of the group is stronger than most of the citizens you meet on the street. And all of them grow stronger with each meeting.

* * *

I called him Jumpy Jack because he always had a problem—even after recovery. For a long spell he wouldn't attend AA meetings, afraid of even making his problem public to a handful. Finally, his wife ordered him to "join AA or get out of the house." He did and the change was spectacular. Jack was a person beset by emotional turmoil over just about every facet of living—and don't blame it all just on drinks. He was jumpier than an outhouse squirrel even in his non-alcoholic days. But when he went to the Sunday AA meeting, he found out everyone had problems.

The group thrashed them out when a member was up tight. So Jumpy Jack joined a Wednesday night group and a Friday night group. "Geeze, I couldn't believe it. By going three hours a week I found out everyone has problems. AA was a release. We talked about our fears, our hopes, our disease—everything. I never relaxed and got out so much garbage from my system in my life. I couldn't live without AA. And my wife couldn't live with me if I didn't have AA. It's more than an organization. It's a way of life."

* * *

And Millie was so fearful somebody would know she was an alcoholic she went into virtual hibernation, until she joined AA. The group was more than a confessional of hopes, dreams, fears, and guilts. It became a wondrous social outlet for her. She met other women and men with whom she had so much in common through the illness that they became fast friends outside the meeting room.

They went hiking, sailing, playing golf together. Through one of the members she met a non-alcoholic young man who became her husband. She never misses a meeting and the members are still her closest companions and leisure pals.

Remember, AA is not some somber, secretive group with weird inclinations and composed of brooding, dark faces. There is little self-pity. Only fresh hope.

It is full of laughs and joy. Imagine if you can a group where the lives of all members have just been saved from death. There is nothing stark or fearful here. A perpetual elation; a soaring of spirits prevails.

And the fact that AA is a non-profit organization; that its members are pledged to help others in all types of duress, makes it so appealing.

The members come from all walks of life. All religions, creeds, political parties are represented. Nobody is too big or too small. There is absolutely no social spheres or plateaus. It is a beautiful, communal body of bright, hopeful, resourceful—and don't forget—courageous people.

There is no charge to join. Its arms are extended 24 hours a day, 365 days a year. A recovering alcoholic would be foolish to try to keep his sobriety without partaking of such a powerful guideline of human gifts.

As one lady said to me, "I've always wanted to talk 'off the record' to my doctor, attorney, minister, car salesman, and real estate agent. Can you imagine one of each belonging to my AA group? It's an unbelievable experience."

Best of all, it's almost universal. Wherever you travel, whenever you are in need, you can find AA. Its huge task force always has someone on the alert, be it just a voice for friendly telephone conversation or the dire need for hospitalization or emergency home care. AA is always there—loving, giving; asking only that you share.

It has been said that if a recovering alcoholic misses one AA meeting he has a problem. If he misses two, he is in danger. If he misses three, the group better look for him in a hospital or jail. I don't put it that strongly. But I know this: AA members who go to meetings consistently build up a reservoir of strength and determination. They gain a perspective so healthy in its appraisal of the world's fortunes, that its members become among the more confident and productive in society.

A little boy once asked his dad what he did at his AA meeting every week.

His dad had a beautiful answer: "I share my life with my friends and my God." It's really that simple.

VIEWPOINT

Alcoholics Anonymous is a source of strength for so many because it is a God-centered and man-involved program. I like to call it the Father of Sobriety. It is a beautifully orientated program which combines self-discipline with constant repetition, which is really the mother of education. It is a program where the lonely and the lost become involved with mutual sufferers of the disease, banding together in a mutual recovery plan in which sharing is the most vital aspect.

It has been said that miracles occur regularly in the AA program. Nobody who has been a part of the program will deny that statement—and today over four million recovering alcoholics around the world adhere to its principles to maintain their health.

The 12 steps combine the fruits of self-knowledge. They inspire one with will power, self-discipline, and motivation. They make one look at himself as he really is—the mirror of one's soul and heart. They implore one to carry the message of love and sharing to others and to make amends to those they have injured. They ask one to ask God for strength to accomplish their mission to be honest with themselves and neighbors.

In essence, the AA creed asks one to love himself, love his companions, and love his God. Actually, what more is there to the code of life?

In the end one comes up with a true responsibility to himself.

I have said that the program contains enough worth and depth to become almost a religion. It does.

I also have said that a person need not be an alcoholic to gain tremendous input from its concepts. That is true. I know ministers and priests who preach its contents from the pulpit in some form every Sunday.

A young man told me: "When they said I couldn't drink again in my life, I could hardly live with myself. I thought of suicide. When I got to know my AA group, I got on my knees and believe it or not, thanked God I was an alcoholic!"

A young woman said: "I hated the world and myself before AA. Today, I feel so secure. I have found new friends and a new life. Mostly, I have found myself. And what I have found is not all that bad. In fact, I have learned to love myself, in a good way."

An old grandmother: "I may only have a few years left, but thank the Lord for AA. Because of it I will accept my fate, knowing I have found true friends and a wonderful way of life. God, how I wished I knew AA 50 years ago."

Below are the official AA versions of the Twelve Steps. Next, my capsule interpretation. It is not necessary that all recovering alcoholics interpret the steps the same. Many may have trouble understanding or feeling comfortable with some steps. This is where the discipline comes in. The steps only become functionally easy from practice, study and soul searching.

None are so difficult but that when the recovering alcoholic says, "I think I've got the disease whipped today," he knows he has immersed himself in each step; a formula so simple and yet so beautifully thorough it defies contradiction or criticism by alcoholics or non-alcoholics.

THE TWELVE STEPS:

Official Version	In 3 Little Words
1. We admitted we were powerless over alcohol — that our lives had become unmanageable.	1. Loss of Freedom
2. Came to believe that a Power greater than ourselves could restore us to sanity.	2. Booze a Problem
3. Made a decision to turn our will and our lives over to the care of God *as we understood Him.*	3. Need Others Help

297

4. Made a searching and fearless moral inventory of ourselves.	4. Know Myself Better
5. Admitted to God, to ourselves, and to another human being the exact nature of our wrongs.	5. Share with Others
6. We're entirely ready to have God remove all these defects of character.	6. Adult or Childlike
7. Humbly asked Him to remove our shortcomings.	7. Please Help Me
8. Made a list of all persons we had harmed, and became willing to make amends to them all.	8. Make My List
9. Made direct amends to such people wherever possible, except when to do so would injure them or others.	9. Pay Back Others
10. Continued to take personal inventory and when we were wrong promptly admitted it.	10. Where Am I?

11. Sought through prayer and meditation to improve our conscious contact with God *as we understood Him,* praying only for knowledge of His will for us and the power to carry that out.

11. On My Knees

12. Having had a spiritual awakening as the result of these Steps, we tried to carry this message to alcoholics, and to practice these principles in all our affairs.

12. Freedom to Function

QUESTION:
ARE ALL AA GROUPS THE SAME—OR SHOULD THE ALCOHOLIC SHOP AROUND?

SELVIG:

Shop around, by all means. Every AA group has its own personality, and they are as diverse as human nature. There are no bad AA groups. But there are AA clubs that are better than others for particular people.

By that I mean, in some areas, they will be made up of older people—mainly senior citizens. In downtown areas you will find more unemployed, unkept, uneducated, transient members. In college towns, you'll find more intellectuals. They cut a swath through Americana, but the area in which they are established still reflects itself on the group.

In some groups, women will feel out of place. In others, the women may predominate. I advise any new member to attend at least four or five different groups. By then I'm sure he will find a particular group which makes him feel most comfortable.

Some groups stress the basic steps, rework them, and stress repetition—almost like a litany. Others stress the moral aspects and some groups the intellectual. Some resemble sharing groups. Some offer more advice.

Some groups are run strictly by procedure. Some integrate new members quickly into the routine. Others let the newcomer observe for several meetings. Some will aim the entire meeting at the newcomer.

Like I say, no two AA groups are alike. But each of them radiates strength. You could gain a great measure from any one of them. The point is: you'll learn more and gain more from the one in which you are most comfortable. Shop around. They all understand. However, don't shop too long or you will end up with no "home" group and no group will get to know the real you, which is so important. It's nice to have a relationship with people who know you as you are and where you feel good about hanging your cap on the clothes rack with freedom.

Examples:

Pete was having an awful time. "I just don't feel at home with some of the clubs. In one they are all do-it-yourself guys who spend a lot of time going over their old drinking escapades and telling how they stopped—20 or 30 years ago. I'm from a rehab center and I just feel uptight in there. I don't think they respect me that much because I didn't do it on my own."

I told him he might have a case. But I also told him he could learn from these older, weather-beaten veterans. I told Pete I'm sure they didn't look down on him as much as he represented a new breed and they were curious.

Pete tried a couple of other groups but drifted back to what he called "my tough old guys." After a few meetings another young rehab graduate showed up, lending strength to Pete. Together they became good friends with the old members, who began asking about their experiences in the hospital.

They knew they were "in" the night the 70-year-old chairman said, "Well, maybe that hospital stuff isn't so bad. I might have wrung out a lot sooner if I had the 'treatment.' " The idea is not to be too blatant or smug about your views. All of these people reach the clubs by a variety of experiences and tribulations. Never try one club, decide you don't like the people, and quit the program. There are AA groups for all kinds of personalities. I know a South Dakota man who drives 40 miles across frozen prairies to attend meetings with the group of his choice.

* * *

I smile when I think of Roger. He shopped around about 800 miles over two-lane roads in Montana to find a meeting he felt "good in." He found his group 83 miles from his home! I told him he was crazy to risk driving over icy roads in the winter that far. His answer was enlightening: "I look forward to the drive—the things I want to bring up. And I look forward to the drive back—rehashing what I heard. Those four hours a week are a real treat. My wife goes along, and meets with the Al-Anon wives. We have great talks going and coming. It's a treat. I'd drive 300 miles a week to find the right AA club."

If it's that important to a member, I decided then and there never again to second-guess a person's inclination to look around for that one particular group in which he feels secure and relaxed.

* * *

There's the case of Louis, a janitor of little education. He complained to me that there were so many intellectuals in his AA group that he hated to open his mouth.

"It never comes out right," he admitted sadly. I told

301

him to look around. Next time I saw him he was beaming. "I found a group, Dick, that's just my kind. All ordinary guys—guys who ain't afraid to talk loud and make some mistakes with the words, yuh know?" Yes, I knew.

* * *

There is a rare problem with some groups which spend more time in helping drunks survive than in preventive work. I attended one of their meetings and all I heard for half the program was this: "Give me a report on Phil, will you Stan? I understand he's back in the tank."

And Stan would tell about the circumstances in minute detail. Then George would report on taking Edward to the care center. And Art would report on picking up Arnie—and the fight he had getting into the car. It was like listening to a police report.

"Where's Nick tonight?" And the answer: "He's slipped again. He got into a brawl in the poolhall and three of us hauled him out." Now these were dedicated good friends. But I had the feeling they were running an emergency drunk service. I got the feeling that they used their camaraderie to assure each other that if they fell off the wagon, somebody certainly would be there to help them back on.

By and large, AA groups are imaginative, creative, spontaneous, and much more interested in helping the sober than picking up the bones in the gutter. Don't get me wrong. They are there to help and will come at all hours of the night. They'll answer phones anytime. They will rush to the aid of a stranger through blizzards or sandstorms.

But the work they do over the table or across the carpet in the quiet atmosphere of a weekly meeting is where the power of the organization really lies. Many groups can put a man back on his feet. But it's AA which knows how to keep him there.

In one particular group I noted that a doctor and a lawyer seemed to vie for attention and try and command the meeting. They were wonderfully enlightened people. But they simply were two very strong persons who had a tendency to be preachy and use a vocabulary which left many of the others puzzled. Eventually the doctor moved to another group. I noted a marked improvement in the original meetings. The lawyer didn't seem to be seeking attention once the other highly skilled professional was gone.

Another point. I've had wives in Al-Anon groups complain that their meetings either lagged or lacked spark or that too many wives smoked. Again, I suggest there is an Al-Anon group for the individual. The wives do not need to go with the husbands to the same meetings and vice versa. This is an extremely personal issue. Go where you feel completely at ease.

But never shop until the choice becomes a problem. All groups have strong points. One very happy, recovering alcoholic of my acquaintance moves among various groups, never staying more than six months. "It's refreshing. I find each group has a powerful message."

Remember, that wherever you go, the AA members share deep love. No one is ever left out or humiliated or snubbed. It is the way of life in AA: love, share, never frown on any member. But, like people, every group has a diverse nature. That's perhaps why it is so healthy and effective.

Every group has its own personality—and they are as diverse as human nature. There are no bad groups. But there are AA clubs that are better than others for particular people.

QUESTION:
CAN AN ALCOHOLIC RECOVER
WITHOUT AA?

SELVIG:

Let me ask a question. Do you think a pet dog can stay healthy without a master? The dog will grow lonely, uncared for, unkept, unloved—and probably bitter. I think that tells the story of AA and the recovering alcoholic. It is possible to accomplish almost anything, including sobriety and recovery, without AA—but highly improbable.

I've heard many old-timers say they did it all by themselves. But the man who says that is usually an unhappy, dry alcoholic, inwardly angry with himself, and doesn't really know how to share his feelings with others.

They may have quit drinking but the disease lurks in the shadows, ready to regain control of them again. Remember—the disease of alcoholism may be controlled in a period of treatment, but it can strike back at the very soul of the alcoholic in a matter of minutes.

The alcoholic is only that one drink away from a repeat attack. But what good does it do an alcoholic to help himself if he isn't happy? He may just as well continue his alcoholic drinking.

The AA is a group of friends—more than anything else. They are there to share your feelings, share you problems, share you destinies. The alcoholic who is trying to recover and doesn't accept this open, warm embrace of human compassion and genuine interest is troubled far more deeply with inner guilt than with anything alcoholism has brought on. He needs psychiatric treatment.

Alcoholics Anonymous is a wonderful tool to not only help recovery but to give the alcoholic self-worth, sustain his confidence, and hone his mind. It offers everything and accepts no payment in return—except your sobriety. It is there that you might enjoy an actual, tangible lifeline. Any alcoholic who turns his back on AA is bordering on the insane thinking which was brought on by his drinking in the first place. You cannot be a completely fulfilled, recovering alcoholic without human help. And AA supplies the very best human aid. I see and sense the strong attending AA, and the weak quit or don't affiliate at all. It takes effort to continue anything. Those who attend not only go for themselves and their own sobriety but to also aid in keeping the AA group alive.

Examples:

Russ was a tough old railroad man who told me, "I quit drinking at 37—when our second son was born. The truth is, I haven't had a happy day since."

I couldn't believe my ears, so I made a study of Russ. Sure enough, he knew nothing nor cared anything for AA. When I suggested he look up a group, he stormed back. "I don't need to listen to a bunch of old drunks like myself give themselves pep talks. I quit. I made the decision. Happy or not, that's all there is to it."

But that wasn't all. Russ's wife confided to me that she had been miserable for well over a decade. "He has no humor. He doesn't know how to have fun or laugh. He can't share anything. He seems to blame the world that he can't drink anymore."

That is the problem with most recovering alcoholics who don't use the gift of AA; they blame the world for their disease. Instead of sharing their good fortune of sobriety and setting an example for other alcoholics, they turn sour on mankind at large. Russ thought he did his family a wondrous favor by going dry. But by not following up with AA he did nobody a favor.

As his wife says, "At least when he drank I could laugh at his antics now and then. Now there is nothing to laugh at. Just glumness and bitterness." A very real tragedy.

* * *

305

Talented Jim is a cartoonist who seemed reasonably well adjusted without AA. He told me, "I have other alcoholic friends and we get in discussions. I really don't need the meetings. They seem to come at the wrong time and eat into my valuable working hours. I do a lot of drawing at home. I hate to break up my concentration with meetings."

I posed a different approach to Jim: "You know, it isn't so much, Jim, what you do for yourself at the meeting as much as what you do for others. A talented, intelligent man like yourself sets a fine example. Why not think of the others you help? Don't just think about yourself.

He gave it a steady whirl for six months and the next time I saw him he was elated. "God, what a great experience. These people do need me. They ask me for advice. They ask me to help their friends. It's the first time in my life I feel wanted and needed by others. It's a great experience.

"The few hours I spend are made up by the fact that I work so much better knowing a lot of people look up to me for advice and help."

See what I mean. AA is a fantastic two-way street. It supplies morale in so many areas.

* * *

A pretty young woman named Marie said she felt uncomfortable being the only feminine member in her group. She stayed away for six weeks, grew irritable, and came back. Gradually, she was made to feel comfortable and eventually became the center of many discussions when men became aware of the problems alcoholism caused their wives. Marie would be able to understand and counsel them from the woman's standpoint.

She told me later that "I found it was tremendous therapy. I was doing something useful. I felt more like a woman than I had in 20 years. Without AA I simply couldn't function. It's a great place to get rid of hangups. When you feel down, it's as soul-cleansing as a confessional. To think it's there and free to anyone who wants to use it!"

In fact, when another woman joined the group, Marie felt a little jealous as she would not be the only woman in the group any more. She talked openly about it and the two are now inseparable.

* * *

Arnie was another "I-did-it-myself" recovering alcoholic. He found himself arguing at AA meetings with younger men who had come out of rehab centers and hospitals.

"I'd go to the meeting feeling good and then get uptight at the newcomers bragging about their experiences in rehab programs. I guess maybe I was jealous of them. Anyway, I quit going to AA for two years. But not a damn thing seemed to go right. I couldn't find 'my kind' to talk with. Nobody really seemed to understand an alcoholic.

"I wasn't comfortable. I made up my mind to go back to AA and get along with the 'new' breed. I vowed to listen more and talk less. Now I've got a dozen guys for close pals, guys who came out of rehab programs. I find the alcoholic has a common sharing with all alcoholics. It's not how a guy got over the disease, it's how he handles himself now that counts."

That's AA. Helping us live our lives day by day. When you say the famed prayer, you realize what enormity it encompasses. *"God, grant me the serenity to accept the things I cannot change, the courage to change the things I can . . . and the wisdom to know the difference."*

It doesn't take an alcoholic long to realize that, if everyone lived by those guidelines, how much more pleasant the world would be.

The wondrous philosophy starts right in the AA group: "Grant me the serenity to accept the things I cannot change."

That means accepting gratefully all the different opinions and personalities involved in AA meetings.

QUESTION:
CAN YOU RECOVER FROM ALCOHOLISM WITHOUT GOING THROUGH A TREATMENT CENTER?

SELVIG:

Yes, but it is a much more difficult process and takes much longer. The alcoholic who has the privilege of going through a treatment center gains knowledge of the disease and the confidence to arrest it. But the average alcoholic who does not go through treatment may need as much as ten years to acquire this. Yes, treatment center programs today are vital, aware, and so far advanced that they can capsulate in a short period of time almost all the facets of healthy sobriety an alcoholic will need.

Oh, there are some practical experiences which must be gained only through daily living with the outside world. But the concentrated therapy of the treatment center today is amazing in its thoroughness and adaptability.

I see a vast difference between recovering alcoholics who went through treatment centers and those who try to do it on their own—or use just AA help. Like I've said many times previously, it is possible. The man or woman who goes through treatment learns much more about the disease and himself than the alcoholic who treats himself.

For one thing, many discover why they became alcoholics—why the disease sought them out. Few do-it-yourselfers can really explain the disease. One of the greatest advantages is that treatment centers bring in the families and expose them to all sides of the disease and its ramifications.

The wife learns how it began and why. The children learn that father is not some kind of ogre in human form.

The relatives and friends learn of the great handicaps that alcoholic has operated under. The alcoholic, too, comes out of treatment knowing that God didn't create any bums. He comes out of treatment knowing why he drank, what alcohol did to him, how his personality was affected, and what he can expect in the future.

He learns hundreds of things which the do-it-yourselfer has to stumble onto—and experiment with. Out of every 10 treatment center patients I have been associated with, most are recovering beautifully. Out of every 10 do-it-yourselfers I've met, rarely have four of them made the grade. And of the four, only perhaps one is truly well oriented to sobriety.

I know that over the years there has been a stigma attached to treatment centers. There was a time when the alcoholic ward had a reputation akin to a mental sanitarium. That wasn't far off target, since the alcoholic is driven insane by alcohol, temporary as it may be.

Today, however, large business firms encourage alcoholic treatment. Many famous celebrities have made public their experience with centers.

A leading newspaper publisher told me, "I credit the treatment centers with saving my papers at least a dozen key editors, writers, and advertising people. They come out not only in fine physical and mental shape—but actually smarter and more creative employees. I almost wish all my employees could take a two-month stay in a treatment center."

That feeling prevails today from coast to coast. I have not met a business executive or plant owner in my travels who would not wholly endorse a treatment center for an alcoholic employee. The billions in man-hours the treatments centers have saved companies will never be known.

Examples:

A truculent fellow, Roger, hated the world. He tried to conquer his illness alone for seven years—with numerous slips. His biggest problem: getting to understand how alcohol changes the mind and personality. His family was embarrassed by him and preferred to pretend he didn't exist.

It wasn't until an AA member urged treatment that Roger grew to understand himself and his relations with others. "It really wasn't until my wife and three daughters spent two weeks with me in treatment in family therapy that I really began to understand the disease," Roger admits. The treatment center today is helping the family as well as the patient.

* * *

The doctor's wife, Lucille, was ashamed of her disease. So much so that even though her physician husband urged treatment, she fought it for years. It wasn't until we had worked with her for three weeks in treatment that she confided, "I was always a leader in class projects in school—always in the forefront. As a doctor's wife, I was shoved to the background, raising children. It wasn't until I came to treatment and studied myself thoroughly and listened to others that I understood what prompted me to try alcohol to feel better.

"Through treatment I also found how to cope with my situation. Now I plan to get back in the whirl of the world and become 'me' again. I found out in treatment my family wants me to take a useful role again now that they are grown. I needed treatment to give me some backbone."

I am not saying all treatment centers are for all people. Like AA groups, there are some that are better than others. But I do say that the family involvement is a very important aspect of the recovery program. If the person has no family, the involvement of other people will suffice.

The treatment center today is one of countless designs. It bolsters ego. It knocks down pride. It builds up courage. It destroys the walls of secrecy. It supplies inspiration. But it makes a point that perspiration is involved.

You work to arrest the disease. The treatment center

gives the alcoholic a chance to study others. Invariably he finds a patient with the same kind of psychological and physical makeup he has. He learns to associate. Going back into the world of sobriety is not easy. I am thoroughly convinced the top treatment centers do a magnificent job of cushioning and conditioning the alcoholic to again become a useful citizen. And the beautiful thing is that rarely today is there a stigma attached to the treatment. Virtually all major insurance policies cover the care.

There is no reason to float helplessly in the sea of alcohol today with so much expert help nearby. The alcoholic who turns his back on a treatment center today is doing a gross injustice to himself and to his family. He is risking his life every day he stays out of treatment.

"I found out from the treatment center that I was no freak—that there were athletes, clergy, professional men all fighting the disease. My wife found out I wasn't a damn gorilla, a natural wife-beater, or a chaser. I was, after all, a sick man—who wanted desperately to get well. And I did."

A woman counselor one time described the value of a treatment center thus: "It is a home. Nobody looks down on you. You're accepted completely—with pimples or warts. And no real home has any more love and understanding. In fact, the understanding in the treatment center goes far beyond what you find in most homes."

A treatment center is where the void created by alcohol is filled by self-respect.

VIEWPOINT

One of the most misdirected statements I have heard out of alcoholic support groups for the spouses and relatives of the diseased is that they do themselves a favor by becoming detached from the sick person. This is not only physically impossible while living with the alcoholic, but also psychologically impossible when you have a loved one on the mind. It is similar to my friend, the ostrich, with his head in the sand. When he comes out of the sand nothing has changed except that he has sand in his eyes as well as the problems he attempted to hide from. Certainly he has avoided a confrontation for the moment but the danger lurks there over his shoulder.

Also, I will never adhere to the premise that the spouse of an alcoholic is as sick as the diseased one. Nobody can be as downcast, empty, alone, weary, tired of being tired, and as mentally whipped as the alcoholic. He is the victim we must concentrate on. The spouse may be harassed and tormented and physically abused—but not insane.

That is the vital difference—insanity of the alcoholic. The spouse of the alcoholic usually maintains a measure of common sense and judgment. They may be strained and she may be at times near a nervous breakdown. But she retains her sanity which the alcoholic has given up.

Thank God for the majority of treatment centers which have instituted a strong family program to go along with the treatment of the alcoholic. A variety of problems can be mended in a short time. Getting the family members together in treatment does a tremendous amount to sweep away strained relations and the anger and hurt which has built up over the years. Consider these salient points:

(1) Family members are shown that they are not the cause of the alcoholism; the bottle is;

(2) The alcoholic needs to know what chaos he brought to his family during his drunken hours to be made fully aware of how important his sobriety is to them—and they, by their presence, to prove their loyalty to him over the years;

(3) Everybody gets involved in the discussions and the "freedom to function" ability becomes the prime part of the recovery, clearing the air of such important facets as separations, the possibility of divorce, and the future acceptance of the alcoholic are brought out in the open;

(4) Family teamwork provides a sense of gratification second to none, in that they are all working toward a simi-

lar goal and sense the importance of every member's contribution;

(5) Everyone is willing to provide support for the alcoholic, a testimony to the fact that there will be little resentment and the chances of complete openness for his indiscretions are excellent;

(6) The family learns that no matter how shabbily they were treated by the alcoholic, he actually feels worse about his disease than they do and is trying to make amends and restitution.

Humility is a word that must have been coined to describe the alcoholic in his early days of recovery. That doesn't mean humiliation as so many feel it does, but instead an "honest appraisal of things."

Thank God for the majority of treatment centers which have instituted a strong family program to go along with the treatment of the alcoholic.

QUESTION:
WHY DO SO MANY RECOVERING ALCOHOLICS BEGIN PREACHING OR RUSH INTO COUNSELING?

SELVIG:

Simple. They are so elated with their sobriety they can't help but want to share it with others.

I admit some are ostentatious crusaders who can become bores. And I've seen a few work too zealously and actually turn off for the time being some other alcoholics who need help. They forget too readily that the

313

alcoholic must feel a part of a decision to get well. But I don't knock the "preachers" and counselors. I'd rather have them out sharing their hopes and new life publicly than living as drunks.

What I tell most zealous newcomers to the roles of sobriety is this:

"Don't push your joys down somebody's throat. Just act natural. Your happiness and light will serve as the best example." On the other hand, many of the patients have become brilliant counselors and leaders in the field. As I've said many times, it often takes an alcoholic to know one. For these, my gratitude. The citizenry is in their debt.

An inexperienced crusader faces one difficult barrier: he must understand that his own conversion to sobriety was difficult and time-consuming. There are no short-cuts. He invariable believes he can hurry up the next man's sobriety. He has trouble understanding that no-body can help the alcoholic finally until he is ready to help himself somewhat, coerced or not.

The "crusaders" as I call them, should busy themselves displaying how happy they are with recovery. They can preach more sense by working their recovery than they can by getting on the podium. The recovering alcoholic's inner glow shows through. His quick smile, his ability to adapt to each day makes him the perfect example to other alcoholics who see the dark side of every day's action and want to change that look with the high feeling.

"Just be yourself. Every day you stay sober, you are preaching in your own way," I tell recovering alcoholics who can hardly wait to rush out and save the world. But don't discount that zeal. From this group come the counselors and the family experts who will help save millions of lives over the years.

Examples:

Angie was a 38-year-old alcoholic, part-time whore and cursed like a field hand. My first thought when I saw her was, "The odds have got to be 100 to 1 against this gal's recovery."

And she had a difficult time with recovery, falling flat on her face in four recovery institutions and discarding her third husband along the way. None of us actually held out much hope.

Today, seven years after her last treatment, she is one of the most respected counselors in the West. She still swears readily. She appears as hard as a tombstone. But because she has been there, she has a remarkable feel for all types of alcoholics. She can be insulting, humorous, compassionate or angry, depending on what her people need. I admire her as much as any woman I have ever met. She is an inspiration.

* * *

The tough little ex-fighter wanted to reform the world when he got out of treatment. He would preach in saloons, at parties, in the filling station—anywhere he thought a drunk might hear. But he was so pushy and so authoritative he repulsed any would-be-decision-maker. He literally frightened those he set out to help.

I finally told him, "Blackie, just live your life. Don't be uptight. It took you years to quit. People just resent you beating on their ears. Your people will see that you're happy and enthusiastic—that's what will do it."

He got the message. He told me later, "I didn't realize I was getting shovy. I just wanted everyone to know how great it was to be sober. I forgot it takes a little time to make that decision." Unfortunately, Blackie, too much time in too many cases.

But before you ridicule or castigate the preacher-type of recovering alcoholic, consider what makes him that way. For years he has lived in trouble of his own making. The bottle blotted out the true world. He forgot about birds, skies, the wind on his face—the comaraderie of loved ones.

Suddenly, he opens up the package and here it all is!

It's like a little boy in his first candy store or bonbon factory. He can't believe so many goodies exist.

So it is with the recovering alcoholic. He sees a bright new world. It's a vision of beauty. He wants to run into the first saloon and drag out the inebriates and shout, "Look here! Look what I've found! See the world—see its wonders!"

It's a natural instinct to want to rush to other alcoholics with the good tidings. He must learn to be patient with these people. The crusader is trying to share—sometimes with overzealousness, sometimes with too much zest. His heart is in the right place. His mouth may not be.

* * *

I like best what a reasonable alcoholic told me in his good mood:

"I decided to come in for treatment for one reason—my best pal Clem seemed to be happy and content all of a sudden. He didn't say anything to me. Just smiled. I could feel something had happened to him. I wanted that to happen to me."

The inner glow of the recovering alcoholic. It is there as surely as if a mining light were attached to his hat. I tell the recovering alcoholic: "Be yourself. Just being you will be enough."

The "crusaders" as I call them should busy themselves displaying how happy they are with recovery. They can preach more sense by working their recovery than they can by getting on the podium. The recovering alcoholic's inner glow shows through.

On the matter of counseling for recovering alcoholics, I stipulate a two-year period I call a time of "grace and learning." I don't believe a person out of treatment can share real recovery to the extent of teaching it until the recovering alcoholic gains healthy self-respect for himself. Then he must experience the support of others. In general, I believe it takes at least 24 months for the recovering alcoholic to reach a level where he completely understands his disease, is completely dedicated to carrying the message to others and feels so secure within himself he impales himself on no psychological or emotional barriers mingling with other drinking alcoholics.

I say this because I know of a very dedicated alcoholic who took on the task of counseling before she was completely sold on her own sobriety and the other alcoholics became a threat to her sobriety. She returned for more treatment and then worked as a secretary for two years. The next time she was ready to counsel and made a tremendous success of it.

Within two years, the recovering alcoholic who wants to counsel should experience more freedom to function without outside activities that involve alcoholics and non-alcoholics alike, including church, home and AA groups. Also, it is generally accepted by psychiatrists and other experts in the alcoholic field that it takes two years for the nervous and physical systems of the recovering alcoholic to return completely to normal.

I think a beautiful thought on this is supplied by an old country doctor who long ago delved into the alcoholic's situation: "Until the recovering alcoholic takes his Greater Power more seriously than he does himself; he should not attempt to preach the sermon of sobriety." Again, in most recovered alcoholics, they have a good grasp of their God-sharing in two years.

Patience is a virtue most difficult for the recovering alcoholic.

The joys of early recovery are perhaps never to be matched. But premature exposure to harsh reality as counseling is can do more damage to the recovering alcoholic and those he counsels than no counseling at all. If the potential to share and help other alcoholics professionally is there, it will come to the fore in two years.

The recovering alcoholic who becomes a counselor can meet with some difficulty, often of his own making. Instead of sharing with other people in the field, he too often takes the "I know it all because I've been there" philosophy. When put in the corner of a professional discussion, he too often lashes back with the standard oldie, "Well, you're not an alcoholic, so how would you know?"

The alcoholic who becomes a counselor has so much to offer. But he must understand that life is an experience to be lived and not a problem to be solved. He must learn to work with medical doctors, psychiatrists, and all the people fighting the disease. It must be a unified team.

I recommend to most recovering alcoholics who are thinking about becoming counselors that they study themselves and consider the counseling position for at least two years of continued sobriety before making a decision. Most recovering alcoholics I have known who became counselors have made outstanding contributions in the field. Some were not ready. Others were never qualified to work with people; proving again that there is no such thing as a preordained recovering alcoholic personality. Alcoholics come in as many types as there are pebbles on the beach.

I like the basic requirements my friend, Dr. Harry Tiebout (first psychiatrist who became enthused about the philosophy of Alcoholics Anonymous) had for those counseling alcoholics:

1. Be firm but not over-bearing

2. Be kind but not soft.

3. Intervention, not on the manifestation of hostility, but on the message from reality.

My advice to those recovering alcoholics who want to

carry the word of joy to other sufferers of the disease: take your time. Make sure of yourself. There always will be alcoholics to help.

**An old country doctor: "Until
the recovering alcoholic takes
his Greater Power more
seriously than he does himself, he
should not attempt to preach
the sermon of sobriety."**

QUESTION:
WHAT DO YOU TELL THE RECOVERING ALCOHOLIC WHO SAYS, "I WAS HAPPIER DRINKING"?

SELVIG:

You tell him he's a damn fool and only kidding himself. Ask him:

"Do you owe everybody in town today?" . . . "Do you still beat up your wife on Saturday nights?" . . . "Do you get fired every six months?" . . . "Do you frighten your children half to death?" . . . "Do you come home with your car's front end smashed in and can't remember how it happened?"

These are just some of the questions you ask the recovering alcoholic who claims he was better off nursing the bottle.

There is only one reason the man or woman will say that she was better drinking: to claim sympathy. They want the loved ones near them to appreciate the ordeal they may be going through—to admire their courage. It's strictly a play on sympathy, a plea for some compassion.

When the husband says, "I was better off drinking," the wife, according to his script, should respond: "Oh, darling, please don't go back to that! I know what a grind it is. We'll all try to help—only please don't threaten to drink again. We couldn't bear it."

Now the hubby knows that he's still the center of the family universe. He again carries a club. It is his old selfish thinking. He is No. 1. He is everything. The world must bow to him.

As I said previously, meet him head on with plain facts, plain questions and you might add:

"Look at yourself in the mirror if you think you were better off drinking. Today you're a man."

That gives him his little hypo of praise and at the same time puts the burden back on him. If he wants to trade what he's accomplished through sobriety, if he wants to trade his health today for the terminal illness of yesterday, then he isn't on the team, but in deep pain and anguish.

I recall the newspaper man who said when somebody asked him if he ever thought about drinking since he had begun recovery:

"Think about it? Let's see. When I get up in the morning the sun looks brighter, the air feels fresher, the laughter of the children is more refreshing. My co-workers look more friendly, my boss more understanding. My family treats me better and the whole world looks rosy. Do I think about drinking? Well, yes, on occasion, but less and less as my sobriety mounts."

The same man added: "You see some recovering alcoholics like me will always yearn a little bit, thinking of these 'good' feelings. But that is only if we can blot out the hardships and sorrow the drinking brought. Actually, it is probably quite normal to think about drinking. But it would be pretty damn abnormal to ever start."

Nobody can say how often or how many alcoholics think about liquor or what it might be like to drink again. That's why I so greatly admire the discipline of the recovering alcoholic. He is a man's man, or if you will—a woman's woman. Subconsciously there may always be that little lingering pang of what it might be to drink alcohol again. But given a moment to pause and appraise his current health, the recovering alcoholic will invariably recall with distaste the turmoils of the past.

I know of a recovering alcoholic who is so turned off by his addiction that at a party recently he picked up his wife's drink by mistake. It had no more than touched his lips when he spat it out on the floor. "It was an instinctive, natural reaction. I might think about a drink—but, thank God, I couldn't get it past my lips."

I think of the radio announcer who one day came to me, occupied with the dark thought that his friends now considered him a loner because he didn't associate with them in bars anymore. I asked him if he thought he was a "loner." With a little prodding, I found out he had made more friendships in Alcoholics Anonymous than he ever had in his alcoholic days. He went to more places with his wife than ever before. He was invited to more parties. We both concluded the only people who might consider him a "loner" were the few barmates who still wasted their lives on the stools. He was having more enjoyment out of life and sharing with more people now than he ever dreamed of in his alcoholic days.

Examples:

Gruff, obstreperous Harold used to make the family spin with his drinking bouts. He had trouble getting so much attention now that he was sober. That was, in part, due to the family's carefully conceived plan that it was better to let Harold set his own pace, without crowding him.

When, after a bad day at the factory, he came home and announced that "everything was better when I was drinking," his wife looked him in the eye and said quietly: "Harold, you know that isn't right. Six months ago today you were sick with a hangover and vowed never to work again. We've got a new car now and you got a raise. Why would you talk like that?"

It sounded so silly coming to him so directly, he

321

grinned. "I guess I was talking like an idiot." It was the last time he mentioned his threat.

* * *

A threat. That's what some recovering alcoholics like to hold over the heads of friends and loved ones. Ernie used to tell his wife, "I'll go back to drinking any time the pressure of bills piles up." It was a threat aimed solely at his wife, trying to get her to keep the budget down.

One day, tiring of the threats, she bought the family a much-needed rug. She announced to Ernie, "I just spent $700 we had saved on a new rug. We'll need a couple of lamps, too. Just because you're sober is no reason we have to live like cave-dwellers. I've got confidence in you to make the payments. In fact, Ernie, I think you can do anything you set out to do."

She turned the tide with a beautiful game-breaker. He was at the same time stunned, surprised, amused and uplifted. The wife had made shambles of his threats, while complimenting him at the same time. That's real diplomacy.

* * *

There was Darlene who used to threaten her husband that she would go back to the bottle if he didn't hire household help. She got a maid. Then she wanted a new car. She got that. One day, her hubby realized he was playing into her hands. It was no good to have a sober wife if the family went down the drain financially.

He took her out for the evening and leveled. "Darlene, since you've quit drinking you're prettier, younger looking, more fun to be with. But I've got news for you: if a sober Darlene means we've got to go bankrupt, you can go right back to the bottle. If you don't think enough of your own health, rather than trying to make a wreck out of me, I can't help you any longer. Your sobriety is what you earned the hard way. Throw it away if you like."

She got the message. A week later she went to work three days a week at a nursery school and loved her new

322

life. She really had become bored. It wasn't the alcohol she craved—just a reason for spouting off.

* * *

Selfishness is difficult to worm out of the system, as it's part of human nature. Selfishness is one of the key menaces to sobriety. And selfishness is what the threat to "drink again" is all about, "taking care of my own needs at the expense of others if necessary."

The alcoholic is looking for sympathy and attention. Those threatened must be firm. They cannot be badgered. They have paid the penalty already. No need to pay the piper again.

Carl's wife called me up and asked, "What should I do? Carl, who has 20 years of sobriety, told me to get his slippers or he would get drunk." I told her to tell him: "Go ahead and get drunk." I ran into Carl a month later and he smilingly said, "You son of a bitch. She called my bluff."

There is only one reason the man or woman will say that she was better drinking: to claim sympathy. They want the loved ones near them to appreciate the ordeal they may be going through—to admire their courage. It's strictly a play on sympathy, a plea for some compassion.

QUESTION:
IS THE SEX LIFE OF RECOVERING ALCOHOLICS ANY BETTER?

SELVIG:

Compared to what? Frankly, usually it's improved by 100 percent. It is the idiot who thinks he or she is a better lover under the influence of alcohol. The vitality, the potency is sapped. The ability to perform, as it is in any action, is reduced by the reaction to the liquor.

The recovering alcoholic should be more patient, warm, tender, responsive, and sharing. It has to be. There is no other way. It's like the golfer thinking he was better with a few martinis. His reactions, timing and sense had been altered.

Take away sense, timing, response, reaction in the love act and you are left threadbare. The recovering alcoholics I have questioned admit to a livelier, healthier sex life.

The mind is keen now, which means the ability to share love experiences is sharper. The instincts are honed considerably. The sensitive erogenous zones are no longer dulled.

Alcoholism slows reaction in drivers, workers, athletes—and it naturally follows: lovers. The drunken woman who thinks she is sexy is repulsive. The drunken man who thinks he is a master is as foolish as he is opinionated on some subject he knows nothing about.

The most ridiculous appraisal an alcoholic can make is that he is a better lover when he's a little bit bashed —because he's more imaginative, relaxed, innovative. Bunk. He has to be clumsier and more selfish, as he is with all other dealings.

The recovering alcoholic who is not improved in his

sex life is suffering from other mental and physical problems relating to sex and may need to seek other professional assistance.

Examples:

"That good-looking Frenchman" they used to say of my friend Claude. "Betcha he gets all the women he wants." Claude was the Casanova of modern days. He never made a move toward his love symbol before having six or seven drinks. Then he was bold, aggressive, almost arrogantly repulsive. But his looks got him many bed partners.

It wasn't until I overheard one of his female companions describe Claude's love-making that I realized how foolish he actually was. "A butcher," is the way she described him. "He's got about as much left after drinking as a wet noodle. There's nothing behind those looks—but bad breath." I had to smile to myself. If the great lover only knew how he was turning them off instead of on!

* * *

A bosomy secretary told me she needed three or four drinks to "feel sexy." I suggested she might have more fun without the alcohol. "Oh, no, my husband and my boss both like me 'hot' with the liquor. It removes my inhibitions." It removed something. Her husband divorced her and the boss fired her, all within six months.

* * *

Then you have the husband who feels he is inadequate and has always feared sex. He has convinced himself that four or five cocktails give him the confidence he needs. His wife told me another story. "Jack is rough and crude. He goes from being sweet to an animal." So much for confidence.

* * *

A man wrote me a letter while in treatment confessing

that the reason he drank was because he felt sexually inadequate. "I can't get my penis up without drinking. Then my imagination goes to work and I can perform."

The truth, sexual experts will tell you, is just the opposite. The man who has been drinking will lack potency and vigor. He may think he's strong and hard. But he literally peters out in a hurry. The wife of the same man told me he collapsed in a stupor more often than completing the sex act after his drinking bouts.

The classical alcoholic lover likes to picture himself as dominating women sexually. It is one of his fantasies. He imagines sweeping them off their feet. Instead, he too often becomes a bumbling klutz. I do not know of a single case where an alcoholic, after drinking, was a better—or even adequate—sex partner. I do know of hundreds of complaints I've had from wives and husbands who contend their drinking sex partner is inadequate, awkward—simply unlovable. The smell of late night booze in close quarters is surpassed in stench only by the wretched fumes of a hangover mouth. Nothing could be less romantic.

Through the years, Hollywood and other media have portrayed the dashing, swashbuckling pirate or playboy as a hard-drinking, two-fisted fighter and lover. But get down to reality. The alcoholic who wants to change his feeling, then, must have an unnatural feeling, too, about sex. If he changes his personality in a matter of minutes, the same aggressiveness which he shows in his talk and actions in public is bound to carry over to his bed partner.

He has to be more selfish, more self-centered. Too often the male today sees himself as a hard-drinking, all-conquering lover. This stereotype portrait is something conjured up in the mind of a script writer seeking to substantiate the male's claim to dominance; or trying to titillate the male into believing there are lovely alcoholic minxes around, with fire in their veins, just waiting to be seduced.

The recovering alcoholics I
have questioned admit to a
livelier, healthier sex life.

QUESTION:
IS THE PRACTICING ALCOHOLIC
UNCOMFORTABLE IN THE COMPANY OF
RECOVERING ALCOHOLICS?

SELVIG:

Certainly. The drinking alcoholic has to be uncomfortable in the company of a recovering alcoholic, first because he fears him and what he represents. He fears him because he is threatened by the possibility that the recovering alcoholic will take his bottle away from him. He fears him, too, because he senses the recovering alcoholic can identify him—because he can identify with him.

He also fears that his own family will observe the sobriety of the recovering alcoholic, admire him and try to foist his recovery on to him.

The guilt and remorse and self-hate which has been slowly destroying him increases. Now there is a comparison as the recovering alcoholic presents a figure that subconsciously the drinking alcoholic is jealous of. Now we have fear combined with jealousy.

Now comes hate. The drinking alcoholic has to hate the man who has done it and who makes him look like a loser in comparison, just as losers learn to hate winners in so many facets of life.

So now we combine the drinking alcoholic's fear, jealousy and hate and we have a highly combustible commodity ready to explode inside himself. So how can we possibly expect a practicing alcoholic to feel comfortable with a recovering alcoholic? He is still confused. The recovering alcoholic has cleared his head and soul of confusion.

The practicing alcoholic is still full of anxieties, doubt, pains, and frustrations and selfishness, all brought on by himself. The recovering alcoholic is handling these bonds. He has the freedom to function. He can will himself, make his own choices. The drinking alcoholic has lost his will. He's lost his judgment. He's lost his ability to turn his back on a substance which is ruining his health.

Frankly, the presence of a recovering alcoholic has to be an embarrassment for the guilt-ridden drunk. He perhaps sees his dream of health and sobriety in front of him. He has to have pangs of regret that he is not able to control his drinking as the recovering alcoholic.

He must be tempted to flee—actually run into the night to escape this threat. Ironically, he subconsciously cries out to be like the sober companion. But the power of the disease drives him further away from help.

He is again caught in a terrible vise of temptations. They are too hard to solve. Better not to see the recovering alcoholic. He represents everything the drunk is not—and secretly wishes to be.

Examples:

Likeable David was certain that even as a non-drinker member of his yacht club, he'd retain his popularity. Listen to his story:

"Gosh, I could hardly wait to get back to the boat and my yacht club pals. I had some real problems when I was drinking and boating—like smashing up the dock on a Sunday afternoon in full view of the dinner crowd. And I ran aground another time, ruining the hull. I figured going back at least the club members would say, 'Well, no more thrill crashes.' But I could feel an icy reception.

"It wasn't my imagination. I got the cold shoulder in the bar. Several friends who always invited my wife and me on yacht parties just ignored us. And I wasn't appointed to the Christmas committee. I knew they resented my sobriety. One wife finally said it all after she got a little drunk. 'Dave, we all get up-tight around you now. We still love you but us old drunks just think you're too straight.' It hurt. I pulled out of the club."

* * *

Same with Joyce, the expert card player. She was invited to every tournament in her home town when she was drinking and as she says, "The loudest one in the party." Upon her return from treatment she explained:

"It was like night and day. A few old friends called. But nobody seemed to want much to do with me socially. Then I got thinking that most of them were pretty heavy drinkers. Margie, an old friend, put it before me, cold turkey. She just said, 'I think everyone is a little frightened. Lots of the girls know they drank more than you did. Now you worry them. It's a case of you playing on their conscience, maybe.' "

Fortunately, Joyce had the resiliency to form another card club with six AA women members. They interested another five or six in a neighboring town and now she says, "We have the best parties ever. We all play better, enjoy life more. And nobody's ever on liquor. No idle gossip. Just sharing. It's beautiful—but gosh, how it hurt at first."

* * *

One of the recovering alcoholics I counseled told me how it was with his football fan club which used to meet once a week, drink up a storm and thus bus out to the game together, drinking heavily enroute. At the game, they would hit the stadium club for more drinks at halftime. It was six solid hours of "buzzing." Listen to him:

"One of our pals came back from treatment. We tried to be friendly. But when he ordered 'plain' coke on the bus, our bartender threw in a shot for old times sake. He spit it out, cursed the bartender and didn't come back in the bus after the game. The next trip he wasn't there. We hung out a sign, 'For Drunks Only.' It wasn't meant to hurt anybody. But 20 hard-drinking guys don't want a 'straight' in the crowd. He might be a helluva guy—but he's a threat. If our wives ever saw a dry among us, we'd all catch holy hell! Now that I've quit drinking booze, I know where my place is. It isn't on the bus. It would just make everyone uncomfortable, including myself."

* * *

And Benny, the bus driver of a baseball fan-trip bus, sees it all. He's an appraising fellow. "I see sober guys try to be regular guys on a busload of drunks. It's murder on the sober guy and tough on the drunks. They figure he's a traitor. I think it's best if he finds other transportation. It can make him damn uptight."

* * *

When a recovering alcoholic said to me, "It's my human right to get on a bar bus to games," I just smiled and patted him on the back. "If you had a chance to get on a bus where there were 40 guys with German measles, would you argue to be a part of them!" He said, "Hell, no." Then I asked, "Isn't getting on a bus of a bunch of drunks about the same thing? You're recovering and they're still boozing it up and maybe a bunch of them are diseased. Why not take a trip out to the game with the healthy people?"

He thought it over and agreed. Really, it is ridiculous to force yourself into a company of people who are edgy with you in their presence. Many places you can associate with heavy drinkers and actually be an inspiration. But when you are in a group whose most important purpose is to get soused, it's sheer folly to wear thick skin and try to make them feel ill at ease. They fear the recovering alcoholic to a point where even their drinks don't taste as good as they think they should.

It can happen with neighbors or at holiday parties with relatives. A recovering alcoholic told me, "I had to quit going to large family parties. There would always be three or four people getting drunk who had to bring up my sobriety. I could kid my way out of it—but it got to be a bore."

I tell recovering alcoholics to go where they are comfortable and where their friends are comfortable. Generally speaking, as I have pointed out, the heavy drinker cares less whether you're holding a peach or a dish of ice cream. But there are particular macho and women's parties where alcoholic drinks are actually a part of the ritual and where an invader is unwanted. That's no place for a recovering alcoholic.

He fears because he is threatened by the possibility that the recovering alcoholic will take his bottle away from him. He fears him, too, because he senses the recovering alcoholic can identify him—because he can identify with him.

QUESTION:
DO SPECIAL EXERCISES OR DIET HELP THE RECOVERING ALCOHOLIC?

SELVIG:

Certainly. Medical experts have told me that when drinking the alcoholic dilates his blood vessels. When he is in a depressive mood, the vessels shrink. Any exercise which helps create the flow of blood makes the recovering alcoholic feel better physically—and mentally.

Consequently, when an alcoholic tells me he has an uptight or abnormal tenseness, I suggest any of many

331

light exercises, depending on age and overall physical condition.

I personally like to jump rope. I am also a great believer in standing on my head, not recklessly but with my body braced in the corner, my feet against the wall. I find this an exhilarating exercise. I call it "Mother Nature's amphetamine."

I also like a brisk walk. Some people jog. Others do exercises sitting or standing or lying.

One of the biggest threats to a recovering alcoholic is to become inactive—physically, socially, mentally. I urge the recovering patients to stay active, but first, undergo a complete physical by a medical doctor. Tell him what exercises you are interested in and seek his advice.

Mental activity is just as important, not just when we feel anxious or strained. But every day we should set aside a little time for reading to improve our intellect, take time to listen to lectures, voluntarily take part in club or group activities and force our mental capabilities to accept new knowledge. Make an effort to take care of ourselves mentally, physically—and spiritually.

I told a recovering alcoholic one day that the perfect way to keep his sobriety was to take a brisk walk in the morning, read an enlightening article later on in the day, converse with at least three new people every day. And then pay a visit to the church of his choice for quiet meditation. In that way, his body, mind and spiritual energies will all be satisfied.

As for diet, let's be sensible. All of us thrive on different diets. Myself, I became an apple advocate. I don't know if an apple a day keeps the doctor away, but it is a refreshing experience for me.

My mind tells me I much prefer to reach for an apple over a piece of cake or even a chunk of roast beef. My appetite doesn't necessarily crave the apple but my sound judgment does—and I believe now my body is so attuned to apples that it would miss them greatly if they were not a major part of my diet.

I don't recommend apples for all recovering alcoholics. In my case, they serve a definite purpose. To each his own.

There are some experts who believe the body of the alcoholic can use Vitamin B early in its recovery. However, as many recovering alcoholics will say, a balanced diet serves them well and they never take vitamin pills. Many doctors also agree with this outlook.

Common sense. That's the key. Only do as much exercise as your body is able to tolerate; follow a normal diet that doesn't put on excessive weight.

An important note of caution:

The early recovery stages of the alcoholic may find him so exuberant over his new "clear head" and "new way of life" that he is full of energy which he feels must be burned up quickly. Too often, his body has not yet caught up with the energy of his mind. In other words, he feels as if he can run up mountain sides—while his body may not be able to get over a footstool. So I urge an important note of caution:

Common sense. The recovering alcoholic must get his body in condition equal to the fresh, happy approach of his mind. Unfortunately, years of drinking may have added poundage, slowed up the body processes to a point where they don't function to the standards set by his mind.

I had a recovering alcoholic tell me, "I felt so good the first week back at work I ran six blocks from the parking lot every morning." A short time later, I noticed him on crutches. He had thrown out a knee. His feet, unfortunately, couldn't keep up with his new-found enthusiasm.

One fellow said, "My friend told me exercise will kill me." Comment: What a pleasant way to go. Don't overdo it but do it. I'd rather have some quality to my life today if I have to reduce the quantity by doing it.

Examples:

A former amateur golf champion named Lonnie was so anxious to get back to the course and the weekend tourneys after completing his treatment, he told me, "That's about all I think about besides my recovery. Gee, Dick, I feel so great I know I could shoot a super round tomorrow."

He had what I call a "false energy charge or false optimism." In other words, he had been away from golf for six months. The feeling of elation and new-found enthusiasm over his sobriety made Lonnie think he could rush out, pick up his clubs, and smash Old Man Par over the head.

He was completely dejected when he shot an 82 in his first round after his treatment. "God, I was awful!" he complained to me. "I almost felt like taking a drink. I couldn't do anything right." I pointed out that it wasn't the sobriety which affected his game. He saw by his inability that he had lost his timing, his rhythm and his coordination. Golf is a game which requires almost constant practice. He admitted I was right—but trying to come back too fast could have caused a very emotional trauma.

* * *

The cross-country runner had the same thing happen. He tried to get back too soon. He thought that by eliminating liquor from his diet he'd automatically get more stamina. He had forgotten too quickly that his body had paid a price for heavy drinking over a three-year period. It needed time to adjust. Like I say, sometimes it takes two years for all the physical and mental adjustments to become a thorough reality in the body.

* * *

I had a close friend explain to me:

"In 8 weeks of treatment, I quit liquor, changed my diet, lost 30 pounds and thought I would automatically feel wonderful when I got back in stride. Instead, the first day going to work was pure hell. The wind cut right through me. I thought it'd blow me away. It wasn't until three months later that I began to feel my old normal strength come back—to match my mental outlook."

It can affect the mental capabilities, too. A writer told me it took about six months to become fully adjusted to his "new feeling." An attorney told me he felt physically and mentally sharp, but to get back into his eight-hour discipline it required a good six to eight weeks of "adjustment."

* * *

I had to chuckle at a patient of mine who went on his first "outing" from the treatment compound after four weeks. He bought a shirt in a shopping center. Then he walked across the way and saw the same shirt advertised for 60 cents less.

He told me he was swept up in a terrible feeling of distrust and fury and began to perspire until he had soaked his clothes. He was so disturbed he couldn't sleep that night. He had to get back and exchange that shirt.

The humor here was that three months before he would have blown $600 at a crap table and laughed it off—in his alcoholic drinking days. The recovering alcoholic will suffer sometimes from a "tight wallet," hating to spend for anything. It is perfectly natural. Now that his mind is clear, his memory will recall all the money he spent foolishly while drinking. He is determined, in many cases, to get it back as quickly as possible. He can even be a bit of a drudge to live with, as wives have pointed out. He can actually become penurious. But I believe that in nine cases out of ten it's simply a natural reaction. After a few months of sobriety he'll understand that his unwillingness to spend was a trigger reaction as his judgment cleared and he assessed his big spending ways when he was drinking.

If the recovering alcoholic remains like the unconverted Scrooge to a degree which troubles the family, his problem should be brought up with his AA group or the spouse's Al-Anon club or with a counselor. It should not persist.

But the common recovering alcoholic's new-found feelings will take some adjusting to.

The man who never cared if he got to work on time may become impatient with himself for not being able to pick up his talents as quickly as he thought, or become impatient with his family and persist in arriving at places not only on time—but early.

The newly-recovering alcoholic will believe his body is now capable of doing things it could not before. He'll rush out and try a strenuous game of tennis the first day home from treatment—and be upset because he can't place the ball. He may even blame his sobriety. He must understand that the reflexes have not had time to catch up with the quickness of his clear mind. It all takes time.

The best advice for a recovering alcoholic who says he can do all things well in a hurry is: "Remember, it took 20-30 years of drinking to turn you into an alcoholic. You can't undo it all in eight or nine weeks."

But the remarkable thing about the disease is how quickly an alcoholic can resume his work and play. And if he only gives himself enough time, he is certain to be better at work and play than he ever was while drinking.

QUESTION:
WHEN IS THE ALCOHOLIC CONSIDERED RECOVERED?

SELVIG:

There are three steps to the recovery process and they involve the ALCOHOLIC, OTHERS (alcoholic and non-alcoholic associates), and THE SUPREME BEING, as one may or may not understand God.

THE BIG THREE: ME, OTHERS, AND GOD:

The order in which the three appear shows one where he is today. The alcoholic's position here doesn't always remain the same. He can be in step one, two or three at different intervals of life.

WHERE ARE YOU TODAY?
IRRESPONSIBLE
OTHERS   ME   GOD

STEP ONE - In this case, other people thinking much more of the alcoholic than he does of himself move in and help him. He cannot imagine anyone thinking much of him, so he is in second place in the order of the three. God is a very remote and really not included in his recovery more than a vague intangible. The alcoholic is in a very intoxicated and sick category—too confused to help himself without the concern and love of others. His greatest helping hand is at the end of other people's arms.

RESPONSIBLE
ME   OTHERS   GOD

STEP TWO - Now the alcoholic is sober and becoming responsible for his own behavior. He is starting to see himself as he is and slowly but surely getting a better feeling about himself. God is more meaningful now. His greatest helping hand is now a combination at the end of his arm and includes others as well. He seeks to help others besides himself. He is sharing.

RECOVERED
ME   GOD   OTHERS

STEP THREE - This is the stage where the alcoholic is recovered. He is fully responsible for his recovery and personal life. He realizes for the first time in his life that he is really number one in his own life for he knows God has made him in His own image and that he needs to ask God for the strength to be honest with himself and others. He is expected to stay sober and the greatest helping hand is at the end of his own arm and how he wields it depends on what he will do and what he becomes.

God becomes a very personal one now and the alcoholic learns to associate comfortably with people from all walks of life, non-alcoholics and alcoholics alike. He has found himself and is very grateful for others who have helped him. He is more honest than he has ever been. He is "free to function." And that is why he's "Recovered." For once we are able to have the freedom of choice to drink or not to drink, we recovering alcoholics won't drink it. When we see God as our strength to be honest with others and ourselves, we will do the right things and not be a bit concerned whether our alcoholism is arrested or cured.

Please remember that all recoveries are based on the one-day-at-a-time plan. An alcoholic is recovered only for the day he doesn't drink. He must always be on guard. There is no guarantee. Every day he needs to thank the Higher Power for giving him his health and clear mind. It is nothing he can take for granted. His sobriety is earned so he must work hard to keep it. He must pray, share and keep his courage at a peak operation. If his faith in himself, his God or his helpers falters, he is in for serious trouble. Each of the three spokes gives the wheel of sobriety strength. None can be permitted to crack.

No other disease can come back and claim you when you knew you were recovered, like alcoholism. You are as far from the disease as making the decision not to take the alcoholic beverage. You are so close that a sip of that beverage once again ignites the tortures.

It was a wise man who said one drink for an alcoholic is too much—and a thousand not enough.

And always guard against over-confidence, over-work, over-exertion. Especially guard your withdrawal from meaningful people in life. These are some of the companions of the dread disease.

Example:

The 62-year-old man named Henry had felt so secure about his alcoholic recovery. He was a director of a treatment center for 11 years. He hadn't had a drink for 23 years. He told me one day, "I don't believe I could force down a drink now without choking. It's a great feeling—to know you're cured, once and for all."

Exactly three months after that statement Henry was informed of the death of his first grandchild. He went to the corner bar and ordered a cola drink. Ten minutes later, as if some unseen hand directed him, he was lifting the glass of whiskey and soda. After the fourth drink he staggered from the bar and was not seen for 70 hours.

Picked up by police, sleeping in his car, Henry said he could not remember a thing that happened after he heard of his grandchild's death. "It was like an invisible force blanked me out. I don't even remember ordering or drinking that whiskey. When I found out I had been drunk, I was crushed." The remorse almost killed Henry.

Here's a frightening case where a man who had recovered for all intents and purposes, was waylaid without defenses because of a crushing emotional blow. The alcohol could not be blamed directly. Henry was ready to be taken by a reoccurrence of the disease. He was susceptible. His mental resistance gone. He failed to share his sadness with his close friends.

* * *

It can strike anyone who isn't thinking clearly 60 seconds out of every minute, 60 minutes out of every hour. A lovely hostess named Mabel had not drunk alcohol in nine years. Tense and overworked one night, she sought relief with a sip of wine.

She was found four days later, almost dead, in her apartment. She had consumed over two quarts of wine. Listen to her tell it:

"My God, it's the most treacherous disease in the

world! Here I was, giving a speech one day at an AA conclave, so proud of my sobriety. If you told me I would be drunk the next evening, I would have said, you are crazy. But I was. Alcoholism is only as far away as the first drink. It's too dangerous to even play with."

* * *

The bartender named Fritz was sober for 38 years. His wife divorced him to run away with another man. Fritz fought back the urge to drink for three days. His story:

"I said I wouldn't give in—I wouldn't crumble. My sobriety was the most valuable commodity I owned. But one night after work, I went home and saw the lonely house. To hell with it—one beer won't hurt. Well, that one beer put me in jail and the hospital. But worse yet, it killed my pride. I lost 38 years of sobriety because I couldn't live one day at a time. It was hell coming back. I swear I'll never drink again. But I said that 20 minutes before the beer." One needs to "not drink now."

* * *

And the 40-year-old housewife who went back to the bottle after five years of sobriety when her husband left her, recalled:

"I used to think the bottle was a friend. I wanted to again. But after two days of drinking, I was so emotionally upset with myself I threw three bottles out the front picture window. The squad car came and took me away. If it hadn't, I would have killed myself. Not over my husband but over the terrible feeling I had about myself."

The recovering alcoholic has no credentials that guarantee his sobriety. He must work on himself, with his God and through others to keep the temptation and the crisis at bay. "Recovering" means only for this minute. Nobody can know the next minute.

"Troups of furies march in the drunkard's triumphs."
Johann Zimmerman

VIEWPOINT

Remember, when we stressed how courageous the recovering alcoholic has to be?

Imagine now if you were ordered by your doctor never again to taste salt—not a grain of it. The salt would generate a killing disease in your body just waiting to spread with a fraction of a gram of the substance.

Imagine, then, that everytime you met socially with friends they nibbled only on peanuts and pretzels. At every turn they were offering you one.

At the meal, the guest next to you said, "Better put a little salt on the salad and that beef. Gives it a real good flavor." And the hostess said, "We have some onion-flavored salt you must try." The dessert came and the hostess urged. "You might like to try a little salt on the dessert. It really does something for it."

Now consider the recovering alcoholic. We all know it is an alcohol-oriented society, drinks at conferences, at lunch, at the club, after golf, before dinner, after dinner, before dancing, and nightcaps at the conclusion.

Billions of gallons of liquor are consumed daily by the world's populace. But it is the one commodity the alcoholic does not dare touch. Not only is his reputation at stake, but the lives of his family and his own health. Even in their wisdom religious leaders and philosophers have said that nearly anything used temperately has a good effect. But the alcoholic cannot so much as take a sip of the beverage.

When people downgrade a recovering alcoholic who suddenly found himself back on the booze, they can't understand it. "But Jack was doing so well. How could he ever drink again?"

Nobody that I can see even imagined what it is like to be a recovering alcoholic in today's society. Certainly he is enjoying life and health like he never has before. But no human beings are more subjected to temptation by their friends in general than the alcoholics.

In movies, plays and television they see constant drinking. They hear at work about the great beer busts.

They hear at church about a wine-tasting dinner. They hear from their teenage children about the beer and clam parties on the beach.

Liquor. Liquor. It is everywhere—but the recovering alcoholic does not dare make a move toward so much as a single swallow.

I so admire the recovering alcoholic remaining staunch. He is a hero worthy of standing ovations from the masses. He is a person who must pray a lot and takes nothing for granted, particularly himself. He must depend on his own fortitude, the help of God and his friends. But he must be himself and fight his daily temptations his own way.

When healthy and thinking clearly, a recovering alcoholic is capable of attaining great heights. He guards well his talents, far better than most. For he knows he is only one alcoholic drink away from insanity which destroys him and those around him.

He is a man the world may be able to turn to. For he has been forged in resiliency, tempered in faith, molded in discipline and polished through necessity.

He is a man you should be happy to call a friend.

The recovering alcoholic teaches society every day what the words will-power or self-determination and God-love and sharing mean. They are his lifeline.

**But no human beings are more
subjected to temptation by
their friends in general than the
alcoholics.**

---

PART V

THE SYNOPSIS

SYNOPSIS

There will be readers of this book, I am sure, who will accuse me of being perhaps too quick to absolve the recovering alcoholic and in praising his courage, to overlook the pain and the anguish he has caused his friends and loved ones. I don't feel I have done this, for the alcoholic pays a tremendous price to gain sobriety.

If, indeed, I show an overabundance of compassion for the struggling alcoholic and his family it is because I acknowledge I am biased toward them. In other words, the alcoholic has not been contaminating others with germs or polluting a community with a plague. It is his behavior, over which he had no control when drinking, which has caused heartache, despair, and pain to those who have come in contact with him as well as himself.

To those who have suffered with the disease of a loved one, I can only extend my heart-felt sympathy. They are brave ones, too. And to the ones who ask: What do I get out of my loved one's return to sobriety?

The gratification of the recovering alcoholic who turns to loved ones and says the simple words, "Thanks," and "I'm sorry" will dissolve the years of frustrations and pain caused in many cases.

They will suddenly discover a warm glow within themselves which only those who have experienced it will understand. The periods of pain will seem insignificant to the joy they are now experiencing.

My feelings in this book stress my love and respect for the loved ones and friends for the amazing loyalty they have shown to the alcoholic through difficult times. I want to make that clear. As much as I love and respect and bask in the recovery of alcoholics, my heart is as warm for the other brave ones who also paid the price of the disease themselves even as it ravaged their alcoholic.

My love for the recovering alcoholics and families goes beyond admiration for their valiant fight against disease.

I have seen so many become—not merely acceptable citizens in our society—but powerful leaders, spreading a goodness and a way of life which transcended all boundaries of race and creed and social barriers.

I am not saying these folks are stronger leaders or better fighters for what they believe in. But because of the fact they have hit bottom, together lived virtually two lives, have seen degradation as close as the mirror, gives them a depth and understanding which perhaps many others do not comprehend.

This does not mean the recovering alcoholic and family are deeper thinkers, more intellectual, or brighter. I am only saying that experience is the greatest teacher and the team has experienced close at hand the best and worst.

They have had to fight for their very existence. They had to go into the jaws of hell, and literally got burned. They had to bare their hurt and despair with the public. They had to take on a humility which would embarrass and discourage many. They had to admit defeat, usually at a time when their friends were reaping the benefits of lifelong pursuits.

The recovering alcoholic and family have had to adjust to a new way of life—one in which the images suddenly are no longer blurred and distorted. Suddenly, they are distinct, sometimes harshly so. The sounds that they could blot out are now everywhere and vibrant. The colors they were not sure of are suddenly there before their eyes in blazing assortment.

The people who shunned them are suddenly not certain. They are engulfed in their uncertainty. Their acquaintances ponder giving them their full trust. They are quite naturally entitled to positions of suspicion by some. Will it happen again? They must conquer all these new challenges. They must assume a new kind of patience and tolerance which they did not allow themselves for perhaps decades. They must take on vast new responsibilities because for years they had blamed accomplices—real and imaginary.

The recovering alcoholic, if he lost a profession, must

346

start anew—not unlike a schoolboy. Again tolerance may be tested when the man who was under him five years ago now assumes the role of an inadequate helpmate to the fresh "new" visionary. New-found beliefs must be tempered, and be met with a mellowness of heart, while adjusting to an exciting, new, challenging world.

Sincerity may be questioned and the alcoholic may even be accused of deceit. Debtors may doubt him. Benefactors may seek favors. The person's very foundation may suddenly assume the fragility of quicksand.

But in the new-gained sobriety the alcoholic is elated in the freedom to function; ecstatic over the fact these challenges are met with a clear mind and healthy body. The problems—that even sobriety can bring forth the first few months—are accepted with a relish and enthusiasm which soon becomes contagious to the community.

The recovering alcoholic, forged in misery, is capable of taking his role alongside any person in society and also in the family.

The victory over the bottle will soon enough win the admiration of the very people who suffered at the hands of the disease—the most cunning, baffling, and powerful disease known to man.

Yes, I offer my unqualified admiration and love to the recovering alcoholic and the family.

They have found a way of strength through honesty which I'm sure the Creator intended all creatures to experience.

With the alcoholic and family it just took more pain, suffering, time, and work.

Keep remembering that the recovering alcoholic is a brave person—in constant battle with the strong, normal temptations. It is also true that it takes brave, strong people among friends, relatives, neighbors, and associates to deal openly with the subject of alcoholism.

So I say, stand up, my recovering alcoholic friends! And stand up, you former accomplices! All of us should be so very, very proud. The alcoholic's sobriety has been earned by all, as it takes a team approach for victory over John Barleycorn.

Now we must all be ourselves—for the original is always better than a copy.

Heed the little boy who said, "Be what you is because if you be what you ain't, then you ain't what you is."

The recovering alcoholic and family and friends represent some of the best qualities of man—the understanding of themselves and the sharing of that understanding with others—in a gift of love.

God bless you and yours as we all walk under the arms of our God, Our Power Greater Than Ourselves, to further victories in our inspiring struggle to find our true selves.

A Note About the Co-Authors

Dick Selvig is renowned wherever alcoholism experts gather. For 23 years Selvig (an alcoholic himself) has worked with the thousands of alcoholics with whom he's come in contact. His fresh, open approach to the disease not only has won over most of his patients—but has created a widespread following in the field.

At Willmar State Hospital in Minnesota, at Heartview Foundation in Mandan, North Dakota, and currently at Fountain Lake Treatment Center in Albert Lea, Minnesota, the Selvig theories and candid approach to the disease are carried by the growing legion of followers.

Author of such well-accepted pieces on the disease as *Alcoholism is a Family Affair* and *How About Your Drinking?* Selvig also has served as adviser to over 200 young counselors and specialists in the field. He has made speeches and has held seminars all over the country on the subject of alcoholism.

The late Dr. Harry Tiebout, noted psychiatrist and an expert on alcoholic behavior, said of Selvig's views on the subject:

"I can add nothing to the views Dick Selvig gives on alcoholism and the recovering alcoholic as a counselor. He says it all."

In the field of alcoholism, Selvig's done it all. An alcoholic at 18 years of age, Selvig drank to "feel bigger and better than the next boy." His drinking brought sorrow to his family and created problems wherever he went. By his mid-twenties he was a threat to society, engaging in drunken brawls, wrecking saloons, and becoming a public nuisance.

Only after countless arrests and threats by the police and judges did Selvig give up the bottle at the age of 28. Subsequently he became a sports writer in Willmar, Minnesota, and as he explains:

"Believe it or not, a municipal judge! They believed that because I had so much experience in court, I'd make a very humane judge. I ran and won. It was a magnificent experience, getting a chance to talk to and advise youth. I owe everything I am to my little hometown of Willmar, Minnesota. It knew me as a little boy and then a drunken troublemaker and gave me a chance to fight for my life and then help others as best I could. I suffered from acute alcoholism from 1939-1949. Any accomplishments during this time were purely coincidental. I was a failure in my educational pursuits at Gustavus Adolphus College in St. Peter, Minnesota. It's a very fine Christian college. Many there tried to aid me but I was too crazy from alcoholism at the time."

Wheelock Whitney, former director of the State of Minnesota's Alcohol and Drug Abuse program and founder of two half-way houses in Minneapolis, says:

"There is only one Dick Selvig. He is a forerunner in the field of alcoholic treatment. He is a brave man with powerful ideas and an irrepressible drive to make them work. I don't believe anyone in this country has a more complete grasp of the alcoholic disease than Selvig."

Mr. Selvig resides with his wife Elsa and a teen-age daughter, Mary, in Albert Lea, Minnesota. He has two additional children, John and Jane.

Don Riley attended the College of St. Thomas, (St. Paul, Minnesota) and the University of Minnesota, (Minneapolis) majoring in journalism and public speaking.

Selvig's co-author, Don Riley, is a well-established sports columnist for the *St. Paul Pioneer Press* newspapers. He is a veteran of 37 years in the journalism field. During this time he has won 18 sports-writing awards and citations and written over 50 articles for national magazines. Excerpts from his controversial column are quoted continually in papers all over the country. He also speaks at inspirational clinics on desire and courage. He currently serves on the board of directors of Granville Halfway House of Minnesota.

Riley has co-authored *How I began Earning $50,000 in Sales at the Age of 36* and *The Gonif . . . Red Rudensky*, the story of notorious safe-cracker Red Rudensky, King of the Cons (Piper Publishing, Inc.).

Riley has also appeared in after-boxing panels on Twin Cities television stations for years, "Hot Seat" television program for four years, nightly sports editorials for WTCN-TV, and talk shows for various radio stations. Riley also has contributed to *Holiday, Ambassador, Male* and *Ring* magazines. He resides in Roseville, Minnesota, with wife Dorothy and daughters Sheila and Shannon.

Riley met Selvig for the first time in the fall of 1974 when he entered Heartview Foundation for treatment of alcoholism.

"When I was introduced to Dick, he was standing on his head in a corner of his office. I thought, 'God, I'm in with a bunch of nuts.' It soon became apparent as I listened to Selvig and his philosophy from his counselors that this man had a knack of saying the right thing in the fewest possible words."

"Later on, Selvig returned to Minnesota and I approached him about the possibility of writing a book. He said, 'Fine, but only if you write it like we see it. Nothing flowery. I think maybe we can help save some lives.' I knew what he meant. He had saved mine."

351

As for his alcoholic escapades, Riley recalls: "I once hired Lassie, the famed movie dog, and rented a 15,000-seat stadium for my daughter's birthday party. I charge that up to six martinis. Another time I sold green beer and corned beef sandwiches at a boxing card on St. Patrick's Day. At one o'clock in the morning I brought 360 unused corned beef sandwiches to the Little Sisters of the Poor. And we had enough green beer left over to sink a battleship. I charge that to three beers and four straight gins."

Selvig says of Riley's co-authorship:

"I love the guy. His enthusiasm is like a raging fire. I say a sentence and he expounds on it. I think he's captured almost all of my opinions on the subject of alcoholism in a fast-paced, hard-hitting way. Riley writes to the point. We have a beautiful relationship: our experiences—and writing enthusiasm. He's a go-getter. Don does much charity work in silence. He's not as angry as he sounds in his newspaper column, as no one could be."